Needle Song

This edition first published 2018 by Fahrenheit Press

ISBN 978-1-912526-13-0

10 9 8 7 6 5 4 3 2 1

www.Fahrenheit-Press.com

F 4 E

Needle Song

By

Russell Day

Fahrenheit Press

For Liz, Harley and Clarissa

Road-Beaten Leathers and Designer Labels

Friday 15 July

Chris Rudjer was hunched over the counter, scouring the appointments book and blocking the light. Doc was fishing.

"How's that posh bit you been knocking around with?"

There was a moment of stillness that centred around the Big Guy. You'd have needed a thin skin to call it a threat, but with someone Chris's size, it paid to listen carefully. Maybe an inch shy of seven foot and a solid twenty-three stone, he carried his own exclusion zone. You ignored it at your own risk.

"You mean Jan?"

"How's Jan?" Doc said.

Where Chris was all road-beaten leathers and tattoos, Jan was designer labels and charge cards. They made an odd couple.

"Not bad, considering." He thumbed over another page of the appointments book, allowing sight of the tattoo on his palm. It was bad work, not ours. I looked away from the smudged ink and Doc caught my eye. It was a fleeting glimpse but long enough to let me know he'd been right. He'd said someone was going to get hurt.

It was one of those moments when I'd rather have worked for someone else.

"Considering?" Doc said.

"Yeah." Chris looked up, frowning. "Oh yeah. I haven't seen you, have I?" He gave us, or at least Doc, his full attention. "Jan's husband killed himself."

"When was this?"

"Last Sunday." Chris appeared to give it some thought before adding, "Early afternoon."

He stopped talking but didn't look away from Doc. Doc was fascinated.

"And he's killed himself?"

"Jan found him on the toilet, bled out. Claret all over the shop. She was in pieces." Chris looked thoughtful again. "Left a note and ... slitch."

He made a slashing motion across his wrist.

Before the day was out, Chris would be under arrest, Jan would be sleeping in my spare room and the men following her would be watching my house.

Friday 13 May

Chris had appeared in The Jericho, with a nervous-looking woman in tow, about two months earlier. I'd been in there with Doc, end-of-the-week broke and set to nurse one pint all night rather than go home. I hadn't paid much mind when Doc's attention flickered to a point over my shoulder – it was his habit to keep an eye on the door – but whatever he'd seen held his interest and his gaze traced a route across to the bar. I craned round and saw Chris scanning the crowd.

Doc muttered, "Ten pounds says he comes to this table."

I told him I'd keep my money. I didn't have ten pounds and bets with Doc were always a bad idea.

Chris spotted me before he spotted Doc – staying out of sight was another of Doc's habits. Chris did a double take before placing me and making his way over. The crowd parted before him. The woman trailed in his wake, staying close and taking whatever comfort that offered.

The Jericho was a biker's pub and the dress code tended towards leathers or miniskirts. What she had on was shortish but not invitingly so and her jacket was cut with style in mind rather than protection. Sexy but not obvious. The word that came to mind was classy. She was out of her element.

When they reached our table, Chris put a hand to the woman's back and drew her forward, presenting her.

"Jan," he said, then after a slight pause, "this is Doctor Slidesmith."

Something about Doc's bearing changed. I couldn't put my finger on it but, somehow, he gave off an air of purpose. Chris might have picked up on the change as well because he cut me a look. I wasn't sure what the look meant so I kept quiet.

Doc nodded to Jan. It was the usual biker's greeting, but he lent it some solemnity. Jan said hello, barely glancing at me. She was struggling with the tattoo running along Doc's cheek. I'd have had trouble with it myself, except I was the one who'd put it there. It was a good piece of work, modesty aside, though why Doc wanted a tattoo of a jawbone and teeth, I couldn't fathom. He already had more teeth than any one human has a right to.

Chris asked Doc if he'd do a tarot reading for Jan. In deference to the deeply spiritual nature of the undertaking, Doc demanded a double Tequila in payment. While the Big Guy headed to the bar, Doc gazed at Jan and unfolded his Cheshire Cat grin. She didn't jump but it was close. He motioned her to sit. Kept up the grin and eye contact.

When he asked her why she wanted a reading, his voice, like his posture, changed slightly. Each word, carefully enunciated, gave the impression that English might not be his first language. His hand slid into his ruin of a leather – long ago white, now road crap grey – and pulled out his tarot cards.

"I thought it might be fun." She'd broken eye contact to watch his hand vanish into his pocket. The tip of her tongue moistened her upper lip. "Chris said you're a kind of witch doctor."

"Do I look like a witch doctor?"

Doc was in his usual uniform: jeans, faded almost white, and a long sleeve tee shirt with *Slidesmith's Tattooing* printed across the shoulders. He'd had seventy printed up to sell in the shop. They'd sold like sandals in the Arctic.

Jan tried for a smile but it was stillborn. Maybe tomorrow, chatting with other classy ladies, this would be a delightful episode of slumming.

That would be tomorrow.

The tarot cards, bound in unbleached linen, were badly worn, if they'd been a normal pack you'd have thrown them away. He offered them to Jan, to shuffle, and she hesitated for a second before taking them. They were slightly larger than a standard deck and she handled them awkwardly. She gave them back and Doc did a smooth one-handed cut before dealing.

He laid five cards, face up, in a cross formation, then studied them in silence until Chris returned. He didn't acknowledge him, or the glass he put on the table, other than to say, "You been telling this lady I'm a witch doctor?"

"Didn't know how to explain," Chris said.

"Voodoo's a religion," Doc said, "same as any other." Then, to Jan, "You ever had a reading?" She shook her head. "Well, understand this, the cards do not deal in absolutes. They won't tell you what number you're thinking of or give you the winner of the Grand National. They are an instrument that allows us to sample the vibrations."

He said *vibrations* with a twist of his hand, he may have meant the universe or the room or just Jan and Chris. Of course, he might have meant nothing at all.

I watched Jan while Doc wheeled out his patter. What he called The Jive. It was always entertaining but I'd seen it before and Jan was easier to look at. And she wasn't buying it. Not at first.

Towards the end, Doc paused his patter and leaned back, frowning. The pause almost grew into a silence. Then abruptly, he reached out and pinned one of the cards down with his index finger.

"Now, this fellow represents causes or reasons. The driving force of this particular tale. This is the Fool. Notice anything?"

Jan craned forward to look closer.

"No," she said.

"The other cards have numbers. The Fool does not. He is zero."

He left another pause.

"Meaning what?"

Doc picked the card from the table then leaned back into his seat again. He addressed the card rather than Jan.

"Well, everyone reads the cards in a different way, interprets them in a different manner. Now, I see The Fool as an outsider, different from the other cards. He has no number because, while belonging to the deck, he is not of the deck. That's why The Fool isn't always a card to be welcomed. Most of us don't want an outsider fooling with our lives."

Jan still wasn't buying it. Not until Doc turned the full glory of his teeth on her and said, "Of course, maybe he wasn't always an outsider. An ex, perhaps? And maybe he's being made a fool. Maybe he does not know he's an ex just yet. Is he going to be the last to know? A note of caution: your Fool is a wild card."

It wouldn't be fair to say the effect was electric but I saw Jan stiffen. Something had landed on target.

Doc wrapped the show up with a chuckle.

"Of course, maybe these are just outdated playing cards and I'm just a skinny tattooist playing parlour games."

Jan managed a laugh but it sounded like a pressure valve.

As soon as Chris and Jan were out the door, Doc, his voice pure north London again, said what I'd been thinking.

"Where the hell did he meet her?"

I suggested a church jumble sale and he laughed.

"You hit a nerve with that stuff about The Fool."

He laughed again.

"Yeah. Well, if Chris wanted happy-ever-after, he should have paid for the good stuff."

He nodded at the Tequila with some disdain. He'd yet to taste it.

"How do you know he didn't?"

"I watched him buying it. The stuff in the optics is crap, Eddy keeps the quality bottles on the top shelf. I'm not bothering with that, you want it?"

Of course, I did. I finally finished off the inch of flat lager I'd been hording and started hording the Tequila instead. Doc wandered off to the bar and returned with a glass I assumed came from the top shelf. They were three deep at the bar but he had a talent for getting served quickly.

He inclined his head towards the door Chris and Jan had just left by.

"*That* is going to end in tears."

"You reckon?"

He nodded.

"You mess about with someone's marriage, people get hurt."

"You think The Fool means she's married?"

Doc gave me a sidelong look and his cheek twitched again. "I think her wedding ring means she's married."

Thursday 7 July

About a week before Chris came in and told us about the dead husband, Jan had come to the shop. I'd not immediately recognised her. She was still expensively dressed but now her look was more obvious. I wasn't complaining, subtlety's wasted on me.

She glanced around the waiting room and there was a flash of nerves again, like the night I'd seen her in The Jericho. Slidesmith's Tattooing was a long way off being a spit and sawdust outfit but it wasn't a pretty boy's palace. We didn't cater to the rich and famous. Clean and well lit, the shop was decked out in red and black, walls covered with photos of customer's tattoos and pictures of Harley-Davidsons.

And there was evidence of Doc's belief system. Various packs of framed tarot were set against purple baize. Leather mojo pouches, containing God-only-knew, hung above every doorframe. He might get huffy about being called a witch doctor but Doc didn't make it easy on himself.

I waited for her to speak, wanting to see if she'd remember me from The Jericho. It doesn't matter how much leg they flash, I don't like people who think they're slumming. She looked away from me before saying anything, stole a glance of the scene outside – expensive black Audi parked behind an ugly black Suzuki. Seeing her car tucked in close to Chris's bike seemed to reassure her.

She smiled and said, "Hello again."

It had taken her a second to place my face but I made allowances for that. If you've got Chris on one side casting his shadow and Doc on the other putting The Jive out, you're not going to make a huge impact.

"Afternoon. You after the Big Guy?"

"Actually, I was hoping to have a word with Doctor Slidesmith."

I glanced at the clock, it had just gone two. Doc didn't generally tattoo for more than four hours at a go. Even the most skilled application involves repeatedly jabbing a needle through the skin. Most tattooists have a few stories about people passing out or throwing up. Doc extended his limit for Chris.

When I opened the flap in the counter to let her through, she made no move to leave the waiting room.

"Oh, Chris said the apprentice would be doing his tattoo. I was hoping to catch Doctor Slidesmith on his own."

An awkward dawn of realisation spread over her face and the nervousness went up a gear.

The apprentice almost pretended not to get what she was asking but I decided not to play games.

Being the apprentice, my work came at a cheaper rate and Chris had booked in with me for that reason. His attitude towards ink mirrored his attitude towards Tequila and he headed to the low shelf first. The massive piece he wanted applied to his back was going to cover up an existing tattoo, one he'd found on a very low shelf.

When Chris decided that morning he wanted the organ grinder and not the monkey, Doc named a figure that made my eyes water. Chris repeated the sum the way most people would repeat a diagnosis of cancer.

"You're going to bleed me dry Doc."

Doc's answer had been to point at the sign above the counter: *Good Work Ain't Cheap & Cheap Work Ain't Good.*

When Chris was out of earshot Doc grinned at me.

"That'll teach him to call me a bloody witch doctor."

I thought about the mojo he handed me when I'd started at the shop but didn't say anything. Genuine belief or affectation? Not expecting a straight answer, I'd never asked.

Now Chris was sat backward on Doc's chair as the design took shape. His head resting on his forearms, he hadn't bothered looking round when I came in. He didn't have that friendly-giant vibe a lot of big men give off. Chris's size had nothing to do with putting other people at ease.

I signalled to Doc that he was wanted outside. He picked up on my attempts at discretion and didn't ask any questions.

To afford the waiting room some privacy, the lower half of the shop window was blacked out. So, when Jan took Doc outside to talk, my view of the exchange – from my seat behind the counter – was of two bobbing heads. I didn't hear the dialogue, Marilyn Manson was baying out of the shop's sound system, but it was clear Jan wanted something that Doc wasn't willing to give. It was also clear that she was persistent. After a few minutes, I saw Doc run his hands through his hair and nod. Jan's expression was fifty-fifty gratitude and relief.

As he came back in, Doc looked at me and rolled his eyes. He went back to Chris's tattoo and Jan waited five minutes before going into the back room to join them. She filled the time sitting on one of the sofas, crossing and uncrossing her legs in a skirt the size of four postage stamps.

After Jan and Chris left that day, Doc started playing it coy.

It had gone five by then and I didn't envy Chris. It was a long session even for him and he eased his leather on with unusual care. Jan left the shop at his side but they parted at his bike. Once again, I watched bobbing heads. Before putting on his helmet he bent down and Jan kissed him on the mouth. She took her time but it was showy rather than intimate. She waited while he started the bike and shook the windows with his departure. She put her head into the shop again. "We're set then?"

This to Doc.

"Yeah," he told her. "Six."

She smiled a goodbye to us and left.

Doc didn't comment and I caught him watching me from the corner of his eye, waiting for me to ask. It crossed my mind that he might have been planning to fool with the Big Guy's posh bit. I wondered if he'd leave me anything in his will to remember him by. I got busy with a sketch pad.

When I didn't bite, he baited the hook a little.

"Don't you want to know how Chris and Lady Muck got together?"

"Not enough to work for it."

I'd only exchanged a few words with Chris, and I'd lodged in his mind as *the apprentice*. Jan I'd literally seen twice. And I was in a bad mood. Doc filled a lot of space and being around him could feel like playing second fiddle in a one-man band. Much as I respected the work his shop put out, I wasn't convinced we'd be having a long association.

Doc told me I was no fun, then volunteered that the star-crossed lovers had met online. That didn't surprise me when I thought about it. Cyberspace was the only space they seemed likely to share. Chris had apparently answered a posting on some dodgy internet site.

"Demure, high-class woman seeks massive intimidating greaser?"

"Oh, better than that," Doc said. "Married lady seeks extra marital adult fun."

The Big Guy had told him there were a load of sites catering for married people looking to play away.

"And now you're meeting up with her?"

Doc laughed.

"Nothing like that, Yakky. I don't touch married women and if I did, I wouldn't tread on Chris's toes. Suicide's not in my nature."

It was unfortunate phrasing given what Chris would tell us a week later.

Friday 15 July

After he'd heard the story about Jan finding her husband's body, Doc swapped the pen he was holding for a pencil. He used it to mark in Chris's next appointment. Pencil, not ink. I didn't think anything of it at the time. Later, it seemed ominous.

A lot of Doc's mystique, a lot of The Jive, worked best in hindsight.

When we'd shut up shop for the day, he asked if I was in any hurry to get home. He'd known me long enough to know the answer. I'd hoped whatever was on his mind could be aired in The Jericho. Instead, he led me down the side of the shop to his flat on the first floor.

Sitting in one of his two armchairs, Doc told me about the back and forth I'd seen though the half-blacked window. Jan had wanted another tarot reading and Doc hadn't wanted to oblige. Leave them wanting more was a main tenant of The Jive. She'd been insistent. She was worried, she needed more information. He'd told her the tarot wasn't the internet, you didn't type in requests and press enter. A wad of cash she produced had left him unmoved. Finally – by chance or stealth – she'd hit a nerve. She asked who else would do a reading for her. Doc told her not to go throwing money at fakers and she sensed a crack in his defences. If he wouldn't do it then somebody else would. At which point, Doc ran his fingers through his hair and agreed.

"Why not let her go someplace else, if you didn't want to do another reading?" I asked.

"She'd have ended up getting striped by some bullshitter." I didn't say anything but apparently Doc could read minds. "Don't be like that. I might Jive a bit now and again but I don't skin people."

The phrase 'skin people' didn't sit too well with me just then. Doc's flat, a separate property over the shop, gave me the creeps.

"You honestly believe a pack of cards can tell the future?"

He was frowning, away inside himself somewhere, and didn't answer immediately.

"It's not that simple," he said.

He unfurled himself from his armchair and stalked across to the wall opposite. He stood in front of the picture there in an act of meditation, or invocation. The picture, according to Doc, was of Ezulie Dantor, a Voodoo spirit. It had been applied directly onto the bare plaster with dark scorings of charcoal. Not Doc's usual style, it looked as if it had been executed in a frenzy. Maybe it had been. Maybe it was only meant to look that way. He was talented enough for either to be the case.

Ezulie Dantor was a black woman with a scarred face. Doc had depicted her running at the viewer with her fist raised. Surrounding her head were seven crudely drawn daggers, their blades facing out, forming a barrier. In the background, a line of headstones, each marked with that circle and arrow symbol that means male. She was attractive, if you like them scary. The image filled the wall top to bottom.

Doc was a great tattooist and a bloody awful interior designer.

"She didn't show anyway," he said this to the picture, not me.

He'd changed again in some way. Like he had the night in

The Jericho putting out The Jive. But this was different again. The Jive was showmanship. The good Doctor Slidesmith in full sail. This was more intense. I'd see him like this on occasion in the shop, absorbed in the ink and the song of the needle. I wouldn't say lost in what he was doing. Lost implies lack of control.

For the first time that evening, it struck me he needed an audience, not to watch him but for him to watch. Like a dial on a machine, not part of the process, just a way of monitoring it.

"Let's put the kettle on," he suddenly announced, breaking the spell.

Tea, along with Voodoo and Harley-Davidson, formed the holy trinity of his religious convictions.

The kitchen was as stark as the rest of the flat but with cabinets on the wall rather than Doc's peculiar décor. Seated at a bare pine table he dealt a hand of tarot.

The cards were the same dog-eared crew he'd used on Jan. I'd seen at least a dozen packs of tarot around, if not framed and on display, then tucked into bookshelves, among volumes on art or crammed in alongside motorcycle manuals. But this was the only pack I'd ever seen him read.

When he'd finished laying the cards, he took a swig of tea from a mug promoting Cadbury's Mini Eggs.

"You can breathe you know?" he said.

I smiled, or maybe grimaced. "Sorry, but you do know how to build an atmosphere," I said. "So, who's this reading for anyway?"

"It's the one Jan wanted."

Doc pushed the sleeves of his shirt up to his elbows, revealing two of his tattoos. On the inside of his right forearm, Baron Samedi, a skeleton in a funereal suit and top hat. On the left, Maman Brigitte, a redhead in an old-fashioned show girl's dress, also with a top hat but showing a lot more leg. They were husband and wife, Voodoo spirits you paid tribute to if you wanted to deal with the dead. I thought of Jan jumping when Doc picked out The Fool.

Thought about Doc noticing her wedding ring. Sometimes rational works, but Doc's rational didn't always work like everyone else's.

"I didn't think you wanted to do another reading for Jan."

Before answering he started dealing the cards. The first showed a heart with three swords pushed through it, the next a ragged couple in front of a stained-glass window. The window had five pentangles worked into its design. Doc frowned and made a soft clicking sound with his tongue.

"That was until she didn't show." I didn't know what that was meant to mean and I held my hands up in a gesture of helplessness. "I arranged to meet her, six o'clock, last Sunday evening."

I still didn't get the point until he repeated 'Sunday' with a heavy emphasis.

The day she was meant to meet Doc and alleviate her worries, was the day her husband died.

There was a low table in Doc's living room. Sitting across from the rendering of Ezulie Dantor, it served as an altar. In contrast to the rest of the flat, it was busy with clutter. Picture frames, candles, odd coins, pewter bowls, other *things*. To my non-believer's eye, it looked as random as the contents of a forgotten drawer. The care taken over its arrangement indicated otherwise.

Some of the rites Doc performed demanded live chickens. He practised sacrificial comprise with eggs. When he'd headed to the altar with a box of free-range offerings, I decided to make my excuses. As he began assembling ingredients, I pulled my leather on and grabbed my crash helmet.

"Doc, before you get into that, I'm going to make a move, 'kay?"

"Yeah sure. I'll see you at the shop tomorrow."

He didn't look round and I made sure I left before I saw what he was doing.

On the way back to my bike, I stroked the leather mojo bag Doc had given me when I'd started working for him. It went with the job. He'd told me to keep it with me and never open it. I kept it zipped into my leather and I'd taken to touching it for luck before I tried to start my pox dog of a Yamaha. That evening the engine caught the first time, which was as close to magic as made no difference. I chalked one up to Doc's mojo hand.

Mornington Crescent

I took a long route home, telling myself it was a nice evening for a ride and that the tension across my shoulders was stiffness from work. Funny the lies we tell only ourselves. I lived about three miles from the shop but managed to put fifteen on the clock before arriving.

The house, my father's, was in the middle of an old terrace. Not classic, just old, one of a row, each one as bland as the next. High-density living, neighbours sleeping a brick's width apart and not knowing each other's names. North London in a nutshell.

Dad was sat on the stairs about a third of the way up. He didn't claim to be stuck but his laboured breathing implied a story to be told.

"Hello," I said. Dad took a couple of heroic gasps but decided the effort of speech was too great and weakly raised a hand, his opening move. "You alright?" I asked it as a greeting rather than an enquiry, subtle difference.

Dad decided his next move quickly and chose badly. He could have gone for the sympathy or pity play. Instead he went for martyrdom, suffering in silence. He held a hand up again and added a brave nod. A man in distress but too proud to let on. I took it at face value and walked straight past him to the kitchen, which was a minor victory to me, at least I think it was. The rules for the game dad played were as clear as those of Mornington Crescent.

The kitchen smelt stale, dad didn't believe in opening windows and a good number of food-smeared plates and a pair of pans waited for attention. I let them wait a bit longer.

I went to the front room and sat facing the over-size television, the blaring screen was the only thing the room hadn't sucked the colour from. Dad came in and made his way to his armchair, sat in it with has much effort as he could. He'd given up on the heavy breathing, conceding a point to me. I had no doubt there'd be a counter play at some stage but I told myself I wasn't worried. Funny the lies we tell only ourselves.

"You had any dinner?" I asked, bellowed, over the TV.

Dad walked right into it.

"Not really." Voice just the right side of accusatory.

I nodded and, without looking away from the screen said, "Load of washing up in the sink."

Bang, I got another point, won a few blessed minutes of peace. Dad broke the silence with a master stroke.

"Your girlfriend rang. I told her you were out."

I nodded, left the room, went upstairs to the bathroom and stood clutching the side of the bath until my knuckles hurt. When I trusted myself to sit with dad again, I asked what she'd wanted. Without looking away from the screen, he shrugged.

"Asked for you. I told her you were out."

I unclenched my fists with an effort and left the room again. Game, set and match to dad.

I'd left home at twenty-one, weighed up wanting to do an art degree against earning potential and enrolled on a nursing course. I managed to pass the first year before accepting it wasn't for me. That I passed the second year was due to Karla.

Karla wasn't my girlfriend, she was my ex. Ex fiancée actually.

I went to my room to make the call. The land line was in the hall and I knew dad would begin hollering questions the moment he heard me dial. In front of a TV anything below ear-splitting was inaudible but a phone conversation in the vicinity turned dad into a bat. I had another motive for using my mobile: it was-pay-as-you-go and low on credit.

"Hello Karla, it's Andy."

"Oh, hi."

I could hear the smile in her voice. I waited a beat and the beat became a pause.

"Dad said you called?"

"Oh, yeah. Thought I'd see how you were. You haven't called for a while."

I hadn't called full stop and it was nice of her not to tell me so.

"Oh. You know, same old same old."

Another beat, another pause.

Eventually she laughed. "This really is sparkling stuff Andy, I hope you're writing it all down."

"Sorry. Been a bit of a day. Friend of a friend of Doc's had some bad news. Doc's been worried."

This time Karla didn't know what to say. She'd struggled to get her head around Doc.

"Are you sure you did the right thing? Dropping the nursing for a tattoo shop?"

"Yeah, I'm sure." I didn't feel the need to justify my decision. "How's nursing working out for you?"

She laughed again. "Hating it."

"Maybe you should try tattooing."

I was struggling for what to say next and, at last, my phone bleeped and a metallic voice told me I had one minute of credit left.

I breathed a sigh of relief and suspected Karla did too.

"Next time you call me first, Andy. Okay?"

"Yeah, I will, I'll – " dead line.

By the beginning of my third year, we were engaged and more or less living together in one room of a three-bedroom bug-hutch. Then dad had a bout of flu that he worried into pneumonia. I took a leave of absence from the course to see him through it. Two months later, convinced that I didn't want to be a nurse, I decided to put a portfolio of work together and find a tattooist to take me on. The piss-poor, short-term income could be offset by moving back into dad's place. Karla would move in too and we'd put the wedding back, say, twelve months. By that time, dad would be fully rehabilitated, Karla's brilliant nursing would be a national sensation and my preternatural skill with a tattoo needle would ensure a career the like of which had never been seen.

I was confidently seeing the Sunday supplements fighting over me for an interview. What journalist wouldn't want an exclusive with the first tattooist to have 'by Royal Appointment', above his door?

I told Karla this, sort of, and we moved in with dad. Three months later the engagement was off, she was back in nursing accommodation and we were having *some time apart.* Ten months now and counting.

I read somewhere that you can catch monkeys with coconuts. You take a coconut shell, cut a small hole in it barely big enough for a monkey's paw. Next you tie the shell down, good and tight, and put some rice in it. Then you wait. Monkey comes along, smells the rice, pushes his paw in and grabs a nice big fistful. Now he can't get his paw out, not unless he lets go of the rice. You can now collect monkey at your leisure. Even in those parts of the world where the natives are going to beat the hairy fucker's brain out and eat him, monkey keeps holding onto that rice. Too stupid and too desperate to think of letting go.

I lay on my bed, which had for a brief time been *our* bed. We hadn't got round to decorating the room but I'd covered most of the wall space with my artwork. Much of it was surreal tattoo imagery but a fair chunk was Karla.

Funny how much like monkeys people can be. Funny how they throw rice at weddings.

I waited awhile before going back downstairs. The front room with dad and the endless TV felt like a prison cell. The news gave way to a film or a series or something. I couldn't have said what, even as I watched it. At regular intervals dad assured me it was bloody rubbish. I asked him why he was watching it and he looked affronted.

"I only have it on for you."

This was his mantra, a vocal tattoo.

My mobile crashed the train of maudlin thoughts before they'd got up steam. It was Doc. I just had time to find this out before dad started bawling questions. I told him it was work and exited before he could reply, then took the conversation outside and sat on my bike.

"Sorry, Doc, go on."

"Got a bit of a big ask mate."

I caught movement from the corner of my eye, dad was watching me through the curtains.

"Go on then."

Dad was mouthing questions and pointing frantically at the phone. The phrase *none of your business* wasn't in his repertoire.

"Think you could stand a house guest for a while? Jan needs somewhere to stay."

I swung one leg over the handle bars so I could sit side saddle, with my back to the window.

"You better tell me what's up."

Big ask, was right. Jan didn't sound like a she'd be a bundle of laughs and as for telling dad we'd have company ...

Doc turned up half an hour later. He was riding his bone white Sportster and Jan was close behind in the black Audi. When I opened the door, they both looked terrible. Doc looked like he'd aged ten years. He'd told Jan to follow him to my place and she'd nearly tail-ended him at every junction and traffic light. Her eyes were swollen and her hands were knotted around a bandana she'd been using as a hanky.

About ten minutes after I'd left his flat, Doc had heard pounding on the door of the shop. He found the Audi slewed across the pavement and Jan near to hysterics. He got her into the waiting room and rearranged her car then, being English and being Doc, made some tea.

She wanted him to do another reading. *Needed* him to do

another reading because the police had arrested Chris and she needed to know what was going to happen. He told her to take it easy, he would do another reading for her, but first he needed to know what had happened. The irony of this statement was lost on them.

She'd been with Chris at his place that evening. At about the time Doc's decorating was giving me the creeps, the police knocked on Chris's door. Two uniforms, one male, one female and both looking for Mr Christopher Rudjer.

Yes, he was Chris Rudjer.

No, he wouldn't like to go to the station and talk about the morning of the tenth.

Yes, he understood he wasn't under arrest.

No, he still wouldn't like to go to the station.

No, he wouldn't care to tell them where he was two weeks ago.

So, they could either arrest him or get off his doorstep and leave him in peace.

They eschewed the leaving him in peace option and arrested him. I got most of this in the back room, mostly from Doc. Jan sat hugging herself and nodding constantly. The only time she broke in was to relate that one of the cops, the 'young one' she called him, had asked if they should handcuff Chris. The older one, the woman and senior of the two, laughed and said, "You fancy trying it? Be my guest."

Jan smiled at this, proud of the episode.

"Not a very smart move though, getting himself arrested," I said. Doc shook his head.

"Right thing to do. This way they've got to charge him or let him go after twenty-four hours. They've also got to supply a lawyer if he wants one. Chris won't say a word without one."

"How do you know?" Jan asked.

Doc's face twitched with one of his rare smiles. "Chris knows the system."

"What if they do charge him?"

Doc gave her a slightly odd look before answering, "He'll have to cross that one when he comes to it. If they had something concrete on him, I think they'd have skipped the nicely nicely bit and nicked him when he answered the door. They're just sniffing around. Tell you something though, they'll have a warrant under way."

Doc watched Jan, looking for a reaction; he took whatever he saw, or didn't, without comment.

An awkward silence fell and Jan broke it by asking where the bathroom was. I walked her to the bottom of the stairs, told her turn left at the top, and went to look in on dad. I'd told him a friend was in trouble and his girlfriend was too upset to spend the night in an empty house. It was as close to the truth as I could handle. He huffed and puffed for a bit but deigned to allow Jan a bed for a few nights.

I returned to Doc, sat at the dinner table shuffling tarot cards.

"You going to do her a reading?"

He shook his head. "Give her a bit of bullshit, try and calm her down." I gave him a look. "What's your problem? You don't even believe in this."

The pack he was manipulating was fresh and made a harsh crackling noise as he riffle-shuffled it. They weren't the cards he kept wrapped in the white linen.

"Fuck what I believe, you believe it. Feeding someone a load of crap you're going to eat yourself is one thing, spouting shite's another."

Doc fixed me with pale eyes and did a one-handed cut repeatedly. It started to get uncomfortable but I was damned if I was going to look away. If he hadn't spooked her with his Jive in the first place, Jan probably wouldn't be in my home causing me hassle.

"I'll make a believer out of you yet, Yakky."

He slipped the cards back into their box and tossed it onto the table. Then produced the linen-wrapped deck from his leather.

I didn't watch the reading. He was right – I didn't believe

in it and I wasn't sure why it bothered me that he was willing to fake it. I made up the spare room while he and Jan hovered over their delusions. Then I sat with dad, figuring if I invested some time in him I might get to bed without any more drama. He slumped in his chair looking abandoned. I asked him what was on and tried to look attentive.

"Some film. Bloody rubbish."

"Do you want to try the other side?"

Dad managed to shrug at great personal cost. "If you want to. I only have it on for you."

And thus the evening progressed.

Doc pulled out all the stops for the reading. It was at least an hour before he knocked on the door and told us he was off. He knew enough to make a fuss over dad for putting Jan up. Dad did his best to be magnanimous and put-upon at the same time. Doc didn't pick up his cues, maybe because he didn't know the script as well as I did. More likely because he just wasn't playing. Card games were more his thing.

Outside the house, Doc's engine started with an enviable lack of coaxing. He must have been worried because he hadn't chained the bike up before shepherding Jan in. Doc would rise from the grave and walk if he thought his Sportster wasn't safe.

"You were right about the reading," he said. Neither of us was looking at the other; we were watching the bike. Its shuddering tick-over gave the impression it was alive. "I was out of order. Taking the easy way out, you know?"

I nodded, acknowledging the apology. "I was just being stroppy. Karla rang earlier, put me in a shitty mood."

Doc patted me on the shoulder and made that half grunt noise blokes use to console each other.

"Tell Jan about it. Might take her mind off Chris."

At the time, I didn't take this on board, just thought it was the sort of thing people say to fill the silence. Which wasn't Doc's style when I thought about it. As he fastened his crash helmet, I told him to ride safe and he gave his Cheshire Cat grin.

"Ezulie Dantor watches over me," he told me.

Before pulling away, he pointed at the house, then touched the cheek bone just under his right eye.

Keep an eye on things.

I went back inside and through to Jan, still sitting at the dinner table. She looked very different to the last time I'd seen her. She'd been crying and was upset, but even allowing for that, she'd changed. Her hair was shorter and less elaborate, hair you could stuff into a crash helmet. The jacket I'd hung in the hall next to mine was a new bike leather, not a fashion item. It was a serious piece of kit, black hide, thick but supple, at a guess I'd have said goat skin and no change from a month's wages. The expensive dresses had given way to tight black tee shirts and jeans. To my eye, a better look. Like most bikers I put a lot of store in low maintenance and high-abrasion resistance.

It had gone eight by then and I didn't know if she'd eaten. Before I could ask, she thanked me for letting her stay. I said it wasn't a problem but told her to say something to dad, otherwise he'd sulk. She didn't question that, just nodded.

"Have you eaten?"

"No. No I haven't," she looked surprised.

I guessed she'd been running on stress since Chris had departed and I told her I'd make a few sandwiches, waved away her offer of help. I checked in on dad to see if he wanted anything. He said he didn't but changed his mind once I was out of the room. I put a filter coffee together with the last of my supply. I figured Jan would be tea-ed out having spent time with Doc.

I wasn't sure what to do with her. I couldn't see her sitting in the front room with dad and his TV and leaving her alone to stew in the back room would have been heartless. In the end I made my excuses to dad and sat with her while she ate.

"You been staying with the Big Guy?"

She nodded and straight away took a huge bite of sandwich, giving herself an excuse not to speak. I let the subject of her sleeping habits go.

"Have you got anything to bring in from the car?" I asked.

She looked alarmed, as if that hadn't occurred to her. "No. I rushed over to Doc as soon as the police took Chris away." I didn't ask for an explanation but she added, "I couldn't think what else to do."

Low maintenance but maybe not so bright. On my to-do list, *get a tarot reading* would've been some way behind *get a solicitor*.

"Did Doc ring the station?"

She nodded. "They wouldn't tell him anything, just said Chris was helping them with an investigation."

I couldn't help but laugh. Jan didn't see the joke.

"Chris, helping the police? He's got ACAB tattooed across his throat."

"ACAB?" she sounded the word out uncertainly. I remembered thinking she was out of her element that night in The Jericho.

"ACAB: all coppers are bastards," I said.

Jan mouthed a silent *oh*. More silence. I began to think we'd have been better off in front of the telly. She sipped her coffee and made an appreciative noise, the way they do in the adverts. Then she asked me if I'd ever had a reading.

"Tarot cards? Never had the urge."

"You don't think there's anything in it?"

"Doc puts a lot of store by the cards but he doesn't push it on anyone." I wasn't sure why she was asking or for that matter why I was being evasive. "He says people should have something to believe in. With him it's Voodoo."

"Chris said he was a witch doctor."

"Yeah, Doc wasn't too impressed with that."

"Then why does he call himself Doc?"

"He is a doctor. He's got a PhD in psychology."

I waited for her to look surprised and say *really?* I was ready to be affronted on Doc's behalf. She just nodded.

"Chris said he was smart."

Which about summed him up. More silence, so we both sipped coffee to cover it.

"It's good of you to put me up."

"No problem." That wasn't exactly true but it was what you're meant to say. "I guess it's hard to go home after what happened?"

She nodded and went blank for a moment.

"Yeah. The police finished whatever they were doing but ... " and she tuned out again. I opened my mouth to speak but thankfully she spoke first. I had no idea what I would have said. "I've been back to get some clothes and things. I looked in the bathroom, you can still see stains. I'll have to get it steam cleaned or something."

"Have you got a key to get into Chris's place, so you can get your clothes?"

She looked up surprised, again. "Most of my things are still in the hotel." She sighed heavily. "I don't know how I'll get them back now."

"Why shouldn't you get them back?"

"I can't pay the bill. The bank stopped all my cards. I haven't got access to any of Peter's accounts. Until the will's read, I'm penniless. Even the car's in his name." Her chest hitched up and down. She struggled to get a grip, succeeded. "I've got nothing. I can't go back to that house, not on my own."

I reached across the table and, feeling stupid, patted her hand, told her she could stay as long as she needed. She tried to smile and started thanking me all over again, I cut it off as gently as I could. "Doc said the cops have to let Chris go after twenty-four hours. Then he'll be back."

This was a long way from what Doc said, but the mention of Chris coming back calmed her. She nodded emphatically.

"The police will see he didn't kill Peter. Chris wouldn't hurt a fly."

I didn't point out that the police don't arrest people for swatting flies.

Saturday 16 July

I woke up to various Karlas smiling, grinning, pouting or sleeping at me from all four walls. Most mornings I entertained thoughts of pulling all the sketches down and bundling them into a bin. I hadn't yet, but some part of me knew it wasn't healthy to wake up in a room surrounded by pictures of your ex. Another part of me said she wouldn't be an ex forever. The optimist was allied to the professional artist, who knew a good life study when he saw one. For the time being, the pictures stayed.

Karla had often commented on my inability to lie in. Sometimes it infuriated her, other times she envied it. She took it as sign of get-up-and-go. I made a point of not disillusioning her. The truth was I always hated waking up. Some part of my mind had earmarked the start of the day as a time for misery and self-doubt. It wasn't something I'd ever been able to shake off, but as I got older, I learned to cope. Rule one was get up and get moving.

Before the morning fug had fully dissipated, I remembered Jan had been foisted upon me. I gritted my teeth, literally, and forced myself to walk to the bathroom. Mentally pulling it together wasn't an option, so I just kept moving.

Keep moving, tough it out, know it will pass.

I went through my morning rituals of showering and shaving. Dad would refer to this as *a shit, a shave and a shampoo*, then burst out laughing. Any sentence with the word shit in it was comedy gold. It was the main reason I kept my hair cropped back to little more than a fizz of stubble – if I didn't need shampoo he might stop saying it. If not, at least I'd have the satisfaction of proving him wrong.

Around six, I could see the coming day for what it was rather than for the disaster it felt like.

Jan surprised me by poking her head out into the landing as I padded back to my room. I asked if I'd woken her but she shook her head.

"I didn't sleep much."

Not surprising given recent events. I was standing with a towel wrapped round my waist and I noticed her eyes flicker over my chest and away to my shoulders. I wondered if she was sizing me up against Chris or just comparing the tattoos. I thought again of her needing ACAB translated.

"Would it be alright to use the shower?"

"Sure. There should be towels in the airing cupboard."

"Will your dad want the bathroom first?"

I shook my head. Dad wouldn't surface for another couple of hours. She vanished back into the spare room and I went to get dressed. I put on fresh underwear and shirt and remembered Jan's clothes, trapped in the hotel. She was on her way to the bathroom as I left my room. Jeans and the crumpled tee shirt that I supposed she'd slept in.

"If you want a fresh tee shirt help yourself." I jerked a thumb to the door of my room. "There's a load in the chest of drawers."

"Is that alright?" She looked startled. "Going through your things?"

"Don't worry about it. There's nothing particularly private hiding away."

I almost added that I kept my wank mags on the wall and pretended they were art, but I didn't. It wasn't her fault Karla had chosen to leave.

While Jan showered I coaxed half a cup of dish water out from the previous night's coffee dregs. The cupboards were pretty much bare so I checked the front room and found the plate of sandwiches I'd made for dad. Cold tea by his chair. It was a matter of faith with dad that I made undrinkable tea. I downed my half cup of swill and put a curling sandwich under the grill.

Jan, when she appeared, had taken me up on my offer and was sporting one of the long sleeve shirts with the shop's logo on the back. Aside from selling badly, the things shrank at an alarming rate, so the fit on her wasn't too far off. I told her to help herself to whatever she could find.

The couple of hours I had in the mornings before dad got up I normally spent drawing. Producing artworks or just competent renderings, like any skill, requires practice. Talent is less than half the story. Jan was sitting, sort of tuned out again, waiting for inspiration or instruction. I tried to imagine how I'd feel in her situation, couldn't.

"Look I've got to finish off a few bits I've been working on. Will you be okay if I leave you to it?"

She looked up from whatever internal landscape she'd been surveying.

"Yes, of course. Sorry, I should get out of your way."

Then she switched off again. I wouldn't swear that she'd even heard me.

I left her in the kitchen and retrieved a sketch pad from my room along with a set of pens. I'd spent about half an hour drawing a couple of dozen eyes when a phone went off. Jan rushed out of the kitchen and searched through the coats and jackets on the rack.

"Hello? Chris?" The desperation in her voice was horrible, so was the disappointment. "Oh. Jeff ... Yes, I'm alright, sort of." There was a long silence as she listened. "No. Not really, no." She caught a breath as if trying to stop herself crying. "Yes, we should but what about Caroline ... okay." Another pause. "Yeah. Okay, tonight, about eight? Okay. Bye."

She began to pace up and down the hallway. I was on the verge of going to see if she was alright when she stopped pacing and I heard a little series of bleeps, followed by a curse and a knock on the open door.

"Come in."

Jan didn't come in, just put her head around the door, the way she had when she'd seen me on the landing. She looked the way she did when Doc gave her The Jive about The

Fool.

"Can I use your phone? Mine hasn't got any credit left."

Snap.

"Use the landline."

The floating head vanished around the edge of the door. On a whim, I drew a pair of eyes and tried to make them look inquisitive.

Jan sounded excited.

"Doc? Doc, you were right he did call, like you said ... now? Okay."

The floating head did a brief encore to tell me she'd see me at the shop. A second later the black Audi pulled away and headed out the top of the road.

Whistles and Bells

When I got to the shop it was locked, but the lights were on and I could see Jan behind the counter, nodding earnestly at something Doc was telling her. They both looked up as I let myself in.

"Kettle's boiled," Doc said.

He spotted the quick look I shot to Jan and gave me the smallest shake of his head in return. I made myself a drink and got to work with the appointments book. Full house, Doc was going to be busy all day. Gina, the shop's part-time tattooist, also had clients booked in for the afternoon and a private session in the evening.

I started cleaning, checking supplies. Doc busied himself preparing for his first customer and Jan sat in the waiting room thumbing through a book of designs. She was more assured than I'd seen her before, very different to the nervous woman in The Jericho or my blank-eyed house guest.

I caught Doc in the back room. He looked to see the door was shut then gave me the Cheshire Cat treatment. "What do you make of Jan?"

The question came out of the blue. His grin went up a couple of notches edging towards manic.

"What do you mean, what do I make of her? Red hair, long legs, no money, living in my spare room."

"Yeah, I know all that, but how did she strike you? What

vibe did you get? And I'll see you right for money."

I was about to say I wasn't worried about that, but I was.

"How did she strike me? Scared, worried." I gave it a bit more thought. "She was hard work to talk to. No spark, you know? But she has got a lot on her plate."

Doc nodded but didn't comment, just waited for more. I was about to tell him I'd given all I had, then he happened to glance at the door again, checking it was still shut. I pictured Jan poking her head around the edge of the spare room door, then the door from the hallway. Not coming in, not showing herself.

"You know what is strange now I come to think of it?" From his expression, I'm pretty sure Doc had an idea what was coming next. "She came across as nervous again, timid."

Doc made a gimme more gesture with his fingertips. The more I thought about it, the less it rang true. She'd had five or six weeks knocking around with Chris, who was your genuine scary bastard. In a state of distress, she'd then run to Doc with his penchant for Voodoo and tarot cards. Why go all shrinking violet around me? I was under no illusion that I was a badass.

"I can't see the woman who was at my place last night hooking up with a total stranger in a biker's pub. She'd have run a mile."

"Puzzler in'it?"

"So, what was all that about this morning? Her running round here first thing?"

"I'll tell you later."

He tapped his watch. Opening time.

Around two, after the last of the morning clients had left, Doc took a wad of notes from the cash box. He counted out my wages and added another fifty.

"Expenses," he said, making a gesture towards Jan who was alternating her time between checking her phone was on and fiddling with one of Doc's tarot packs. He handed a second wad of notes to her. She tried to refuse. He held up a hand to her protests.

"You can pay me back when this shit is sorted. Anyway, think of it as a bribe, 'cos I'm going to be asking you a favour."

Once Jan headed out with the cash to stock up on a few things, I went around the local pizza place and bought a family size box of ill health.

"Let's have the goods then," I said when I'd finished my first quarter.

Doc wiped his fingers on a paper towel, settled back into the sofa.

"It was her brother in-law called this morning. She's going to meet with him tonight."

"Is this the first time he's been in touch?"

"Yep."

Peter Keller had been on a slab for almost a week.

"Has Jan tried to reach him?"

Doc shook his head. I thought about my sister and her husband. If my sister was found dead, how long would Gary go before he made contact? A day, two on the outside? I hadn't spoken with my sister in three years.

"Not a close family then?"

"Or too close," Doc suggested.

"Spell it out, eh? Use short words." Doc took another slice of pizza and, ever the showman, kept me hanging while he chewed. By the time he'd finished, the penny had dropped. "Mr brother-in-law has a wife?" A nod. "And the wife isn't too keen on him seeing Jan?" Another nod. "Because Mr brother-in-law and Jan have a bit of form?"

"By Jove, I think he's got it."

"She told you this?" Doc pointed at one of the framed sets of tarot, his mouth was full of pizza again. "The reading at my place last night?"

He nodded, held up a finger before I could say anything else. For a man with so many teeth, he chewed at a sedate pace.

"You really were spot on about me bullshitting," he said

after a heroic swallow. "If I had just given her some mooey to chill her out, we wouldn't know any of this."

"Hang on a minute. She said on the phone you told her he was going to call today, how'd you work that?"

He went for the pizza but I pulled the box away. The Jive was wearing thin. I told him to spare me the melodrama.

"First thing, she didn't say anything about calling today. She said, 'he called like you said'. You've picked up on her amazement and your memory's added a few whistles and bells."

I gave him the pizza back and replayed the phone conversation in my head. Conceded he was right.

"And you didn't really tell her he was going to call, did you?"

Doc pulled a face and waggled his hand. "Not outright. The cards suggested things, pointed to possibilities. One of those possibilities came to pass. Jan's memory did what yours did; whistles and bells. *Someone close to you and Peter is thinking about you and trying to reach you*, becomes, *your brother-in-law is going to call.* But that's only after the phone call's happened of course." He picked up another piece of pizza then put it back, decided not to bother with a prop. "If she'd had a letter from him in a month's time, she'd probably still have connected it to what I told her last night."

"And the other possibilities that come to nothing ... "

"Get forgotten."

"So how is this different to you giving her the mooey?"

"If I'd used that deck you saw me shuffling, I wouldn't have been doing a reading. I'd have just been fannying about with a pack of cards." He shrugged, one of the few times I'd seen Doc at a loss. "I don't really understand it myself. I don't always know how the things I do actually work."

"You really think there something in it? Voodoo, tarot?"

"Well, yesterday we didn't know Peter Keller had a brother. This morning? We know his name, his wife's name, what his ex-mistress had for breakfast and where he's going to be at eight o'clock this evening."

Abracadabra.

Jan came back to the shop a little after three. There was no trace of nerves about her now. She didn't bat an eye at the pair of over-pierced Goths poring through the tattoo books. Neither of the Goths gave her a glance, other than to sneak a quick look at her arse as she walked by. I was on the phone with a customer. I acknowledged her with a look and she waited by the counter.

"I was wondering if I could go back to the house," she said as soon as I put the phone down, "I picked up some groceries, thought I should restock your fridge."

"Thanks. Sure, go back to the house if you want. Dad'll let you in."

She smiled, leaned across the counter a little way. I thought she was about to peck me on the cheek and I jerked back slightly. She looked around at the Goths and dropped her voice, "These are the bits Doc asked me to get." She slid a paper bag – its neck folded over on itself half a dozen times – across the counter. Still in a near whisper, "Would Doc mind if I borrowed a pack of his cards?"

I had a quick root through the shelves and came across a newish looking box that, if the packaging was to be believed, contained an art nouveau tarot pack.

"These do?"

Jan slipped the pack into her jacket like it was contraband. When she'd left, I rang my home number and warned dad she was heading back.

We were sat in the waiting room. Doc was sloughed in the sofa nearest the door, positioned so he'd see anyone coming in before they'd see him. The lights were still on but the shop was officially closed for the day. Gina had a private session going; it was my turn to chaperone and Doc was waiting for Jan.

The twilight sky was resisting nightfall but playing a losing game. Doc wasn't talkative and I wasn't in the mood to draw him out, spending time in the same building as Gina was always a chore. The paper bag Jan had left was resting in his lap. He hadn't opened it but it was on display and that suggested he wanted me to ask about it. Like I said, I wasn't in the mood.

A few stragglers from the home-time commute drove past, one of them trailing bad music through their car stereo.

"You fancy a bet?" Doc suddenly piped up.

I'd been quietly sketching him without his knowledge and held up the pad to compare image to reality. I'd flattered him somewhat.

"A bet with you?"

My decline was implicit.

"Where is your sense of adventure, Yak?"

I told him it was way behind my sense of financial survival, and he fell silent again. He'd sussed I was drawing him and his posture became self-conscious. I closed the pad on principle and tucked my pencil behind my ear. Silence.

I broke first.

"Alright. Bet on what?"

Doc tried to affect indifference and I told him he wasn't pretty enough to play hard to get.

"Charming. I am willing to bet that within two minutes of Jan getting to our door, either a white Ford Focus or a silver Honda Civic will drive past that very window."

He pointed at the half-painted shop front. "Really?"

The skeletal tattoo on his cheek twitched with a satisfied smile. "Oh, now you're intrigued."

"You saying someone's following her?"

He leaned out of the sofa some way, dropped the man of mystery act.

"I'm pretty sure. When she turned up here last night, she damn near parked around a lamp post. I moved the car for her and I happened to see saw some guy in a white Ford Focus, parked up on the other side of the street. He stayed there until Jan followed me back to your place. I told you she nearly shunted me a couple of times on the way over? I spent more time looking over my shoulder than I did looking at the road."

"And the white Ford Focus was following?" Doc nodded. "And the silver Honda Civic?"

"I'm not so sure about that one. When I left your place last night, I had a quick look up and down the road. I didn't see the Ford but there was a Honda with someone sat in it. There was a silver Honda Civic about a hundred metres from the shop this morning. I spotted it a bit before you got in."

"But you're not sure it was the same one?"

He shook his head. "Common enough car. I'm pretty sure about the Focus through."

"Police, you reckon?"

"I don't think so. Suspicious death. It's not a murder investigation yet and if it is, they've got Chris to play with." He rubbed the edge of his jaw, stared into the middle distance. "I keep coming back to the Five of Pentangles. Money."

"Losing me here."

"There's a will to be read at some point. That may mean she's about to inherit a fair sum and a good-sized chunk of real estate. Where there's money, there's people wanting to get hold of it or trying to keep hold of it."

Doc went quiet again and slouched back into the sofa. After a while he motioned towards my sketch pad. "You going to show me that, as your professional mentor and all?"

"If you'll tell me what's in the bag."

He tossed the bag on the table and scooped up the pad, regarded the incomplete portrait with approval.

"Screw what you say. I am pretty enough to play hard to get."

The bag contained tubs of makeup.

Jan's black Audi purred past the window and we waited. Two cars passed by, then a silver Honda Civic. I heard Doc click his tongue and mutter something but I wasn't really paying attention. I went to the window and watched the car. Sure enough, it pulled over and parked.

"You think we should tell Jan?" I asked.

Doc had gone back to examining my drawing of him.

"I don't think it'll achieve anything other than scaring her. We know they're there, they don't know we know. I say we play dumb."

Jan walked into the shop, gave me a nod, biker style.

"Ready?" Doc asked without preamble.

"Yeah, I'm ready." She didn't sound sure. "Thanks for doing this."

I waited, with little hope, for someone to explain what was happening. My hopes were fully realised.

Doc: "Did you ring the police station?"

Jan nodded.

"Same thing, 'Mr Rudjer is aiding us with an inquiry'."

Doc checked the clock hung just above the counter. Twenty past six.

"They'll have to let him go or charge him pretty soon. I'm guessing they'll let him go and be waiting at his flat with a warrant to search it." Jan looked despondent at this and Doc added, "Can't see them finding much." Then he turned to me. "I'll be able to reach you here or at your place, yeah?"

I nodded and didn't think to ask why he might need to.

"We better hurry up," Jan said.

Doc picked up the bag of makeup.

"We got time for this?"

"If we get a move on."

With that they went out the door and a minute or two later I heard them moving about in the flat above.

Twenty minutes later I had a glimpse of Doc, in the passenger seat of the Audi, wearing a white shirt with a collar. A minute later the silver Honda Civic followed.

Family Affairs

After leaving me chaperoning Gina, Doc and Jan had gone to Doc's flat. Doc shaved and changed into his one and only button-down collared shirt. An item reserved for funerals and interviews with bank managers. Then Jan applied the heavy-duty makeup to his right cheek, covering the jawbone and teeth tattoo. She did a good job. Anyone who spotted it for what it was would probably assume it was covering a birth mark.

Doc clocked the Honda Civic as soon as it left the curb and kept to his decision to keep Jan in the dark. She had enough to keep her on edge. The closer they got to her home – if she still thought of it that way – the more she withdrew.

The estate the house was built on was an oasis of wealth in a middle-class desert. The first indication that they were hitting the money were the signs reading PRIVATE ROAD. The second was the road itself turning into a mass of craters and rubble. The whole housing complex was privately owned, meaning the road and pavement didn't get maintained by the council. Meaning everyone should pay, meaning no one did.

Jan nursed the Audi over the decaying tarmac and began to fidget. Doc didn't comment on it, assumed she was just upset returning to the house. And of course, she was about to have an embarrassing meeting with a married man she'd slept with.

The estate glistered with the trappings of wealth, all of it new. Keller's house, or what had been Keller's house, was at the rear of the estate, backing onto a golf course.

To get to the house they had to drive through what looked like a wooden five-bar gate. In fact, it was a steel barrier painted to blend into the country house look the builders had aimed for. The pretence was given away by streaks of rust breaking through at the weld points. A keypad mounted on a steel post waited for a code.

While Jan tapped in the sequence of numbers, Doc looked for the silver Civic but couldn't see it. Another car however was parked a little way behind them. The only vehicle, aside from theirs, not tucked away on its private drive. The steel five-bar swung away with a series of jerks and Jan drove through. The other car came to life and followed.

"Jeffry?" Doc asked.

Jan nodded, tight lipped for a moment.

"And Caroline. Oh God. What a bloody mess."

The driveway led just far enough from the road to hide the frontage of the house. Jan parked next to an ageing Mitsubishi 4x4. Jeffry Keller and his wife pulled in behind and the surviving Keller stepped down from his own 4x4. A gleaming Range Rover that hadn't left the showroom floor more than a month before.

Doc couldn't help but notice the surviving Keller's size. He wasn't in the Chris Rudjer's league, but he was in no danger of being mistaken for a midget. He towered over the woman who stepped from the passenger side.

Jan made for the oak-panel doors and began tapping away at another keypad. From somewhere in the house an alarm sounded a long note then cut off. Jan finally looked around at the couple, offered a thin smile and disappeared through the door without waiting to see what reaction it got. The man followed her, glancing at Doc, the woman close behind, face carefully blank.

The entrance hall was kitted out in off-the-shelf

inoffensive. Three or four marble tables prowled around the edges of the floor, vases overflowed with silk flowers that had been colour keyed with the walls. There was a huge photo, printed onto canvas, of Jan done up to the nines next to a man about ten years her senior. The photo and the expensive silk flowers were lit by spotlights.

The little group passed through into a large reception room. This too was decorated in expensive bland. Jan was centre stage in more canvas print photos, professional studio shots like the one in the hall.

On one of the marble tables was a notice from the police informing Jan that in her absence they had affected an entrance to the property and carried out a search. She barely glanced at.

She sat at the end of a four-seater sofa – one of a pair – perched on its edge, knees together and ankles neatly crossed. It was a posture matching one of the posed photos. Without the elaborately styled hair and the trophy-wife designer dress it looked incongruous. Possibly realising this, she pushed herself further back in her seat and uncrossed her ankles.

"Sorry, I haven't been here in days, there probably isn't any milk for tea or coffee. Would anyone like something stronger?"

She motioned to a lacquered cabinet. Jeffry Keller shifted uncomfortably and shook his head; his wife favoured Jan with a glare. Doc asked if there was any Tequila. The cabinet contained a vast array of spirits and all the correct glasses. Doc found a bottle of Casa Noble with an unbroken seal and filled a whiskey tumbler to the two thirds mark.

"Shall we sit?" Jan said. Caroline ignored the comment. Jeffry sat stiffly on the edge of the other sofa. "This is Doctor Slidesmith, he's a friend of mine."

Caroline snorted at the remark and gave Doc a sour look as he held a hand out to her husband.

"Please, just James."

Keller stood again to make sure he was looming over Doc

before taking the offered hand. His grip was barely the right side of crushing.

"Jeffry Keller." There was no suggestion that Doc could use his first name.

He was around fifty-five, with a rugby player's build that was becoming flaccid bulk. He stayed standing until Doc had taken a seat.

"This is a bit awkward, Jan," Keller started. "I didn't want to say this over the phone and Caroline wanted to be here when you were told."

He paused, either thinking of what to say next or waiting for Jan to reply. For the first time Caroline spoke, her voice as sour as her expression,

"Oh, for God's sake, just get on with it."

She pulled a pack of cigarettes from a handbag, put one in her mouth and lit it with a silver lighter. The breath she pulled in as she applied the flame was sharp and angry, half the cigarette turned to ash. Doc noted the polished surfaces and the lack of ashtrays.

Caroline was about the same age as her husband. Noticeably kicking back at the ageing process, she almost looked ready to be photographed for one of the canvas prints. Keller glanced at his wife then at Doc. If he was looking for some sign of male solidarity, he didn't get it.

Doc sipped the Tequila.

The ash fell on the sofa.

"The house ... " Keller started again and again stopped.

Jan, who was avoiding looking at Caroline, spoke up, "I don't know what's going to happen with the house. Because the police are still investigating the ... the ... " She looked up towards a corner of the room. Doc assumed she was directing her gaze towards the bathroom. "Because of *that*, the will hasn't been read yet."

"The house won't be in the will," Keller said carefully, looking like he wanted the ground to swallow him. "The house isn't ... wasn't ... Peter's to put in a will."

"No. It's ours," Caroline said without taking the cigarette

from her mouth. She smiled for the first time, lips stretched across her teeth like a scar.

"It's mine," Keller corrected. He didn't hold her eye for long. "Pete made some bad investments, very bad. He came to me for money, about a year ago."

There was another silence and something hung in the air. Caroline fired up another cigarette after throwing the stub of the first one into the fireplace.

"I gave it to him but he must have lost that too. Then he came back to me wanting more. I didn't want to just throw more money into a black hole. I made another loan on condition that he signed this place over." He looked around the room, trying to indicate the whole property. "Peter was on borrowed time. This has been in my name since February."

Doc sipped the Casa Noble and watched Jan's reaction. She met the loss of the house stoically but the mention of February made her tense and she glanced at Caroline.

Caroline's scar of a smile became a victory grimace.

"So, you can get your things together and find somewhere else."

Jeffry gave her a look, fast and dirty. Fast enough that she didn't see it.

"I'm not expecting you to move out immediately," he told Jan.

Caroline opened her mouth to put forward a different opinion but caught Doc watching her and contented herself with flicking more ash.

"I'm not living here currently," Jan addressed some middle distance. "I can leave tonight."

Keller began to protest, but his wife talked over him, "If she wants to leave now, Jeffry, then let her. She's no reason to stay."

Keller looked again like he wanted the ground to open.

"Caroline, for pity's sake."

"What? For pity's sake, what, exactly?"

Doc, veteran people watcher, was ready to settle down for

the show, but Jan cut the cabaret short by standing up.

"James, would you help me pack? Most of my things are in ... "

Instead of finishing the sentence she looked up to the ceiling again. Doc, with some regret, followed her from the room. As they reached the landing, they heard Jeffry and Caroline leave the house, arguing in whispers. The front door slammed.

Jan began collecting clothes from a bank of built-in wardrobes. Doc asked if she wanted him to get anything from the en suite bathroom. She looked puzzled by the question, then realised why he was asking.

"This isn't where it happened. Peter ... it was in the guest room."

She finished packing in silence, filled a soft leather hold-all and a Samsonite case. It barely made a dent in the room's inventory. She didn't show any concern about leaving the designer clothing behind. Doc carried the large case down the stairs for her.

On the doorstep, Jan began working her key ring, taking the house keys off. She only had two, a Yale and a long deadlock key.

"They might as well take these now."

Doc asked her if she was sure. "I'd want to know more about the legal ins and outs before I moved house."

"I've got no money to put up a challenge. If it's not above board, I'm sure it's something the solicitor will raise when the will's read." She met Doc's eye. "Anyway, I don't want to live here."

She reached to the keypad but before she tapped the alarm code in, Doc patted his pockets.

"Sorry. Left something behind. Do you mind?"

Jan let him in and stepped into the hall too, maybe to get away from the sight-line of Caroline who was leaning against the bonnet of the Range Rover smoking another cigarette. Doc, without turning any lights on, vanished into the reception room and reappeared a minute later with the bottle of Casa Noble.

Jeffry Keller was propping the driver's door of his car open. Caroline was sizing the house up. The tip of her cigarette glowed brighter each time she pulled on it.

"Do you want me to hand the keys over?" Doc asked.

"Please."

Doc found his wallet and drew out one of his business cards, pulled out a pen.

"Better give me the number for the alarm then."

Jan nodded and showed no emotion as she set the alarm, reciting each number aloud. Doc wrote down four digits.

While he took the keys over to the Range Rover, Jan retreated to her own car. The Audi seemed to hold Jeffry's attention, his expression was hard to read in the fading light, but Doc suspected he still had things to say.

Caroline had her hand out. She regarded Doc coolly but took the proffered keys with a half-smile.

"Thank you."

She didn't pocket the keys or drop them into her handbag. She clutched them together in her fist. It may have been her husband's name on the deeds, but evidently it was her prize. Doc passed over the business card.

"Number for the alarm," he said.

"Okay," Jeffry said and pulled himself into the driver's seat tugging the seatbelt across him. As his door softly thudded shut, Caroline spat a look towards Jan. "If you're with that one, you'd better watch yourself."

Doc half turned but changed his mind and said softly, "Something I should know?"

She snorted twin blasts of smoke then jabbed the hot end of the cigarette towards Jan.

"She's a slag, that one. Nothing but a – " Doc waited but Caroline had composed herself. She let the end of her cigarette fall between them and extinguished it with a twist of her shoe. "You'll see soon enough Mr ... ?"

"Slidesmith," Doc said. "My name and number are on the

card."

Caroline nodded and stepped from the front of the car to the passenger's door.

Jan's Audi was blocked in by the Range Rover and they sat waiting for Jeffry to pull away. He'd tried to reverse back along the driveway but given up after two attempts. Driving wasn't Jeffry's forte. Jan was checking her phone.

"Still nothing from Chris," she said. "I've tried ringing him. I just get, 'The number you have called is unavailable'."

"Not much we can do right now," Doc told her.

The Range Rover lumbered through a three-point turn. She allowed the Kellers to get far ahead before slipping the Audi into drive.

"Well, that was delightful," Doc said once they were under way.

They'd picked the Honda Civic up again almost as soon as they left the private estate and rejoined the public highway.

"I've had worse times with Caroline."

"You two ever get on?"

Jan thought before answering, "We were civil. Had the same social circle, coffee mornings, ladies who lunch." She pretended to plant big kisses on somebody's cheeks. "Mmmwah ... mmmwah ... daaarling you look gooorgeous. It was all about winning. Who had the biggest house, who had the most expensive shoes. It's hard to be friends when you're keeping score."

"Who'd win?"

"In our little clique? Caroline was always in the top set. I was barely in the club. I was the newer model though."

"Come again."

"I was youngest. Trophy wives aren't like wine, their vintage doesn't improve with age." She fell silent and Doc let the silence hang, waiting for her to fill it. "Jeffry always had an eye for me and Caroline knew it, she got protective."

"And that added fuel to the flame?"

"I suppose so, yes. I'm not proud of sleeping with Jeffry

but with women like Caroline, it's hard to take it seriously, hard to imagine them caring enough to be hurt."

"Because the husband's just another way of keeping score?"

"Exactly."

"So, one point to you."

Jan nodded. "But now I'm a homeless widow. Game, set and match to Caroline."

While Jan parked the car, Doc came into the shop. He just caught me before I left for home. Gina had left twenty minutes earlier, leaving me and her client to arrange the next appointment. She'd grunted something to the client and blessed me with a frown by way of a good night.

The client had been a middle-aged woman with a woeful expression. At a guess, I'd say the tattoo had been more private than intimate. Gina was a good choice for things like that; she never asked questions and never got curious. I nodded a greeting to Doc and collected my helmet and gloves. I wanted to get away. I'd picked up the mood of the shop by osmosis.

"Any word from Chris?" Doc asked.

"No. Would he call here?"

"He might, if he's out and wondering where Jan is."

Personally, I questioned if Chris would be wondering.

"Might be worth belling the cop shop," I suggested, but Doc was already moving around the counter to the shop's phone. Jan came in just as he hung up. She must have guessed what he'd been doing because she looked at him hopefully.

"The police said he's out. They let him go," he glanced at the clock, "over two hours ago."

I found myself homing in on Jan's expression. Like they say, misery loves company. As I expected, she looked crestfallen.

"Then where is he, why hasn't he called?"

I didn't say anything and neither did Doc. I'd have lain

money that we were thinking the same thing. Jan looked from one of us to the other. I thought again about her hovering behind the doors at my place, waiting to be told the rules before making a move. She sat herself down on one of the sofas and faded out for a few beats.

"I think I'll go round Chris's gaff," Doc said finally. More to me than Jan.

Jan looked up at him, was about to speak, then didn't. I felt bad for her. Maybe it hadn't occurred to her that Chris had a list of priorities she wasn't on.

When she found her voice again, she said, "Do you want me to drive you?"

Doc drew in a deep breath, buying time to think, and at last shook his head.

"No. I better go on my own." Jan, waiting for reassurance, didn't look away. "If there's more trouble brewing, Chris wouldn't thank me for dragging you into it."

I don't know if she believed that line of Jive but she was willing to take whatever was on offer.

"I'll ring you as soon as I've got news okay? I'll ring you at Yakky's place."

He left the shop and headed to his flat.

Jan settled back into the sofa, switched off again. I went to the shop door and looked left and right. The Audi was tucked behind a white builder's van. The silver Honda Civic was parked thirty yards further up on the opposite side of the road. I stroked the mojo a couple of times and went back to Jan.

"You alright to drive?" She looked up, distracted, and nodded. "Let's make tracks then."

Jan moved slowly to the door. I locked up and told her to go ahead. My bike was just outside the shop and I sat astride it, letting the engine warm up, and watching the silver Honda in the rear-view mirror. Angry that it would be following Jan to my home, I indulged a fantasy of beating the driver senseless. In the mirror, Jan's car exited left at the top of the road. As she began the turn, the Honda moved away from the kerb.

Keller dead in a pool of blood and Chris arrested. Now a woman, who'd been involved with both, was sleeping in my dad's spare room, and people we didn't know were tracking her there. I gave the mojo another stroke before pulling away.

I made it home before Jan. I'd slipped the bike along the outside line of traffic as she waited at a red light. The Civic was two cars behind and I was careful not to look at the driver as I rolled by.

Jan didn't notice me when I drew up beside her at the head of the queue. I wasn't surprised; people behind steering wheels normally blot out their surroundings. Wound clock-spring tight, she was holding it together but it was costing her. I remembered Doc's account of riding with her behind him, and when the light changed, I dropped the clutch and put some distance between us.

The phone sounded as soon as I got through the door. I got to it before the second ring. It wasn't fast enough to stop a bleating round of, "The phone. The phone, Andy. Andy, the phone."

"I've got it, Dad," I bellowed at the wall of sound from the front room, hand clamped over the mouth piece.

"Hello, Yakky?"

"Yeah, hello."

More bleating: who is it, who's there, what do they want, Andy? Andy, Andy, *Andy!* Christ, I hated that name. My shoulders inched up my neck as the homecoming tension settled in. Dad made it to the front room door then sagged dramatically against the frame.

"You there, Yakky?" from the phone.

I almost started laughing but didn't. If I started, I might

not stop until they medicated me. Possibly from a safe distance using a dart gun.

"I'm here, give me a minute." I guided dad, still gasping questions, back to his chair. "Hello, Doc. I'm with you now."

"I'm at Chris's drum. His bike's still here but there's no sign of him."

"He might have headed straight to a pub."

Doc clicked his tongue, then he said, "Is Jan with you?"

"Not yet."

I explained about leaving her at the lights. Behind me I heard the TV launch into the news at ten.

"I'm not sure what the deal is between those two," Doc said. "Jan's in a state after everything that's happened. She might just be trying to hold on to anyone who's handy. Chris might just be convenient."

"You think Chris is avoiding her?"

"I think he might not even know she's worried. When they met, she was just looking for a leg over. He might not think it's moved beyond that. If he doesn't know she's been calling the cop shop looking for him, he'll probably think she's just moved on."

"So, what do I tell her when she gets here?"

"Tell her I'll call if I find him. In the meantime, I'm going to put a note through his door to call me or Jan."

"Have you tried the neighbours?"

"Yeah. No joy. I'm going to head down The Jericho, see if anyone's seen him."

I thought about another evening with a grieving widow and a sulking father.

I told him I'd join him there.

"I'll wait 'til Jan gets in; tell her what's happening."

"Okay. Ask her if Chris took anything with him when he was arrested."

"Like what?"

"Money, wallet, phone."

"Okay, I'll ask her."

"One last thing, Yak: tell Jan not to answer any calls from Jeffry or Caroline. Let it go to answerphone when they ring."

"*When* they ring?"

"Yep. It's your round by the way."

Dead line.

The Jericho was heaving, somebody was having a birthday and celebrating big time. I don't know what time the serious drinking started, but no one I saw was going to make it to closing time.

Doc was nowhere to be seen, but I'd parked up next to his Sportster so I knew he was close. I forced my way to the bar and shouted myself hoarse to get a barmaid's attention.

"Tequila. The expensive one." I jabbed a finger at the top shelf. "Double."

I handed over a note and turned away from the bar straight into the glare of Doc's teeth.

"Thanks," he roared and melted through the crowd like smoke, taking the Tequila with him. I followed him back to the relative quiet of the street.

A trio of guys in bike leathers were gathered around our bikes, cooing over Doc's Sportster. My bike didn't get admirers, just sympathisers.

"Any word on Chris?" I asked.

"Nothing. Did you find out if he had any money on him?"

"Jan didn't know for sure. She said he left his jacket behind when he went off with the police. His wallet's probably in it."

Once it became clear Doc wasn't going to offer an explanation I asked why it was important.

"Only time I ever got pulled in by the police they kept me overnight then slung me out at six o'clock on a Sunday morning, no money, no phone. I ended up walking five miles home."

"So, if they threw Chris out on the tiles four hours ago, he could still be walking?"

Doc nodded.

"I should have thought of that in the first place. I think I got a bit caught up in the drama."

"Jan's worry rubbing off?"

"Maybe. Still, something's not right."

"I wonder why Chris left his jacket behind."

"I thought that."

Chris had spent time with the police before, not on amicable terms. He'd have known to take his wallet, at least cash for a cab or train fare. I'd been wondering if Jan was over estimating her position in Chris's life, I could have got that arse about face. Perhaps Chris had left everything behind expecting Jan to wait in his flat, expecting her to know the drill when your old man got arrested.

"Did you put a note through his door, or on it?" I asked.

"Through it. You thinking he left his keys?"

My jacket had half a dozen pockets, all of them held something, keys, phone, loose change. If I left the house without it, I'd be in limbo. It was the blokey biker equivalent of a handbag.

"We best get over to Chris's place again," Doc said.

Chris's flat was the bottom floor of a maisonette. I didn't know if he owned it or rented it from the council but it was unmistakably his. The handkerchief front garden was concreted over and stained in a dozen places with cancers of oil. His matt black Suzuki stood guarding the front window, locked down to a pair of steel eyelets. Doc rang the doorbell and we stood in silence waiting. Nothing.

My mobile had a torch on it. I shone it through the letter box and saw Chris's jacket hanging in the hall. Doc wrote: *Chris, call Jan or Doc ASAP* on another business card and wedged it into the door jamb.

After a spell of pointless silence, he said, "You fancy a ride? I'd like to take another look at Jan's place."

I followed Doc back to the new-moneyed estate and cursed the state of the private road as we babied our bikes over it.

A security light came on as we landed on Keller's drive. I left my helmet and gloves on my seat and waited for Doc to chain up his Sportster. I didn't ask who was going to see it, let alone steal it.

"Now what?" I asked when he'd finished.

He was looking over the frontage of the house; it was big but not huge. The Mitsubishi I'd parked beside was an older model with a crease along the driver's door. It was wearing road tyres and a good growth of rust. There wasn't any mud on it.

"Just want to sniff around a bit. What you think of the place?"

"Needs a bit of work. That front gate's on its last legs." I jerked my head at the make believe off-roader. "And what's this for, patrolling the grounds?"

The gardens had been carefully laid out to give the impression that they rolled away into the distance. If you took the trouble to look, the flood lights were casting most of their light on the golf course next door.

"Yeah. That's what I thought. Shall we go inside?"

"How? Jan gave the keys to her in-laws."

Doc gave me one of his more disturbing grins, held up a pair of keys on a ring.

Jan hadn't given the keys back, Doc had. Only he hadn't. While he'd been back in the house stealing the Tequila, he'd separated two of his own keys from their ring. Caroline Keller's spiteful victory grip had been wasted. She'd been holding the keys to the shop. When the switch was discovered, it could be passed off as an honest mistake. The discovery, when it came, was likely to result in Jan getting a phone call. One she'd been primed to ignore.

I asked what all the cloak and dagger was in aid of.

"The code number for the alarm's on the back of my card. When Jan doesn't answer they'll probably try me next. I want a chat with Caroline."

"Why?"

Teasing information from Doc was getting on my nerves

and I was beginning to regret coming along for the ride.

"Caroline's got a knife out for Jan and I want to hear her story." Doc slipped into the house and took a second to realise I hadn't followed. "You coming?"

"Not until I know why we're here."

He found a light switch and a ridiculous number of spotlights came on in the entrance hall. I squinted as my eyes adjusted from night vision to white-out.

"If Jan's husband didn't kill himself, then someone else did. I want to look around a bit"

"We've here to play detective?"

Doc vanished into the house leaving me to decide whether to follow him or not. I stepped into the hall, annoyed with myself for not leaving.

"You don't think the police will have done all this?" I asked when I caught up with him.

The Jive was gone now; he wasn't grinning.

"The police want a warm body so they can clear the books and meet their quotas. I'm looking to keep my mate out of the dock."

"Seriously, you think they'd frame him?"

Doc headed up the supersize staircase. In the house this one was pretending to be, it would have been one of a pair.

"I think Chris is an easy option to get the job done. Criminal record, history of violence. And I doubt if he made any friends at the station today. Policemen are human too. They cut corners, decide things with their gut not their brain."

I didn't bother asking if they'd be better off deciding things with tarot cards.

"Alright," I said, "let's say Chris is the cop's number one choice for dirty deeds. What are we going to find that the police haven't?"

"I don't know. All I know is the police are looking to prove some bugger did it. We've trying to prove someone didn't."

Doc took a pair of black latex gloves from his jacket,

black being the colour of choice for tattooists because they hide smears of ink and blood. He threw a second pair to me.

"Is this legal?"

It was a question I should have asked at the door.

"If anyone asks, Jan wanted us to pick something up for her. We've not forcing an entry because we've got a set of keys and the number to the alarm."

"Then why'd you bring gloves?"

"I always carry a couple of pairs, saves getting covered in shit if I've got to fiddle with the bike on the side of the road."

"Your prints will be all over the place already."

"Yeah, but most of the house isn't a crime scene."

Doc gave me a grin that was high on enamel and low on reassurance.

We had to open a few doors before finding the guest room where Peter Keller died. We knew we'd found it by the silver-grey dusting of fingerprinting medium the police had left behind. That and the trail of footprints on the cream carpet, which led from the door of the en suite. The footprints became vague smudges after four or five steps. Someone had paddled in a lot of blood before leaving the bathroom.

The guest room was too big to be comfortable and not big enough to be impressive. The architect had tried to hide this in plain sight by sheathing the bank of fitted wardrobes with mirrored glass. They reflected a largely empty room and a lot of beige paint. Other than the bed, the only furniture was a lady's dressing table and chair. The bed was a king-size that someone, I guessed the police, had stripped, revealing a cheap box-spring mattress.

Doc tapped his knuckles on the mirrored door he was nearest to.

"What do you make of these?"

A pair of handprints had been captured in silver-grey. Someone big had left them there.

"Chris?"

"That's what I'd have said before I met the lovely Jeffry Keller."

"Mister brother-in-law then?"

"I don't know about that. I'm just wondering if Jan's got a thing about big men. How'd you reckon the prints got here?"

"Someone leaning against the wardrobe?"

"Or … "

Doc leaned on another of the mirrored doors, mimicking the placement of the handprints. I wasn't any wiser until he made thrusting movements with his hips. The light dawned on a mental picture I could have lived without.

"Well okay, but so what? It's a bedroom, that's what people do."

Doc moved away from the wardrobe doors and mused on the prints.

"It's the position that strikes me."

"Jan gets it from behind. Like I said, it's a bedroom."

Doc gave me a grin that would have got most people sectioned.

"Go stand behind the bathroom door and look through the crack. Tell me what you see."

Resistance was useless. I got into position and pulled the door nearly closed. My view of the room was as close to complete as made no difference. I was looking out at a wall of mirrors and what I couldn't see directly was visible in reflection. If the dear departed Peter Keller was behind that door he'd see Jan and whoever getting it on.

"You see the palm prints?" Doc asked.

It was hard not to – they were central to my line of sight. If Peter had stood where I was, he might as well have been sitting on the edge of the bed.

"Are you thinking he caught Jan at it then killed himself?"

Doc shook his head.

"Don't see it myself, do you?"

I gave it some thought. It wouldn't have been my reaction. Keller sees his wife, up against the mirror, getting her brains screwed out, loses it and goes for Chris. To me that made more sense than suicide. It was a scenario could have gone south real quick.

"Keller storms, in all guns blazing. Chris drops him," I said.

"I don't see that either," Doc said, "but I'd guess it's what the cops are going for."

He joined me and put the bathroom's array of spotlights on.

"You saying it *was* suicide then?"

Doc looked around the bathroom and didn't answer straight away.

"The only thing I'd swear to is Chris ain't a killer."

I hardly knew Chris and wouldn't swear to anything about him.

"I'm talking about an accident, not a murder."

Doc wasn't having it.

"If Chris had self-defenced Keller to death they'd still be scraping him off the walls."

I could see the truth of that. Even a clean kill was likely to leave traces. Something that might not work in the Big Guy's favour. Blood all over the walls could be construed as self-defence. A clean bedroom with a dead body in the bathroom looks like you took a little time planning things.

The bathroom was slightly smaller than the shop and fitted out in marble and polished chrome. The metallic grey powder had been dusted on almost any surface capable of holding a fingerprint. The blood bath someone had walked into the carpet had been cleaned up but the vanity unit, four foot from the toilet, had a brown witness mark smeared over its side. Whoever had done the cleaning hadn't done a great job. Or opened a window – the air was toxic with industrial cleaner.

The floor was black slate squares, each separated from the next by half an inch of grouting. The grouting had soaked up stains and provided a map of blood loss.

Doc looked around the en suite.

"What you think?" he asked.

"Think about what?"

He made a long sweeping motion with his arms: the crime scene.

"Let's go with the suicide option. This look right to you?"

I wondered why I'd been appointed expert status, but since we were already there, I rolled with it. I thought about how I'd go about killing myself. I'd probably opt for an enclosed space and a running engine. Sit down, fade away and let someone find me. If I was going to be found in possibly the world's biggest bathroom ...

"Toilet's a hard way to do it, if you sit on a toilet, then slash your wrists you're going to get weaker, start to topple, reflexes try and keep you upright, not an easy route. If I was going to end it all, I'd be looking to just slip away peacefully. That or go out with a bang."

"Bang?"

"Find your wife cheating in your own bedroom with its shiny mirrors and its tasteful cream carpet? If you wanted to send a message, you'd bleed out all over the bed, make it nice and clear what had driven you to it. Slip away gently or go bang. Toilet seat don't feel right either way." I pointed at the bathtub. "Nice warm bath, lay back, drift off. That's where most wrist slashers do it. Water slows down the blood clotting too."

"If we're talking about disguising a murder?" Doc asked.

"Still don't see why you'd pick a toilet. I'd think it'd be easier to dump a body in a bath than get one to sit up to order. And why the bathroom at all? Easier to leave the body in the bedroom."

Most people don't want to handle stiffs more than they have to. You take the route of least resistance.

Doc nodded his agreement. Which was great, we'd established it wasn't murder *or* suicide.

Back in the entrance hall was the photo portrait of Jan and her late husband. They were both booted and suited. Peter slightly in the foreground, his chunky gold watch doing its best to draw focus from his middle-aged spread. Jan had been caught with her eyes turned to her husband, smiling warmly, hand on his shoulder. He was staring straight out to the camera, feet shoulder-width apart. His head was titled back slightly, possibly to hide the beginnings of a double chin, possibly to give the impression of assurance.

"Strike you as the modest type?" Doc asked. It was a question that didn't need an answer.

He walked through to the big reception room. Like the bedroom, it was too big to be comfortable and not big enough to take your breath away.

"Looks like he thought a lot of Jan," I said.

"You think?"

I swept a hand around gesturing to more portraits, these ones solo shots of Jan.

"As an artist, Yakky, would you say any of these look remotely like Jan?"

Photography's never really caught my interest, pencil line or inks have always been my thing, but casting my *artistic* eye over the pictures, I saw what Doc meant. Jan, at least the Jan on the walls, would've looked at home on the cover of *Vogue.* Not a hair out of place, makeup that must have taken hours. The photographer might as well have taken pictures of a shop window dummy. An expensive shop window, of course.

Doc revisited the drinks cabinet and checked through the bottles again. I asked him if having the keys and alarm code provided legal precedent for raiding the booze.

"We'll tell the judge we're just a pair of happy-go-lucky scamps. There's no more Tequila anyway. Plenty of pricey-looking Scotch through if you fancy it."

"More a lager drinker myself."

I trailed after Doc to the kitchen. He went through the drawers and opened the cabinets. I watched him and wondered how much the yards of granite had cost. There was a pair of fridges, six-foot-high and a cool silver-blue colour, one of them fronted with a glass door.

Doc directed me to it.

"There's the lager."

The glass front was displaying a range of bottled lagers with fancy labels. It took me a while to find one in English. The bottom shelf had a dozen bottles of mixers and a similar number of miniature cans. I thought about slipping a few bottles into my jacket but decided against it. I wasn't much of a drinker. Doc pulled open the door on the other fridge, the one with the usual solid front.

"Look at this."

I recoiled at the smell. Jan had been living either at Chris's place or in a hotel since the death and the contents of the fridge were getting ripe. Luckily it was mostly empty. One of the few things in it was three tins of cheap lager clinging to the plastic net thing that holds a six-pack together. There was a bottle of white wine in the door, next to a carton of milk that had ambitions to be cheese. I knew nothing about wine but I suspected the good stuff doesn't come with a screw top.

Doc took the bottle and looked at it with a critical eye.

"Bit different to those."

He used the bottle of plonk as a pointer. There was an island unit dominating the kitchen, a rack with a dozen bottles on it sitting centre stage. Doc put the cheap wine back in the fridge and before he shut the door, I noticed a tin of cola nestled behind the lager. It was another cut-price supermarket brand.

"Why would you buy the cheapo economy junk when you've got a stockpile of the real McCoy?" Doc asked.

"If Jeff's being honest, Peter had money problems. Perhaps he couldn't afford the good gear anymore."

"So why not drink what you've got? If you've got a taste for the finer things, why spend money you don't have on rubbish you're going to gag on?"

"Maybe the cheap stuff's for the staff. I'd bet there was a cleaner and a gardener. The great and the good get the branded splendour and the help get the crap."

I had a paper round for a year or so when I was a kid. Come Christmas I went hunting for tips – the bigger the house, the smaller the tip.

"Don't explain the wine. Who gives the gardener a glass of wine?"

"Okay. If Chris was round here, maybe he brought it over."

I was thinking about the bottom-shelf Tequila Doc had bridled at. Bringing cheap booze for a quickie with a married woman wasn't out of the question. Doc shook his head.

"I can see him buying cheap plonk and cut-price beer but he wouldn't leave half a six-pack behind."

We both thought the same thing at that point. I broke the silence. "He might have hightailed it out of here with other things on his mind."

Doc sighed and for a second looked slightly desperate.

"Chris didn't kill him. You'll have to take my word on this, Yakky. Chris can be a handful when the mood takes him, but he's no killer."

He held my gaze until it got uncomfortable. I was getting an inkling of how Jan would have felt having her tarot read. I took a degree of pride in how effective my tattooing of his face had been.

"Look, Doc, if you're that certain about it, I'll go with it. Okay?"

Doc graced me with his least disturbing grin and said, "Thanks. Thanks man."

"But ... Chris still might have left here at warp factor five if he was with Jan when she found the body. Tough guy or not, I don't see him waiting around for the blue crew to show."

"Yeah. I'll buy that. We'll ask the tight bastard when we find him."

He carried on looking through the cupboards, pulling a few jars out at random. Again, no-brand basic stuff and not much of it. The acres of granite and the six-burner hob didn't get much work. I took another look at the glass fridge. Once I got past being impressed with the range of pretty labels, I saw it was almost empty. The bottles were pulled to the front, making the shelves look full. A bowl of fruits sitting on a corner cabinet turned out to be wax. It was like standing in a doll's house.

Doc left the kitchen and went through to the hall. He pulled open another door.

"Now what?" I was working up to a bad mood, angry at myself for following Doc on this jaunt and unsettled by the house.

"This looks like an office."

Doc vanished into the room but I didn't follow him.

I propped up the door frame and watched from the hall. A small gesture of independence that didn't make me feel better.

The office was a fair size. Lots of shelf space, and a faux antique desk that could have doubled as a pool table. This room had been dusted for fingerprints, too. Doc was opening drawers again and in a particularly deep one, found another stash of bottles. Vodka this time and, again, cheap stuff.

Doc held up a bottle that was nine tenths done.

"Will the real Mr Keller please stand up?"

I could see what he meant. This was the first room we'd seen that felt genuine. An ageing computer monitor, ugly and functional, was sitting on the desk. Cables trailed from the back of it and lay meaningless on the desk top. No keyboard, no computer. The room smelt of skin and sweat – someone had spent many many hours in there.

"Looks like the police took his computer. Printer too, I'd say."

Doc nodded at a space on one of the shelves, bordered on one side by an open box of ink cartridges and on the other by a block of paper.

There was a sheen of dusting medium along the front edge of the shelf. I didn't know if it was there by design or accident.

Doc put the vodka back in the drawer, pushed it shut and looked around him, frowning. On one wall was a framed, poster-sized map of the world, a political map, not the kind you'd normally put up with aesthetics in mind. Next to it was a print of a super yacht, moored somewhere the extremely rich went to get sunburn. The print and the map were in cheap clip frames and both were faded with age. Doc and I both stared at them without comment. I found the two pictures strangely sad for some reason.

Doc used the opening bars of Tequila as a ringtone. When it went off we both jumped. In the stillness of the dead man's office, the ring sounded incredibly loud.

It was Chris.

Biker in a Tie

When Doc ended the call with Chris, he tipped an imaginary hat to me.

"You were right on the money – keys *are* in his jacket. He assumed Jan would wait at his flat."

"Where's he calling from?"

"Neighbour." He pulled up a number on his mobile, told me, "Going to let Jan know."

"Chris didn't call her?"

"Her number's in his phone."

That was doubtless in his jacket too. Jan answered and we heard the TV blaring in the background and the flustered rigmarole of dad having a phone conversation by proxy. I caught Doc flicking a look at me from the corner of his eye, trying not to laugh. I exited the room, embarrassed on dad's behalf.

I waited in the hallway under the photo portrait of the happy couple, tried to gauge what they were thinking about. I couldn't come up with any ideas. Like the cover-shot photos in the reception room the picture had captured the surface image and nothing more.

Doc came out of the office, tucking his phone away, straight-faced and apologetic.

"Sorry Yak, laughing at your old man. I didn't mean anything by it."

"Forget it. I want to laugh myself sometimes. He goes into one every time the phone rings. I can't get a bloody word in when Karla calls. *Who is it? What do they want? Why are they calling at this time of night? Where're they calling from? How long they going to be?*' I sighed, the humour lost on me at that point. "Every fucking time."

Doc gave me the patent blokey slap on the shoulder.

"Family, eh?"

"Yeah," I said, "family."

Doc told me Jan sounded relieved when he called. She'd left Chris's flat in a rush, trying to find Doc, and hadn't thought about collecting house keys. He told her we'd all meet at Chris's and see about getting his door open before the Big Guy kicked it off its hinges. We hammered the bikes across town like the oil crisis never happened.

I expected the black Audi to be waiting for us when we arrived but it wasn't. We parked up on the hard standing and before we had our helmets off, Chris had joined us. He was in jeans and a sleeveless muscle shirt. I thought a night in the cells must have suited him because he was in good spirits, then he saw we were alone.

"Where's Jan?" he said by way of greeting. "You did call her?"

"Yeah, I called her. She's on her way over."

Chris looked back at Doc with his head cocked to one side, waiting for an explanation.

"She stayed over at my place," I said.

Something about the way Chris navigated the hard standing on his way to me put me on guard. I clambered off my bike, making sure I kept it between us, thinking for a second that my time had come. Then it stopped. Chris realised he'd put the wind up me and gave me what he thought was a reassuring smile. He had fewer teeth than Doc; it didn't help.

"Thanks man, I really appreciate that."

"When did you get back?" Doc asked him, chaining the Sportster up.

"I called you as soon as I found your card." The good

spirits had evaporated. "Left the cop shop then remembered I didn't have me poxy wallet. I'd left everything in my jacket, phone, keys, the lot. I've had to walk miles. Bloody police." He scowled around at the world in general. Then to me, "Has Jan been alright?"

"Worried about you, but she's okay."

Chris nodded and tried another smile. I wished he wouldn't.

"Did she say if she's got my keys?" he said to Doc, who was already at the front door.

"She ain't got them. You're locked out and that is official. Luckily for you, I'm a skinny sod."

He slid his leather off, then eased his arm into the letter box, twisted himself into an odd position, hunting for the lock on the inside. It took him a minute or so but the door cracked open.

Jan pulled up just as Chris was about to step into his hallway. They didn't speak. Jan, if I'm any judge, was close to tears. She threw her arms around the Big Guy and pressed her face into his chest. Chris engulfed her with massive arms and kissed the crown of her head. He nearly dislocated his neck to get down so far. I walked to the doorway to give them space, spectating felt dirty. Doc was watching their embrace from the cover of the unlit hall.

"Looks like Chris has got it pretty bad," I commented, uncomfortable to find Doc had turned voyeur.

"Yeah, I think you're about to get your spare room back."

He sounded far off, deep in thought.

"Something wrong?" I asked.

Chris was murmuring something into the top of Jan's head. Doc finally turned away.

"Not really, I was just wondering why it took her so long to get here."

He must have been leaning against the switch because the light came on without him appearing to move. It made me jump and he favoured me with a grin.

"You going to put the kettle on or what?" he shouted at

the expanse of the Big Guy's back.

Chris and Jan tried not to separate as they came through the front door. The door was barely large enough for Chris on his own so the idea was a non-starter. They both found this funny.

Again, I'd followed Doc into someone else's home. I couldn't see why we were hanging around. The door was open and love's young dream were reunited. Our work was done.

In the living room Doc dropped his jacket on the floor and plonked himself into an ancient armchair facing a TV screen. The flat was open plan and the living space segued into a kitchen diner. I sat at a bare pine table that rocked slightly when I put my elbows on it.

The flat lacked the starkness of Doc's place but I had the impression Chris could move out without a backward glance.

Doc caught my eye and shook a can at me. It sloshed gently and he put it back by the side of the armchair. Chris must have been sat having a drink when the police arrived. It wasn't fancy but it was a branded lager, not the budget stuff in Keller's fridge.

Doc settled himself deeper into the chair. I thought he was making some sort of point sitting in the Big Guy's place. Then I took in the layout of the room. The chair was against the wall, close to the hinged side of the door. When Chris and Jan finally came in from the hall, I was the first thing they saw. Doc took a second to locate because the open door shielded him from view. The effortless way Doc homed in on these locations was unnerving.

Chris didn't put the kettle on but Jan did. She also took the abandoned beer can to the bin. As soon as he'd been found, Doc had moved over to the table with me. The Big Guy vanished briefly and came back in a fresh tee shirt that would have fitted me twice. Jan pulled a similar vanishing act as the kettle boiled and reappeared in loose fitting combat trousers and tight-fitting vest top. After doling out the drinks, she sat at the table, packing herself close to Chris.

Doc asked what had happened with the plod.

"They asked a lot of questions and I told them I wasn't saying anything." Chris shrugged, shoulders like tectonic plates. "What can I tell you? *Blah blah blah.* You know what they're like."

"Why'd they pull you in?"

It didn't occur to anyone that this was none of his business. Jan, I figured, at least had some reason for sitting at the table. She'd pulled Doc into her life when she turned up asking for help. Chris only called because Doc wedged a card in his door telling him to. Yet there we were, gathered around the table, holding court.

Chris drained his can and absently crushed it into something the size of a walnut.

"The police don't think Jan's husband did himself in," Chris said. "They said *suspicious circumstances* and *manslaughter* quite a lot."

Jan went pale. I thought the relief of Chris making it home had made her forget the depth of trouble he was possibly in. She grabbed one of his hands and squeezed it.

"Manslaughter?" Doc asked.

Chris nodded. "They've got my prints in the ... "

"Bedroom," Jan finished. She gave Chris a dopy my-hero smile.

"The bedroom next to the bathroom where he killed himself."

I kept my eye on Jan more than Chris. Which wasn't hard to do, but a view worth killing for? If the only thing between you and her was Peter Keller with his wax fruit and off-the-shelf good taste? She hadn't batted an eyelid at the mention of her husband's death, and she'd found the body. The stains on the bedroom carpet implied she found him in a blood bath.

"What do the police think happened?"

Chris asked Jan to get him another lager. She kissed his head as she got up from the table.

"The police think Peter caught us in the bedroom. They

were playing good cop bad cop."

He laughed without any humour.

"So, what was good cop saying?" Doc asked.

"She was going for a self-defence story. Enraged husband comes out all guns blazing and I lose it. Then I try and make it look like suicide."

Doc nodded; we'd worked through that idea.

"Bad cop?"

"He just kept on saying they knew it wasn't suicide and they knew I was involved."

Jan returned with two lagers, put one in front of Chris and opened the second for herself. She took a long pull straight from the can.

"Why are they so sure it's not suicide?" I asked.

Chris looked at me a beat too long and I thought I'd broken the spell of Doc irresistible will. Then Chris's eye flickered towards Jan. I'd trodden on some toes one way or another.

"They said some things about way the body was found."

"Like?" Doc said.

Chris ignored both of us, turned to Jan.

"You okay with this, hon?"

Blank-faced, she took another pull at the lager and nodded. "It's okay. We need people on our side."

Chris didn't turn back to Doc immediately. He may have been processing the meaning of *our* side. Chris Rudjer, republic of one, looked to be expanding the borders.

"Good cop said the note they'd found didn't add up. Bad cop came out with some snide remark about the blade he'd used. Something about, *'You really didn't think out that Stanley knife too well, did you?'"* He looked over to Jan again, checking her reaction. So far there hadn't been one. "The pair of them kept saying how convenient it was Jan had messed up the evidence."

Bingo. Jan shuddered and her head dropped so she was staring at the tabletop. Chris stopped talking. I guessed there was more to be said, but I didn't want to risk jinxing the mood. Doc arrived at the same conclusion and changed tack.

"Why didn't you take your wallet? You know what the police are like."

"When I told the coppers that turned up here to either arrest me or piss off, I didn't think they'd actually do it." He shuffled his chair around a little so he was even closer to Jan and put an arm across her shoulders. "I nearly grabbed my leather then I remembered it had a knife in the pocket, figured if I got searched ... " He gave Jan's shoulders a squeeze and stood up. "Which reminds me."

Chris went out to the hall and searched though his jacket, Jan busied herself with her lager again.

"Knife?"

At one time, knives had been so common among bikers they were practically national dress. This had largely died out, in Britain at least, as the laws tightened. Carry a blade more than three inches long, you're nicked. Any knife with a blade that locks open, you're nicked. Any knife that opens automatically, you're nicked.

"Since when do you carry a knife?" Doc called out. Chris didn't answer, just came back into the room holding exhibit A.

He unfolded it and it locked open with a sharp click that was worth up to four years and five grand. It was a nice bit of kit, fairly small, designed for lightness, the handle peppered with cut-outs. The blade was satin-white ceramic. Possession of a knife that size might normally come to nothing. Possession of a knife while under arrest for involvement in a suspicious death? You might want to leave that one off your CV.

"Christ almighty, Chris, if the police had found that on you ... " Doc left the sentence hanging.

"Well, that's why I left without my leather isn't it?"

He'd takin umbrage at Doc's tone.

"Since when you carrying a blade anyway?" Doc asked.

"I gave it to him," Jan said. "It was ... a sort of present."

"Next time, a tie eh?" Doc told her, she didn't get it.

Me and Chris did. *What do you call a biker in a tie? The accused.*

It was gone midnight when I headed home. Surprisingly, I thought, Jan left with me. Doc started to ask something, more about the knife I think, but Chris motioned silently to Jan. The picture of contrition, regretting her choice of gifts. I wanted to tell her not to bleed over it. Beyond Chris's long walk home, no real harm had been done. But I'm no good at the soothing platitude bit, and it was the Big Guy's job.

Doc wanted to talk more with Chris. Chris was more concerned about Jan. This was all conveyed by meaningful looks and head jerks. I broke the impasse by announcing I'd had it for the night and was heading home. As I stood up and pulled my leather on, Chris put a hand on Jan's shoulder. She didn't look up, just leaned her head over and cradled his hand under her cheek. On Chris's hand I could make out the word JUST, one letter on each finger. It was his variation on the traditional Love and Hate knuckle tattoos; his read JUST HATE.

"Listen hon, I've got a few things to talk to Doc about and I've got a lot to do tomorrow. Why don't you go back with Yakky, get some kip and I'll give you a bell in the morning before I go to work, okay?"

I couldn't see Jan liking this idea and I put my exit speed up a gear, eager to get out of the flat before the weeping and wailing began. Doc, at a more relaxed pace, joined me on the hard standing. He settled his weight on to the seat of Chris's bike. Over his shoulder, through the net curtain, I could make out the shapes of Chris and Jan. Their moments were calm and gentle, not what I'd expected.

"You won't be getting your spare room back just yet. you alright about that?" I told him it was no problem. "Really?"

I looked away from the kitchen sink drama and turned to Doc. Again, he was positioned so anyone coming through the door would have to look for him. Back to the lighted window, cast in darkness.

"She's no trouble."

Doc was silent and I began wheeling my bike backward to the road. He peeled himself away from the shadows and stood close to me, watching the front door.

"If you get a chance to talk to Jan when you get home, see if you can find out why she took so long about getting here tonight."

I asked why, but only for form's sake. I wanted to point out I was my own man who didn't do his bidding without good cause, but I knew what he was wondering.

"Doesn't it strike you as odd? All the fretting about Chris and – "

"And then she drags her heels about getting over here. Yeah, odd."

I watched the window some more. The room was empty now.

"Do you think she's going to come out shouting the odds or bawling her eyes out?" Doc asked me.

"I was just wondering that exact thing. You read minds now as well as cards?"

Doc laughed. "If I could read *your* mind I'd impress myself."

I was going to let the statement hang but couldn't. "What's that mean?"

"Nothing, you're just a hard person to read. You don't give off many signals."

"Is that good or bad?"

I could feel the grin coming off Doc's teeth. "It lends a certain fascination."

I decided he was taking the piss and we both watched the front door in silence. When it opened, all we could see was Chris silhouetted by the hallway light. After a while Jan's smaller silhouette emerged from him, like a blob of oil in one of those lava lamps.

Chris said, "You go on hon, it's alright. I'm fine."

"Okay, I will. You don't have to worry."

She sounded happy, excited even.

"I'm not worried."

They embraced, parted, embraced again, kissed, parted again. Jan was walking on air.

"What'd you read into that then?" I said from the corner of my mouth.

Doc didn't answer.

I waited for Jan to pull away from the curb and nodded a good night to Doc as he went back into Chris's flat. I didn't leave her at the lights this time. I followed the Audi all the way back to my place. Moderate pace, caught a few red lights, still the journey took less than ten minutes.

Doc and I had cut a rather dashing swath getting back from the Keller house but the trip had still taken the better part of half an hour. She should have been sat on Chris's doorstep for at least fifteen minutes before we arrived.

There wasn't a parking space outside my house so Jan parked a couple of doors away. I waited on the bike until she walked up to the front door and passed her my house keys.

"Let yourself in, I'm going to get some juice."

She looked puzzled until I rapped my knuckled on the fuel tank.

"Should I make a decent coffee?" she asked.

I gave her a thumbs-up and rode off. The nearest filling station was two streets away in a straight line. I filled the tank up, threw caution to the wind and decided to buy a Mars bar with the change. I took a roundabout route on the way back so I could come into my street from the top again. I couldn't see the Honda Civic but there was a white Ford Focus parked six doors up from my house.

I chained the bike up before leaving it in the front garden. Putting petrol in probably doubled its value.

Jan was in the dining room sitting at the table. The tarot cards she'd borrowed from Doc's collection were spread out in front of her and she was consulting a page of handwritten notes.

"Coffee's in the machine," she told me brightly and made

to get up.

I waved her back to her seat, said I'd get it. I noticed she didn't have a cup on the table for herself.

"You having one?"

"Please. Milk no sugar."

Easy to remember, it was how I took it.

Jan had told me she'd gone shopping with the money Doc had given her. The fridge was now nicely packed with an assortment of supermarket-own brands. Thankfully she'd bought full fat milk. Dad moaned like Billy-O at anything less. There was also an opened bag of filter coffee folded over and tucked into the fridge door. Colombian, one of the better brands.

I took a seat across from her rather than directly opposite, I'd been spending too much time with Doc. I took a sip of the coffee and nodded with approval.

"Nice."

Jan smiled a thank you and took a small sip of her own.

"Yeah, Colombian's the best."

"Well, not everyone would agree with me on this, but I love Ethiopian."

"Don't think I've ever tried it."

"They don't sell it in many places. I get it when I see it."

Jan turned one of the tarot cards, pulled a face and consulted her notes.

"You really getting into that?" I asked.

"I never gave it any thought until I met Doc." She drifted off a little. "That night he did a reading for me, in the pub, he knew things about me that he couldn't have known. How would he know I was married and ... "

She left something unsaid – 'and cheating' was my guess. I didn't pursue it. That first meeting, Doc hadn't used the words marriage or husband. He talked about The Fool and made a few guesses. Now Jan was filling in the blanks. Hindsight, despite rumours to the contrary, was not twenty-twenty.

I considered telling her about her wedding ring but in the

end just said, "I think the secret's got more to do with Doc than with the cards."

Jan nodded then smiled; it suited her.

"Chris said he's a smart one."

"True enough." Since the subject of Chris had come up, I said, "Did you have trouble getting over there tonight? We were waiting a while for you."

I didn't like pretending to be casual. It felt underhanded. Jan answered without looking up from the cards, took in more coffee.

"Oh, I was just caught up helping your father."

"What with?"

When Jan had answered the call from Doc, we both heard dad's TV on the line, listened to his barrage of questions. She must have been in the front room when she got the call.

"Oh, nothing much, just helped him get upstairs. Doc called just as he was about to get ready for bed."

I could imagine dad making the most of a willing helper. She was lucky she got away at all. The silence dragged on too long and I realised she was waiting for me to say something. I didn't feel like obliging. Dad adored being the martyr, always overplayed it. If she wanted to cast me in the role of uncaring son, I'd let her. She'd see the lay of the land in a few days.

When I didn't speak, Jan turned over another card and frowned at it, put it down carefully in the centre of the cross pattern she'd set out.

"Lot of Swords," she said. I misunderstood her intonation at first and thought Lot of Swords was the name of a card, like Queen of Wands or Knight of Cups. "That's the fourth Sword I've drawn."

I looked over the cards. There were about ten of them on the table.

"And Swords mean what?"

"Communication, intellect and strife."

"All at once?" She looked up and I wondered if my scepticism was making her feel foolish. I felt a flash of guilt.

I wouldn't try and pick holes if Doc was reading cards. I knew he could run rings around any rational argument I might put his way. "I mean, how do you know what the card is meant to be saying?"

"Doc says the cards are guides, pointers to things that we'd see if you knew where to look. Or they turn you to face things you're trying to hide from."

I nodded as if what she'd said made any kind of sense.

"So, what do you think those Swords mean?"

Jan sighed, turned another card, the Page of Swords.

"Strife," she said.

"Given the shit you've been through, I'd be amazed if you could see anything else."

"According to Doc, the real skill of it is getting under the surface."

I took a gulp of coffee and Jan followed suit.

"Easy for him to say. You found your husband's body. No small thing to cope with."

She took another swig of coffee, using the mug as a distraction. I remembered how she looked when I passed her at the traffic light. She looked the same now, tightly wound, held together with frayed nerves.

"I don't know if I *am* coping with it. Sometimes it doesn't feel real, then something brings it back and it's the only thing I can think of."

She did that tuning out thing again, stared at some point beyond the room we were in. I think I knew what she was seeing.

"Sorry, didn't mean to dredge it up again."

Jan sucked in a deep breath, dragged herself back and began pulling the cards together.

"It's alright. It's a hard subject to steer clear of."

"Doc's worried about Chris. He thinks the police are going to pin it on him because he's an easy mark."

"But he didn't do it. Chris couldn't have done it. Does he really think they'd do that?"

Then the tears came. She didn't gush, didn't become

hysterical, but the way she cried was unsettling. Something about it made me feel predatory for being there. I tried not to look at her but that made me feel a coward.

"You got an alibi for him?"

She shook her head and it struck me what was wrong about how she cried. She didn't close her eyes, just carried on watching me with tears streaming down her cheeks.

"I can't give him an alibi."

She said it like it was a personal failing not a fact. Then I twigged.

"You were both in the house when he died?"

Wide eyed, tears streaming, she nodded.

"We were right in the next room."

The Big Guy

Sunday 17 July

My mobile woke me up. It was Doc.

"Morning, Yak, you still asleep?"

He sounded surprised. Eight a.m. Late by my standards.

"Yeah, long night."

"Really?"

The way he said it implied something.

"Yeah, Jan and me got talking."

Pause, then Doc said, "Talking?"

I got what he was implying at last and managed to raise a degree of indignation.

"I've had about three hours' sleep because your mate's girlfriend kept me up all night crying and reading tarot cards. If you've got something to say, then fucking say it."

If I'd been on the land line, I would have most likely slammed the receiver down. Mobiles don't lend themselves to such dramatics.

"Sorry, you're right. I'm out of order."

"Forget it."

I swung my legs out of bed and stood up, held my stomach in for the sake of the many Karlas watching from the walls. One was escaping, hanging at an angle from a blue-tac corner. It was one of the last I'd drawn before she'd moved out. It had been a full-length pin-up style piece. Karla as a sexy nurse, looking at me over her shoulder, all legs and come-hither. The subsequent sense of humour failure had been fairly impressive. I'd done some editing with the scissors, turned the full body study into a portrait. I straightened the picture and pressed the blue-tac firmly into place, wondered if I could recreate the original drawing from memory.

"Any chance of you coming over?" Doc said.

"To the flat?"

It wasn't really a question.

"Yeah. About an hour?"

I pulled my jeans and tee shirt on for the journey to the shower, in case Jan was about. We'd been up late but we'd also packed away a vast quantity of coffee. Between the caffeine and her state of mind, I doubted she slept peacefully.

I looked at myself in the bathroom mirror and considered what Doc said about signals. My chest and shoulders swam with coloured ink and my back was in the process of being filled by Gina. But, it all ended at the tee shirt line. People only saw what I chose for them to see.

I limited my morning coffee intake to one mug; the bag of Colombian was almost empty. Jan and dad didn't appear and I took a certain pleasure in leaving them together. Now that he'd cast her as carer to his patient, I didn't doubt Jan would soon find out why I didn't dote on him.

Doc's mojo failed me and I spent a frustrating ten minutes coaxing the Yamaha to life. My mood wasn't improved by seeing the silver Honda. It was early enough that the heat of the day hadn't kicked in and there was a fog of condensation on the windscreen.

"The kettle's just boiled," Doc said. "You want one?"

I declined and let Doc lead me to his front room. As I expected, tarot cards were laid out in front of his armchair. I glanced at them without much interest, though one of them caught my eye: The Hanged Man. The altar had been in use too. A mess of eggs and what looked like ash had been mixed up in the pewter offering bowl.

Doc lowered himself carefully into the armchair. He

looked like he'd been up most of the night as well. There was a mug of tea on the floor beside the chair along with a glass and a bottle of Casa Noble, presumably the one Doc lifted from the Keller house.

"Breakfast?" I asked.

"More a late supper. You want some?"

The idea of drinking spirits that early in the day turned my stomach. Doc was made of sterner stuff.

After a swig of tea, Doc said, "Did you find out why Jan didn't beat us to the Big Guy's drum?"

"Yeah, she said – "

He held up a hand. "Let me take a stab in the dark. She got waylaid by your dad?"

"You read that in the cards? Or in a wedding ring?"

"Little bit of both." He held his hands up at chest height and waggled his fingers, as if he'd just pulled off a conjuring trick. When I didn't react, he switched the teeth off. "You're a little ray of sunshine this morning."

"I've not had a good night. Despite what you may think."

"Again, my apologies for that."

I was too tired to do a bad mood justice. And I was grudgingly impressed.

"How did you know about Jan and my dad?"

"You said something about mind reading, remember?"

"Yeah, and you said I don't give off signals."

"When I said that to you, it sort of rang a bell." He tapped his forehead. "It got me thinking about something you said, about Jan being timid at your place. How did she strike you that first night we saw her? When Chris asked me to do a reading?"

"Rich girl out for a bit of slumming."

Doc nodded. "That's what I thought. Then a couple of weeks with the Big Guy ... "

Doc grinned an invitation for me to finish the sentence.

"Couple of weeks with the Big Guy and she's all black denim and lager straight from the tin."

"Then, when Chris gets pulled in, she runs round here to

me. Now she's learning the tarot and asking me about making mojos."

Peter Keller had had the perfect trophy wife – slinky, classy, ill at ease down The Jericho. To Chris Rudjer, she was a righteous biker old lady. For Doc, she became a Voodoo acolyte. I got a blank.

I remembered speaking to her in the hallway with a towel around my waist. At the time, I thought she was sizing me up against Chris or just comparing our ink. Maybe she was trying to read my tattoos, pick up a signal.

"I still don't see how you knew she'd be tied up with dad."

"I didn't know, it just seemed possible. Every time I ring your house your dad's butting in, desperate to be included. When I called Jan yesterday, she got the same treatment. She'd been sitting with him and he was loving the attention. I figured he'd do his best to get more." Doc gave me a knowing look. "If she'd been held up by something dramatic or she'd given you a story that didn't ring true, you'd have told me as soon as you landed. You didn't bother mentioning Jan until I asked. Bit of observation, bit of guess work."

He waggled his fingers like a conjurer again.

Abracadabra.

Trophy wife. Biker babe. Voodoo doll. Attentive nurse.

"Why did you assume I'd slept with her?"

The glare off his teeth almost gave me snow blindness. He sat forward in his chair and picked up the Casa Noble.

"When we landed at Chris's last night, and he found out Jan had been staying at your place, you noticed his reaction?"

"I thought he was about to lump me one."

"Yeah, I thought he was. It got me curious. I've known Chris a good while, having a hot flush because a lady friend wasn't there for one night? Really not his style."

He poured himself a modest amount of Casa Noble.

"I expect he felt threatened by my stunning good looks."

Doc toasted me with his glass before giving me the story

he'd got from Chris.

Chris hadn't wanted to talk in front of Jan. I'd thought he was worried about upsetting her by mentioning her husband. It was more about sparing her blushes.

Chris had a few trust issues. It didn't surprise me. He'd met his girlfriend on a web-site promoting infidelity. It wasn't the best starting point for a relationship, not if you valued monogamy. Doc had pointed this out, asked him what he expected. Chris admitted the hypocrisy of the situation. He didn't have a problem when he was the bit on the side. Things looked different once he became the main man.

Doc pulled his usual trick of providing a silence and waiting for someone else to fill it. Chris started on the lager in earnest. He wasn't drinking to get drunk; it was Dutch courage. He surprised Doc by looking embarrassed.

"This is a bit awkward for me," Chris said.

Doc told him if he'd sooner talk to the police, he was happy to leave. He'd go home and bake Chris a cake and even put a file in it. Then he sat back and folded his arms.

Chris sunk another lager before telling the story. He asked Doc if he knew a fella who went by the name of Jock, a long streak of piss who fancied himself. Doc drew a blank but I knew him. Jock was English; he'd been christened Howard Strap and baptised Jock Strap the minute he started school. I knew him from a snooker hall I'd played in a few years earlier. He liked to think he was a bit of a hustler. He also liked to think he was a lady's man. Doc nodded when I said this. He asked what I made of the bloke.

"Sleaze bag. Talks non-stop about the women he's had. Mentions the army now and again, wants you to ask about his military record."

Doc took a sip of Tequila, pondered this before nodding to himself and carrying on with the story.

Jock worked at the same printing plant as Chris. He tended to gravitate towards the Big Guy and bend his ear with stories about women and partying. One lunchtime, when they were sat in the tea room, Jock handed Chris his mobile.

"I think this one's looking for you."

The phone showed a page from a married-dating site, opened at Jan's profile – twenty-nine years old, non-smoker, slim, redhead. Before Chris could read much more, Jock scrolled up the page to Jan's picture. He expanded the fingernail size image so it filled the screen. Both men were impressed.

"Hot to trot as well, I'd say," Jock commented.

Chris handed the mobile back.

"And you can tell, can you?"

The sarcasm was lost on Jock. He scrolled the screen a few times and held it in front of Chris. Under the heading *ideal partner*, it read,

I am looking for a genuine person. London based and ideally North of the river. Appearance wise, I'm not holding out for film star looks but I like my men v.big and v.tall. I'm willing to see where this goes but initially I'm just looking for uncomplicated extramarital adult fun.

"Uncomplicated extramarital adult fun," Jock recited reverently. "You don't see that come up very often."

"I thought that was the point of these sites."

Jock made a disgusted sound and took the phone out of Chris's face, began scrolling again.

"That's what they want you to think." He pulled up another profile at random. He read it briefly before proffering the screen to Chris. "Then all you get is this."

Again, before Chris had time to read what he was being shown, Jock took it away.

"Friendship, companionship, mutual interests." He brooded over the phone, began scrolling. He located Jan's profile once more, expanded the photo again. "But this one," he waved the phone around, "is looking for uncomplicated adult fun." He turned the screen to Chris.

"And she's put up a public photo. Dirty."

The site gave members the option of using an anonymous avatar to signpost their profiles. If the profile generated interest, the user could choose to reveal a password via a personal reply. The password would allow access to their photo. Most profiles didn't include a photo for general viewing.

"I'm telling you, my friend, this woman is panting for it." Chris told him best of luck but Jock shook his head. "She's not going to go for me. She wants 'em big and tall." Jock was neither. He leered at Chris. "Very big."

"Even if she is, and assuming that photo's genuine, I'm not paying good money joining some hook-up site."

"You don't need to. I'll send her a message. I'll just give her your email instead of mine. If she contacts you, then you take it from there." Chris, who'd learned a trick or two from his long association with Doc, didn't answer. Finally Jock filled the silence. "If you get anywhere though, I'd like to know about it." Chris told him he'd think it over. "Well you'll have to let me know soon. My membership runs out this weekend. I'm not putting another week's wages into this."

Jock turned the phone to face Chris again. Jan was pictured head tilted slightly to one side, tip of her tongue at the corner of her mouth. Her shoulders were bare, giving the impression she was naked.

"Go on then, send her a message."

Three days later Chris got an email asking for a photo and some more details. The night Doc and I saw them at The Jericho had been their first meeting. Chris had suggested he wait outside an agreed location on his bike. Jan could drive by and just keep driving if she didn't like what she saw. Chris suggested The Jericho as the location. He'd picked his local for practical reasons. If Jan just drove by, at least he could go in for a pint.

When Jan did make contact, he got the feeling the edginess of a biker's pub was turning her on. He figured he'd take it up a notch when he spotted Doc's bike parked outside,.

"When we left the pub, I asked her what she'd like to do. I thought she'd want to get something to eat, bit of chit-chat, you know?"

Jan had put her fingers on Chris's cheeks and held them there for a few seconds. Looking him in the eye she told him calmly, "Your place. You're too big for the back seat of my car."

Chris was surprised when she actually followed him to his flat. He had begun to think she was playing out some game and would drive off once he was under way. But Jock had been right – Jan was hot to trot.

"We barely made it to the bedroom. She didn't even get undressed, just whipped her knickers off and, wham, she was all over me."

"Worse ways to spend an evening," Doc said.

"Much worse, but ... the second we're done," he clicked his fingers, "she's gone. Thank you, that was great, g'night then, and out the door she goes, didn't even pick her drawers up."

Another lager tin got turned into a walnut. He added it to the little hill of scrap metal on the table. Chris was waiting for Doc to say something.

"Sounds cold."

Chris began fiddling with the tins. "I thought she just fancied a bit of rough. Then once she'd scratched the itch – "

"Back home to hubby?"

Chris told Doc to hang on. He moved the debris of cans to one side and put a laptop on the table. While it was booting up, he went back to the fridge and found it empty of lager. He came back with a bottle of vodka and two glasses. When Doc declined, Chris ignored both glasses and drank from the bottle.

Chris had saved the emails from Jan in a dedicated folder. He spun the computer around so it faced Doc and turned in his seat so he wouldn't have to watch Doc reading them.

Morning Stud,

I dropped some things at your place last night. Would you like me to cum and collect them?

Or would you like to keep them?

It won't happen again. Next time we meet I won't be wearing any.

When?

Jan XXX

Morning Stud,

Hope I didn't wake your neighbours. I suppose it's only fair if I did. After all I had you up most of the night.

I still didn't pick up what I dropped last Thursday, did I?

When should I cum and GET IT?

Jan XXX

There were more messages. Doc spared Chris the embarrassment of reading them all. The other few he skimmed were in the same vein. They alluded to the previous meeting and suggested another one. Doc turned the computer back to Chris, who left the machine on but folded the screen down.

"Sounds like Christmas."

"Not saying it wasn't fun but it was freaking me out a bit too." The vodka took another hit. "We'd meet up somewhere for a drink, usually The Jericho, and she'd be on me like a cheap suit. She wasn't acting too smart if she wanted her husband kept in the dark."

"I'm guessing Peter Keller didn't get down The Jericho much."

Chris shrugged. "Yeah, but even so, she was showing out like no one's business." He sighed. "You can call me a hypocrite for this if you like, but if she'd been my wife carrying on like that, I'd have put her in the ground."

"But as she wasn't your wife?"

"Like you said, Christmas."

The thing really troubling Chris was Jan's vanishing act at the end of the night. Three, four o'clock in the morning, no matter, out the door she went. Into the black Audi and away. Doc asked how long that had gone on. About two weeks. Then she calmed down slightly and would sometimes stay until morning. Even then she left as soon as she woke up. Chris started on the vodka again. Doc waited him out.

Finally Chris said, "That's when she started getting a bit screwy."

"Screwy?"

"Odd. She didn't want to clean herself up after we'd finished. When she stayed over she'd sleep in her clothes. Get out of bed next morning, maybe have a cup of tea, then vroom. Gone. The state she'd leave here in, makeup smeared round her face, hair all over the shop." More vodka. This was Chris's cue to leave things unsaid. Doc waited.

Chris turned to look at Doc again. Trying to gauge his reaction to what he was being told. Whatever Doc's face had told him, Chris made some sort of decision and put the top on the bottle of vodka.

"It got a bit kinky. A couple of weeks before her husband topped himself, she was round here every night. She stayed over most nights. She'd ask me to pull out and cum on her." Doc kept his face carefully blank. "If we had another go in the morning she'd want another spraying. Then she'd drive home covered in it." He managed a laugh. "You should have seen the curtains twitching when she left."

"But you went on meeting up with her?"

"I don't lose much sleep worrying what the neighbours think. And it was great, in a way. Like having my own personal porn star. Cheap to run too – I didn't have to wine and dine her."

Another uncomfortable pause.

"But?"

"I like her, Doc. Simple as that. But, I had the feeling what she was doing with me wasn't really important. What she got off on was cheating, screwing around behind her husband's back. This is going to sound stupid, but I was feeling sort of used."

Doc leaned forward in his armchair and tapped the tarot card that had caught my eye when I came in. The Hanged Man. He didn't offer an explanation and I refused to ask.

"That's why you thought Jan and me might have been at it last night?"

"Well, you're single and Jan might have some sort of fetish for infidelity."

I wasn't impressed with the assumption that I'd jump at the first offer of sex.

"Even if she did put out to me, which she didn't by the way, I wouldn't bed a woman in her state. She's in bits."

"I know, Yak, I'm sorry, I'm sorry. But she is a good-looking woman, and if half of what Chris told me is true, resisting her might test the old moral fibre."

I tried to rage but my heart wasn't in it. I may have been riding for the moral high ground but, if Jan had offered herself, would I have said no?

"So why did Chris send her to stay at my place last night?"

"Show of trust. Having her spend the night in another man's house was a display of faith." He rolled his eyes. "Go figure."

"If those two were going at it round Chris's place all the time, why are his prints all over Keller's bedroom?"

Doc drained his glass before up ending it on the top of the bottle. His way of closing the bar.

"A week or so before Keller tops himself," Chris told Doc, "I get this."

He opened the laptop's screen again, tapped a few keys and turned it towards Doc.

Hey Stud,

Want a change of scene? Husband's away for the weekend. The little wimp's leaving the marriage bed unattended.

Want to cum over.
Jan XXX

Doc clicked his tongue.

"How many times did you go over there?" Chris held up three fingers. "Same kind of performance?"

"Not the first time. It was a lot calmer."

Chris first went over to the Keller house on a Saturday afternoon. He complained about nursing his bike over the neglected private road.

"So, Jan didn't drive over and collect you?"

Chris told him no, he'd ridden over just after noon. Jan had told him she'd make them lunch. She met him at the door naked and they christened the dining table before eating. To Chris's relief, she cleaned up before preparing their meal. He stayed until mid-morning the next day.

"We talked a lot. Before that, we'd meet up, Jan would make an exhibition of herself, then we'd head off to bed. It was nice to relax with her for a bit."

"And that's all you did?"

Chris shook his head. "Did the usual. She insisted we did it in the main bedroom. The marriage bed." Chris gave a helpless look. "It's what she was into. At least on the home turf she had a shower afterwards."

The next email arrived late Sunday night.

Hi BIG Boy,

Great to finally make proper use of the master bedroom.

Pity the little wimp couldn't see us, he might have picked up a few tips.

Did you enjoy lunch? Service on the dining table has given me an appetite.

Shall I cum round tonight?

Jan XXX

When she came around it was business as usual. She knocked on Chris's door in a designer dress and raced away the next morning wearing a dry-cleaning bill. That had been the schedule through the week and on Saturday morning another email appeared. By now Chris was checking his email account five or six times a day.

Hello Stud,

Thanks for last night. I'll have to throw those stockings away (naughty).

The cleaner put crisp new sheets on the bed. Want to cum over and help soften them up?

Hubby left an hour ago and won't be back until Monday.

Jan XXX

Chris had duly ridden over on his Suzuki. The weekend followed the same pattern as the previous one. Chatting and watching films on Peter Keller's home-cinema TV, then up to his bed to screw his wife.

"This is when she goes really weird on me," Chris said.

They'd had a longish evening together. Chris was splayed out on a massive sofa skimming the endless channels, and Jan was curled up with his arm around her reading a magazine. Surprisingly domestic given the situation. One of them, and Chris couldn't say which, had suggested they go to bed.

Jan pecked his cheek.

"Give me a couple of minutes to get ready. Then come up."

She'd flipped the switch from contented domesticity to sexual jungle in the blink of an eye. Made her way from the TV room shedding clothes as she went. Chris gave her ten minutes before following.

He found her sat at the head of the marriage bed. She'd changed into a black velvet dress that fastened down the front; the Big Guy reckoned about forty tiny pearl buttons held it together. Jan had one foot on the floor and the other on the edge of the bed with the dress rucked up around her hips. She told him it was hard to get the dress off and she needed help with the buttons. Then she'd pulled the knife out.

"The one you've been carrying?"

"Yeah. She opens it and nips off one of the little buttons. Then she offers the thing to me and says *cut away lover, open it up*, some shit like."

Chris had taken the knife and closed it. He was going to put it on the night stand but thought again and slipped it into the hip pocket of his jeans.

"Not my scene, Doc, not by a long fucking way."

He told Jan much the same, though less bluntly. Added a few tips on personal survival and the wisdom of handing men knives then asking them to start cutting.

Doc and Chris lapsed into silence. Chris must have been deep in thought because he jumped when Doc spoke.

"How did she take it?"

"Me not playing knife games? She was okay about it. I think she was glad I wasn't up for it."

"After getting it all set up?" Doc considered this. "That must have been a let-down. I'd have expected a bad reaction to that."

Again, Chris was having trouble meeting Doc's eye.

"It wasn't the end of the fun. If she was into getting her dress ruined, it worked out alright. She ripped it open down the front and she'll never get the stains out."

"So, why you carrying the knife?"

"I'm not carrying it, I put it in my pocket to get it out the way. I didn't think about it again until the next morning. I felt it in my jeans pocket as I was about to ride off."

"You didn't give it back?"

"Didn't want to leave it with her. I know that's stupid, but I didn't like the idea of her playing about with it. So, I slipped it in my leather and forgot about it. Then I got nicked. Thank Christ I remembered it was there."

"What have you done with it now?"

Chris nodded towards the kitchenette. "Put it in the cutlery drawer."

Doc began pulling the tarot cards together.

"Weird," I said.

Doc gave me a Cheshire grin.

"Very." He began binding the deck in its white linen. "Do you want to know what's really bothering me though? Those emails."

Before I could answer, Tequila reverberated around the room. Doc pulled his phone out, listened with a tight smile. Before he spoke back he looked up at me and mouthed, *show time.*

"Caroline. Oh, I'm so glad you rang. I've given you the wrong keys, haven't I?"

He'd changed his voice, nothing hugely different, just a softening of his accent. Less of the London crow call. He didn't sound like someone sitting four foot away from a Voodoo altar having Tequila for breakfast.

"What? The gate won't open?" Doc listened, or at least didn't speak, for a moment. "What does the card say? I know, my hand writing's awful. Have you tried sevens instead of ones?"

He was enjoying himself, riding the crest of a full-tilt Jive. He lifted one bony arm above his head, fingers splayed wide, and began a countdown. Five-four-three-two-one ... an indigent squawk from the phone's earpiece. Doc linked finger to thumb, zero.

"Still not opening?" he asked innocently.

I left him to whatever game he was playing and wandered through to the kitchen to reboil the kettle. When I went back to the front room he was off the phone and tidying the altar.

"Can you hold the fort with Gina tomorrow?"

I told him I could if I had to, didn't relish the prospect. When I asked why, his tight smile relaxed into something almost humorous and he told me he had a date.

Then he suddenly laughed and added, "I'll have to do my makeup."

Back Story

Monday 18 July

I went through the appointments book to see if Gina could take one or two of Doc clients. Then I made phone calls and left messages to find out if people minded switching tattooist, or just wanted to rebook.

Doc came to the shop as I was putting the open sign out on the pavement. He was wearing his interview clothes, his festering white leather draped over one arm.

"Gina's going to be here before eleven. If you can put any of my appointments on to her – "

"I've already done all that."

The prospect of a full day with Gina already had my back up, micromanagement I could do without. Signals or no, Doc saw it was the time to step back.

"Good. I've just rung Jan. I'm heading round to your place. I'm pretty sure she'll explain to your old man but do you want to tell him I'll be round?"

I thought about Jan, playing nurse maid to dad, and shook my head. If she was as good at switching between personas as we suspected, she'd already be telling him what to expect.

"What you need Jan for?"

By way of an answer Doc touched the jawbone tattoo.

"Makeup isn't one of my talents." He began looking around the shop, then, with an effort, stopped himself. He pulled on his leather. "And I need to borrow her motor. I get the impression Caroline's not a motorcycle person."

Gina pulled up on a nondescript Jap bike. It was a hack, something you'd ride to get from A to B rather than a machine you'd get involved with. She looked around the waiting area and jerked her head at the young woman on the sofa. I nodded an affirmation that she was her first client.

She was booked in for a straightforward piece. Bread and butter work, known as flash. Not very exciting and often the sort of thing that comes free with a hangover. Gina ran it off in about forty minutes. Even for a piece of straightforward flash that's impressive.

The young woman didn't look particularly happy when she came to settle up. Tattoos are personal, your skin, your markings, but someone else makes those marks for you. For some people the quality of the finished piece is only part of the process. The experience of being tattooed is something they carry away as much as the fact of their tattoo. If that's the way you feel, Gina isn't going to be your first choice of artist.

I cleaned up the back room, prepped what I could. Then we waited. We didn't talk, I asked if she wanted a tea, she grunted something that might have been a please. That was it for an hour. The time of the next appoint came and went without sight or sound of the customer. We gave him fifteen minutes before I called him. He told me he'd changed his mind, asked if he could have the deposit back, didn't like the answer.

I suggested putting in a few hours on my back piece. About eighty percent of my tattoos were Gina's work. The lack of involvement was, for me, part of the attraction. The markings I carried were mine and mine alone. I didn't want another artist's interpretation coming between my images and the needle that applied them. Gina also didn't care what she put down, never asked *are you sure?* Or *what does this mean?*

I had the business with Chris on my mind more that I knew. When Gina fired up the needle and touched it to my shoulder blade I got a mental picture of Jan. I saw again the way her eyes roamed over my chest and shoulders, trying to read them. Few people had seen all the pretty ink I'd had punched into my skin. Discounting the two other tattooists, who put a few hours in, the count was four. Including me. Jan who couldn't read them, Gina who wasn't interested and Karla. I'd never *shown* my tattoos to any of them – they just happened to see them.

Doc knew I carried a lot of ink that I didn't parade. That's why he called me Yakky. It was short for Yakuza, Japanese gangsters known for their massive tattoos worn behind respectable outer clothing. I couldn't tell if he was trying to wind me up so I'd show him, or just winding me up because it was in his nature.

Buzz, buzz, buzz. Needle song, hypnotic almost. Gina didn't break what I thought of as the spell. Twice she asked me to okay the colour of an ink, other than that, silence. After an hour of so she made a departure from the norm.

"Is Doc in trouble?"

It was so unusual for her to speak that it took a moment to filter through that she'd asked me something.

"I don't think so. Chris is up to his neck in it though."

The buzzing stopped.

"Chris?"

"The Big Guy."

I waited for the buzzing to start. In vain.

"I know who Chris is. What's he done?"

I sat up. "He took up with this married piece. Hubby turns up dead as disco and Chris fits the frame." Gina squinted at me when I said this. I glanced at the clock, rounded it up to an hour and decided I could dress the fresh wound myself. Gina made no move to get out of my way, so I was sort of trapped in the dentist's chair. "Doc's got it into his head he can do a better job than the police. Now I've got the married piece round my drum and Doc's off playing Columbo."

Gina added a sour frown to the squint and finally leaned

back.

When I did move to get up, she put her hand on my chest.

"Turn round, I can get this finished today." I shuffled around in the confined space, straddled the chair again. The buzzing started. "You think Chris did it."

It wasn't a question.

"Chris has form."

He was also in the house when Peter Keller shuffled off to join the choir invisible. I didn't say this to Gina.

"Chris gave someone a clout. That's a long way from a murder."

I didn't answer. I was trying to tune back into the needle song. Gina worked without further comment for a while. I could feel her tension though, the rhythm of strokes across my skin more staccato than before.

"Did Doc ever tell you why we got divorced?"

"No, never discussed it."

I hadn't known they'd been married. There was another pause. I think Gina was trying to work what I did or didn't know about her and Doc. Well good luck with that one sister. If Doc couldn't figure out what I was thinking I doubted any bugger alive could.

"I found out he'd offered Chris a thousand pounds to beat someone up. It never happened because Chris told him to get lost."

I waited for something else, it wasn't forthcoming.

"So?"

Gina snorted. Objecting to explaining herself, or maybe just to talking to me. "He's got his own moral compass. People don't see it because they can't get past the way he looks and the way he doesn't give a shit what they think. Doc knows that. So should you."

It was the longest speech I'd heard from her.

"Why should I know it? I barely know the guy."

Gina made the snorting noise again. "Because you three are all the bloody same." The buzzing stopped again. "You have a face you put on so nobody gets inside and no one can see what's there." I heard her move away from me and pull her latex gloves off. I made to get up from the chair but she snapped, "Stay there."

She cleaned my back up and applied antiseptic ointment. She finished up by taping cling film over the area, then left the room without another word.

I cleaned the equipment trolley. Threw away disposables, put reusables into the autoclave. When I went back into the shop, Gina was putting her jacket on and patting herself down, hunting for keys.

"I'll be back at four."

"What do I owe you? I'll nip down the bank."

Gina shook her head. "You can have that one on the house. But I want to tell you something." I figured she wasn't about to pledge undying love, but I also figured if she wanted to insult me then tattooing me had paid for the privilege. "Chris wears a face and people don't see past it, but he's not hiding anything. You ... "

And she walked out. Either words failed her or she'd said all she needed.

I left the shop open and manned the desk. If anyone came in I'd book them in for another day. Since I was the only one there, I pulled up a playlist of music I actually wanted to hear. I didn't realise I was trembling until I put my hand on the computer mouse.

Doc didn't show again that day. Gina came back at four. We didn't mention our earlier exchange. I'd been to the bank and drawn out enough to pay for two hours of Gina's time. I'd taken the cling film off after an hour and cleaned the fresh work with cold water. I'd normally do this in the shower but had to make do with paper towels in the customer's toilet. I checked my new ink out in the back room. We had mirrors set up for customers to do the same.

Gina reproduced my design perfectly. If it was possible to tattoo your own back, it was exactly how I would have done it. I assumed she stopped working on it because she got the hump. Turned out she finished it.

"Keep it," Gina said when I proffered the money.

"Take it. It makes it mine."

My design, my skin, my tattoo. If I didn't pay for it, part of it was Gina's. That wasn't the way I wanted it. Gina took the money and stuffed it into her pocket.

"Suit yourself."

I got back home after a long winding ride. Some evenings, particularly in summer, even the crappy Yamaha was hard to leave behind. That night it took an effort to climb off the bike and haul it into its space in front of the house. Jan's Audi was parked, badly, just opposite. The silver Honda Civic was parked two cars away. I wondered if they were getting sloppy about following at a safe distance, then I remembered Doc probably parked up there when he returned from his 'date'. The Honda had most likely been there all day, staking out Jan.

The TV noise blasted through the front door as I opened it. I waited for dad's bleating. When it didn't come I went straight to the kitchen and put a coffee on. I could feel the material of my tee shirt sticking to my upper back, so while the coffee machine steamed I went to change. I threw the stained shirt, blood and ink, into the washing machine. I lathered my back with fresh ointment and found my loosest tee shirt. The spare room door was open. I glanced around it but Jan wasn't there.

I went back downstairs and looked in on dad. He had his I'm-not-well look on. There was a pillow under each arm and a duvet spread over him. Too deep in character to speak, he acknowledged me with a weak lift of the head, half-closed eyes flickering. Jan had brought a chair from the dining table set and was sitting by the patient's side.

"I think he may have a temperature."

"Feel so hot," dad managed to murmur. I pointed out it was the middle of July and he was wrapped in a duvet.

Without missing a beat, he mumbled, "I was so cold."

The stage was dressed much as I expected. Mug of cold tea, barely touched bowl of soup, thick with dissolving bread. Dad favoured the sick-room look. Jan looked at me with a worried expression and blinked a couple of times. I couldn't help thinking of a frozen computer screen.

"You guys eaten?" I asked.

Dad, seeing he was about to lose fifty percent of his audience, stalled for time by pretending not to hear and bleating pointless questions. I asked Jan directly if she wanted anything to eat. When she said she'd eaten I collected the crockery and took it to the kitchen.

I heard Jan following and made a bet with myself: first thing she'd say on entering the kitchen was how good the coffee smelt. I won the bet and told her to help herself. Maybe I was getting paranoid, but I could almost feel her scrabbling to get a hold of something.

"Your motor's back outside," I said. "Did you speak to Doc?"

She shook her head, mirroring the way I stood, propping up a work surface with her backside, holding her coffee in both hands.

"He gave me the keys back, grabbed his bike gear and left. He's been gone about two hours. Didn't he go back to the shop?"

"No."

I didn't doubt I'd get a call at some point. If Caroline had given him something to think about, he'd be back in his flat, reading tarot cards and sacrificing eggs.

"Where do you think he's gone?"

I nearly told her he'd probably gone for an omelette. "Hard to tell with Doc. Don't sweat on it, he can take care of himself."

"I don't think your dad's too unwell."

I had that feeling again she was scrabbling, trying to catch something.

"He can take care of himself too."

She tuned out for a moment. Came back.
called for you, about half an hour before you got .
was about the time I'd have got home if I hadn't be
around wishing I had somewhere to go. "Karla?"

Jan paused, and I think she was waiting for me to slip some information into the silence. Doc's acolyte was coming along nicely.

"Did she say anything?"

"Just asked if you were in. I said I'd ask you to ring her back."

At this point dad rallied enough to start bleating. Jan switched quickly into nurse mode and vanished into the front room. I opened the fridge but didn't feel hungry. I put another coffee together.

The fresh tee shirt began to cling to the ointment on my back. The sensation wasn't particularly unpleasant but if Jan wasn't there, I'd have taken the shirt off and been spared it altogether. I thought about Gina, Doc's ex-wife.

Chris wears a face people can't see past. But you ...

But I what?

I emptied my first coffee just in time for the machine to finish producing its second. I decided it was time to ring Karla and I went to the hall to grab the handset, then changed my mind. At the foot of the stairs the tee shirt sticking to my back really started to get on my nerves. I turned right and headed to the shower.

I was still in the shower when the phone rang and I nearly fell down the stairs, trying to pull the towel around my waist one handed as I descended. Something felt wrong when I put the receiver to my ear. I'd picked it up with my left hand but pressed it to my right ear out of habit. I was also leaning towards dad's door listening to the noise of the telly rather than the voice on the line. No bleating questions from dad. He must have been flat out keeping Jan busy.

"Hello?"

"So, your phone's not been disconnected then?"

Karla. I straightened up, away from the door, as if I was

following the sound of her voice, which I suppose I was. In the process of untwisting myself I lost the struggle with the towel, then cracked my elbow on the phone table bending to retrieve it. The sounds must have been picked up on the line, because Karla asked what was going on.

She sounded worried.

Funny the things that can make you happy.

Finally, standing upright, phone to my left ear, towel round my waist, I could speak.

"It's okay, I just got out of the shower and I'm trying to be modest with an escaping towel."

She laughed and I realised how much I missed that.

"Are you trying to get a girl excited with visions of your firm young body all wet and glistering?"

I told her the only bits of my body that were firm and young were a couple of corns. I won another laugh.

Standing in the hall I could see into the kitchen. Karla's laughter and the smell of good coffee. I felt something collapse over me. Relaxation, so alien I didn't recognise it at first.

"Look, Karla, give me a minute to get dry and I'll call you back."

She paused for a beat before answering, "Andy ... you never call."

Sadness in her voice. I still held a big enough space in her life to cause pain.

"Two minutes. Five, absolute max. On my word."

She paused again, then, "Okay. But you call back."

Quietly, again sad. Oh, the power.

I didn't manage two minutes, but I didn't go to the full five. I padded back to the phone dialled Karla's number, then waited for the ringing tone before getting a coffee. The ringing tone purred over five cycles before she picked up, the belief that she wasn't going to answer grew stronger with each one.

"Andy. You called back."

She sounded happy with a faint whiff of accusation. I was

too relieved to take offence so I played wounded instead.

"Your lack of faith causes me pain, it truly does."

"Have you got a cold or something? Your voice sounds off."

I was holding the receiver against my ear with my shoulder. My hands were both easing the jug from the coffee machine.

"No, I'm just trying to talk on a phone and pour coffee at the same time."

"A man who can multitask. My hero."

"Ah shucks ma'am, taint nuttin'."

I freed the jug and could finally devote an opposable thumb to the art of conversation. I added milk. It did little to change the brew's colour but did make it a drinkable temperature. I took a mouthful as I sat down at the kitchen table and my reaction was audible.

"Now what have you done?"

"Nothing, just made this coffee a bit strong."

"If *you're* saying it's a bit strong it'll probably give you chemical burns."

"I need the boost." I paused and came to a decision. "I just spent the whole day in the shop with Gina. I've earned a lift."

"Have you eaten?"

"No. I can't be bothered with food when I'm wound up. Do you think that says something important about my state of mind?"

Karla had zero tolerance for psychobabble, less still for my full caffeine diet.

"It says your state of mind should drink less coffee."

"Well that's a very deep insight. Have you ever thought of becoming a therapist?"

"I'll stick with shoplifting, it's more honest and the hours are better. And you drink too much coffee, it gives you high blood pressure."

Since the stuff I was drinking probably corroded arteries, I changed the subject.

"You still drinking herbal tea, the distillation of middle-class pretension? That whirring sound you hear is Marx spinning in his grave."

"Well, if Marx turns up at my place at least I can look him in the eye and tell him I'm not oppressing the underpaid farm workers of Colombia."

"Well if he turns up here at least he'll get a decent coffee."

"Fascist swine."

"How did we get from *my hero* to *fascist swine*?"

"That's what comes from being a couple." She meant, from *having been* a couple. I almost asked her if it was a Freudian slip. "Who was that answered the phone when I called before?"

She made it sound very casual, but it came hot on the heels of the remark about being a couple. I assumed it was loaded and handled it carefully.

"Friend of Doc's is having a bit of trouble. That was his old lady you spoke to. She's got nowhere to live at the moment."

I mentally played back what I'd said. I'd not really told her anything. There was a brief silence.

"So your place is pretty crowded," she said.

It didn't come across as a question or a statement. I wasn't sure how to respond.

"Not really. Dad's decided he's ill again and Jan's fool enough to play Florence Nightingale."

"So you've got the night off? Only I've not got a shift tomorrow."

I asked her if she had something in mind and there was another silence – this one definitely packing something.

"How about I come over and keep you safe from marauding old ladies?"

I went back to the bathroom and added a second shave to that day's tally of ablutions. Then I swapped my jeans for a clean pair of black combats. I even put fresh linen on the bed. I stood and waited in the kitchen finishing the coffee.

My hands were trembling again and conceded Karla was right about my drinking habits.

I got to the front door just as Jan came out of the living room.

I turned and said, "It's okay, it's for me."

She didn't withdraw straight away and I waited pointedly, not answering the bell. Once she was back in the sensory wipeout of dad's orbit, I opened the door to Karla.

She hadn't pulled out all the stops, but she'd made the effort and unlike mine it had worked to good effect. She was wearing a simple red dress and black (I learnt later) stockings. Her hair was shorter and darker than when I'd last seen her and she'd put on just a touch of makeup. Karla was always pretty good at pressing the right buttons. I wanted to say something witty about my combats and tee shirt but thought I'd most likely sound crass. She pecked me on the cheek and allowed herself to be ushered into the kitchen.

"Still the kitchen?"

"Yeah. Still the kitchen. I live here how many years now, and I still feel like I'm a health visitor?"

"Any chance of a drink?" she said by way of an answer. "And just so you know, I'm not doing it on the kitchen table."

I contrived to look disappointed.

"For this I shaved?"

Jan arched an eyebrow and found another button.

"Well? So did I."

The part of my mind that wasn't set to stupid mercifully took over, and I stopped thinking about what to say next.

It was good. It wasn't Hollywood so there was no romantic soundtrack. By the same token it wasn't French cinema, so it wasn't followed by a suicide pact.

Karla was propped up against a pillow. She was smiling to herself and pouring vodka into a plastic coke bottle. It looked to make about half a litre of fifty-fifty mix. No great drinker, I lamented the loss of the coke, but I wasn't about to say so. When she'd finished swirling the mixture together, I groped under the bed to find her glass. I found it but she took a swig from the bottle and shook her head.

"I've already blown the lady-like look for today. You're quiet."

"You worn me out woman." Which was at least half true. I took a sip from the bottle when she offered but needed something I could glug back. "Fancy a coffee?"

Karla choked on the next swig of booze and sprayed my fresh linen with fizz.

"Jesus Christ. Are you scared of snoring or something? Take a nap, get your energy back."

She struck one of her pin-up poses.

"If I nap now I'll be out for hours."

"So do it. I'm not about to run off with your collection of vintage tee shirts."

"I'm thirsty."

She pressed the vodka and coke to me again. I declined and made to get out of the bed.

"Stay there, I'll get something." She pushed me down into the pillows and told me, "Conserve your strength. I mean it."

She slipped the red dress on and started towards the door, the small of her back showing through the unfastened zip. Watching her leave the room half naked, knowing she'd be coming back for more, was bittersweet. I felt good, really good, for the first time in months. I also felt it was more than likely an interlude.

Caffeine levels and habit woke me before anyone else in the house. Even with Karla in the bed next to me, my morning dose of despair forced me to start the day. The tee shirt I'd slept in was rank with sweat and ink. I balled it up and threw it at the laundry bin. I put my jeans back on with yet another fresh tee shirt.

I thought it would be nice to take Karla breakfast in bed, then remembered the state the bed was in and decided to put a real breakfast together at the dining table. The washing up from the night before included most of the house's crockery. If I was planning on doing the breakfast thing right, I was going to have to do the dishes first. As I was checking the front room for stray plates, I saw Karla's red VW parked directly outside the window.

A slightly built man with the beginnings of a paunch was bent at an odd angle in front of the car. He stood straight and I saw he was holding a mobile phone. I watched him check the image on the screen then pocket it. He took a quick look around and walked away. I moved closer to the window and watched him climb into a white Ford Focus parked about five doors up. Karla's number plate wasn't visible from where the Ford was parked and it had only just got light enough to take pictures without using a flash.

I'd stopped breathing. I didn't notice until I had to gasp in a sudden gulp of air.

Thirteen

Tuesday 19 July

I rang Doc's flat and waited while the ring tone cycled over and over. Finally Doc answered, voice crocking.

"Bloody hell, Yakky. Don't you ever sleep?" I listened and heard things getting shifted about. Guessed he was getting up. "Gina left an envelope for you."

"Really?"

"Yeah. Money in it. Said to you tell you, she don't want to be a part of it. That make any sense to you?" I told him it did. "You going to explain it to me? She came up here last night giving me a hard time."

"Really?"

There was a long pause. I could hear him thinking.

"You and Gina had a ruck?"

"I don't know what we had, but let's just say we didn't share a beautiful moment." I heard him laugh softly. Then I asked him, "Are you going to be in the shop today? 'Cos I'm going to be late."

There was a cord of tension in Doc's voice when he replied, "What's going on here Yakky? Talk to me."

"Karla stayed here last night. Now I've just seen Jan's little friend in the Ford Focus taking pictures of her number plate. I'm about to go and have words."

"Don't," Doc said. "Let's calm down a bit and take a second to think." I gave him a second to think. I did less well in the calming down stakes. I was at the window staring at the white car. I don't know if I was hoping to calm down or tip over into blind fury. "Yakky, you still there?"

I had to take two tries at answering. My throat had locked.

"Yeh."

"Go wake Jan up. Tell her to get round to my place ASAP, tell her I want to see her. When she goes, the creep outside will follow her. When you know it's clear, you can take Karla home without them being any wiser."

I took a few breaths, saw the sense of what he was saying.

"Okay. But, Doc, these guys are outside my house, now they're sniffing around Karla. I am not happy."

"Get Jan out. Get Karla clear. We'll sort this out, sort it without going off half-cocked."

Blind obedience must go with the Voodoo acolyte gig. Jan didn't bat an eyelid when I woke her at stupid o'clock and told her Doc wanted to see her. She was up and out the house in under ten minutes. I watched her Audi from my bedroom window. Doc was right: the Ford Focus followed her out of my street. I looked around for the Honda on the off chance the bastards had started double handing the shifts. No sign.

Karla enjoyed the breakfast and I assured her I'd call her soon. I did a good job covering how wound up I was, or Karla did a good job pretending not to notice. Either way I walked her to her car and watched her out of sight. I considered riding after her to make sure she got home safely, but common sense made a rare appearance. I forced myself not to have coffee. I was shaking as it was. I did the washing up. Focused on each item as I cleaned and dried. Forced myself to calm down.

The white Ford was parked closer to the shop than usual. I wondered again if they were getting sloppy. I cast a quick look at the driver's seat as I rode past. Empty.

I went to the shop first, it was still locked up with no sign of movement. I slipped up to Doc's flat and Jan answered the door. She looked worried – welcome to the party. Doc was in the kitchen, cards lay out on the table. I barely looked at them but did register they were the art nouveau pack Jan used.

I waited for Doc to speak.

"Karla get off okay?"

His attention was more on Jan than me. She'd taken a seat opposite him and began working the cards. I didn't answer Doc's question and when he looked up at me, I tilted my head in the direction of the front room. Jan was too busy with the tarot to notice him nod and get up.

The altar was clean, the front room as welcoming as ever.

"You told her about the guys following her?" Doc nodded. "She got any idea who they are?"

"Not a clue. She was scared when I told her, really shaky."

I felt the anger building again and swallowed it back down.

"Now what?"

Doc gave one of his tight smiles. He flopped down into one of the armchairs and stared past me at the charcoal drawing on the wall. Unlike me, Ezulie Dantor wasn't making any attempt to hold in the rage.

"I think we should wait until it's dark. I reckon if Jan drives over to the Delmount Estate, we can find somewhere out of sight to have a word."

I waited a bit, hoping something else was coming.

"That's it? We have a word?"

Doc held up a hand, pacifying.

"As far as we know, they've been tracking Jan for three or four days, right? That's since I saw them. They might have been there for weeks for all we know. But I'm betting they ain't police."

I agreed, whoever these guys where, they weren't cops. They were too crap at it to be trained. Even with government cuts, the police could probably round up more than two cars.

"These jokers are alternating days. I reckon they're doing twelve hours a piece. Then they drive home, something to eat, bit of a kip, then back to it. Twelve hours sat in a car. Couple of days of that ... these guys ain't going to be top of their game. We let the wanker in the Ford stew until it's dark, then we ask him a few questions."

I pointed out that two cars could still be more than two people. Doc shook his head, held up two fingers.

"Middle-aged guy with a bit of a gut and a younger fella with a wispy beard, blonde. I've been keeping an eye on them."

Middle-aged, gut. That was the one taking pictures of Jan's car.

"I'd say they're going to change shifts before dark," I said. "That creep with the Ford's been on since at least five thirty."

That was about the time I saw him.

"Like I said, these guys have been at it for days. Even at the start of the shift, I'd bet he's going to be next to useless. I'm sure these guys are private detectives. Cheap ones, small time."

I took the room's other chair. Talking it through was easing my nerves and Doc was making sense. Watching Jan, watching anyone, twenty-four-seven was no easy task. Any organisation with the resources to do the job right wouldn't send just two people. Even so, someone was paying, even if they weren't paying much. Who? For that matter, why?

"You still think this is an insurance company trying to avoid a pay out?"

Doc shook his head.

"Not anymore. If an insurance company had sent them it'd be all about money. What we know about Jan's husband ... " He pulled a face. "I don't think his business dealings had anything like the clout to make it worthwhile. And again, these guys are Mickey Mouse. If insurance brokers were chasing big money, they'd use better people."

"This is about the death then?"

I kept my voice on the low side, aware that Jan was in the kitchen. The lack of furniture and carpets made the whole flat into a resonating chamber, sound carried.

"I can't see what else."

"The house is gone, but what about capital. If she stands to inherit a mint."

Doc shook his head. I suspected he was thinking about the same as me. Our snoop around Keller's place hadn't left the impression of untold wealth.

"Well," Doc gave me a full beam Cat grin, "on the up side, it looks like we're not the only ones that don't trust the police. It's nice to know we're not just being paranoid."

I rang dad from the shop around eleven and told him I'd be home late. His steady whine of complaint assured me he was fine. The shop was busy, Doc was fully booked. Gina was due to come in at three to begin a sleeve for a new customer. I had a run-of-the-mill piece to apply. It was her first tattoo and she asked a lot of questions. Jan came to man the desk while I was in the back room slinging the ink. The tarot cards arrived with her.

At half-twelve Jan got a call from Chris and she vanished to brighten his lunch hour. The Audi left the road, double time, followed by Middle Age Gut in his white Ford.

"So who's paying them?" I asked when we had the shop to ourselves.

I didn't think he knew; I was talking to myself really. Doc answered anyway.

"Someone with a fair bit of money. Even low-rent people need paying. Day and night, four or five days, even Mickey Mouse won't be that cheap. Talking of which."

He fumbled in a hip pocket, produced a crumpled envelope and offered it to me. Gina's money.

"I don't want it."

"Gina said to give it to you."

I didn't move to take it, so he dropped it on the counter. I explained it was payment for the back piece.

"Gina said she didn't want it," Doc told me, "said she 'didn't want to be a part of it'."

He did his silence thing, maybe waiting for me to explain that too. We both stood in the silence with the envelope on the counter between us. Doc let up when the kettle began to steam.

"Look, Yak," he said over his shoulder, "I've known Gina a long time. That money's her way of saying sorry. It's the nearest you'll ever get to an apology from her."

I told him Gina had nothing to apologise for. Doc rolled his eyes and put a mug in front of me.

"You two did have a ruck then?"

"She wanted to know what you were up to. I told her Chris was in trouble, and you were playing Columbo. She's with you; Chris is a paragon of virtue. I'm meant to know that just by looking at him."

"Gina's got a lot of time for Chris."

"Yeah, I get that. Chris has got his own moral compass apparently. That's what your ex-wife tells me."

The statement hung in the air and I watched Doc to see if he'd react.

He blew out a mouthful of air through pursed lips.

"Gina tends to keep quiet about our bit of history. I keep schtum for her sake. Nothing sinister about it."

"Well Gina's got it in her head that Chris is a choir boy because he wouldn't knock the shit out of someone for a grand."

Doc didn't answer for a while.

"That's one of the reasons I know Chris didn't kill anyone," he said. "I asked him to give someone a slap, didn't want them killed or maimed, nothing close. Just a couple of bruises. Chris looked at me like I'd crawled out from under a stone and said, 'What do you think I am? Go fuck yourself?'."

Doc made an open hand gesture, *there you have it.*

A man with his own moral compass. The tattoo I'd seen on Chris's palm, the day he'd told us about Jan becoming a widow, was an ornate number thirteen. Thirteen carries a few meanings. Luck, good and bad, or the thirteenth letter of the alphabet, M, standing for marijuana or motorcycle. For a few, the thirteen means twelve plus one. Twelve members of the jury plus the judge. This can be a show of independence, following your own rules, a law unto yourself. It can also mean the wearer is judge and jury, dispensing his own justice.

I thought about the evening outside Chris's flat, when he'd found out Jan had spent the night at my place. I wondered what form of judicial review Chris would favour.

"That's it, is it, all the proof you need? Well bully for you. Meanwhile I've got people watching my house, sniffing round Karla."

"Tonight, we'll find out what the deal is. Even if we don't find out who sent them, I think they'll back off once they know we've rumbled them."

He tilted his head at me, wanting some kind of response.

"If I see either of those clowns outside my place again, Jan can get herself somewhere else to sleep. I feel sorry for her but putting my family at risk because I choose to trust you? Not going to happen."

"I understand that. Tonight, we'll get it sorted."

The plan was simple, if only by virtue of being thin on details. Once it was dark, Jan, Doc and me would get into the black Audi. Doc would be driving. Once he was sure we were being followed he'd take the car out to the Delmount industrial estate and find a stretch of dark road. Once we saw our tail park up, me and Doc would confront him. If I hadn't seen Middle Age Gut taking an interest in Karla's car, I'd have raised a few questions about why we needed to do this without witnesses.

"Bingo," said Doc. Jan made to look over her shoulder. "Don't turn round. I'd hate to tip them off."

Jan's head snapped back so fast it made me wince.

"Which one is it?" I asked. I was packed into the back seat.

"Honda Civic," Doc said. "You were right about them changing over."

We headed towards Delmount. I found I could get a reasonable view of the traffic behind us if I sloughed in my seat and kept an eye on the driver's-side mirror. The Civic was never more than two cars away. At one point it was directly behind us. That they were so bad at what they were doing made it worse.

By the time we hit the industrial estate it was mostly deserted. The units there were occupied mainly by small businesses and few of them operated through the night. Doc did a circuit of the estate, keeping to the access roads because they weren't covered by security cameras. We passed a lorry park with a lot of sodium street lamps and a single arctic passing the night. There were no lights showing from the cab. About fifty yards after the lorry park the road branched. Right took you around the rest of the estate; left vanished into an unused plot of waste land. The streetlights ran out where the road split. Doc pointed into the darkness of the left fork.

"How about there?"

"Cool," I said. My stomach was knotted.

Doc pulled over into the glow of light from the lorry park. In the mirror, I saw the Civic slow to a crawl, as the driver tried not to catch up. The car had its lights off, which made it more obvious. Doc turned in the driver's seat.

"Okay," he said, "get out the car and make a big show of walking away. I'll take matey boy around the estate again. Once he's out the way double back and hide." He had his full Cheshire Cat on. "Make sure your phone's on."

I nodded and struggled from the back seat, slapped the roof of the Audi the way people do when they've got out of a friend's car. Then I walked back towards the Civic. I avoided looking at it, affecting an interest in the HGV in the lorry park. I expect I overdid it, but we weren't dealing with MI6. Doc drove off, round to the right, and the Civic followed. When the cars were out of sight behind the blocks of industrial units, I spun on my heel and headed back to the unlit stretch of road. A little way after the road forked to the left it died in a field of rubble and brambles. The only sign of use was a pair of burnt out cars. I waited at the mouth of the road, pressed back into a tangle of foliage trying to bring a chain-link fence down. I pulled on black latex gloves and waited. I didn't have to wait long before my phone rang.

Jan was on the line.

"We're nearly there. Is it clear?"

"Yeah, clear. I'm at the entrance to the road, out of sight."

I heard something muffled, and assumed she'd covered the mouthpiece to speak to Doc. Then she came back.

"Good. Doc says don't hang up."

As she said that, I saw the Audi approaching. It was moving faster, not hammering it, but definitely shifting. Making things happen quicker gave the guy following less time to think.

The Audi hauled a left into the dead end, slipped into the dark. Doc killed the lights and engine. If he'd given it any thought, the Civic driver would have known the car wasn't going to get away. He could have parked out of the way, on the access road, waited for the Audi to come back out. He realised his mistake pretty fast.

The Civic hung a left into the disused road and straight away pulled over to park. As chance would have it, he gained a little bit of cover by tucking his car behind one of the burnt-out wrecks. Like Doc, he shut down the engine. I briefly heard music playing before he snuffed out the radio.

I put the phone to my ear.

"He's about ten yards from me and he's got the windows rolled down."

Which meant we could reach in and unlock the doors if need be. Doc came on the line.

"He's parked on the left, yeah?"

"Yep. Driver's door is on the off side."

"Let's do it."

"Okay."

The line went dead.

Doc started the Audi and put the lights back on. He reversed the way he'd come, went a little way past the Civic, paused, then put it in first and pulled up alongside it. The passenger side of the Audi was tight to the driver's side of the Civic, blocking the door.

We timed it well. The guy in the driver's seat flicked his head to the right just as the Audi pulled up. By the time he looked left I'd unlocked the door and was sitting next to him.

The car stank of old food and someone who'd only just stopped being a teenager. I gave the guy behind the wheel my best don't-fuck-with-me look. His mouth opened and closed a couple of times but nothing came out. He found his voice as Doc opened the rear door and climbed in.

"What do you think you're doing?"

He did his best to sound outraged. He didn't do it very well.

"That's what we're asking you," Doc said. I could hear him smiling. This, more than the situation, made me angry again. I wasn't seeing the humour in any of this. "Now, why are you following my friend Jan?"

"I got no idea what you're talking about." He was trying hard to keep his head still, trying to keep contact with Doc. Doing what he could to appear sincere. There was one of Doc's silences but it drew out nothing useful. The guy repeated himself, "I don't know what you mean. I got no idea."

"You just followed us around an empty industrial estate, twice, then down a dead end." Doc shifted on the back seat, moved into the driver's personal space. "Why? Looking for some dogging action?"

The driver giggled, either nerves or an attempt to ingratiate himself. The silence in the car swallowed the sound whole.

"Why are you following Jan Keller?" Doc asked again.

The driver let out a sigh. He sounded tired. Worn out

tired, not bored. Doc was right about back-to-back twelve-hour shifts, they're a killer. Ask any nurse.

"I'm being paid to. Someone wants to know what she gets up to, that's all I can say."

We waited but nothing else was forthcoming.

Doc said, "Who's paying you?"

In the gloom, I saw the outline of the driver's head shake. "I'm not saying anything else. More than my job's worth."

I felt something inside me shift. The anger had been there all day, since I'd seen Middle Age Gut snooping with his mobile, but it had been aimless. Now it changed, became pointed. I reached up to the car's roof light and switched it on. The driver watched me. He was still nervous, but now he had an air of defiance to him. Maybe deciding the line he was going to take had made him feel in control.

I reached into a pocket of my leather, pulled out the Stanley knife. I held it in front of me to make sure he'd seen it then thumbed the blade open and thrust it towards him. He jerked away and came to a stop pressed hard against the door pillar, then jammed his head back into the seat rest as far as he could. He wound up with nowhere to go and the tip of the blade just under the angle of his jaw. His head was craned back so he was looking straight up to heaven. Eyes wide.

"Jesus Christ," he squeaked.

We waited a moment. Jesus didn't show, so we carried on without him.

"Talk." It was a grunt, my throat was locked. I managed to turn my head enough to see Doc. The Cheshire Cat grin was gone. I wasn't sure if I was talking to the driver or to him. "Talk."

"Who's paying you?" Doc asked again, the driver was making hissing sounds, sucking in terrified breaths that whistled through his teeth.

I gave the knife a tiny twist and a pin point of blood became a trickle.

"Mrs Keller. Her sister-in-law."

He squealed this in one breath, made it a single word. It took me a second to make sense of it. Caroline.

"Why?"

The answer was another squeal, this time too long to be decoded. Doc put a hand on my forearm and spoke slowly to me, "Give the boy some air, Yakky. Let him talk."

He put an emphasis on the word *boy,* I guessed for my benefit. The driver was young, no more than twenty. Fear made him look younger still. I pulled the knife back a little way but he didn't move his head away from the door pillar. His eyes swivelled down from heaven, down to me.

"Your mate, one in the white Ford, he was taking pictures of my old lady's number plate. Why?" He didn't speak straight away, just looked scared and sucked in air. "Why?"

"He's got a contact, they get him addresses from number plates."

"What do you mean contact? Police?"

I had the knife at his neck again. He tried to shake his head, remembered the blade was there.

"Not police. Just some dude works at the DVLC. My uncle knows him from way back."

I leaned closer. "Uncle?"

"My uncle Ken, it's his firm. I'm working for him."

I took a deep breath and clicked the knife shut. I put it back in my leather, sat back and gave him some room. He still didn't move away from the space he'd fitted himself in. Doc looked at me, raised his eyebrows, *you finished?* I nodded.

"What's your name?" Doc asked. The driver twisted his neck enough to get a look at him.

"Steve."

"You've been following a friend of ours, Steve. We just want to know why." Doc waited, letting this sink in. Steve flicked a look at me, caught my eye and quickly looked away again. "I've got a few questions that's all, you going to talk to me?"

"Yeah."

Steve was breathing hard, almost hyperventilating.

"How long have you been following Jan?" Doc asked.

"About a week."

The answer had come so fast I suspected it had bypassed his brain completely. Doc must have been to be thinking the same thing.

"A week. Since Tuesday?"

Steve nodded eagerly, then shook his head.

"Friday."

Five days.

"So, what have you been doing exactly?"

Scared as he was, Steve almost laughed. The answer was, *not much.*

Steve's career in surveillance had started on Friday, cash in hand. Until then, Ken's detective agency had consisted of Ken, an online advert and a mobile phone. Ken's normal line of business was tracking down used cars for repossession. He had a circle of second hand car dealers who put work his way. They tended to specialise in extending credit to the uncreditworthy. When the payments stopped Ken slipped some money to his contact at the DVLA and his contact provided an address. Ken, whose real talent was getting into cars and hotwiring them, then carried out a repossession. All this depended on the car being legally registered, which it seldom was.

His other source of income was contacting distant relatives of people who'd died intestate. He'd convince them they were in danger of missing out on a substantial inheritance. Then he'd offer them the details of their dearly beloved, and previously unknown, relative. His condolences came free. The information they needed to stake their claim had a price.

Caroline Keller's commission for a twenty-four-hour surveillance gig came out of the blue. Uncle Ken accepted the job without batting an eye then called his nephew. Steve went from unemployed to private investigator in the course of a phone call. Ken's detective agency was cheap, and you got what you paid for. Steve was told, *follow the tart in the black*

Audi, make a note of where she goes and at what time, and take the odd picture. Ken typed up the page of notes and sent Caroline a daily up-date.

"Why's she want Jan followed?" Doc's next question.

"She thinks your friend killed her own husband. She thinks we're going to be able to prove it." Doc sat back in his seat, thinking. Steve, rattled by the silence, began to gabble, "We don't have a clue though. We wouldn't know where to start. Ken thinks it's funny. We're just stringing this Keller woman along. Taking her money until see figures out we don't know what we're – " Steve cut off like a switch had been flicked when Doc made a shushing noise.

"Why does she think Jan killed her husband?"

Steve took a breath before answering, trying to calm himself.

"She had a copy of the police report. The police are saying it was murder, she's convinced it was your friend."

"Why, what did the report say?"

"I don't know," Steve said then looked wildly between Doc and me, close to panic. "I didn't read it. Honest to God I don't know."

Doc put a hand on Steve's shoulder and shushed him again, quite softly. Steve clamed up again and began weeping.

"Do you and your uncle have a copy of this report?" Steve shook his head. "Mrs Keller didn't give you a copy? Really?"

Steve began crying in earnest.

"She did, but Ken threw it away. He didn't want it, said if the police got involved, it'd look bad."

Doc nodded, told Steve he believed him. So did I. Police reports about ongoing investigations don't get put into general circulation, not without some funny business taking place.

"Okay Steve," Doc said, "calm down and listen. You go back to your uncle and you tell him, the ride on the gravy train is over. You guys tell Mrs Keller you're not working for her anymore. You got that?" Steve nodded his head frantically. "Now give my friend your wallet and your mobile."

"There in the glove box," Steve said without opening his eyes. I opened the glove box; they were there along with a digital camera, sitting on a jumble of notebooks and music CDs. I handed the wallet to Doc and picked up the one notebook that looked like it'd been used. It was the spiral bound type, some of its pages turned back, out of the way. The page on display was headed with the date and divided into four columns: *LEFT: TIME: ARRIVED: TIME:*. There were three entries, the last one only half an entry. *LEFT: tattoo parlour. TIME: 19:48.* I wondered if Steve would be adding *ARRIVED: Dead end road in the middle of an industrial estate.*

I turned the digital camera on and checked through the memory. After I'd seen a dozen or so blurred pictures of Jan entering or leaving various front doors, mine mainly, I deleted everything. The phone needed a PIN number to unlock it. Steve told me it when I asked. I checked he was telling me the truth then turned the phone off and put it my pocket.

"Okay, Steve," Doc said, "here's your wallet." His bony hand held the wallet alongside Steve's face. He opened one eye enough to see it and put his hand over it. Doc let him take the wallet. "I've taken your driving licence. I'll put it in the post to you tomorrow once I've made a note of the address. That way, if we need to get in touch, we'll know where to find you. You understand?"

"Yeah. Yeah, I get it."

Steve he was getting himself under control now, the tears had stopped and his breathing was slowing towards normal. He could see it was nearly over.

"You'll get your phone back too."

Doc slid along the seat and opened his door. I listen to him walk around the Honda and get back into the Audi.

"Keys," I said. Steve turned to look at me but kept himself as far away as the space allowed.

"Keys?"

"Give me the car keys."

"Oh, man, look it's my uncle's – "

I'd hit him before I even thought about it. My fist connected square on his left ear, his head rebounded off the door pillar and he pulled himself into a tight ball on the driver seat. The next two punches landed somewhere around his head but with nothing like the force of the first. I was bent over him then and the car's roof stopped me pulling my arm back. It was probably lucky for both of us.

He was crying again, trying to speak, "Take them, take them."

I reached past him and fumbled the keys from the ignition, then I pulled him upright. He had his eyes tight shut again. A picture of Jan popped into my head, sitting at my dining table crying with her eyes open. Ever watchful.

"If I ever see you outside my house again, or sniffing round my old lady again, I'll kill you. You got that?"

He managed to nod. "I won't, I won't. Okay? I swear to God, I won't."

"Same goes for your uncle. You tell him."

I got out of the car and threw the keys into the patch of waste ground. I didn't hear them land. Doc had got out of the Audi again and was watching me.

We drove back to the shop in silence. Jan didn't look at me or Doc the whole way. It occurred to me she would have been watching from the passenger seat of the Audi the whole time.

Ever watchful.

Doc pulled up outside the shop. As he and I got out the car, Jan's phone rang. I'd seen her send a text during the drive back from the Delmount estate. I leaned against the car, tried to slow my breathing. The shaking was down to a tremor. I could feel Doc watching me.

"You alright?" He used the voice people use when they find meths drinkers collapsed in the underpass.

I nodded, but then said, "No, not really."

Doc made a muttered reply I didn't catch then I heard him unlocking the door to the shop. We left Jan to her phone call. He stood back and let me pass into the waiting room. I stepped between the sofas and went behind the counter, fumbled in the gloom, locating my helmet and gloves.

"When did *you* start carrying a shiv?" Doc's voice seemed to come from thin air.

Following his usual routine, he'd slipped into the shop and straight to the point of maximum obscurity.

"Always have."

"Any reason why?"

I turned on the light above the counter so I didn't have to talk to a disembodied voice. Doc was just inside the door, leaning against the wall.

"Handy tool."

I normally had half a dozen pencils in my pockets. I shaped the leads so I could vary my shading techniques. Nine out of ten judges wouldn't buy that plea. I didn't imagine Doc had either, but he didn't say so.

"If I was you, I'd lose the habit for a while."

From what Steve had told us, Uncle Ken worked on the edge of legal. Best case, Ken would shrug and move on to the next deal. Worse case, Ken and Steve run to the police. Edge of legal or not, a complaint that came with bruises, blood loss and the perpetrator's name and address is the stuff charging officers dream of.

"You fancy a cup of tea?" Doc asked.

I didn't, my stomach was clenched tight, but I didn't want to go home either. I put my lid and gloves on the counter.

"Yeah, I'll do it."

I watched my hands as I filled the kettle and sorted out a pair of mugs. The tremor was almost gone. I wondered where all that anger had gone, where it had come from. Steve had followed Jan to my house and I'd held a knife to his throat. I told myself I was looking after the people close to me. I didn't buy that any more than nine out of ten judges would.

Doc had left the wall and settled into the sofa least visible to the street.

"I think we've seen the last of Steve and Ken," he remarked when I put his mug on the table.

"Good." I felt through my pocket, found Steve's mobile next to my knife. "You want this?"

As Doc leaned forward to take it, the shop door opened. Jan was hiding behind the door again, appearing in the room as a floating head.

"Yakky?" She didn't wait for a response. "I'm going to sleep over at Chris's flat tonight, okay?"

"Sure. I'll see you later."

She nodded at Doc, and the door shut. The Audi left. Doc and I both watched the window.

After a minute, he said, "You scared her."

"I scared me. I don't know where that came from."

Doc nodded and took a mouthful of tea. I followed suit, realised my throat ached.

"Why'd you punch him?"

"I told him to give me the car keys. He started to say it wasn't his car and I just ... bang."

I felt sick thinking about it again. He was only a kid. What would I have done if I'd still been holding the knife? Best guess was ten years. Doc suddenly stood up.

"I think we both need a real drink. Let's put a dent in that bottle of Casa Noble."

I settled myself in the armchair Doc normally used. This meant I was facing the mural of Ezulie Dantor and the head stones. Atonement? Doc came in from the kitchen with a pair of glasses and the Tequila. He poured generous measures.

"Remember," he said as he handed me one, "sip, don't glug."

It was largely wasted on me – quality or cheap stuff, I

couldn't tell. All the same, I appreciated the burn as it went down. Doc toasted me and took a sip, then he poured a shot into the pewter offering bowl on the altar. He took the armchair opposite.

"Let's have that knife," he said.

"I was planning to drop it in a litter bin on the way home."

Doc shook his head. "Let's pretend the police are on the way here, right now."

I went with the flow and picked my jacket off the floor, pulled the knife out. I'd had it years and I surprised myself by not wanting to give it up.

Doc took the knife apart and emptied the spare blades from the handle. None of them were new and all of them had my prints on them. Doc studied the components checking them, I assumed, for blood. Satisfied there was none, he wiped everything clean with a bandana. He put it all back together without gloves and I pointed out his prints were now all over it.

"Nothing suspicious about that. I'll put it in a drawer with a couple of screwdrivers. If anyone looks, my knife, with my prints, in with my tools."

He was better at this stuff than I was. Doc vanished into the hall and I heard a drawer open and close in his bedroom, then the clank and whir of a printer waking up. When he came back he was carrying a laptop. After glancing at the driver's licence we'd taken from Steve, he tapped away at the keyboard for a couple of minutes. He read back what he'd written;

Dear Mr Steven Bruton,

Please find enclosed your driving licence and a mobile phone that I believe may be yours.

I found these items lying on the pavement near my shop. As the phone and licence were together, I assumed they were dropped at the same time.

Hope you have not lost too much sleep worrying.

Yours sincerely,
Dr J. Slidesmith

"Why all the bullshit?"

Doc grinned and must have pressed print because the printer in the bedroom started up.

"This way, if Holmes and Watson go to the police, all they've got is a polite letter from a Good Samaritan. Meanwhile, I have a legitimate reason to have Steve's address in the recycle bin of my computer."

The licence and one of Doc's business cards went into an envelope. Doc scrolled through the list of numbers on Steve's phone.

Without looking up, he asked, "You want to talk about tonight?"

"Not really."

"Don't bottle it up too long."

I shook my head, took another sip, and a shudder ran the length of my spine.

"I'm not, I just need a bit of distance on it, sort it out a bit."

I tapped the side of my head for emphasis.

Doc nodded. "Just remember, when you want to talk, I'm here. I'm good at listening."

"Does Steve have Ken's number in that phone?"

"Expect so," Doc said. He glanced up from the little screen. "Think we should ring him?"

I was picturing Steve stranded in the empty industrial estate, still in tears.

"We should tell him where to find his nephew."

Doc considered this, and carried on scrolling through the store of numbers. He didn't say at the time, but Ken's number had been filed under U, listed as *Uncle Kenny*. There was a mobile and a landline number. The mobile went straight to voicemail; the land line rang half a dozen times before an answerphone message. Doc hung up and hit redial three times before Ken picked up. I could just make out a groggy voice on the end of the line.

"Hello Ken," Doc said, "I'm a friend of the woman you and your nephew, Steve, have been following. Now, I've spoken to Steven about this matter, along with one of my associates. We told him what I'm telling you. You no longer work for Mrs Keller. If you don't understand this, go and talk to your nephew, because my associate made it clear to him exactly what the situation is."

Confused sounds from the mobile.

Doc listened, briefly, then, "Do you know the Delmount industrial estate? Go around the access road; there's a lorry park with an HGV sat in it. Just past that, there's a road leading to an empty plot. Your car's on the road and the keys are in the empty plot. I'd go there now if I was you, 'cos Steve's going to need someone to drive him home."

Ken must have asked for the name of the estate again, because Doc said, "Delmount. You know it? Good. Now, understand this, Kenneth, if I need to talk to you again, I'll be doing it in person."

With that he broke the connection.

When I pointed out the exchange had been less than reassuring, Doc's cheek twitched into one of his tight smiles. He leaned forward in his chair.

"Look, Yakky, you're upset and feeling guilty about what you did to Steve, is that fair enough?" I knocked back the last of my drink and nodded. "I get that, and I respect you for it. Believe me, if you could put a knife to someone's throat and feel good about it, you wouldn't be sitting in my home, drinking my best Tequila."

He took my empty glass and refilled it. As he did, Steve's phone began to ring. Doc put it to his ear. A slightly panicked voice said, "Hello, Steve?"

"He's on the Delmount industrial estate Ken," Doc said. "I already told you that." He turned the phone off then carried on talking to me. "Don't mix up feeling bad with being wrong."

He topped up his own measure and held it up to me like a

toast. He didn't move to drink and I saw he was waiting for me to respond. I was in the dark but, as so often with Doc, I went along for the ride and we tapped glasses. Doc copied Ken's numbers into his phone and Uncle Kenny became Snoopy. The phone joined the licence in the envelope. The envelope was sealed.

"I think we might have made a bit of progress this evening. To be blunt about it, I don't think The Jive was going to work on Steve, too subtle."

"Where as my mindless brutality – "

Doc stopped me talking, reached over and put a hand on my shoulder.

"Yakky. I'm not going to pretend I know you that well. I don't and I doubt if anyone else does. But you're not a brute. Any more than Chris is, any more than I am. We all carry anger, it's an emotion like any other. And sometimes it gets past the thought process. Learn from what happened, then move on."

I think he felt a bit self-conscious about this speech. He snapped out a Cheshire Cat grin then hide behind his glass.

"Anyway," he carried on, "light a candle for Steve if you must, but don't waste any sympathy on Ken. Main point of tonight was to scare the bastard away, and I think it's best he stays scared. So, no disrespect to your humanitarian side, but my call to Ken was not about therapy." I made to say something, but he held up a hand. "Ken's on his way to Delmount now, maybe he finds Steve and they go home and count their blessings, along with the money they've screwed out of Caroline Keller. Maybe Steve's walking home already, without his phone, and Ken gets to drive around all night worrying. Either way, Jan and Karla get left out of the picture. Who knows, perhaps Steve decides against a career that involves stalking innocent women."

"How is any of this progress?"

"We now know Caroline Keller gave Ken a copy of a police report." He made a spooling motion with his fingertips, the motion you make if you want someone to turn the engine over.

If Caroline had a copy of the police report to give away, she was likely to have one she'd kept. In the wake of my day with Gina and night with Karla, I'd forgotten about Doc's date.

"You met with Mrs Keller yesterday," I said after a while.

Doc tipped his glass to me. "Here's to progress."

Peter and the Slag

The day Gina and I had been watching the shop, Doc took Caroline out for a Jive. They'd met at a point roughly midway between the Keller house and Doc's flat. Caroline mentioned a coffee shop but Doc suggested he buy her lunch. He put it to her that this was his way of apologising for the 'mix-up' with the keys. The fact she agreed was testament to Doc's peculiar brand of charm. His take on it was less flattering, to both parties. Caroline was lonely and looking for somewhere to vent. She also liked the idea of being taken to lunch a by a man of Jan's acquaintance.

Caroline was older than Jan, fifteen years was Doc's estimate. Even so, the physical resemblance between them was striking. At least between the woman Doc had lunch with and Jan as she appeared in the trophy-wife portraits. Both were good-looking women and while Caroline wasn't dressed to the nines, she clearly seldom aimed for anything beneath a high seven.

The restaurant she'd suggested was small, overly bright, and set the diners out like exhibits. It smelt of money rather than food. Caroline was already seated, studying the menu and waiting for Doc. When he arrived she gave him a false smile. Doc again apologised about the keys and thanked her for meeting with him. Caroline brushed aside his apologies with a delicate laugh and offered her own thanks for being taken to lunch. Both gestures were as genuine as the smile.

"Have you ordered?" Doc asked.

"No, I waited for you."

"Not too long, I hope."

Another shallow smile. "A few minutes."

There was a half-litre bottle of sparkling water on the table. Caroline had already put away two thirds of it. Doc asked if she wanted a starter and wasn't surprised when she didn't. What Caroline did order came with plenty of garnish, zero calories and financial advice on how to meet the cost.

Doc gave a joyless laugh. "She was looking after her figure the way surgeons look after their hands. I don't think it was vanity. She was tending to her career."

The development plan of a professional trophy wife? Grow old in splendour with your wealthy husband or catch a divorce settlement the size of the national debt. If hubby's got a roving eye, I'd guess you go for option two. If your main asset is looking good on an arm, you've got a limited window of opportunity. Timing is all. And while you're listening to the clock tick, and watching the newer models strut their stuff, you fill up with a pint of water before every meal and judge the food by the number of calories.

When they exchanged keys, Caroline produced the business card, the one with the wrong alarm code on it. Doc took the card, exchanged it for a fresh one on which he'd already, very carefully, printed the real number. He crumpled up the old card and slipped it into his pocket, leaving no record that the two numbers bore no resemblance.

"My handwriting's awful," he told her.

Caroline cut her tiny salad into tiny pieces, chewed each speck until Doc's jaw began to ache in sympathy. Between bites she was eager to talk. Talking meant she wasn't eating.

"When we met the other night, you said I should watch myself?" Doc prompted her.

Caroline, consented to stop chewing and actually swallowed. She washed down the morsel with half a glass of water.

"Jan, is a little tart. She's out for whatever she can get, and she will fuck anyone she thinks can move her up a rung." Her tone was clipped, matter of fact.

It sounded rehearsed, or at least oft repeated. Caroline paused, waiting for Doc to ask for details.

There was, Doc thought, a power play taking place. She needed the keys and the alarm code, so they were here. Doc acquiesced gracefully, dressed the meeting, and the exchange, as a luncheon date. He didn't think she'd be such a magnanimous victor if he admitted to needing something she had.

"This is something very personal between you and your ..." Instead of saying husband, Doc left the sentence to hang.

He busied himself with his own meal. Caroline couldn't handle the silence.

"I think you're entitled to know the sort of person you're getting involved with, Mr Slidesmith."

Doc smiled indulgently. "Then please, carry on. And it's Doctor Slidesmith actually, but please, call me James."

According to Caroline, the late Peter Keller had fallen under Jan's spell. Details of how they'd met were sketchy. One day he was a bachelor, the next, a fiancé. Their first public outing had been a charity benefit. Seating arrangements reflected size of donation, reflected social rank. Caroline's husband was a top table guest, his brother was less impressive. How close Jeffry and Peter Keller were, Doc couldn't gauge. Before seats were taken for dinner, and the hierarchy properly enforced, the elder Keller was kind enough to seek Peter out for a chat.

"Jan was standing there like butter wouldn't melt," Caroline recounted. "I remember thinking she was out of Peter's league. I thought he'd hired her from one of those escort agencies."

Doc waited for a snide comment about Jan and escort girls, but Caroline restrained herself.

After introductions, Peter announced the engagement. Jan proudly, though modestly, showed them the engagement ring. Caroline, with some satisfaction, told Doc that Poor

Peter had bought a ring almost identical to her own. Doc threw a stone into the pool to see where the ripples went.

"Sounds like Peter was carrying a torch for you."

He watched Caroline carefully. The idea pleased her, but she shook her head with a laugh. She tried for a youthful girlish sound but her nicotine habit showed through. After another pinch of her meal and another half glass of water, she said, "I don't think Peter was bothered about me. He just wanted to show Jeffry he could keep up. Jeffry had always been more successful."

Doc threw another stone. "You and Jan look quite alike, I hope you don't mind my saying that. I did think you might be sisters."

"A few people thought that. We played on it sometimes. If we knew we'd all be going to the same do, we'd get together and coordinate outfits."

Jan was taken under the wing, introduced into the right set. Caroline didn't say she was shown her place, but that was the subtext. Then, Jan forgot her place.

"Of course, it was Peter I felt sorry for," Caroline assured Doc. "Poor Peter."

Doc asked what she meant. He had the feeling she needed to salvage some pride.

"Well," Caroline began, then paused to summon a waiter and another bottle of water. "I think these things usually are harder on the man, especially in such a young marriage. For Jeffry and me, it was a blip."

She waved her hand in a dismissive way and almost dropped her fork.

"So, you and Jeffry moved on?"

Caroline nodded, but took another tiny forkful to chew. Doc feigned an interest in his own meal and left her to find her footing.

"For Peter it was awful, truly awful," Caroline finally said.

Doc could see what the conversation was costing her and let her take the reins.

"Because his brother and his wife ... "

"Well, Jeffry wasn't just his brother. He was the alpha male. The older brother, wealthier, more successful. Jeffry was the better catch. Poor Peter, all he had – "

She ducked for cover behind more chewing. Doc filled in the blank. All Poor Peter had was an imitation of his brother's wife. Only the imitation was younger and sexier. He rephrased this for Caroline's consumption.

"Your husband made a fool of himself?"

Caroline gratefully fell in line with this view. Jeffry had indeed made a fool of himself. Ageing male, enticed by a tart almost half his age, had fallen from grace. He dealt with his guilt the way he dealt with most things. By opening his wallet. Doc listened patiently to a detailed list of the high-price amends Jeffry had made.

"Jeffry felt horrible."

After saying this Caroline fell silent. Doc watched her, and concluded that for the first time since sitting down, she was actually thinking something over.

"Even after bailing Peter out, he felt bad. Poor Peter, he never did have Jeffry's business flair. He was a hard worker, no one could say otherwise, but he was never going to be one of the big boys."

Doc waited, aware that Caroline was wandering from her set list of grievances concerning Jan. She was pondering something again.

He suggested, cautiously, "Did Jeffry blame himself? For Peter getting out of his depth, I mean. Little brother trying to keep up with him and not quite managing?"

Caroline nodded, liking the notion. She looked earnestly at Doc, pleased to find someone who understood.

"You know, James, I think that's it exactly. I think, when Peter came over to ask about a loan," she put a heavy emphasis on loan, "Jeffry must have been torn in half. Knowing how badly he'd been hurt, I can't imagine what Peter must have put himself through, going cap in hand to Jeffry. Jeffry was thrilled to see him again, but the circumstances, well ... "

"You mean Jeffry felt bad, about feeling good, that his brother's misfortune had brought them back together?"

"Yes." She caught Doc's eye again, she looked genuinely upset, rather than righteously outraged. "That little slag ruined them both."

Caroline managed to avoid about three quarters of her plate, but she thanked him for lunch as Doc walked her back to her car. The restaurant was on a gentrified high street, rebranded as a village. There were half a dozen competitors that would have produced better food. None of them could have topped the price.

Her car was a silver-blue Porsche hard top. Doc complimented her on it and she gave him a real smile for the first time.

"Jeffry wants to trade it in for something newer. But I won't let him." She patted the roof, the way you'd pet a dog. The brief flash of pleasure passed, and she sighed deeply. "James, you seem like a decent man. You might think I'm the world's biggest bitch and perhaps I am, but Jan is a vicious little slag. I don't know what she is to you but believe me: you are nothing to her. Nothing."

"You blame her for Peter's death?"

"Absolutely."

Caroline's car didn't go with the ladies-that-lunch bit. It was too masculine. Fun little coupe, or a Chelsea tractor, would have been a better fit. The silver-blue Porsche was a driver's car. Doc hadn't expected that; he also hadn't expected her to peck a kiss on his check before she drove off.

He held up the bottle of Casa Noble for my inspection – two good shots left.

"Shall we?" I nodded, and he divided the spirit between us. "When we got to her car, there was a load of bird shit across the bonnet. She pulls a packet of tissues out of her handbag and cleans it off herself."

He took a thoughtful sip of Tequila, sober expressioned.

"You're easy to impress, Doc. Some posh bint has to clean her own car? Wow."

"What I mean is, she appreciates the finer things. Really, appreciates them. She knows that Porsche is a quality machine, knows enough to enjoy what it is rather than what other people think of it. Then, she sits in the priciest restaurant she can find, drinking water and eating two bits of lettuce. All the time, knowing what she's missing out on. I think it's sad, all that effort pretending she's happy."

Maybe the alcohol was making us maudlin, but I found myself feeling sorry for a woman I'd never met. I thought about Peter Keller's house, and all the money he'd joylessly spent on it. What had Jan told Doc about sleeping with Caroline's husband? Just a way of keeping score.

"Do you think Caroline really believes Jan killed her husband? I mean, murdered him."

"She's willing to pay out for Ken and Steve to follow her."

Mention of the private detectives made me think of something. If Caroline had been getting daily updates and photos, I couldn't see how she failed to see through Doc's Jive. Doc tapped his cheek, the jawbone tattoo.

"Best disguise in the world. Somebody gives a description of me ... "

He made the spooling sign with his fingers. First thing anyone would say, *bloody great tattoo across his face.* Cover the tattoo and, suddenly, the description was of someone else.

Ken was photographing number plates with a mobile. Steve had a basic pocket camera in the glove box. Pictures of Doc leaving a doorway on the other side of the road were going to be grainy shapes, particularly if they were copies churned out on a home printer.

Take Doc out of his jeans and threadbare leather, add a little makeup and Caroline was having lunch with a nicely groomed business man, not a biker with a facial tattoo.

He left the room and I heard drawers opening in his bedroom. When he came back he was holding a box of charcoal pencils and a pack of tarot cards. He pushed the cards into the back pocket of his jeans and, on the wall opposite the room's only window, began marking out some kind of the diagram.

He worked quickly, drawing lines that connected points that had some significance only to him. In the centre of the wall, he wrote two uppercase letters: *P* and *K*. He'd written *C.Kell* slightly smaller, near the centre of the construction. Next to it, he scrawled: *Slag Fuck ?*, an arrow ran from the question mark to the *PK*.

I asked him what he was doing.

"I can't keep all this straight in my head. I need to see it," he said, still working, absorbed the way he sometimes got when tattooing. Caught up in the needle song.

"Okay, I'm going to shoot off."

"You sure?" Doc asked.

I was very sure. I could see him edging towards one of his weirder episodes and I wasn't up to it

"Just tell me one thing before I go?" I pointed at his scrawling. "*C.Kell, slag fuck, question mark*. Give me a clue, eh?"

"C. Keller. Caroline," Doc said. "She told me Jan was a slag a couple of times. But she only called her a slag when she was getting emotional. It's not the type of word bandied about amongst the coffee morning set."

I ran the word through my head a few times and could see what he meant. It was offensive, it was meant to be, but it was also crude. The sort of vocabulary used in self-consciously gritty dramas set on run down council estates. Not the lexicon of people like the Kellers. Or at least, not the people the Kellers wanted to be.

"It's was different when she said Jan would fuck anybody. She said fuck in a very deliberate way. Made it sound like the sort of thing she'd only say in extreme circumstances." He shook his head, *no sale*. "The question mark just means think about it."

He started with the charcoal again. This time adding dates.

I followed the arrow, saw what *PK* stood for.

"You mean Peter Keller and Caroline were both posing?"

Doc stopped again, but didn't turn around this time. He still had the piece of charcoal raised, ready to carry on.

"Yeah. I think Pete was pretending to be a big-time player and struggling to keep up with his brother. I think Caroline wants everyone to think she's to the manor born. I'd lay good money, she's more to the rough end of the manor born."

"You think that's important?"

"I don't know. I keep thinking about Jan, playing roles, tip-toeing around and learning the rules."

"Maybe the rules Caroline and Poor Peter played by were a bit hard to pick up?"

Doc nodded, head moving in time to the strokes he was making with the charcoal.

"Or she learnt them too well."

He put a heavy circle around *C.Kell*, linked this to another circle. In the second circle he wrote: *J.Kell.* Linked this back to *PK.* His movements were getting faster.

I left him to it and rode home. I did two passes of the street looking for Steve or Ken. Was cheered by their absence. I checked on the kitchen before I checked on dad. The sink was full of washing up, so I knew he'd eaten. I went and sat with him for the rest of the evening. I hoped the wall of sound would bludgeon my mind into submission but it didn't.

To the list of disturbing images running across my brain, I added Doc's latest efforts at interior design. I wondered if Jan felt better, safer, now she was with Chris. I also wondered if she'd tell him what had upset her.

The Writing on the Wall

Wednesday 20 July

Mindful of the alcohol I'd consumed, and not wanting to add dehydration to my morning ritual, I drank a litre of water before getting to bed. My bladder woke me up just after four a.m.

When I tried to get back to sleep, my mind's eye kept seeing Steve, pinned against the side of his car. I gave it up as a bad lot after about fifteen minutes.

It was still dark when I came out of the shower. I made a huge breakfast and burned a hole in my coffee supply. I tried to draw out a few designs I'd had ideas for, but my concentration was shot. Steve kept intruding on my thoughts. I cleaned the kitchen, tidied the front room, set about assembling a full English breakfast for dad. Kept moving and avoided thinking. I ran out of distractions long before dad was due to make an appearance and prowled around the house aimlessly. Finally, I picked up a sketch pad again and drew Steve from memory.

I was hoping for some kind of mental purge. Get Steve onto a sheet of paper so he wasn't in my head. I normally drew faces big enough to fill an A4 page, but I couldn't do that with Steve. He became an image the size of a passport photo. I'd drawn it hunched over the dining room table, tight, locked into a ball. When it was finished my shoulders and neck hurt. As therapy went, it wasn't great.

By the time dad was up I'd filled a couple of A3 sketch sheets with more or less random images. Including various knives and the en suite bathroom reflected in a mirror. I considered taking them to Doc, seeing what his PhD in psychology made of them. But given the state of his walls I decided against it.

I fried dad's breakfast for him and made him a mug of tea that he drank almost a third of before declaring it horrible. It was close enough to count as a win.

I got to the shop before Doc. Another busy day, I had a couple of my own clients, and Doc was booked solid into the evening.

Ten o'clock came and went.

Doc appeared about a minute before his first customer. He set to work with no more than a cursory glance around the studio. I could have taken this as a compliment but decided to worry instead. When lunch time rolled around Doc put a note in the window, *back at two.*

Perhaps it was frequent exposure but Doc's flat seemed less creepy. He deposited me in the front room and dragged himself to the kitchen. I squatted on my hunches, back to the window, tried to take in what had Doc made on the wall.

He'd added a lot to it after I'd left. Various tarot cards were fixed into the design, along with a brace of mojos. A couple of candles were burning on the altar and the offering bowels were full. The room had a sharp burnt smell that was over laid with bleach. Doc's old cards, the reading pack, were spread out in the centre of the room. I was glad I'd left him to it.

He came back from the kitchen with two mugs of tea and a couple of sandwiches. He dropped into the nearest armchair, yawned hugely and gestured to the wall.

"What do you think?"

I thought the whole room needed a coat of paint.

I said, "What are the numbers along the top?"

At the top left corner of the wall was written *2Y*, then a symbol similar to the return key on a computer keyboard, an arrow bending back on itself.

"Two years back. Six months back, and so on," Doc said. "Timeline."

I looked again; it still took me a while to figure out the meanings. *2Y*-arrow symbol, two years ago. Going to the right, the next entry was *1Y9M*-arrow symbol, one year and nine months. The next entry after that was *6M*-arrow symbol. The entry furthest to the right was easier to decipher, *19/7.* July 19, the day before.

"You got it?" Doc asked me, after I'd studied it for a time.

I nodded. From each point on the timeline an arrow dropped, ending at a drawing, or a written note, or sometimes a tarot card. With my mouth full of sandwich I pointed at the top left corner and wiggled my finger up and down. Doc got my meaning.

"Two years ago Jan and Jeffry Keller have an affair."

This was represented on the wall by *JK + Jan* printed neatly in charcoal. Below this was a pinned a tarot card, The Lovers. This card had been pulled from a modern pack, artsy and printed on glossy stock.

"Okay," I said, "got that. The next one?"

The next one was three months later, marked at a year and nine months ago. The line drawn from this point ended at *PK* contact *JK (loan/gift).* Above this was pinned the Five of Pentangles. This card was from a more traditional deck.

"Three months later, Peter Keller makes contact with his brother asking for money. Jeffry told Jan, the night I went back to the house with her, that he made Peter a loan. A loan that was never repaid. When I had lunch with Caroline, she implied the money was a gift, or at least money Jeffry expected to lose."

Doc's notations were beginning to make sense. The next mark, six months ago, was the initials *PK* and The Ruined Tower.

The Ruined Tower showed a tower being struck by lightning, stricken bodies falling to the ground. It was from the modern, glossy pack. Peter Keller is in ruins and his house, his castle, is signed over to his brother. Doc

confirmed my interpretation.

"Why are you using different packs of cards?"

"The arty-farty ones can be taken at face value, more or less. Jeff and Jan were lovers, Peter loses his house. The older ones are more about the meanings. Or they came up when I did a reading."

Now I had a taste of Doc's strange logic, the wall started to look less random. I began to see layers of order to it. The bottom layer, just above the skirting board, had a lot of question marks.

"Bottom far left?"

This was the Hanged Man and another card I didn't recognise, mounted upside down. Between the cards was a clutter of question marks. Doc was slumped low in the armchair and looked ready to sleep.

"That's Jan and the Big Guy," he said. "I said on that first night we saw them, how did they hook up?"

"Dodgy website, via that sleazebag, Jock."

Doc shook his head then reached in his pocket and pulled out his phone. After tapping away for a minute he handed it to me. It was showing the inbox of an email account, in the name of SkinKitten. The inbox had twelve messages, all from Sally Hart. I picked one at random and opened it. It was telling SkinKitten that Bull-Sigh had sent a virtual kiss. I opened another. This said that four hunky men had viewed SkinKitten's profile. There was a hyperlink to follow if SkinKitten wanted to know more. The hyperlink took me to a login page.

Doc was watching me navigate the phone.

"Username: SkinKitten. One word, capital es, capital kay. Password: Garbo78, capital gee, no spaces."

"What is this?"

Doc laughed and motioned to have the phone back. The webpage I'd opened contained a welcome message from Seductive Secrets. It also informed SkinKitten that there were nine unread messages waiting, that Tallyman76 had sent a virtual gift and five other members had sent virtual kisses.

"Married dating site. I signed up to see what kind of response it got. I'll tell you, as a bloke I can't pull a muscle. As a woman, I'm beating them off with a stick."

At around one o'clock in the morning Doc had finished the wall. He'd sat, much as I had, regarding his handiwork and pondering the layer of question marked symbols. He kept circling back to Chris and Jan. The Hanged Man and The High Priestess, inverted. Jock finding Jan's profile and pushing it to Chris was only half the story.

Doc googled cheating sites to see how the system worked but the sites were pretty well locked. The only way in was to become a member.

"Why pretend you're a woman?"

"It costs an arm and a leg for men to join up. Women get free membership for life. Market forces."

Sex sells. Mainly it sells to men. Nine times out of ten a woman can just give it away. Men face more of a struggle. Doc told me he'd joined Seductive Secrets and set up a fresh email account, as recommended by the site. This was around quarter to two. By five to two, his fake profile had received six replies. The details he'd put down were more of less those of Jan's posting.

Doc fiddled with his phone, clicked his tongue as he calculated something.

"I've been on this site for, just gone, twenty-four hours. I've already had eighteen guys sniffing around. Correction, nineteen, another one's just sent me a response."

He turned the phone to me. I found myself looking at a photo of a young man, wearing dark glasses and a pair of Speedo budgie smugglers. I told Doc he could do worse. He considered the picture through narrowed eyes.

"I'll put him in the maybe pile." He closed the phone and jammed it back into his pocket. "Question still is, why Chris? I can't imagine Jan got fewer responses than me."

"Jan was picky. Looking for someone big, huge."

"I put the same. Chris ain't the only big boy out there."

"Could be he's just the biggest so far."

All we knew of Jan's involvement with the marriage dating site was what we heard from Chris. For all Chris knew, he might have been the latest in a dynasty of oversize lovers. Doc shook his head when I put this forward.

"Look at the timeline."

He hauled himself out of the armchair, stepped carefully over the tarot cards and tapped a point near the ceiling marked: *2M*-arrow symbol-(*mid-May*). Two months ago. The line leading from this ended at a simple notation: *CR and Jan, first meeting.* The next was marked: *10/7.* The day Jan found Peter's body.

"According to Chris," Doc said, "he and Jan spent practically every night together, from the night they hooked up, to the night Keller died." He moved back to his armchair. He didn't sit back in it, just perched on the edge of the cushion. "I don't see where she'd have time to take on anyone else."

"That only covers two months. Jan might have been picking guys off that website since she got back from honeymoon. Let's say she goes for them really, really big. That narrows the field. If you take creeps like Jock out of the picture, that narrows the field. She may well have an inbox full of men, but once she whittles out the chancers, the weirdoes and anyone under six-foot-five, she might only be looking at three or four."

Doc sat back at last. Made that clicking noise with his tongue. He considered what I'd said, then shook his head.

"I still don't see her picking Chris."

"We don't really know her, do we?"

Doc pulled a face, pantomiming not knowing how to put something into words. "That's what I mean in a way. We said before, she adopts roles to play. When we saw her the first night in The Jericho, she was still in trophy-wife mode."

"Okay. She's in trophy-wife mode. Maybe that role demands a bit of rough trade."

"So, why the website? From what Chris told me, she ain't

shy. With that attitude she could go into any pub, any night of the week, and fill her boots. Why go to the trouble of filtering out all the online sleaze bags, and answering emails, and all the other shite?"

I was about to suggest safety, but a second's thought knocked the idea on its back. If safety was a prime concern, nothing about picking Chris made sense.

"The other thing is the timing," Doc said. "They meet and six weeks later Peter Keller's dead."

"You think the death was planned?"

Doc stood up again and began moving around the room. Looking at the wall from different angles. He came to rest in front of the tarot cards he'd spread on the floor. He held one up so I could see it. The Hanged Man.

"However I look at this," Doc swept his arm through the air, vaguely indicating the wall, "I keep coming back to Chris. Something changed when Chris got involved. Now Keller's dead."

The sentence hung like a noose. I think we were both waiting for the other to speak. In the end I broke the silence.

"You beginning to think Chris was involved?"

Doc put the Hanged Man back into its place on the spread.

"He's involved. We're all involved. That don't mean he killed anyone. But something about Chris and Jan don't ring true. And the emails, I don't get that."

I didn't say anything. Not because any of it sounded particularly ominous, just because the sudden change of subject had thrown me out of gear. Doc didn't add anymore, he was back to studying the tarot.

"Doc? Emails?"

Doc pointed at the wall again, some point high up, I assumed he meant the timeline.

"First night, Jan and Chris get it on. Next morning he gets an email, *you're the best, let's do it again.* Then the next time and the next time and the next time. Why?"

"Was Chris sending answers?" Doc nodded. "Well then,

they're setting up the next meet. What's the problem?"

"They got it on every day for six weeks. Even if she didn't sleep at Chris's place, she'd be leaving in the small hours. Surely, you just say, *same again tonight?*"

"Could be Jan's a bit on the needy side?"

"Not the way Chris tells it. He said she'd often be out the door before he'd got his breath back. Needy people tend to hang around for a bit of reassurance."

I couldn't see the significance of sending, or not sending, copious emails. I wondered what I'd do if Karla started talking dirty to me via the internet. I didn't see it happening somehow. She'd bitten my head off for drawing her as a nurse wearing suspenders. Doc returned to his tarot.

"You willing to give up your spare room again?" he asked, out of the blue.

Chris was on his haunches, back against the shop door. When he saw us coming out of the alley he levered himself upright and headed straight to me. Doc made to stand between us but I put a hand on his shoulder and eased him out of the way. I figured one of us should stay conscious so there'd be someone to call the ambulance. Chris's colossal left arm reached out and went round the back of my neck. I had a moment of absolute calm as I waited for the elbow to slam into my face.

"I owe you one, Yakky. Good man."

The bear hug was brief; Chris slapped me on the back, his hand covering an insane amount of my shoulders.

He let me go and turned to Doc.

"You should have told me Jan was being followed."

I couldn't tell if he was upset at Doc. I was too busy staying upright. My knees had gone weak. Doc unlocked the shop and flipped the sign back to open.

"You're in enough trouble as it is," he said then ushered Chris into the waiting room. "Anyway, Yakky had it covered."

I waited for my pulse to get back down to double figures

before going into the shop. It took a while.

Doc was behind the counter and Chris was perched on the arm of one of the sofas, his weight was crushing it out of shape. They both turned as I walked in.

"The police have been around Chris's gaff," Doc said. "Jan told them she didn't know where he was and shut the door."

Chris nodded and made a humourless sort of half laugh. "She rang me at work, figured they'd be there before too long."

I agreed but didn't say so; there wasn't any point. Doc reached under the counter and pulled out a leather pouch, bound tight with wire, and a pack of tarot cards.

"Take these," he told Chris, who looked puzzled.

"Why?"

"You're going to be stuck in a cell. You'll need spiritual comfort."

Chris knew enough of Doc's habits to just go with the flow. He took the pouch and the cards, stowed them in his leather. He turned to me again.

"I don't want Jan stuck in the flat on her lonesome, you know? She alright to stay at your place again?"

"Sure," I said, and thought about Doc hunched over his tarot spread, holding the Hanged Man. Asking me the same question.

Abracadabra.

Nobody said it out loud but we started preparing for Chris to be charged. Doc got on the phone to Gina and put Chris on desk duties until she arrived. I was dispatched to Chris's flat. He told me to expect the police to be on his street. I touched my mojo and chalked up another one to Doc when the Yam started first go.

Chris was right about the cops. Three doors down from the flat, two uniforms, a man and a woman, were sat in an unmarked car. I parked facing away from the curb. More by chance than design, I was positioned so I caught the police car in my rearview mirror. As I killed the engine, the driver's door began to open, then was pulled shut again. If someone had taken me for Chris it had been a short-lived error.

Jan was at the door before I was. She looked rough, red eyes and the shakes. I'd been ready for her to press herself against the wall as I passed. Instead she looked at me with hopeless eyes.

"Doc called, he said Chris is going to go to the police."

It wasn't a question, but it sounded like she wanted to be told different.

"Yeah. Chris and Doc talked it over. Doc thinks it's for the best."

Jan finally broke eye contact.

"Okay."

She sounded resigned. We moved from the hallway to the living room. Chris's laptop was waiting on the sofa. This was what I'd come for. Doc asked me to collect it before the police took it away during the search we were sure was coming.

"Did you check your phone?" I asked Jan.

When he called her to tell her Chris was at the shop, Doc said to delete any texts to or from Chris, along with any voicemail. Jan told me she'd purged her phone. I suggested losing any emails as well but she said she didn't have any.

I got ready to leave again, now with the laptop zipped into the front of my leather. Jan stopped me as the door. Put a hand on my arm.

"Chris called, just before you got here. He wants me to stay at your house again, said he'd feel better knowing I was safe." I nodded, not knowing what she expected me to say. "Is it okay? Staying again?"

"Not a problem."

She squeezed my arm.

"Thank you. Really, Yakky, thank you."

"It's not a problem. I'm sorry I scared you last night, knocking that kid about. I didn't mean to do that."

She hung onto my arm. "Chris said he'd have done the

same. I'm ... I'm glad they've gone."

She let me go at last. We didn't say anything else and she closed the door as soon as I was through it.

When I got back to the shop, Gina was behind the counter, looking as good for business as Chris had been. I hadn't seen her since she'd finished my back piece and relations were no more cordial. Someone I'd booked in a few weeks before was waiting for his slot. He looked miserable too. The door to the back room was ajar and I could hear Doc's tattoo gun buzzing away. I assumed Gina was aware of what was happening. So, when she looked up to glare at me, I mouthed, *Chris?* She pointed up, to the flat above.

I knocked on the door. Chris opened it and handed me his laptop. He beckoned me inside with a jerk of his head and we ended up staring at Doc's wall.

"Any idea what all this is about?"

"Doc said he couldn't keep track of everything, needed to visualise it."

He whistled softly through his teeth. "This is what the inside of Doc's head looks like? Glad I don't live there."

Amen to that. Chris reached out and touched a Death card pinned next to the initials, PK. It was mounted dead centre of the wall.

"Peter?" I nodded. "Stuff at the bottom, that what's worrying Doc most?" I nodded again. He'd picked up the timeline and most of the notations after a moment's consideration. He knew the topography of Doc's mind better than he may have wanted to. "This the to-do list?"

He was pointing to the right of Peter Keller's death. I hadn't recognised it because it was composed of symbols, sketches and abbreviations, but it was a bullet pointed list. I moved closer and tried to figure out some of the meanings. The first entry was marked, *Get cop.rep CK poss. JK*

Chris got there a lot quicker.

"Police report?"

"Yep. Get report from Caroline, or possibly Jeffry."

"What police report?"

I explained what had gone down with Steve, didn't spare the details. When I'd finished he looked at me for a couple of beats, then around the room.

"Glad you fuckers are on my side." I took it as a compliment. "What's two?"

Notation two was, *£ PK JK M6* followed by the arrow symbol.

"Peter Keller's brother lent him money. Peter went back for more six months ago."

Chris nodded slowly, still staring at the wall. "Tick the last one I guess."

Bottom of the list just said: CR laptop/phone (password). He took out his mobile and deliberately dropped it on the armchair, next to the laptop.

"I've given Doc the passwords already." He looked over the wall again. "When did Doc do all this?"

"Last night."

Before the police had even got to Chris's flat, Doc had mapped out what to do. I saw him again in my mind's eye, leaning over the cards. Holding up the Hanged Man.

"Don't miss a trick, does he?" the Big Guy said, then sighed and closed his eyes for a second. He turned to me. "Can I ask you one more favour? I don't want to leave my bike outside my flat while I'm ... away. If you can give me a ride to my place, I'll leave it in Doc's yard."

Getting Chris back to his flat aged me ten years. Not everyone makes a good pillion, and a bad pillion, twice your size, makes for an interesting ride. He asked me to park up behind the two cops. I was grateful to pullover. As he got off the bike I felt the rear end spring up, freed of his weight.

The uniforms were out to meet him before Chris had unstrapped his lid, which he deposited on the roof of their car. One of them took this as an aggressive move and pulled an extendable baton from his belt. The other, who had the car between her and Chris, kept an eye on me. I stayed on the bike, hands on the grips. The engine was still running and I was ready to drop the clutch and beat a retreat. Getting on the business end of a police baton didn't figure in my plans.

Chris lifted his hands, kept them at shoulder height, palms out.

"I know you're here to arrest me. I'm going to come quietly, but will you give me a minute to let my old lady know what's happening?"

The cop with the baton relaxed a notch. He put the weapon back in its holster, but I noticed his other hand was resting on a canister of pepper spray. The other cop still had her attention on me.

"Couple of minutes, that's all," Chris said, still talking to baton cop. "Walk me to the door if you have to. I won't be doing a runner."

They told him to make it quick. Chris made his way to his flat with Baton Cop following a few steps behind. He waited at the pavement as Chris walked up to his door. The cop who'd stayed by the car cast a look at them then turned back to me.

"Thanks for that," I said, flicking a glance towards the flat.

Chris and Jan where holding onto each other in the doorway. Female Cop looked over her shoulder at them.

"Bit of an odd couple," she said.

"They say love is blind."

The cop nodded, turned back to me and asked the question on everybody's lips, "How'd they meet up?" I shrugged and she looked pissed off, or possibly disappointed. "You clowns don't make it easy on yourselves, do you?"

I couldn't think of anything to say to that so I watched Chris and Jan vanish into the flat. PC Baton used his personal radio to report something to base. After a minute or so, when a helicopter dangling a rope ladder didn't appear over the horizon, he came back to the car and gave me a quick once over.

"You were here before," he said.

"That's right."

"Why?" I stayed blank faced and shook my head, aware that I was talking, or rather not talking, to a man with an extendable baton in his belt. "I asked you a question."

"And I exercised my right not to answer it."

I crossed my arms to show I wasn't playing. It also pinned my hands down so the cops wouldn't see them shake.

"Save your breath, Nich," Female Cop told him, "They're all playing it stupid."

After that we waited in companionable silence. Not that we had to wait long. We all turned to the sound of Chris's door closing. He'd left Jan inside and was walking back towards the car. He presented himself to the cops.

"Okay, ready when you are."

"Alright, Chris, get in the back," Female Cop told him.

Nobody mentioned handcuffs but, as Chris got into the back of the car, PC Baton did that hand on top of the head thing. Maybe it made him feel good. Chris caught my eye and gave me a crooked smile. I expected the car to drive away but it didn't. The Big Guy twisted round enough to look at me and wave, deliberately, *get out of here.* I lifted a hand back to him and took off.

Dad was sitting on the stairs when I got in from work. I spent a few minutes standing him up, and dutifully witnessed his heroic descent of six steps. After much puffing and blowing he was back in front of his telly. In accordance with family tradition he assured me it was bloody rubbish.

I had an hour of ear-splitting sitcoms then went into the kitchen for a breather. He said he didn't want anything to eat. Not unless I did. I threw a pair of frozen pies into the cooker. I went for oven chips rather than baked beans. If you're cooking for the bin you go for stuff that's easy to scrape off a plate, call it the smart move. I ate mine without tasting it. I watched dad push his around and eat four chips, chewing them like they were made of clay.

Jan knocked on the door about ten o'clock, and something approaching a smile bounced across dad's face. She'd parked the Audi at a jaunty angle and she'd been crying. Now she looked empty, used up. I took the holdall she was carrying and noted how light it was. We didn't say anything. I led her up the stairs and dropped the holdall in the spare room. On the way back down I met dad making his way up and turned him around. He was caught between hurt and outrage.

I pressed through the bluster and worked hard at being gentle.

"Let her get some sleep, Dad. She's had a rough day."

"I was, I was – "

"Dad. I know what you were doing. You know what you were doing. Let her get some sleep."

We sat in silence, while the TV deafened us.

The Why of It

Thursday 21 July

I spent the night alternating guilt over Steve with worry about Jan. Doc's amateur detective spiel was rubbing off on me. When I finally fell asleep it was the small hours. The small hours plus about twenty minutes when I woke up again. I decided to fill the coffee machine and wait it out until morning.

Jan came into the kitchen around seven, wearing spray-on jeans and a too-small vest top. She asked if she could make herself some breakfast. I told her to go right ahead. When she bent over to get milk from the bottom of the fridge door, I caught myself staring. She didn't head towards the coffee machine but worked her way through a box of cornflakes.

She confirmed what Doc had suspected. Not long after Chris had waved me off, his flat had been searched. Another four cops arrived, two more uniforms and a suit. They were as polite and civil as the circumstances allowed but they meant business. The Suit asked repeatedly about Chris's movements, and Jan, who was getting the hang of the old lady bit, ignored him. She sat at the pine table, where we'd all sat a few nights before, and watched. Blank faced and silent. She didn't say as much, but I suspect the silence worried the Suit, because after ten minutes or so he sent one of the uniforms out of the flat. He was replaced shortly afterwards by a WPC who sat with Jan and made reassuring noises. As Jan put it: *Joan came and sat with me again.*

"Joan?"

"Joan Rix, police woman."

Baton Cop's lady friend I assumed. I made Doc's spooling motion. Jan didn't get the idea.

"What do you mean she sat with you *again*?"

"When I found Peter. Joan was one the officers that came to the house. She was very kind."

Jan abruptly stopped speaking and shuddered. She looked exhausted but I didn't think it was about lack of sleep.

I remembered WPC Rix commenting on Chris and Jan being an odd couple. I should have twigged then they'd met before. Jan had been dressing from the House-of-Biker summer collection for weeks – that version of Jan being with Chris made sense. Jan, as Joan would have first seen her, in her trophy-wife setting, was a different proposition.

"Did she question you?"

"Only general things. *Was I okay, should she make tea?* Stuff like that. I was civil. Chris told me not to talk to them but I didn't think that would do any harm."

I assured it was fine. "Chris meant don't answer questions that was all." Jan was still wide eyed with worry. "You did okay, honestly."

She blinked once; it made me think of a camera shutter. Then the moment was over and she went back to eating cornflakes. I felt embarrassed, the way I'd feel if someone caught sight of me naked. While I retreated to the warm embrace of the coffee machine, Jan, tonelessly, announced, "They took the knife away. They put it in an evidence bag."

She meant the ceramic knife she'd given Chris to cut her dress with. Dad's entrance saved me the trouble of replying. He played it slow, coming into the kitchen in pyjamas and dressing gown, managing to make the journey from hallway to kitchen table both heroic and pathetic. He over played the coughing a bit, otherwise, BAFTA material all the way.

The shop was open when I got there. Doc was tucked behind the counter, only in view if you looked. He had the appointments book out and was frowning at it. I'd checked the bookings before I left the previous day. Two pieces of flash in the morning and the beginnings of a sleeve for the afternoon. We weren't due to be busy.

He looked up when he heard me enter and gave me the standard biker nod.

"How was Jan?"

I told him she was frazzled but keeping it together. Doc clicked his tongue thoughtfully and commented that Jan was tougher than she looked. I didn't agree but couldn't be bothered arguing the point. I recounted the sparse details she'd given me about the search. Once dad turned up it was pointless trying to talk to her anymore. She was sucked whole into his tiny orbit of need.

We made the obligatory mugs of tea and I started prepping the back room. Doc followed me in, double checking my work without knowing he was doing it.

"Chris put a guy through a window a few years back," he said. "The arresting officer was a woman. I'm wondering if it's this Rix character."

I hadn't thought anything of it at the time, but I remembered Rix used the Big Guy's first name. When he came back to the police car, she said, *alright Chris, get in the back*. Not in a friendly way, but not in that patronising tone most coppers reserve for first names. I told Doc and he nodded, clicking his tongue. Something else Rix had said came to mind.

"I told her thanks for letting Chris go into his flat to see Jan. She asked me how they'd met, when I didn't tell her anything, she looked kind of pissed off and said something like, *you guys don't make it easy on yourselves.*"

Doc stopped fussing around the shop and stared at some point that was nowhere close. "Do you think we've got a cop who's on our side?"

I wasn't sure if he was asking me or just thinking aloud.

Either way I didn't answer. I thought he was clutching at straws. The police always want you to talk.

Doc handed both the pieces of flash over to me and I later heard him apologising profusely into the phone as he rescheduled the sleeve. He skulked behind the counter all morning manning the phone and reading tarot.

When I came out of the back room with the second client, freshly inked, Doc was already shutting up shop.

I left, pulling on my leather, trying to convince myself I intended to get on my bike. Of course, I didn't. Going with Doc back to his flat was as inevitable as the tarot reading that followed. Doc was smart, I didn't doubt it, but his intelligence was hard to reconcile with a devotion to something so meaningless.

I took an armchair, angry at myself for being there, and watched as he laid out the familiar cross. He carefully laid each card in its place and studied it at length, all the time knowing that had he performed one more shuffle, the selection he was seeing would have been totally different.

There were no curtains. The room was flooded with natural light. Yet, it felt dark and colourless, as if the flat, or the things that took place there, absorbed the brightness. Or rejected it. The anger went up a notch when I realised I was spooked.

When the Hanged Man appeared, Doc broke his steady rhythm, laid the next two cards in quick succession. After the Hanged Man, The Fool. After The Fool, Death.

"Did you fix that?"

It came out more harshly than I'd expected and the barren hardness of the surroundings supplied an echo to make it harsher still.

Doc started slightly but turned to me with a Cheshire Cat grin.

"If I could deal cards to order, I'd give up tattooing and take up poker." I didn't say anything back. He laughed softly. "What's got you rattled?"

I indicated the last three cards he'd put in the spread. He asked me what I thought they meant.

"Hanged Man is Chris. The Fool is Peter Keller. Death is Death."

Doc picked up the Hanged Man. He fiddled with the card, making it rotate around his fingertips. It looked like the figure in the picture was dancing. Then he stopped and the figure was still.

He allowed himself a dramatic pause before saying, "What you see, Yakky?"

"The Hanged Man. A tarot card."

With his free hand he made the spooling motion. Turn the engine over. *Think*.

"Okay, line drawing, woodcut style. A man in outdated clothing hanging from a tree."

"So, what does that mean?"

"I don't know. I don't read tarot, I don't know what they're meant to tell you."

"Forget tarot, and forget science and magic." He danced the Hanged Man around his fingertips again. "This is just a piece of card stock, with a drawing on the front. Stop looking at it like a rationalist and look at it like an artist. What does the drawing say?"

I looked at the card again. It was a fairly basic image, but skilfully done. A man suspended by his left ankle, if you looked more closely, not from a tree but from a structure, something that had been purpose-built. The man's left leg was straight, his weight pulling it taunt. The right leg was crossed, heel cocked behind the knee. The face was placid.

"It's somebody being punished, or tormented. It doesn't look like it's working, or the guy's just a real hard bastard and he's toughing it out." I looked at Doc. I was waiting for some reaction. "Is that why you're taking this card to mean Chris?"

"Not really. What I see with the Hanged Man is somebody going through an ordeal. Could be a punishment being inflicted on him. Could be an act of contrition he's volunteered for. What strikes me is the set of the body. The Hanged Man doesn't thrash aimlessly or give up and hang limp. He's learning, getting stronger, not weaker."

He stopped talking. Like the night he'd talked me through the aftermath of pulling the knife, he was embarrassed by his own gravitas.

"I don't really get the Chris connection," I said.

"I think Chris's been on a steep learning curve for the last few months. If I hadn't seen the Hanged Man come up I wouldn't be thinking about Chris in these terms either."

Just to show him I could be annoying too, I made the spooling motion. Yeah, I had the moves. Doc abandoned the reading and started to pull the cards back into the pack. What he said next caught me by surprise.

"I'm with Caroline. Jan's acted like a slag. She throws herself at Chris, and, from what he said, she wasn't making any effort to keep it quiet. Then she's firing off emails full of snide comments about her husband. All the time she's taking hubby's money and living in his big house."

It would have been a lot of people's view of Jan's behaviour but hearing it from Doc put my back up.

"It takes two to tango, Doc. Your mate Chris didn't have a gun at his head, he could have said no."

Doc was still sitting, cross legged on the floor. His head was tilted slightly to look up at me and I saw his eyes flit to one of the armrests of my chair. I hadn't noticed, my right hand was balled into a fist.

"Well, I'm glad I took that knife off you," he said evenly.

I uncurled my hand and flexed the fingers, turned away from his narrow gaze.

"I'm sorry. But I don't see there's any need to talk about her like that."

Doc regarded me thoughtfully for a couple of beats and shook his head.

"Yakky, you're missing my point. It's Chris I'm talking about and, no, I'm not holding him up as a paragon of virtue. He hasn't behaved well and he admits he's been a hypocrite." Doc got up from the floor and dropped into the other armchair. "Even so, he's seen Jan in a poor light and I think two months ago he'd have said what I've just said: slag. Now, hubby's come over all dead, and the two love birds are ready to start picking curtains."

I was still in the dark.

"So what are you saying, Chris is in love, where's this tie in to your Hanged Man?"

I wasn't shouting, but I was talking too fast. Making a question into a confrontation.

"I don't know about Chris being in love but my point is a couple of months ago, Chris was chugging along more or less happily. Now he's in a police cell with a murder charge being floated about, and *he's* fretting about *Jan's* welfare."

"And you think he's learning something from all this, like your Hanged Man?"

"I think so. I love Chris to bits, but I doubt if he'd have seen past the slag label if he hadn't gone through all this crap with Jan."

"Much good this learning curve's doing him."

Doc cocked an eyebrow at me. "He's better able to entertain the idea that people don't come in black and white. Better able to see that a woman, who acts out sexually, acts outside of the social norms, is not diminished as an individual. Is not any less deserving of respect and consideration, nor any less able to experience emotional highs and lows. I'd call that growth, maturity." He turned his attention to the ceiling. "You know Yak, if all this shit had been going down when I was doing my doctorate, I'd be a professor by now."

"Or you'd have a career writing greetings cards."

He flicked me the vee and announced he was going to put the kettle on. When he went into the kitchen, he didn't come back until the tea was made and he didn't call out to me or speak. It was unusual, and I assumed he was giving me time to get myself together. Getting wound up, by Doc calling Jan a slag, had surprised us both.

I tried to decipher the fresh additions to the wall and worried about how much of the night he'd dedicated to doing it. The last entry on the to-do list had been dated and scored through. Chris's laptop and phone were sitting under the altar. Yesterday's date had been added to the timeline, the line leading from it ended at: *Search, Jan back to Yak's*. The most striking change was the addition of a bright orange post-it note stuck at the top of the to-do list. It highlighted the entry about getting the police report. Something as mundane as a post-it note set against the madness of Doc's wall jarred on the vision.

Doc came into the room with tea in one hand, and the tarot pack in the other. He abandoned the cards in favour of a charcoal pencil and began adding to the wall. Under, Jan Back to Yak's, he added a drawing of the lock knife. He drew an arrow connecting the knife to a point a on the timeline, slightly ahead of *10/7*.

Doc looked at the new entry for a long time then said, "I missed a trick there."

He tapped the new question mark with the end of his pencil.

"Because the police took the knife?"

"Because it was out of the blue. Why a knife, and why then?"

I fell silent again as he stepped back from the wall. He dropped, gracelessly, into a cross leg position and put the tea and pencil aside. The white linen was laid out, the cards followed.

The knife had slipped into the story barely noticed. Up until then, Jan and Chris had been enjoying a normal, if frantic, sex life. A week before she found a bled-out corpse, Jan decided she wanted to play kinky games. What we'd heard of Chris and Jan's antics were odd enough to mask the strangeness of her giving him a knife.

My eye fell to the centre piece of Doc's wall: Peter Keller's death. One of the arrows that emanated from it snaked to the to-do list. The entry read: *Get Jan's story.*

Yak/Gina? I asked Doc what that meant.

Eyes closed as he shuffled the deck, he said, "We need to know what happened after Chris left Jan's place on the fifth, when she found the body."

I'd guessed that bit.

"Yak stroke Gina?"

Doc started dealing cards. I caught myself watching to see which cards came up and made a point of looking elsewhere.

"I think you or Gina might get better results than me," Doc said, still not looking up. "Jan knows me too well."

"Isn't that a good thing?"

"I don't think so. I think she's got me sussed." Doc broke off for a while, studied a card. "She'll tell me what I want to hear."

The faithful acolyte parroting their lines, I could see that.

"What do you want to hear?"

"I don't know, but I think Jan might. She's very, very sharp."

I tried to follow the logic of that statement but like a lot of Doc's logic, it defeated me. I could sympathise with Jan's acolyte gig. Being around Doc felt like an act of faith.

"You don't trust her, do you?"

He didn't answer immediately, weighed up the answer. "I trust the version of Jan that I know. But she was a different woman when she found Peter Keller's corpse." He fell silent and stared into space, tapping the edge of a card against his chin. "There's no point me asking her about that night. The Jan I know wasn't there."

"You mean she's blotted it out?"

He shook his head and put the card in its position. "Nothing that simple. People perceive things in different ways. Two people walk down the same street, past the same shops and houses. Ask them to describe it, and you get two totally different accounts."

Doc talks to acolyte Jan, and in effect, gets a hand-me-down account of finding Peter in the bathroom. The events of the night filtered by the woman she is now, facts twisted by how that woman perceives events around her.

If I was in the market for some psychobabble and I was given a big enough budget, I might, *might*, buy that. I still couldn't see why I'd have any more success than Doc.

"Jan hasn't reinvented herself for you, or Gina. Gina she hasn't really met and you don't give her anything to build on."

We were back to my signals again, or lack of. The whole spiel sounded farfetched to me, but no one else was coming up with any other plans to get Chris sprung.

"So, who's the lucky winner, me or Gina?"

Doc turned to look directly at me. He still held the deck of cards in his right hand. Without looking at it, he executed a one-handed cut and turned over the top card, glanced at it, and grinned hugely. The card showed a man on a galloping horse, holding up a sword. It was upside down, inverted, to use his term, but I could still read the title. The Knight of Swords.

"Guess it's down to you, mate."

At some point, I asked Doc if I could borrow some paper. I wanted to jot down the bare bones of the crime wall; he told me to look in the bedroom. In keeping with the rest of the flat, the room was stark. One wall was taken up with a fitted wardrobe. The other walls were lost to books, row upon row of them. The smell of old paper permeated the room.

The shelf set above the door was a depository for anything related to Harley-Davidson. The bottom shelves opposite the cot bed were a mix of art tombs and coffee table photography. The rest appeared random but I didn't doubt there was a strict logic to their order. Knowing Doc, I didn't bother trying to work it out. Stephen Hawking was shoulder to shoulder with books on the history of burlesque. Richard Dawkins and Ben Goldarce jostled for space with yellowing books on Voodoo. I recognised a few Miss Marple titles; these spouted multitudes of bookmarks and were sitting demurely alongside expensive looking texts on clinical psychology.

Aside from the bed – a metal framed foldaway thing, made up with a painfully white cotton sheet and a rolled up sleeping bag – the room's only furniture was an ancient bureau. On it were a printer and a framed picture of Doc and Gina outside a registry office. I took some paper from the printer's tray and went back to the living room. I said I'd been impressed with the library. Doc looked almost embarrassed.

"I keep meaning to have a clear out, but every time I throw a book away, I decide I want to re-read it, then I end up buying another copy. Cheaper to hold on to them."

"The Miss Marples look like they've had a few readings."

"Some men dream of glamorous movie stars. I dream of Miss Jane Marple."

The single photograph in his bedroom told a different tale but I let it go.

"Okay, I'll bite. Why the Miss Marple fetish?"

Doc switched off The Jive and gave me an apprising look. He was about to tell me something deeply personal.

"Miss Marple's all about the villain's mind. She gets her man by knowing what goes on in here." He tapped his forehead. "Why put the body in the library? Why use poison? Why do it at half past three on New Year's Eve? Why do it at all? People get into the how-it-was-done stuff, for me it's always been the why of it. If you can see why something happened, you can work backwards to the how. You ever hear people bang on about motiveless crime?" I opened my mouth to reply but didn't get time. "No such thing, all crimes have a motive. A lot of the time people lose sight of that because they get motive tangled up with reason. They think accepting someone had a motive means accepting they were justified, but that's crap. The courts make that distinction all the time. Collecting the money is a motive for making a fake insurance claim; it's not a justification. Three teenagers beat a stranger to death; there is no justification. But there will be a motive." He got up again and went back to the wall. "That's why these are niggling me."

He'd lowered himself to his haunches to get level with the base layer of his wall. The layer with the question marks. He pulled a charcoal pencil from behind his ear and added another drawing of the lock knife, much larger than the one he'd put in the timeline. He worked quickly but executed a detailed piece of work. I let my attention lapse long enough to envy his talent. He finished with a question mark.

Assuming I was reading the symbols, cards and abbreviations right, the lower strata now read,

-Why did Jan pick Chris?

-Why all the emails?

-Why take Chris to her house?

-Why the guest room?

-Why the knife?

-Why was Peter Keller killed?

I put that on my piece of printer paper, along with the timeline.

"You think Jan's going to tell me about finding the body?"

Doc, now standing in front of the to-do list, nodded without turning.

"Yeah. She's in your house, eating out of your kitchen and sleeping in your spare room. Tell her it'll be helping Chris out."

"I'll have a go."

"I'm going to get on to this." He pulled the orange post it note down and stuffed it deep in his pocket. His hand reappeared with his mobile.

"Caroline?" I asked as he began scrolling the numbers. "You going to need Jan to make you up?"

"Not this time." He put the phone to his ear. I could just hear the ringing tone. "I think a bit of freak out might not go amiss."

"I'll get going, see if I can get Jan to talk to me. If I can pry her away from dad."

Doc told me to hang on and left the room with the phone still held to his ear. He came back in just as his call was answered, and he switched to his Caroline voice.

"Hello, Caroline. It's James." He listened with that tight little smile, enjoying himself. In his free hand he held an old Dictaphone, the type that uses miniature cassette tapes. He handed it to me, covered the end of the phone. "Get it on tape."

Then he was back to Caroline and setting up another date.

I turned the recorder over and popped open a little panel on the back – it needed batteries. I caught Doc's eye, and mouthed: *really?* The Cheshire Cat nodded back. I left him to his roll, glad to get away.

I took a long route home via a superstore so I could pick up the batteries. I tested the batteries and recorder before leaving the car park. The recorder was probably top of the range in its day, and the sound quality was surprisingly good considering its size. It must have been a throwback to Doc's time at university. The tape in it had been used to record a lecture. There was a background burble of ambient noise but the speaker's voice was easy to make out. I recorded myself counting to ten.

All of which was fine, but I wondered how Jan would feel. Being asked to recount details of finding her husband's body wasn't likely to be the best part of her day. I didn't think me recording it would make it any easier. I pressed record once more, put the machine in my pocket and, again, counted to ten. When I played it back all I could hear was the built-in microphone rubbing against my pocket lining. I delayed going home by pretending to think about what to do.

Jan was throwing herself into the nursing role like a lemming off a cliff. As I poked my head into the front room, she was coaxing dad to eat 'a little soup'. She wasn't stupid; I don't doubt she was fully aware of the amount he'd eaten. I also didn't doubt the amount he'd eaten was colossal. Jan acknowledged me from the corner of her eye, gave me a don't-worry-I've-got-it-covered look.

The coffee machine was dry as a bone so I made a pot of toxic waste to counteract the tea I drank at Doc's. I ended up taking some of Jan's self-imposed load out of purely practical considerations. If I didn't help, she'd have passed out from exhaustion before I got to speak to her.

Dad was rocking and rolling like Elvis. Stretched out on the sofa, supported on an avalanche of pillows, his expression flickered unsteadily between suffering and ecstasy. Jan didn't have a nurse's uniform, but she'd done what she could. She'd lost the black denims in favour of combats. The skin-tight vest top had been ditched for a modest white blouse, a remnant, I suspected, of Peter Keller's time.

Once we'd got dad to bed, Jan took a shower and I cooked. It was nothing special but I suspected her devotion to duty excluded a meal break, so it wouldn't go to waste.

Our dining table was the type that could be extended by pulling the two-piece top apart and slotting a third section into the gap. The extension piece was stored out of sight just under the assembled top pieces. If you knew it was there, it could serve as a shelf. I rested the Dictaphone on it, hit record and counted to ten. The play-back wasn't perfect but it was audible. The problem was you could hear the noise the recorder made when you sat at the table. I got the radio I usually kept in the kitchen and set it on the fireplace, set a place for Jan just in front of it. After a fruitless search for music that wasn't plastic pop or easy listening, I tuned it to a news channel. I marked my place at the table by putting a half-finished mug of coffee next to my knife and fork. Then I pressed record again and waited for Jan to join me.

Karla often commented that I wasn't very romantic. She had a point.

I drank another pot of coffee. I don't know what did a better job of keeping me awake, the caffeine or the stomach ache. I finished transcribing the tape at about one in the morning and emailed a copy to Doc. I didn't really want a copy of it on my computer but decided not to delete it until I was sure he'd received it. It was around three when I got to sleep. I heard Jan shifting about just before I dropped off.

From: andy909@locomail.com
To: [Doc]nettle78@hotmail.com

Transcript of conversation with Jan. Thursday, 21st July. I've put observations in brackets where I thought they might be relevant.

Me – I'm surprised your head's not spinning round and round. Lot seems to have happen at once.

Jan – What do you mean?

Me – Last couple of months, taking up with Chris, losing your husband, losing the house, Chris getting arrested, twice. Lot of adjustments to make. Not much in the way of luck, leastways not much in the way of good luck.

Jan – It's not all been bad. It's been great being with Chris, and you and Doc have been very kind.

Me – Even so. I mean, Chris told Doc it was you that found your husband's body. I can't even think what that must have been like.

Jan – That was horrible.

Me – You want to talk about it? Doc's always telling me I need to talk more. Perhaps he's right, if I got more shit out in the open I might be able to sleep better.

Jan – You don't sleep well?

Me – Nah. Not since I was a teenager. You?

(Long pause before Jan answers.)

Jan – I wish I didn't sleep at all really. I have bad dreams and can't wake up.

Me – You mean dreams about your husband?

(Long pause. Jan watches me carefully as she answers.)

Jan – Not really Peter, I've never really dreamt about Peter. Isn't that funny, shouldn't that be what I have nightmares about?

Me – I don't think should or shouldn't comes into it. People are all different. I started training to be a nurse a few years ago, had to lay out bodies once or twice. Only thing that ever bothered me was this one time I was cleaning a man's face. I used these little sponge-on-a-stick things to clean some gunk from his mouth and one of his teeth came free, just came out and hung from his mouth. I didn't freak out but something about it upset me. For a long time I'd get a picture of that tooth just popping into my mind for no reason. Sorry, that probably sounds stupid compared to what you went through.

Jan – No, I think I know what you mean. I really did freak out, I fell, slipped on the blood, but that's not what pops into my head. It's the little blade I keep seeing.

Me – The blade he used to ... to do it?

Jan – I suppose it was. I never thought about that before but it must have been. I thought it was a razor blade at first. (Long pause while she tunes out.) I was scared it was going to stick in his foot. That's what pops into my mind: Pete's foot with that silly little blade stuck in the heel. It didn't even go near his foot.

Me – Where was it?

Jan – Just in front of the toilet bowl. That's why I slipped over it I think. I was trying to pull Pete up and I noticed that blade laying there. I was scared he'd tread on it so I sort of tugged him towards me, away from the toilet. That's when I fell, I slipped on the ... on the blood. I held onto Pete and he fell on top of me. Funny thing is I was thrashing about trying to get out from under him but a part of me was still worrying about getting cut on that blade.

(Long pause. Jan stares into space.)

Me – You alright?

Jan – (Blinks and shakes her head, as if she's clearing it.) That's when I understood he was dead. I knew as soon as I saw him, just the colour of his skin, like putty, and all that blood. But until he fell on me I couldn't understand it.

Me – You landed in the blood? Christ.

Jan – I couldn't believe how much of it there was. It went everywhere. It was cold like jelly. Felt horrible.

Me – Jesus.

Jan – It felt like I was pinned down for hours. I kept thrashing around trying to get out.

(Jan starts crying. She doesn't close her eyes but continues to watch me

while tears are streaming down her face.)

When I finally got out, I mean out from under him, I couldn't stand. I tried to get up but I just folded, my knees gave way, I was squatting on the floor in shock, like some silly bitch in a soap opera. I couldn't think.

(Long pause. Jan isn't looking at me anymore, she's drifted off. She's speaking in a low voice almost to herself.)

Then I couldn't look at the ... at Peter. When I was a little girl I was scared of this wardrobe in my bedroom. The doors were made of some strange kind of wood that had lots of knots and lines in it. When the doors were closed they looked like a face. Two of the knots looked like eyes. If the doors were open, it was okay. I'd always leave them open before I got into bed. When they ... if someone shut them, I'd sit up in bed, too scared to look at them. I played a game. I knew I'd have to look at the doors, I didn't want to look at them, but I couldn't stand not knowing what they were doing. So, I'd look around the room and try to find something in the room that was different from the last time I was in it. I'd see how many I could find before I couldn't stand it anymore and I'd have to look at the doors. I'd set a number. When I found that amount of differences, I'd peek at the door. Then I'd look away again.

(Jan, still crying, looks at me again.)

So I did that. Five. When I found five new things in the bathroom, I'd look at Peter again.

(Pause.)

Me – Did you find them?

Jan – One: Pete's Watermark pen was on the vanity cabinet. Two: that silly little blade. Three: The bottle of Scotch was half gone. Four: The note propped up behind the tap.

(Jan gives a sharp laugh)

Then I sort of cheated, because I looked at Peter and he made five. Then I ran out of the room and called the police.

Me – What did you tell them?

Jan – My husband's dead. He's killed himself. They kept me on the phone for a long time. Trying to keep me calm I suppose.

(Jan stops crying. She seems to be talking to herself again.)

When I got off the phone I went back to the bathroom. I went back to be with Peter. I thought that's what I should do.

(Jan stops talking.)

Me – Did you read the note?

Jan – The police showed it to me later. I couldn't recite it word for word but he'd blamed me basically. 'Can't carry on, you've broken my heart', something like that. He'd printed it out on the stationary he used for the business, very expensive. He'd used half a sheet. Typical Pete. Even on his suicide note he cut costs.

Me – How long before the police turned up?

Jan – An ambulance crew arrived first but it could have been hours for all I know. I went back to sit with Peter, with his body, and I lost track of time. When they did come I realised I wasn't dressed so I grabbed my dressing gown to put on. I don't know why, but it wasn't until then that I saw all the blood I had on me. When I opened the door I was having hysterics, trying to wipe it off and screaming about Peter being dead. I don't know how long that went on for. Then Joan got there, Joan was sweet. She took me to one side and talked me down, made me tea of course. Her partner was a bit more gung-ho.

Me – How do you mean, was she giving you a hard time?

Jan – It was a he. He didn't give me a hard time, he was just a bit hyped up. As Joan was leading me into the front room and trying to calm me down he went charging up the stairs.

Me – Was he with Rix again when they came to Chris's flat yesterday?

Jan – I don't know, I only saw Joan. Why?

Me – I was waiting by the police car when they let Chris come in to see you. That was Joan Rix's call. Her partner was a youngish bloke; he looked like he was itching to pull out his baton and play tough guy.

Jan – The man with Joan that day was *younger than her. I think she was in charge. I remember when he came back downstairs, we were in the kitchen, then Joan was making tea. He rushed in and announced the upstairs was clear. Joan rolled her eyes like he was being a bit of a prat. I don't think I was meant to see.*

Me – So the Action Hero went and found the ... found your husband, you didn't have to show them?

Jan – The ambulance crew showed him. I didn't go back to the bathroom. Joan asked if I wanted to call anyone and the only person I could think of was Chris. I called his mobile and he came over right away.

(She starts crying again)

I wish I'd kept him out of it, I really do.

Me – Don't beat yourself up. His prints were all over the place, they'd have pulled him in sooner or later. You do know he's got a record don't you?

Jan – He told me, little sod had it coming. I know they would have found prints but if I hadn't called Chris I don't think they'd have questioned Pete's death.

Me – How do you work that out?

(Jan takes a deep breath with her eyes closed. She's switched from tears to outrage very quickly.)

Jan – A police doctor arrived at some point to formally declare Peter dead. There was another policeman was with him, Joan called him Sarg. She went to the hall to speak to them both just as Chris got there. We all heard his bike pulling up. Joan was different once she'd seen him. She'd already asked me a lot of questions but she kept telling me it was all just routine, but once Chris was there, I could see her antennae were up.

Me – She said to me you were an odd couple.

Jan – It wasn't that, she recognised him. She was one of the police who pulled Chris in when he was arrested for putting that guy through a window. Chris barely gave her a glance but I could see her mind was going nineteen to the dozen. Anyway, she left me with Chris and went upstairs. Chris just held me for a while not saying anything, then he took me to the utility room and turned the shower on. I couldn't bear seeing the blood running off me and I froze. He cleaned me up and wrapped me in a towel.

(Jan's calmer now. She seems to have got over the outrage. Now she just looks sad.)

There was a load of clothes in the dryer so I had something to put on at least. Me and Chris went to the lounge and sat on the sofa. Chris just kept telling me not to worry, everything was going to be alright. He just held me close up against him and kept saying everything would be fine.

After a while I saw Joan was standing in the doorway, watching us. Once she saw I'd noticed her, she came and sat down opposite us. She was still being kind, being very gentle, but something was different. I could tell she was suspicious. I didn't know then that she knew Chris. I thought she'd just taken a set against him because of how he looks.

Then she started asking me if Chris and I were good friends, was he a friend of Peter's. Stuff like that. She was trying to make it sound casual but I felt Chris tense up. He wouldn't answer, he just shrugged or ignored her altogether. She took down my story about finding Pete, she was trying to get me alone, away from Chris, to do it. But I wouldn't let him go. Maybe I should have, I don't know.

Me – You think Rix wouldn't have questioned the suicide if she hadn't seen you were involved with Chris?

Jan – Yeah. When Chris appeared Joan started looking for problems.

Me – And found some.

Jan – But she has to be wrong. Chris didn't kill Pete. I just know he didn't.

Nasty Word

Friday 22 July

Doc was hidden away behind the counter. There was tea made and, unusually for him, music playing through the shop. I didn't recognise the singer or the song and I didn't bother asking. Slow and mournful blues leaves me cold. I've never advocated giving misery a sound track.

"You look like shit," he said, by way of a greeting.

"Yeah, think I died in the night."

Doc toasted me with his mug. "My condolences."

I poured a tea I didn't want and examined the appointments book. It was going to be a full day. For the first time the prospect made my heart sink. The business with Chris and Jan, and I suppose Peter Keller, had become my focus. That in itself was enough to bring me down.

"Mind if I change the music?"

Doc nodded and I shut the soul-deadening lament down and replaced it with some Dr Feelgood, a blues band, but their vibe was different. Even as the cancer had picked him away until he could barely stand, Lee Brilleaux had grabbed bad luck by the throat and sang defiance, not defeat. I let the opening bars of 'All Through the City' batter their way into the shop and turned back to Doc.

"Well, I've had a bedtime story off a widow and two hours' sleep," I said. "What's your beauty regime?"

He gave me a wince that might have been an attempted

smile.

"I met up with Caroline again."

He rubbed a hand across his face, as if he was trying to scrub away the tiredness. I noticed he kept the hand to his face when he started talking again. I don't know if he was aware of it, but he was masking the tattoo on his cheek.

"No joy on the police report?"

Another wince. "Oh, I think she's going to let us have that, it's just," he stopped and scrubbed his face again, "something else."

He didn't elaborate on what the something else was and I didn't ask. I pulled the Dictaphone from my leather. He looked at it curiously.

"You got something?"

I put the little machine on the counter.

"The recording's not great so I made a transcript of it. I emailed it to you about two o'clock this morning."

Doc became animated. He reclaimed the computer and went to his emails. He read the attached document then printed off a copy, re-reading it from the screen while the printer clanked away. I left him to it and went to buy some milk. I picked up a jar of instant coffee too. I hate the stuff but I needed caffeine.

When I got back Doc had the copy of my transcript in front of him and was matching the words on the page to the sounds on the tape. He told me I'd done well, but before I could ask him if he thought it'd help, he shut the player off and nodded a greeting to a point somewhere behind me. The first client of the day had followed me in.

The day dragged. I was dog tired and feeling lousy about taping Jan. Doc was quiet, working mostly in silence. I don't know if the punters picked up on the atmosphere but the shop was a pretty cheerless place. The moment the last customer left, Doc brought in the shop sign from out front and threw the lock on the door. Once we'd cleaned up the back room he asked if I fancied going down The Jericho. I wasn't really in the mood for more of Doc's company but the prospect of heading home held even less joy, so I agreed.

Doc was sipping a lager. I'd skipped the booze in favour of caffeine-rich cola. We were crammed into one of his corners. A copy of the transcript was out on the table and he was frowning in concentration. Eventually he folded the printout into four and slipped it into a pocket. He looked around the pub.

"Quiet in here tonight," he commented.

There was a big rally over Reading way and a lot of the regulars would have taken off for the weekend. I'd have liked to have been doing the same. I was wishing I'd turned down the invite and just headed for home. Doc had something he wanted to say and the fact he didn't come out with it was putting me on edge. He often played it close to his chest, but this was different.

"I thought I'd have heard from Chris by now," he said and looked at his watch. "Been over forty-eight hours."

I nodded as if I knew, but I hadn't kept a track of things. Time seemed fluid.

"Would he be able to contact you?" I asked.

"He's allowed a phone call."

"Would he use it to call you?"

Doc sipped his pint again before answering. "Me or Jan. I'm sure if he'd spoken to her I'd have heard about it."

We fell into silence. I people watched while Doc stared at his pint. After a few minutes I got to thinking about Jan, stuck at home with the make-believe patient. A combination of guilt for leaving her there and the desire for better company made me reach for my phone. I waved it at Doc to get his attention,

"Shall I give Jan a bell?" Doc sighed and did that odd scrubbing his face thing again. "Should I take that as a no?"

"No, call her. See if she wants to come over."

When she answered, dad's interruptions were barely audible over the TV. The conversation made a dent in my phone's credit because Jan had to relay it, blow by blow, to dad. I've no idea if she wanted to come out for a drink or not, but once dad got wind of the notion he went into overdrive. Doc probably couldn't hear the details but the squawks coming from my phone were hard to misinterpret.

"No show?" he asked. I rolled my eyes in answer. "Duty calls, I guess."

I followed his lead and finished my drink, when he pointed at my glass in invitation I shook my head. I'd had enough of the half dead pub and strained company.

"I'm going to take the bike for a shake down, clear my head before getting back to the family estate."

"Got anywhere in mind?"

"I might take a blast down the duel carriage way. See if that burger van by the industrial estate's still open."

I didn't shake off Doc's company in the end. We caned it down the A road together, weaving between HGVs and the last of the straggling commuters. I took the lead and did my best to outpace him but my shit rag Yam was no match for his Sportster. The gleaming white bike stuck to me effortlessly and pulled up ahead of me at the counter of the burger van. Doc dismounted and stretched as if we'd just covered a hundred miles rather than a twenty-mile dash.

"Don't do that enough," he said, words muffled as he pulled off the full-face helmet. "Just ride for the hell of it I mean."

He had a buzz on, sometimes you need to just ride. It's easy to get so caught up in the business of paying the bills that you forget what you're slaving for. Just ride.

I ordered up a duet of cheeseburgers and teas then settled into one of the lawn chairs set out in front of the van. There were three more chairs and a matching table. The set had once been white plastic, now it was grey with road crap and diesel fumes. Doc was in another of the chairs, fidgeting. I wasn't sure if he was still buzzing or just unable to relax without cover. Lay-bys tend to be a bit short on dark corners.

We started on the burgers as a phalanx of bikes, mostly

Harleys, swarmed across the adjacent roundabout, probably heading to the M25 and out onto the rally. Because Harley obsessives have a supernatural ability to spot a vee twin, Doc, or at least his bike, received three or four waving salutes as the pack hammered past. Doc took a pride in his beloved 'Garbo' but didn't like to be part of the show. He returned the recognition with a tepid clenched fist of solidarity.

The gesture brought something to mind I couldn't quite catch, the feeling you get when you hear a song you can't place.

Doc pulled the folded transcript out again and started re-reading it while he chewed. I passed the time watching my bike leak oil.

"How accurate is this?" he asked, nodding at the print off. "There was a fair bit of the tape I couldn't make out."

"It's spot on."

I got it all down less than an hour after Jan told it to me. It was still fresh in my mind and I listened to it through head-phones. It still wasn't great but better than through the Dictaphone speaker.

"Did she know you were recording?"

I shook my head but didn't elaborate. Doc's look didn't weaver. I turned away, back to the growing oil stain under my engine, and took another bite of my cheeseburger. What he said next surprised me a little.

"I wish Chris had found someone else to screw around with."

He'd decided he was going to keep Chris out of nick and I'd never questioned his motives, but this was the first time he didn't seem to be enjoying himself – the episode with me and young Steve aside. His dedication to The Jive didn't always sit well with me and there was a small satisfaction in seeing him subdued.

"Playing Miss Marple not as much fun as you expected, eh?"

The words hit home and Doc cringed. It came out

sounding more caustic than I'd meant it to. I apologised and blamed the remark on being knackered. Doc shook his head.

"No, you're right, Yakky, you're right." He looked at some point in the middle distance and sighed. "I think I got carried away, being clever and feeling all righteous."

Again, he did the scrubbing thing, rubbing at his face.

"Is this about your meeting with Caroline?"

He nodded, still looking into middle distance. "I didn't conduct myself very well."

Caroline Keller had agreed to meet up again. That part had been easy, easier than it would have been for me. Doc's had one of those personalities people were drawn to. I've met plenty of that type over the years and generally don't take to them. Too many of them think the world's there for their convenience and too many people offer up their friendship as proof. Doc had a bit more substance to him than that, perhaps you'd call it depth.

He'd phoned Caroline expecting to go to voicemail and join a thousand coffee morning invites. When she actually picked up, he was surprised and they quickly arranged a second date. Doc simply told her he wanted to speak to her, *something had come up*.

Doc did one of his long chewing sessions on his cheeseburger. He wasn't building tension; he was trying to delay telling the story.

"Lonely woman," he said.

Doc had suggested they meet for another meal at a place he was familiar with, a slightly pompous gastropub where he'd create a ripple. Then he purposely reserved a table right in the middle of things, centre stage.

He went slightly more up-market than his usual wardrobe but skipped the makeup, went for a *touch of freak out*, as he put it. Caroline showed up fashionably late and, naturally, hadn't been able to find him. He'd found the part of the bar least visible from the door, probably with his eyes shut. Caroline stewed in her own body language for a while; she wasn't arrogant but she was certainly assured.

"I didn't have much of a plan," Doc told me, "I wanted to get a bit of a feel for her mood."

So, he'd watched her assurance decay a little at a time. She made her entrance and waited to be claimed and when that didn't happen, she made a few scans of the tables and bar. Doc took note of how long it took her to get uncomfortable. Longer than most, he concluded.

She took a place at the bar and ordered something that came straight from optic to hand. Doc let her get to the bottom of the glass before approaching. He did allow himself one smile while recounting the meeting.

"She nearly dropped the glass when she clocked this." He touched my tattoo work on his cheek. "Mind you, she recovered well."

There was more silence disguised as a bout of chewing.

"Not exactly a freak out then?" I prompted when it started to get on my nerves.

"No. She just looked sort of disappointed."

"So, it wasn't going to plan?"

"It wasn't that exactly. I wanted to put her off her stride but ... " He'd run out of burger by that time, so he took a long thoughtful pull on his tea. " ... disappointed? I hadn't seen that coming."

"You think she took a shine to you over lunch, was on the lookout for something?"

"No, nothing like that. I think she was just looking forward to spending time with someone she could talk to."

"And she couldn't talk to someone with a tattoo?"

Doc cast me a look. "Put your hackles down Yakky, you know what I mean. When I was giving it the sharp-dressed man bit and feeding her expensive lettuce she thought we'd made a bit of a connection." He shooed away a fly circling the stains on the table top. When it made a second pass he flicked at it viciously with his hand. "Then she sees me again and that's out the window."

For whatever reason, Caroline had stayed with the dinner

option rather than bailing out. The meal followed the same routine as the lunch, count calories and fill up on water. Maybe because of Doc's new look, or some belated sense of discretion, Caroline didn't mention Jan. Conversation was stilted and strictly small. The conversation was too sparse for any natural openings to arise so Doc waited through a half a dozen torturous bites of food before speaking directly.

"I need a copy of the police report."

She didn't reply, carried on chewing and gave a quizzical look. She wasn't much of an actress and Doc knew too much about the script.

He put his cutlery down and steepled his fingers.

"Tuesday night a friend of mine had a chat with a young man called Steve. Steve and his uncle Ken were meant to find proof that Jan killed Poor Peter. Steve said you gave them a copy of the police report." He let this sink in for a couple of beats. Faux bewilderment gave way to genuine surprise. "Did Kenny give his notice by the way?"

Caroline gave up any pretence of enjoying her evening and pushed the abandoned meal to one side. "He rang me first thing Wednesday morning. Told me something had come up." Caroline glared. "What did you do, buy him off?"

"All that Muppet did was take your money and run off a few pictures. Bad ones. We did you a favour getting them off your payroll."

She picked up the undercurrent of things unsaid. Like Jan, Caroline wasn't stupid. Nor was she easily cowed.

"That woman can pull one serious dirty look when she needs to," Doc told me, a note of admiration in his voice.

The meeting was a juggling act for Doc. He was depending on Caroline's self-image to keep her from storming out. The people she wanted to be didn't have hissy fits in public and set the lesser orders tutting.

Caroline had wanted to know why she should produce a copy of the report.

"You paid for the privilege of giving Ken a copy that he threw in the bin. If you want to know what happened to

Poor Peter, I'm your best bet. And it won't cost you a penny."

She glared at him. It was a good effort but for Doc tense silence counted as the home game. Even so, she put up a fight. Then she announced she wanted a vodka and tonic. Again, there was a vein of admiration in is voice.

"Really broke my stride. Clever."

I made the patented spooling motion with my hand. "Explain, oh wise one. Short words eh? We're losing the light."

The echo of a Cheshire Cat padded across his face. It was a skinny specimen compared to its forebears; still it was a good sign.

Doc explained his asylum logic. He saw two possible outcomes to their sparring match. Outcome one, capitulation and giving up the goods, or at least beginning negotiations. Outcome two, sticking her bottom lip out and saying, shan't. I suggested she could have waited him out and carried on staring, Doc dismissed the notion. Few people sit easily with silence, and even if she was one of them, Caroline was still at a disadvantage. The well-groomed women and the freak show had been a point of interest since they took centre stage. A hostile bout of wordless glaring was going to draw viewers as effectively as a full melt down, which she didn't want.

In that setting, Caroline was the player with most to lose. Which is why asking for the drink was a smart move. It turned the tables, made Doc into the one with the choice – do as he was told or stick his lip out and cry shan't.

In the world according to Doc, this put him on the back foot. If he didn't get his dinner guest her drink he'd become a petty bully, revelling in a cheap power play. If he gets her the drink then, in effect, he loses control of the situation. A couple, however mismatched, squabbling about a round of drinks is likely to become invisible. The witnesses drinking in an angry woman's public melt down were the same people who'd look away in embarrassment and give a couple some privacy to have their domestic. Doc was impressed with the subtly of her game.

It sounded like bollocks to me.

"Christ almighty, Doc, did you consider she might have just wanted a stiff drink? You think shit like this every time you have a chat? Being in your head must be exhausting."

Doc twisted position to get the low hanging sun out of his eyes. I hadn't been joking about losing the light.

"Everyone thinks like that. Anything you do, anything you say, your brain is doing a ton plus." It was evidently a subject he'd given a lot of thought to. "Nothing is ever just *because*; there is always, always, a reason. There's nothing sinister about it, it just is. The human mind is complex and calculating and vast. It never stops and most of the time we don't take any notice, we just call it instinct."

Doc got her a vodka and tonic. Sitting in the lay-by, he looked like shit. He dry washed his face again, hands against his stubble sounding like sandpaper, then he went quiet. We watched late evening HGVs grinding along the A road, the brittle sound of their engines bounced around the concrete landscape, perversely making the place seem isolated.

"Are we nearly there yet?" I asked.

Doc took a lungful of north London industrial grade air in through his teeth.

"Yeah, I think so."

He stopped playing Mr Nice Guy, which was how he put it.

From the bar, he'd called across the heads of the other customers, "Caroline, you want *slim-line* tonic?"

It was as calculating as it was low. Caroline flinched at the remark, eyebrows inched up at surrounding tables. It was a combination of dig and message.

She didn't touch the drink, didn't look at it after Doc put it on the table. Neither of them bothered with the silent treatment a second time.

"A friend of mine has been arrested. The police think he killed Poor Peter. I want to know why. I need a copy of that report."

Caroline changed position, pushed away from the table edge. She looked back at Doc coolly, concern not part of her agenda. Doc mirrored her, then decided this was a mistake. Now, leaning back from each other and exchanging reproachful looks, they become a couple having an embarrassing domestic. The audience, as he guessed they would, politely turned away.

"As I said, why should I give you the report?"

"To keep an innocent man out of prison, maybe?"

"You lay down with dogs, you get up with fleas." Caroline gave a sour smile.

"Guilt by association," Doc said. "Honestly, you're happy with that? Chris gets his leg over a few times with your sister-in-law then they trot off and top Poor Peter?"

"If your friend got himself mixed up with that little slag then they'll both have to live with the consequences. Call it poetic justice. She tried taking my husband, now the police have taken her bit-on-the-side."

"Meanwhile Poor Peter's killer gets away with it."

Caroline half twisted in her seat so she could prop one elbow on the back of her chair. It was an oddly masculine posture, out of character. Doc saw it as a chink in the armour. I could feel we were getting to the crux of what was unsettling him because he explained his thinking, instead of making me tease it out of him.

"She sat like this." He demonstrated, cocking one elbow up and back. He twirled his hand around in a lazy circle, then used it to bring an invisible cigarette to his lips. "She needed a smoke, but it wasn't just the nicotine addiction kicking in, she was getting aggressive. When civilised people start using the reptilian brain to do the thinking, you've got the upper hand."

Unless they're swinging a club of course, or holding a knife to your neck. Caroline, lacking a blunt instrument, made a bid for the moral high ground.

"Stop saying *Poor Peter* in that patronising way. The man's dead, show some respect."

Her hand twitched before remembering it wasn't holding a cigarette.

Doc had reminded her that Poor Peter was her term, that she'd offered the man no respect when he had a pulse. And he gave her a snide laugh.

In the darkening lay-by he sighed deeply.

"Not how Miss Marple would have handled it."

I couldn't make out his expression in the gloom, but I'm fairly sure he wasn't joking. He told Caroline she'd won. She had the bigger house and more money in the bank and Jan had nothing.

Caroline saw his snide laugh and raised him a sneer. "Jan should have done her homework. If she'd kept an eye on Peter's accounts she'd have known there was nothing to inherit. She could have saved your friend the trouble of killing him. If he's in trouble, you can blame her, not me."

Doc lifted a hand in the twilight and pointed a finger into the sky, cocked his thumb and mimed dropping the hammer.

"Bang," he said softly.

"Husband's accounts?"

He nodded.

Detectives, even bad ones, cost money if you want them pulling off twenty-four-hour-a-day surveillance. Jan hadn't known Peter was broke. Something Caroline regarded as a basic mistake. Husband's personal accounts? No such thing. Huge expenditure on petty spite? No problem. I nodded in the darkness as the light dawned.

"You blackmailed her?"

"Nasty word," he said as affirmation.

"Does your husband watch his accounts as closely as you?" Doc asked her, quietly.

He more or less had his fingers crossed – if she was going to melt down and storm out she'd have done it then. She stayed put and stayed still, answer enough. Doc pulled closer into the table and clasped his hands in front of him.

"Bottom line, you don't have the resources or the

connections to get hold of a police report from an ongoing investigation. If you did, you'd have known better than to hire monkeys like Steve and Ken. This means Jeffry got hold of the report, and he can't have done that legally. Now, because of you, Jeffry's dealing in illegal documents is in danger of going public."

He let this sink in while Caroline made calculations. If Jeffry was sufficiently well-connected to pull police reports it was possible he could smooth over a few questions about legality. But it would cost him somewhere along the line, things like that always did.

Doc won.

"You little shit."

At that point, safe in the belly of The Jive, Doc barely felt the words roll off his back. Magnanimous in victory, he offered reassurance.

"Let me have a copy of the report. I get what I need, Jeffry's none the wiser and you never see me again." In the face of her furious glare he added, "Everybody's happy."

"This ends here, is that clear? If you're harbouring any ideas of sniffing around me trying to get money – "

Doc held his hands up.

"Mutually assured destruction. If the police find I'm holding a copy of one their reports I'd be in as much trouble as you and Jeffry."

Which was almost the opposite of true. With a copy of the report to back up his claim Doc could cause ripples, without it, he'd just be a scruffy weirdo mouthing off. However he'd come by the report, Jeffry wasn't likely to have paid with plastic and been issued a receipt. Had Caroline gone home and confessed all, Jeffry could have put a match to the report and told Doc to do his worst. Doc was gambling she'd weigh the domestic fallout against his, fairly modest, request. That and she'd be too angry to think it through.

We abandoned the plastic chairs when the burger van closed for the night. We drifted back to the bikes while the maître d' locked his dining room away and drove off. I straddled my Yam and rocked it between my legs, trying to gauge how much petrol was in the tank by the sloshing sound. Sod all plus fumes.

"I take it she agreed to make you a copy?"

"She's going to scan it and email it to me. She'll have to do it while Jeffry's out of the house, might be a day or two." He swung a leg over his own bike and sat stroking the fuel tank. "That's assuming she doesn't change her mind and tell Jeff."

I thought we might find out about that the hard way. Jeffry Keller had connections that could bring forth official Met documents. He might also have connections that could bring forth gentlemen with low foreheads, big sticks and limited conversation.

I ran a thumb over the mojo, and the engine fired on the fifth try. I pulled my helmet on quickly before the God of Crap Motorcycles changed his mind and shut me down again. The ride home was subdued. I followed the Sportster at a distance so I could listen to my own engine. I wasn't hearing much good news.

The house was quiet when I got in. Dad's efforts must have exhausted both him and Jan. I went into the front room and stretched out on the sofa. Without the TV's screaming overture and dad's litany of complaints, the room felt almost serene. The tiredness was bone deep but my mind wouldn't let up.

I was with Doc; I wished Chris had pulled someone else out of cyberspace. I wondered how he was coping with being locked up. I knew I'd be bouncing off the walls. The weight of what we were trying to do was getting heavier. Not only for Chris. He said he was glad me and Doc were on his side, faith again, of a type. I hoped it was less misplaced than Doc's mumbo jumbo.

I was glad when my mobile buzzed and demanded attention.

"Caroline just emailed the goods to me."

Doc's voice was flat and I assumed he'd found something damning in the report.

"Not good?"

"Haven't read it yet, it's quite a big download. You expecting something in particular?"

"No. I just thought you'd be more upbeat about getting it."

"Keep thinking about how I got it." Brief pause then, "Can you get in early tomorrow, say eight?"

"Yeah, no sweat. Get some sleep through, will you?"

He assured me he would and told me to do the same. I broke the connection and dropped the mobile on the sofa. I felt flat too. Getting the report had seemed important when Chris and I stood together deciphering the bizarre notations on Doc's wall. Now we'd actually got it, I was totting up the cost.

Maybe Doc was right and Voodoo was the way to go. If the Buddhists had it right, we were laying down a lot of bad karma.

Four Skinny Fingers' Worth of Progress

Saturday 23 July

Neither Jan nor dad had made an appearance before I left the house that morning.

After waking up on the sofa and yelping with pain, I spent ten minutes in the shower, alternating scalding water with cold. Once my spine loosened up enough to let me dress without crying, I made an attempt on breakfast.

Supplies in the kitchen were non-existent but the bin was fully stocked. Dad would go hungry before conceding I could produce an edible meal; Jan had fed him most of the kitchen in less than twenty-four hours. My upper back sent me another needle of pain when I slammed the fridge door.

Black coffee and bile, most important meal of the day.

I scraped the last of my cash from my wallet and left it on the kitchen table with a note suggesting Jan go shopping.

At Doc's flat I found the front door swinging. Logic told me he'd left it open to cool the flat. That reptilian part of my brain, however, provided a crew of Keller-backed heavies to kick it open and beat the crap out of Doc. I took a deep breath and listened for sounds of violence or pain. When neither was in evidence I stepped in cautiously and called out, 'morning'. Five minutes later I'd been promoted from apprentice tattooist to chief coroner.

"You been on this all night?"

"No." Doc shook his head without looking up from the carpet of paperwork he was studying. "I only printed this lot off this morning. Kettle's just boiled if you want one."

I went to the kitchen and sought out a mug.

"You want me to close the front door?"

"No. I'm trying to let some air in."

It wasn't doing a lot of good. The air outside was heavy with moist heat; it felt like you could take a handful and wring it out. Back in the living room I found a space on the floor and mirrored Doc's cross-legged pose. Both armchairs had been pushed back against the walls to make floor space. There was a lot of paper.

"Is this all from Caroline?"

"Uh-huh." He looked up at me and his eyes widened. "Christ, did you sleep at all?"

"Yeah, I just didn't have time to do my makeup."

I wasn't looking my best. Sleeping on the sofa in the shape of a paper clip didn't suit me. Doc regarded me for a few seconds and decided I was either okay or beyond help.

"I think our Jeffry's got some well-appointed friends." He waved a hand across the collection of paper. "This is the attending officer's report, the scene of crime officer's report, the post-mortem report, a transcript of Jan's nine-nine-nine call and a copy of Chris's old charge sheet."

Doc selected a small stack of pages. He handed them to me.

"Post-mortem," he said. "More your field than mine. You trained as a nurse."

I pointed out this was two years of making beds and washing commodes. It was an exaggeration, though not a big one. I was vaguely familiar with medical terms and had a fading knowledge of anatomy. Doc told me to pick someone better qualified and did a slow scan of the room to drive the point home. I started reading.

I read the post-mortem through, circling words I needed to look up. After I'd gathered sufficient evidence of my ignorance, I asked Doc if I could boot up his computer. I dredged memories of my student days to come up with a reliable website, and filled in the blanks. Once I'd translated all the technical terms and deciphered all the three-letter abbreviations that medics hold so dear, I wrote up my layman's summary as a set of bullet points. I hoped Doc would have some thoughts on what I'd scribed. If it added anything useful to our pool of knowledge, I couldn't see it.

Doc took the stack back from me, my pencil-written notes fitted easily on the back of a single sheet. He sank back into his cross-legged position as I struggled to my feet. My back had taken the chance to start seizing again.

As Doc read I rolled my shoulders and looked over the crime wall. It had grown, the right border creeping closer towards the adjacent wall. The new growth consisted mainly of tarot cards and Roman numerals, arranged in a column.

The column had been segregated from the bulk of the wall with a charcoal line. Heavily scored in black at the top of the column was XII, beneath it III. Next to the III was a small curved arrow. The rest of the column was a similar shrine to crystal clarity.

I went and put the kettle on again, helped myself to some toast while I was at it. Doc joined me in the kitchen while I waited for the second round to pop up.

"Spot the problem?" he asked, sitting himself at the kitchen table and dropping the post-mortem report in front of him. He'd put it face down so my notations were visible. I propped myself against the sink and shook my head. I was more concerned with eating than thinking at that point. Doc looked amused. "Don't they feed you at home?"

"Dad's disowned me. Jan's his son now."

It was meant to be a joke but it came out wrong.

Doc tapped the page, drawing my attention to the bullet points I'd made. I leaned closer, still eating, to see what he was getting at.

Wounds:

WRIST. L: radial artery, 1cm Deep, 1.5 cm Long, 3mm at widest point. Triangle shaped

CROCK OF ARM. L: brachial artery, 4cm D, 5cm L, oval shape, tearing at ends.

CROCK OF ARM. L: small flesh wound 1.5cm D 2cm L, 3mm at widest point. Triangle shaped

KNEE. R, minor abrasion, no bruising.

Doc had made a notation of his own, he'd underlined, *3mm at widest point*. I was about to tell him I still wasn't getting it when I suddenly did.

"The blade Jan found doesn't match the wounds."

"Bullseye."

Murder or suicide, we'd assumed the Stanley blade Jan had found had been the one to commit the deed. The width of the wounds suggested something else had been used.

The blades used in Stanley knives were little more than beefed up razor blades. They didn't run to 3mm thick and weren't triangular in cross section. Triangle-shaped wounds suggested the tip of a real knife, wide on the top tapering to an edge. Something like the lock knife Jan had given the Big Guy.

"How accurate would those measurements be?" Doc asked me.

"At a guess, given the depth, I'd say fairly accurate. The blade would have gone right through the skin and fat layer into the connective tissue. The connective tissue's not that elastic, it doesn't spring back."

Doc nodded, acknowledging my superior knowledge. I held up my hands, alarmed at the gravity he was giving to my half-arsed musings.

"I know this is isn't expert testimony Yak, but you're still the best we got. So ... "

He made the spooling motion. The gesture was becoming one of my least favourite things.

I picked my notes up again and read them back to myself. I finished the toast while I was at it.

"Even if the width of the blade is off, I say we can declare the Stanley blade innocent."

I rifled back into the report, rechecking what I'd read.

"*Wound at antecubital fossa, elliptical, 40mm in depth ... tearing evident at distal and proximal ends*. If, *if*, I'm reading this right, then this cut was the daddy. The blade's gone in deep and taken out of the brachial artery. The tearing at the ends means the skin's torn apart rather than cut. I think that means the blade was twisted."

Doc was quick on the uptake and I didn't have to wait long for a reaction. Jan had described a Stanley blade, not a complete Stanley knife. Doc held his finger and thumb pinched tightly together, as you'd place them if you were gripping a Stanley blade. He nodded, clicking his tongue.

Gouging a hole into the crock of your arm with a Stanley blade pinched between your fingertips would be close to impossible. If you managed it at all, you'd slice your fingers to ribbons. The report made no mention of injuries to Keller's hands. I put the papers back on the table. Doc picked them up and knocked the edges together to tidy them.

"You think that's why the police are ruling out suicide?" I asked.

"I think that's just part of it."

He started back to the living room and I followed. He didn't sit down again, just bent from the waist and deposited the tidied post-mortem papers on a patch of clear floor. He took a moment to select a couple of fresh sheets and handed them to me.

One of them was a page from the transcript of Jan's story. The other was a confusing block of text that filled a side of A4. Doc had marked about half a dozen points with yellow highlighter. He tapped one of them with a finger. My transcript was similarly highlighted and I spotted the connection straight away.

There were no fingerprints on the bottle of Scotch. The one Jan had noticed was half empty. There was a bottle in the bathroom, and at some point, or so it appeared to Jan, someone had drunk from it. Someone who then wiped their prints away.

"And the note," Doc said and singled out another highlighter smear.

The words *ink-jet printed note* glowed under the yellow ink. The next selected line of words read, *signature obscured by brown staining*. Medico-legal documents state known facts, not conjecture. So, brown staining, not blood. At least not without some test results.

I remembered Jan's comment about the half sheet of paper, even for his suicide note Peter had been counting the cost. I tried to picture someone, anyone, sitting in their office to knock out, *goodbye cruel world*, then cutting the page in half. Then taking the note to the other side of the house and propping it behind the spotlessly clean tap, but not before the signature's been bled on.

For all Doc's efforts and soul searching, all we'd done was conclude it wasn't suicide. Something the police decided the minute they'd seen Chris.

"We'd better get to work," Doc said.

For a moment I thought he meant get to work on proving Chris's innocence, but it was another one of his mental gear changes that left me lagging. It was time to open the shop, get back to our day jobs and get the needles singing.

Jan rang me on the shop line about an hour before we closed. She'd found my mobile down the back of the sofa when Karla had tried to reach me. Karla had called the landline first.

Jan, of course, had answered both calls.

There was an uncomfortable pause. I couldn't hear dad or the TV in the background. Super Nurse had left her patient to make this call.

"I told her you were at work and might be home late, because of the business with Chris." She took a long breath. "I don't know what I said but she sounded upset."

"What did she say?"

"She said, 'tell him he's too old to be playing cops and robbers'." She paused rather than finished, not wanting to say the next bit. "And she told me the next time I'm in your bedroom, I should wear less scent. Then she hung up."

I waved away a round of apologies from Jan, told her it didn't matter, surprised myself when I realised I meant it.

Karla wouldn't listen when I tried to explain about Jan going into my bedroom to borrow a tee shirt. It didn't sound very plausible even if it she had. I dialled a second time after she'd hung up on me. Pride or fatigue forbade a third attempt.

Doc was too caught up with our game of cops and robbers to offer much sympathy and I didn't court him for any. Karla and I had been circling each other for months without resolving things. Perhaps it was time.

After we locked up the shop, Doc and I went back to his flat and got on with it.

"I haven't paid you this week."

The comment brought me back; I'd been drifting. The documents had stopped making sense and turned into blocks of random words. Doc had his back to me when I looked up and I thought he was kneeling before his altar. In fact he was pulling up a floorboard. I put aside the sheet I'd been trying to read and pulled myself from the armchair. I had to pick my way over to Doc's corner. The amount of paper on the floor had increased as I'd printed out my own copies. It had also spread as we tried to compile the mess of information into a coherent whole. We had little success.

The floorboard was a snug fit. Doc worked it free by means of a knot hole that allowed him to get a finger in and pull. When the board was out, he gently stood it against the wall. The space under the floor appeared to be empty but a faint smell wafted from it. I hadn't smelt mothballs in years. Doc put an arm deep into the gap and felt around. What came out was a polythene bundle about two foot long.

He unwrapped it and watched me for a moment before shaking his head.

"You got a real poker face on you, Yakky, you know that?"

If he was impressed with my lack of reaction he shouldn't have been. I wasn't playing it cool, just struck dumb. The bundle contained more cash than I'd ever seen and a sawn-off shotgun.

"What's with the mothballs?"

The smell burst out once the polythene came away, and one of the little white spheres rolled away under the altar.

"Don't want my savings getting eaten." He selected one of the smaller rolls of notes. There were about thirty in all, each tightly bound with a rubber band. "And gun oil has an odour all its own. I thought the mothballs might confuse any sniffer dogs." He looked embarrassed. "Chalk it up to paranoia."

He freed the notes from their band and counted out my wages, then counted out some more.

"Jan's food and board," he said. I took the money with a nod and pushed it deep into my hip pocket. Doc regarded me from his crouched position on the floor. "Honestly, mothballs? I pull out a shotgun and a ton of moola, and that's your only question?"

"Figured it was the only one you'd give a straight answer to."

He thought this over.

"Yeah, fair point."

When the board was pressed back into its gap, you couldn't tell it had been moved. Without saying any more about the money, or the gun, Doc stood up. He arched his back and twisted, making his spine crackle.

"I need something to eat, Yak. Let's take a break, stretch our legs."

We headed to the pizza place across the road, intending to take something back to the flat, but the shop was full of lairy teenagers, acting drunker then they were. Neither of us was in the mood, so we stretched our legs a little more than we planned. We wound up sitting in an Indian restaurant with a grandiose title and a pricing policy that dissuaded half-cut adolescents. Aside from a loved-up couple making mooneyes at each other we had the place to ourselves. Half a dozen waiters stood eyeing the empty tables, bracing themselves for a late evening rush or a round of redundancies.

After we ordered I borrowed Doc's mobile. I rang Jan hoping I'd catch her away from dad, another three-way drama over the ether didn't appeal. For the first time that day I got lucky and she picked up the call in the kitchen. When I told her I was with Doc, and wouldn't be back anytime soon, she took the nurse bit down a notch and asked if we'd got anything that'd help Chris. I gave Doc his phone back then got sick of listening to his Jive. I finally went to the toilet to get away from it.

The food had arrived to when I got back to the table. Mouth too full to speak, Doc pointed at his meal and gave a thumbs-up. The food was pretty good as I constantly told the flotilla of waiters.

Once our stomachs had been pandered to a bit, we were back to the job at hand.

"We're getting nowhere," I said, and assured our waiter the meal was fine for the third time.

"I wouldn't say that."

"So, where *have* we got?"

Doc put his cutlery down and started listing things on his fingers.

"One: We now have the stuff from Caroline. Two: We have a pretty good idea why the police are treating it as murder. That means we have a better idea what we've up against, and what we need to do. Three: We have some idea of the nature of Peter Keller and his relationship with his family. Four: We have access to Jan, who was in the house when Peter died."

Four skinny fingers' worth of progress. He picked up his

cutlery and resumed eating. The points were all true but I still didn't see where they took us. I thought of Karla's judgement. Playing cops and robbers. From where I was sitting, it looked like the cops were ahead on points.

"You don't think the police have all that, and more?"

Doc shock his head, didn't answer until he'd finished his mouthful.

"Jan and Chris will talk to us; they won't talk to the law. And the police are wrong footing themselves. They think they've got their man and all they need to do is send him down. It doesn't matter what they have or haven't got – they're not looking at it anymore."

I wasn't inclined to dismiss the abilities of the police so quickly. Even if they were as blinkered as Doc liked to think, they still had more resources than us. More manpower, more training, more experience, more equipment.

"Even if Chris is giving the cops the silent treatment that's hardly helping, is it? He can't talk to us either while he's in a cell."

"Chris'll be in touch."

"You didn't sound so cocksure about that yesterday."

Doc was chewing away at a naan bread, thankfully he didn't make a production number out of it. He gulped it down with a swig of his larger.

"Yeah. Well yesterday I was no use to anyone. Back on track now." He tapped himself on the forehead and mopped sauce with the remains of the naan. "Chris is just playing silly buggers with the police. I'm betting when he gets fed up staring out coppers he'll demand his phone call and ring me. Me or Jan."

With surprising delicacy, he bit off enough naan to feed small a horse.

"I'd have thought he'd have done that by now to put Jan's mind at rest."

Doc pulled an exasperated face, hamming it up. "The Jan Chris knows?"

He had a point. The Jan waiting for Chris was rock-steady-righteous-old-lady Jan. It still seemed a callous way to conduct his love life, but who I was to judge?

"You think she'll be able to play that role for long?"

"I don't think it's a matter of playing a role. She lives it. That's what her life is."

After taking another mouthful of food, he reached into his leather. I thought the tarot cards were about to get an outing, instead he pulled out the transcript I'd made of my talk with Jan. Doc hesitated before unfolding the sheets. I could see he was thinking by the tempo of his chewing. He cleared a space on the table and set the pages down facing me.

Doc put his finger on a section of dialogue. "Remember that?"

I read the first few lines of the bit he was pointing at. "Yeah, she had a wardrobe and when the doors were shut they looked like a face."

"Probably walnut burr, it was big in the thirties. They'd use two sheets of veneer cut from the same stock then set them up side by side, usually on cabinet doors. You'd end up with a symmetrical design. If the veneer had knot holes, they'd make you think of a pair of eyes and your mind filled in the blanks. *Everybody* had a wardrobe with a face."

I figured the lecture on cabinet making was a different version of chewing. I listened hoping the point was on its way. When Doc took a mouthful of rice and started on his usual delaying routine, I smacked the transcript with my knuckles.

"If it wasn't for me playing tricks with Jan we wouldn't have this." I held Doc's gaze. "If it's giving us something, I'm entitled to know. You're not the only one around here with a fucking conscious, you know."

And I didn't have Voodoo spirits at the end of an altar to forgive my sins. Doc wasn't fazed by my outburst but he nodded and finally swallowed.

"I know Yak, I know. But what I'm saying now goes no further, this isn't mine to share. You get me?"

I didn't have a clue what that meant but I nodded anyway. Doc tapped the sheet of paper again, put his finger at a particular point.

"Read that bit through, tell me if you think it's accurate."

I picked up the page and read it.

When the doors were closed they looked like a face. Two of the knots looked like eyes. If the doors were open, it was okay. I'd always leave them open before I got into bed. When they ... if someone shut them, I'd sit up in bed, too scared to look at them. I played a game. I knew I'd have to look at the doors, I didn't want to look at them, but I couldn't stand not knowing what they were doing. So I'd look around the room and try to find something in the room that was different from the last time I was in it. I'd see how many I could find before I couldn't stand it anymore and I'd have to look at the doors. I'd set a number. When I found that amount of differences, I'd peek at the door. Then I'd look away again.

"I typed this up when it was still fresh in my mind and I was working from the tape." I put the page back on the table with the rest of the transcript. "If it's on the page, it's what was said."

"I thought it would be."

Doc's attention flickered around the near empty restaurant before he continued. He leaned forward and there was an implicit invitation that I debated ignoring but didn't. We ended up huddled over the transcript, looking like the lovebirds at the other table. I hoped the atmosphere at the other table was less tense.

"This stuff about someone closing the doors. On that part of the tape, her voice isn't clear, it sounds like she having a hard time keeping it together."

"Yeah." I remembered how upset she was by then, also remembered how bad the recording was. "She was talking about sitting in the bathroom with her dead husband, covered in blood. I'm surprised she could talk about it at all."

Doc made a noise that indicated agreement, but he made it sound like it wasn't important.

"I'll give you that, but it's what she says, more than how she says it."

He turned the page slightly to read a section aloud.

"'When they ... if someone shut them, I'd sit up in bed, too scared to look at them'. She changes from, *when they* to *if someone.* I get the feeling she's covering something up or at least trying to keep something buried." He quoted another line. "'I'd look around the room and try to find something in the room that was different from the last time I was in it'. The wording's suggestive."

He clicked his tongue a couple of times, thinking.

"Suggestive?" I prompted.

I also promised myself I'd punch him if he made the spooling motion.

"'The last time I was in it'. She's talking about her bedroom as a kid. This business with the doors sounds as if it was a fairly regular thing. If she was in that room then she was worried about the face in the doors. But she says *the last time* she was in the room, not the night before or last night. Most kids sleep in the same place every night. I get the idea she was moved between different rooms."

I couldn't see why it was bothering him.

"And the bit about changing *when* to *if*?"

Doc shook his head, corrected me.

"*When they,* to, *if someone.* That's a big change in terms of concept. She changed from two or more people definitely doing something to an individual possibly doing something. Again, it feels to me as if she keeping something back. Or down."

"You're making this sound sinister."

"Well, I could be totally wrong here." He made this sound comically unlikely. At the time it needled me. "You ever heard of dissociative identity disorder, Yakky?"

"No, of course I haven't."

"It used to be called multiple personality disorder. If

somebody's got it, they section off chunks of their memory and character. They protect themselves by electively forgetting the bad times. Trouble is the mind is vast and all the crap they've pushed away doesn't vanish, it just gets lost for a time. Lay on some trauma, bit too much stress and, pow, the bad times come back. When the bad times start coming back, someone with dissociative identity disorder reacts by switching to an entirely different personality. They become someone else, someone without the bad memories."

"And you think Jan's got this?"

Doc shook his head. "No, no, but the way Jan switches between characters put me in mind of it. The idea of dropping who you are so easily, letting go of what make you, you ... " He stopped, stared at the pages on the table. After a while he folded up the transcript and put it back into his leather. "I wasn't expecting anything about Jan's childhood to come up on the tape. When I read that bit of the transcript, it sent up a flare. Especially when she got on to the game she'd play."

"That freaked me out when she said it. She doesn't want to look at the face in the door, so she makes a game up to distract herself. But the prize, if she wins the game, is to look at the door. Lose-lose situation."

"She had to look at the door so she'd know the face in it hadn't moved. Playing the game didn't change that but it would have given her some semblance of control over what was going on." Doc grimaced. "Good survival skill."

It went quiet again. It was beginning to feel like the previous night in the lay-by. We both chewed in silence. I sat on my impatience and allowed him his thinking time. At the back of my mind though, I opened a mental door and let Karla in. She quickly moved from the back of my mind to the forefront. I almost missed what Doc finally said, but it filtered through enough to hit a nerve.

"I wasn't sure about bringing this up. People often have a problem relating to someone once they know they've had some sort of trauma. It's almost a form of envy."

I snapped out of my scrutiny of a possible future without Karla. "Well if you don't think I'm up to the fucking job, put an ad in the paper."

Doc looked startled. "Christ, Yakky – "

"Christ, nothing. I've got Jan shacked up my spare room while Karla gets the hump about it. I'm spending all my time hand in glove with you, trying to get your mate out of the shit. And the way we've going, we'll be lucky if we don't end up in the cell next to him." I sat back in my seat and held Doc's eye. "I'm in this up to the hilt and I didn't ask for any of it, okay? So, if you've got a better volunteer, go and fucking patronise them."

Doc finished his lager and raised a hand to get a waiter. He had to wait all of two seconds. He ordered himself another and pointed at my glass in mute enquiry. I shook my head.

"Sorry," he said simply when the waiter had retreated. "I'm still feeling bad about the way I treated Caroline, now I feel like I'm about to tell you something that isn't my business."

Doc saw the waiter approaching with his drink and waited until he delivered it before speaking again.

"As I said, I might be wrong."

"But you don't think so?"

"No, I don't. I think Jan's behaviour is a survival tactic. She's like a chameleon. She blends in so she doesn't get eaten. Most of us do that in a limited way. Jan's taking it to an extreme. I read of similar behaviour in abuse victims. They have a horror movie for a childhood and, as adults, they adopt roles that allow them to avoid further grief, allow them to survive. Looking at the way Jan is then reading about her bedtime routine as a kid," he paused and sighed deeply, "I'm pretty sure she suffered a lot of abuse from more than one person. I think possibly a group of people."

"Doc, you're reading a hell of a lot into a few remarks. Remarks she made when she was tired, worried about Chris and in the middle of recounting something horrible."

"Stressed, in other words."

He reached behind him and pulled out the transcript again. He took a while to find the section he wanted. He didn't place it on the table this time. He read something first to himself then, aloud, to me.

"This is what Jan says she did after getting off the phone to the police. 'I went back to the bathroom. I went back to be with Peter. I thought that's what I should do'. Do you see what I'm getting at here? This is a woman who just waved off her lover at the front door. Then she's found her husband's body in a pool of blood. Blood that she's then got covered in. Remember what I said about stress triggering bad memories? How people with dissociative identify disorder cope by switching to a new personality? I think something like that happened here. Jan is stressed like we can't imagine and she starts playing that bizarre game. The way she did when she was a child."

He left a gap in the dialogue and looked at me to see if I knew the next line.

"The bad memories are back. She's regressed to her childhood."

Doc made his fingers into an imaginary gun and fired, *bullseye*. "So, she plays the game. Like I said, it's a survival strategy. The game allows her to gain control and do what has to be done. Not check the face on the wardrobe now, but look at Peter. Or, to think of it another way, to look at the immediate situation, bring her back from the past."

"Then she makes the call and goes back into the bathroom, because she thinks that's what she should do."

"She goes back into character."

Goes back to being the trophy wife to Peter Keller. Because it's safer to be trophy-wife-Jan in a room full of Peter's blood than little-girl-Jan peeking at the face in the door and waiting for God knows what.

I could see why Doc was reluctant to talk about it.

The waiters had been stricken at the sudden end to our meal.

We'd called for the bill and reassured them again that everything was fine. I peeled my share of the bill from the wages I'd got earlier. When he paid his half, Doc had pulled his wallet from his boot and took out a thick wad of notes.

When we passed the pizza shop again the lairy teenagers had been replaced with a twenty-four-hour glazier's van. At the mouth of the alley that led to the flat Doc broke away and went to check the shop was unmolested. I went on into the yard and waited on the steel landing at the top of the external staircase. The sun was lower in the sky now, taking some of the day's sticky grey heat with it.

I wondered if Doc's thoughts on Jan were right. I respected his intelligence, more so when I could see it forming a logical chain. I wished he'd pulled out his cards and given me some Jive instead of a reasoned process of deduction.

Doc came stomping up the metal stairs and let us in. Didn't mention any damage to the shop. I went in behind him, wasn't surprised when he made a beeline for the kettle.

"Want a brew?"

"Please." I sat at his table as he made tea. "What you want to do next?"

We'd both read all the documents Caroline had sent, twice over. I still wasn't convinced we had anything worth a damn.

"I think we should get it in order, so we can see any points that cross." He squinted at one of the mugs he was holding and decided it needed cleaning before use. "Then we need to work out how it was done."

"The murder?" He turned from the sink nodding and I asked him, "What was all that bullshit with the floorboard about?"

It was one of the rare occasions I managed to surprise him. "What about it?"

"Doc, I know you are one smart fucker. I get that, I really do. But – come here." I went to the living room, picked my way across the debris on the floor and turned to make sure he'd followed me. "Your mind works in ways other people's don't." I opened my arms to encompass Ezulie Dantor and the crime wall. "And even when you're being bat shit crazy you're a better artist than me at my best. No contest Doc, you is the man. But that doesn't mean I'm stupid. So, don't patronise me and don't give me your bloody Jive." I noticed something – I wasn't breathing hard. I felt as though I should have been; I wanted to be angry. "You didn't need to get money from under the floor to pay me. When you pulled your wallet out at the Indian it was packed with cash. So, what's with pulling up the floor and dragging out the buried treasure?"

Doc put his hands up, almost grinned, maybe thought better of it.

"You've put lot on the line since Jan and Chris went shit shaped. I know you're doing it mainly on my word that the Big Guy's innocent. So, you trust me. I showed you the money, and the gun, because I wanted to show I trust you too. Call it a compliment."

It was gone one when I got home and the light was still on downstairs. As I wrestled the bike into the yard, the front door opened and Jan came out. My first thought was something must have happened. I brought myself up short and took a moment to consider Doc had been right. Thinking Jan might have a history of abuse changed the way I saw her. A week beforehand, when she was being followed, my reaction had been resentment. Now I jumped because she stayed up late and opened the door for me. I forced myself to stay calm.

If she had been abused my late-in-the day pity wasn't about to change anything.

"You're burning the midnight oil," I said as I hung my leather on the rack.

Jan walked backwards into the hall as I came in. I couldn't make sense of her expression, it looked out of place. Then it struck me she was nervous. Nervous-excited, like she'd been the first time I'd seen her, trailing Chris and getting the darker end of The Jive.

She said, "Anything?"

Anything that might help Chris. I wondered what her expression would be if I said no. My stomach did another roll in anticipation. I didn't know if I'd have felt the same before listening to Doc's analysis of her childhood.

"Doc's managed to get a copy of the police report," I told her.

I hoped that would impress her enough to keep her happy. I also hoped she wouldn't ask what good it had done us. She didn't ask anything. The acolyte had learned the way of silence.

"It's going to be pretty useful," I hedged.

I avoided looking at her by pretending to check if my gloves were inside my helmet.

"I did a bit of shopping. Sorry but I used up all the money you left."

"Don't apologise, that's what I left it for."

We did a strange dance in the confines of the hall. When I turned and moved towards the kitchen she stepped into my path, thinking I was heading to the front room. I didn't want to push past her and for some reason saying excuse me would have seemed odd. After a few hesitant steps, I found myself in the front room facing the TV. I sunk into dad's chair.

Jan settled on the arm of the sofa.

"Have you read the report? What do the police say?"

I threw her the only bone I could think to offer and repeated Doc's speech to me in the curry house. We actually had the police report, we had a handle on what the police thought and had the advantage of knowing they were wrong. To my horror Jan's chest hitched and her breathing caught. I thought she was about to cry.

"I know it's not much but it's progress," I said.

I left the depths of dad's chair and stood next to the sofa, wishing I was anywhere else. She was doing her best not to cry, eyes open as ever. When I put my hand on her shoulder something gave way and the tears started to flow. There was nothing sad about it – it was anger.

"He didn't do it," she said, "he didn't do it." Again and again like a mantra.

I stepped in closer and put my hand to the back of her head. She surprised me by putting her arms around my waist and pressing herself into my side. The strain to keep my balance set my back aching again, and I was aware of how close she was to my groin. When I looked down some distant corner of my mind registered that she had finally closed her eyes.

She pulled herself together quickly and apologised. I told her I understood, told her she was probably tired. Mention of fatigue set off a Pavlovian response any dog could be proud of, and I wound up brewing coffee.

Jan, now sitting at the kitchen table, dried her eyes on a handful of kitchen roll then fiddled it into confetti. She'd blown a chunk of the budget on the Ethiopian coffee I'd said I favoured. A lot had happened since that conversation but, as a fellow addict would, she'd remembered it. Yet she declined the coffee I made. That distant corner of my mind filed this fact next to her change of crying habits.

Double Dealing

Sunday 24 July

There was another uncomfortable moment with Jan before she headed for bed. She'd given me back my mobile, which I'd forgotten about, and asked if everything was okay with Karla.

"It's fine," I said, she kept on looking at me so I made an effort and smiled. "Really it's not a problem."

I don't think I convinced her any more than I'd convinced myself. She returned my smile with one of her own, just as forced, then squeezed my arm. It was a strange gesture, removed and familiar all at once.

I listened to her climb the stairs, waited to hear the bathroom door pulled shut. Then I opened my mobile and checked for messages, texts or missed calls. Nothing. On a whim, I pulled up the log of outgoing calls and, when I found nothing I didn't expect, felt a twinge of guilt for checking. I tried to shake the feeling off by reminding myself that Jan was possibly holding out on us about the events of Sunday the tenth. Then I felt guilty about thinking that too. I finished off the pot of Ethiopian and thereafter could put all such feelings down to impending stomach ulcers.

Once I'd put the phone on charge I made myself leave it downstairs. I'm not a big phone user really. My contacts list is small and I give my number out like the taxman gives out refunds. But my phone does serve as a photo album. I knew if I started fiddling with it I'd start deleting pictures I might want back later. I went up the stairs and you'd have barely noticed the moment of hesitation outside my bedroom door.

I shut the door behind me and stared back at a hundred Karlas. I told myself I'd pick one good portrait that I'd put in a frame. Those showing artistic merit I'd gather together for my portfolio and the rest were for the bin.

The solitary candidate for the frame was easy to pick. So easy I managed to pick nine. After thirty minutes or so I grabbed one from the shortlist at random, put the others face down on the bed. The sexy nurse sketch that had upset Karla went in the bin along with a few other pin-up-style efforts. They'd have looked okay in my portfolio but they'd have felt intrusive on general release. In the end, I broke my initial ruling and kept two pictures to display and haunt myself with. One was a three-quarter profile that I spent long hours on and was worth keeping on its own merit. The other was a nude study in which I'd reimagined her with full sleeve tattoos and a back piece.

I thought long and hard about discarding it. Bittersweet. Close to perfect from my point of view but a long way from what I'd had.

My head hit the pillow. I didn't dream and I didn't wake up again until almost seven.

I reclaimed by mobile from its charger and checked it for missed calls and texts. Doc had texted. At four oh seven,

U awake Yak?

Then at four ten,

Call me when you get this.

I checked the time; it was twenty to eight. I put some more Ethiopian on to brew. Drinking the first cup of the day allowed Doc another ten minutes before he learnt the error of texting insomniacs. I used the landline in the hall to save credit. Doc took a while to pick up.

"You ordered an early morning wake-up call?"

"Is that you Yakky?"

His voice was thick with sleep.

"Yeah. I just picked up your text. What's up?" I heard a muffled thump, like he'd been sat up and then dropped back like a stone. He muttered a curse. "Want me to call back when you're awake?"

"No, no just hang on a sec."

I heard creaking sounds and assumed he'd got out of bed. To judge by the noises I heard he was moving from one room to another. I made a guess that he was heading towards the kettle.

"Can you talk?" Meaning, *is Jan there?* I told him I was the only one up. "Had a thought in the small hours." There was a subtle change in the acoustics, an echo on Doc's voice that suggested he'd moved into the living room. "Why haven't the police been in contact with Jan about Peter's body? He's been dead two weeks and they've done the post-mortem. Shouldn't he have been buried or cremated by now? You must have seen people leaving feet first when you were doing the student bit in the hospitals."

I had, but once the porters had wheeled the body away, our part was done and we moved on to the next one. One that still had a pulse. I said as much to Doc.

"Sounds jolly," he said. I agreed; it had its moments. "So, just give me your best guess."

Again, I found myself in the undeserved role of expert.

"Most people want it done quickly, in a few days. Different cultures, religions, might do it differently. Two weeks does seem a long time though. Someone's dragging their heels. But this is a murder investigation. The police could be hanging on to Keller until the case is resolved."

Doc's tongue clicked as he pondered.

"I reckon they'd still be talking to the next of kin. Letting them know they'd have to hold off on the funeral."

"You think something funny's going on?"

I heard movement from the spare room.

"I might just be on edge but I think we've been ignoring Peter Keller. We're overlooking something. For one thing, why hasn't Jan been spending more time with the police? Next to Chris, she's probably top of the list of suspects."

The noises from upstairs were more earnest. I knew from moments of ruined intimacy how sound travelled between the floors of the house. In the brief months Karla and I shared the house with dad, we'd had more than one episode of cringing embarrassment. I winced as Karla took up centre stage in my head again.

"We've going to have to wrap this up Doc."

"Okay. Look can I come over later? I want to see Jan. I can run a few things by you both. You'll get what I mean."

That would have been a first. I told him to get round soonish and I'd do him breakfast, fry up an olive branch or two.

Jan came into the kitchen dressed more for her biker chick persona than her faux nurse engagement. The over-tight jeans were back, topped off with one of my old shop tee shirts, which remarkably had managed to shrink even more. After I washed it once I had to make a cut in the neck to get it over my head. Now, by accident or design, the cut had deepened a good few inches. The show this made of her cleavage also emphasised the slump of her shoulders. Her smile didn't match her body language.

"You're busy," she said, with a non-reflective brightness.

I looked up from slicing potatoes.

"I thought I'd do everyone a decent breakfast. Doc's heading over as well."

She asked if she could anything to help. I asked her to lay the big table in the back room. If we were going to do the thing we might as well do it right. Also, dad's attention-seeking was easier to cope with given a bit of elbow room.

I heard the Sportster draw up outside just as I was making a pot of tea. He'd probably smelt the stuff. Dad timed his descent of the stairs so he came into sight as I opened the front door. Doc made a suitable fuss and Jan leapt in to help with the mammoth journey down the last three steps. Between them they eased him, huffing and puffing, into the back room.

We didn't eat in silence but dad hijacked every line of conversation. When we'd finished eating Jan helped me clear the table and we grabbed a breather in the kitchen. It didn't last long. Doc came in to tell us dad needed the toilet. Jan made to go but I motioned her to stay.

Dad was disappointed when I appeared in the doorway but accepted the game was over with relative grace. When we got downstairs again the TV was on in the front room and a cup of tea was next to his chair. I listened to his detailed account of why his breakfast had been inedible then left him to work his way through the pile of biscuits Jan had provided.

Doc and Jan were sitting at the kitchen table. Doc was finishing off the fried bread dad had rejected.

"You should open a cafe," he said.

I acknowledged the compliment with a small bow and started on the washing up. Jan made to help and I told her it was alright. Before she could argue, Doc asked her if she had her tarot to hand. She left without a word and made her way to the spare room.

"Is she – " Doc began, and I held a finger to my lips. In answer to his look I pointed up to the ceiling then to my ear. If he got the idea or not I couldn't say but he came over to the sink and kept his voice low. "Is she still tuning out around you, going blank?"

I gave it a little thought then shook my head. She hadn't last night or that morning.

"Why?"

Doc turned so he was facing the doorway. "I thought she seemed different around you today ... " He trailed off, lapsed into thought. I left him to it and carried on stripping oil off the cutlery. We heard Jan coming back down, Doc whispered to me, "I think she'd got you pegged."

"Is that a problem?"

"Don't know."

Then Jan was back in the room, clutching her tarot deck.

Normally I'd have given the show a miss but I was curious about where this was leading. Doc wouldn't leave home without his own tarot cards any more than he'd leave without trousers. If he was consulting another pack he wasn't reading, he was Jiving.

Jan was learning the ways of Voodoo and card reading with alarming enthusiasm, but I knew more about the ways of Doc.

She sat at the head of the kitchen table and Doc pulled another chair around so he was angled on the corner, at her right hand. He made several, entirely pointless, adjustments to his position before settling. I didn't know if he was building an atmosphere or fidgeting with his conscious. I caught his eye as Jan became engrossed in shuffling her cards. He pulled a pained face at me but quickly returned his attention to his pupil.

"Do you shuffle a set number of times?"

Jan looked surprised at the question then concerned.

"I haven't been. Should I?"

Doc reassured her with a tiny shake of his head.

"People do it differently. I'm the same as you, shuffle 'til the shuffling's done, then stop. You feel when it's right."

She smiled, pleased she'd given an agreeable answer, and shuffled the cards four or five times more. She didn't close her eyes the way Doc did, but she seemed oblivious to everything in the room.

As she was about to lay the first card, Doc interrupted again, "Tiny point." Jan stopped, the deck ready in her hand. "I think it's worth using a cloth of some kind, like my square of linen. When you read, you lay the cards on it. When the cards are resting, you wrap them in it."

His tone was apologetic but the way he held himself conveyed an air of serious business.

Jan had on her nervous-excited look.

"Does it have to be linen?"

"No. You can use anything, as long as it's opaque. Opaque cloth acts as a barrier." He may have thought he was laying it on a bit thick because he cracked a believable smile. "It also helps keep the cards clean. Something personal is always a good idea."

At these last words Jan gave a little jump. "I've got one of Chris's bandannas upstairs."

"Perfect, do you know where it is?" Doc held out a hand, a silent offer to hold the cards while she went to look.

"I know where it is. I won't be a second."

She gave him the pack to hold and went to fetch the bandanna. Doc listened, head cocked, as she climbed the stairs. He dug into his jeans and pulled out another pack of tarot cards. He gently took the newcomers out of their box and switched them for Jan's. With Jan's original cards hidden in his pocket, Doc cast a guilty glance at the door. He turned to me, like I could grant absolution, and mouthed, *sorry*.

It was all bullshit but I still didn't like it.

"That is bad fucking juju, Doc."

He looked sheepish. That gave me a degree of satisfaction.

The art nouveau tarot cards Jan used went in for streaming hair and flowing robes in a big way. Chris's old Motörhead bandanna set them off a treat.

I stood watching her set out the familiar cross pattern. It was apparent what Doc had done. The order of cards had been prearranged and each move turned up a member of the cast. The Fool, The Hanged Man, The Ruined Tower, The Five of Pentangles, they all duly appeared. Along with Death and The Lovers, of course.

Jan wasn't scared but her strange nervous-excited look was painful to see. If there looked to be any risk of her getting sanguine, Doc would ramp up the tension with a soft hiss or a murmur of concern. For the first time since I'd known her, she looked genuinely happy; delighted with the sudden power she'd found. I went to check on dad, not wanting to test my temper by staying in the kitchen.

I stayed in the front room and watched an episode of something about the fire service. Thirty minutes felt like enough time for Doc's preordained divination to take place. When the credits rolled I got off the sofa and asked dad if he wanted another cup of tea. *Only if Jan made it.*

Back in the kitchen, Doc was presiding over a religious experience. The cards had been stacked in a neat pile and laid in the middle of Chris's bandanna. Jan looked shell shocked and was breathing like an obscene phone caller. Tea making was probably beyond her at that point, so I set the kettle to boil.

"Does that mean Jeffry's going to be in touch again?" Jan asked.

She was talking to Doc, of course. I was behind her and I don't think she'd noticed I was in the room.

Doc deliberated before answering, finally said, "Tarot cards very rarely deal with absolutes." Depends who does the dealing, I thought. Doc glanced up as if he'd read my mind. "But, I think we can take the Ten of Pentangles as a reference to Jeffry or Peter."

Jan must have understood this. She nodded the way you do when you've been told something you already know.

"Maybe it could refer to both of them."

Doc looked surprised then thoughtful, as if this hadn't occurred to him. If he was faking the reaction then he had a promising career on the stage. Pleased with this response, Jan carried on.

"If the Ten of Pentangles is appearing to show the culmination of events it could be saying my connection with the Keller family is over and done. That would tie in with Death appearing."

The tarot card Death, Doc had once told me, did not necessarily mean a life ending. It referred to change or transition. It could also mean a beginning or an ending.

Given that an image as definite as death could suggest two polar opposites, I questioned the purpose of shuffling the bloody things.

"Is that how you're reading it?" Doc asked.

He came over as a wiser hand gently pointing the truer path. Jan faltered a bit but didn't give up her ground easily.

"I think so, yes." She pursued her lips and, reverently, placed her hands on the tarot deck. "If the Ten of Pentangles is a reference to money and control, then it could be either Jeffry or Pete but both of them are in my past. If Death means an end it could be expressing breaking away entirely. If it means a fresh beginning, it could mean a new life with Chris."

Doc, in an unusual move, didn't leave a silence for Jan to fall into. I could tell he was back peddling. In retrospect, it was almost funny seeing Doc outsmart himself. At the time I wasn't amused. The stakes were high in the game he was playing, and I was struggling with seeing Jan manipulated.

"The cards aren't there to maintain the status quo. Once you lay out the cards, you stop being passive." Doc leaned in closer. "You don't twist the symbols 'til they tell you what you want to hear. Did you see anything in the spread that pointed to a choice?" His intonation made it sound like a question but he was telling her, no, she hadn't. "You're talking about choosing the Big Guy over the likes of the Kellers. In short, do nothing, let the Kellers fade away and wait for Chris. I didn't see that from the cards that appeared. The Hanged Man was there with the Ten of Pentangles. The Fool was there too, he's still part of this story. Death means change, maybe an end or a beginning. But change, not stagnation."

Doc sat back in his chair again and regarded Jan expectantly.

She hesitated, then said, "You think something is going to happen? Something involving Jeffry?"

"There's no point doing a reading just to sit and wait. Reading a spread to then just watch events unfold around you isn't tarot, it's voyeurism." Jan still looked like she was out of the loop. Doc smiled kindly, although my tattoo work on his cheek turned it into a manic leer. "You've consulted the cards. Whatever they have to give, they have given. Now you need to make use of what you've seen. Now we have to act." He sat back with an open-hands gesture, as if he was passing something over to her. "It's time to wrap the cards up and let them rest."

Especially since she'd shuffle them if she did another reading, and undo all Doc's work. The acolyte dutifully wrapped the bandanna around the switched deck and pushed them to one side. She unconsciously mirrored Doc's over-to-you gesture.

"But I don't know what I should do."

That was okay, Doc had a few ideas.

House Call

The upshot was Jan and I would go round to her old home. Not unreasonably, she'd asked why. Doc had rapped the table where she'd done the tarot reading.

"Peter, your in-laws, Chris. They all have connections with that house. It's also where a lot of big changes took place." He avoided looking at me and added. "It seems logical."

Jan swallowed this line of bullshit, I swallowed something else entirely.

"What do I do once I'm there?" Jan said.

"Just play it by ear." He paused for a fraction then added, "You'll have Yakky with you."

Jan didn't reply to that but she did turn and give me a weak smile, all doe eyes and gratitude, and she did ask why Doc wouldn't be joining us. He was uncomfortable with the question but told her about blackmailing Caroline. The account he gave her was brief.

"I've burned my bridges there. If I show up, she'll have kittens. I'm hoping if you turn up with Yakky, she'll keep things civil."

I was hoping the same. If Jeffry Keller was there to see his wife opening the door and having a meltdown, I'd rather not co-star in the scene. Friends on the force worried me a damn sight more than card tricks.

Jan digested our impeding sojourn while I made dad a tea. I nudged her back to the present and asked her if she'd take it to him.

"If he thinks you made it, he'll drink it."

She took the mug form me and went to deliver it. Doc followed her with his eyes. She disappeared into the noise of dad's TV and Doc turned to me shaking his head in admiration.

"Wow."

"Letching's not usually your style," I said.

He pulled a wounded expression.

"Didn't you notice the way she moved? Between here and the next room, she changed the way she walks. It's like she became someone else between here and the end of the hall."

"I thought you were just looking at her arse." In fairness, she did fill her jeans nicely. "Messed up though isn't it, having to change like that?"

Doc considered the point for a moment, then said, "Humans survive. That's just the way she does it." I didn't say anything, and he studied my face for a couple of seconds. "I know that sounds cold but I don't mean it that way. What she's doing is amazing, it's ... wonderful."

"Wonderful? It like she's been wiped away. She only exists when someone's there to write her a script."

We both cast a look to the front room. Jan had yet to escape dad's orbit.

"Think about it Yakky, trying to learn that skill, the sheer energy involved, the sacrifice. Think how high the stakes must have been if putting herself through that was the best option."

"So how is that wonderful?"

"Because it worked; she's still standing. Whatever she's been through, and I think she been through more than we can imagine, she's survived it. The fact she's made it through is wonderful."

I didn't say anything to that either and we let it go. It was funny how we'd swapped positions about Jan. When the shit had first hit the fan, Doc had been far more concerned about her than I had. Now he was talking about her in the abstract, as if her past turned her from an individual into a case study. Meanwhile, I couldn't disengage from her.

Doc didn't sit at the table again; he drank his tea standing next to me. We were both keeping an eye on the hallway, watching for Jan. He asked me again about her tuning out.

"She didn't last night, hasn't today."

I told him about the night before – Jan grabbing me around the waist and crying with her eyes closed. Something about it bothered me, that and the coffee she'd bought but didn't drink.

"Like I said, I think she's got you pegged, she's got a role she can fit to you." I made the spooling motion. "People don't cry with their eyes open. When I read that in your transcript it really sent up a flare. Crying with your eyes open takes effort, and I'd say it's not a knack you'd develop without a lot of practice."

Doc, who probably spent half his life waiting for people to catch up, allowed me some thinking time while he finished his tea. Why would you cry with your eyes open? Same reason you'd make yourself look at the face in the wardrobe doors. So you'd know what was happening. Ever watchful, keeping those eyes open, keeping that guard up.

"Speak to me, Yak."

"So why'd she start closing her eyes?"

Doc laughed softly and I heard something click in my neck when I snapped round to look at him.

"Calm down man, I'm not laughing about this. It's just funny that you don't get it."

"Don't get what?"

The calming down bit wasn't going well. It didn't help that Doc laughed again.

"The moment someone gets snotty about tattoos or bikers you're up on your high horse so quick you get vertigo. Then you can't see past your own sour puss. She's got you pegged for Sir Galahad, her knight in shining armour. She can shut her eyes and cry when you're there because she knows you'll do your best to keep her safe."

"Oh, do fuck off."

Doc looked like he was about to laugh again but held it in.

"Okay, if you won't take credit for being one of the good guys, look at like this. You spend about twenty seconds of your life talking to her. Then, when everything goes tits up, you give her a place to stay. You open your home, you feed her. You even sort out the guy following her."

"I don't remember her being too thrilled about it at the time." If I remembered correctly, she'd high tailed it round to Chris. Looked at me like I was liable to explode. "And that was nothing to do with her, that was about Karla."

I thought Doc was going to ask if I was sure it was about that. He just shrugged.

"Don't matter. Chris told her he'd have done the same, so it gets the golden seal of approval. And it's about Karla, so what? You're still charging in to the aid of a fair maiden."

I didn't know if I believed it or not but I knew I didn't want to be anyone's hero. All my heroes were bastards.

"You're one of the good guys Yakky, live with it."

"You've got me pegged too?"

"Christ, no." I caught the glare of Doc's grin in the corner of my eye. "I'm just telling you how Jan models her role to fit you. That helps it along too."

He nodded towards the hallway and the thunder of the TV.

"Dad?"

"Yeah. No offense, but if you can live with him without recourse to violence or a straightjacket, you must have one hell of a sense of duty."

My pokerfaced lack of signals gave Jan little to work with. What she had amounted to: looks after people and likes coffee. The coffee addiction hadn't helped her, which was probably why I didn't have to share my supplies anymore. But looking after people I cared about was a different matter. Doc was warming to the subject but Jan re-emerged from the front room.

There endth the first lesson.

"Don't go right now." Doc was sitting at the table again. As Jan had come out of the front room, he seemed to have appeared there, without covering the ground in between. The secret service stuff was grating on me. "If Jeffry and Caroline are there, let them have a nice relaxed morning, it'll make things easier if you don't ruin their breakfast."

I knew he was stalling. He hadn't gone to the trouble of the hi-jacking Jan's tarot reading without some motive. Just playing it by ear wasn't on the cards. He took his phone out to check the time. Pretended to think.

"Give it 'til around two, yeah? Meantime, if you don't mind Yak, I need some help on a mechanical matter."

Which I took to be our cue to leave. I nearly asked Jan if she wanted to come along for the ride, just to watch Doc try and talk her out of it.

I only reason I didn't was that I knew he'd have a line of Jive ready prepared.

We rode past the shop and into the alley beside it. Doc parked the Sportster in his yard, out of sight of the road. He didn't lock it up in its steel shed, but he did put a chain around its front wheel and fork. He looked surprised that I'd ridden into the yard with him.

"Can I scrounge some oil?" I asked. The Yam, my boots and anywhere I parked were an oil slick. If it wasn't leaking the stuff it was burning it.

"In the shed," he told me, "help yourself."

He threw me a ring of keys. The shed wasn't huge. It was there to store his bike and tools and the limited space was doled out with military precession. The oil he had was the petrochemical equivalent of Casa Noble. Fully synthetic, the seriously good stuff. Doc was looking over the Yam when I came out the shed.

"When you'd last give this thing a full oil change?"

"Just before my voice broke."

Doc went into the shed and came out again with a drain

pan and a socket set, told me to do it right.

Black sludge oozed from the sump like an infection. Oil from a good engine smells a bit like toast, from a bad engine it smells of burnt carbon. Take a guess.

"What's the plan?" I sat back on my haunches and waited for the last of the ruined oil to seep out. I didn't get an answer and looked over my shoulder at Doc. He was sitting side ways on the Sportster watching me work. "Come on, you got something on your mind."

"I do but a lot of it's down to you and I don't think you're going to like it."

I checked the tension of my drive chain and began sorting through the sockets. They were cleaner than most people's cutlery. Using them on my rig felt like a crime.

"Go on."

"I want you to get Jan talking again. About the night Peter died, about the night with Chris."

I didn't like it. I could also see a flaw in it.

"You said Jan's got me pegged, now she's got a role she can play to me."

"Yeah, but that's not the problem, she's got you down as Knight Errant, intent on keeping Helpless Maidens free from dragons. I think she'll off-load her woes on you in a shot."

"The problem is, what then?"

"I think whatever she says is going to colour that way. Tilted, so you can see her as a victim."

"What's the point of me talking to her then? If what you're thinking's right she'll sell me a sob story to get me on side."

Doc clicked his tongue. I turned my attention back to my chain and made a few minuscule adjustments that wouldn't make a scrap of different to the bike, but made me feel better.

"If she's on the level, I mean *if* she's innocent, I think she'll tell you the truth," Doc said. "But, it'll be the truth coloured by the lens of the role she's in. I'm saying be aware.

Harden yourself to it."

"If she's going to tell the truth why don't you talk to her. Surely the Voodoo acolyte's going to confess all to the High Doctor."

He didn't respond. At first I thought he was pissed off, taking offence at the slight on his beliefs. But after a while he gave me an unconvincing smile.

"I don't think she trusts me and she'll hold out on telling me anything at all. She trusts you and frankly that's a weakness."

I wiped my hands down the thighs of my jeans. Then poured three litres of finest oil into the fiery pits of my engine. Doc had told me – on more than one occasion – that Voodoo was the religion of survival. And Jan was a survivor. Voodoo-Acolyte-Jan had found a way to make survival her religion. She was going to be even more guarded and watchful, than my Jan.

If Voodoo-Jan knew Doc had switched the tarot pack on her, she'd have understood, probably even approved. But she wouldn't open up.

I offered what was left of his oil back to Doc but he waved it away. I wasn't about to refuse. Dirt and charity were currently the only things holding the bike together.

"Tea?"

I accepted that too and scrubbed at my hands while Doc brewed up. I hadn't learned his trick of carrying latex gloves around.

By the time I'd finished with the sink Doc was sitting in one of the armchairs sorting through a pack of tarot cards. It was the set he'd sleight-of-handed away from Jan. He was examining each card, front and back, before transferring it to a pile on the floor. He glanced up as I came into the room.

"Tea's there."

He nodded to the other armchair and the mug sitting beside it. When it was obvious he wasn't going to explain I asked what he was doing. He put a card on the floor, stared intently at the next one.

"I just want to be sure Jan didn't mark this deck so she could ID it."

Voodoo might have been the religion of survival, but Doc was a High Priest at The Church of the Eternally Paranoid.

"Is that why you always use that beaten up old pack of yours, you think someone might switch them?"

He shook his head, transferred another card to the pile.

"That's mainly a comfort thing, like an old leather, something that's worn to your shape. The security check's just a useful extra."

We didn't speak again until he was happy the deck was clean.

"How long had you been planning that switch you pulled on Jan?"

"I set it up after we spoke on the phone this morning."

"And you just happened to have another pack of those cards lying around?"

"When Jan took that pack, I ordered a replacement set on-line. They arrived a couple of days ago."

I debated whether to believe him. Doc didn't accumulate clutter as a rule but he did own a lot of Tarot cards, perhaps he'd genuinely wanted to fill the gap in his collection. Or he'd simply stockpiled tools on the off chance he'd spot a way to exploit Jan's interest. I shook off the musings. It was all bullshit anyway.

"What do you want us to at the house?" I asked and wondered when Jan and I had become *us*.

"Have a good look around that bathroom and bedroom set-up. We can plead Chris's case all we want, but if we can't show how Peter wound up dead, then the Big Guy's going down."

Which might mean putting Jan in his place. I remembered my jibe to Doc, about playing Miss Marple not being as much fun as he'd thought. I asked him what I was meant to be looking for and he let me have one of his less reassuring grins.

"Not a clue. One thing though, see if there's any post

there for Jan, something official. I can't believe no one's had anything to tell her in the last fortnight."

I agreed to what he was asking, and with the sentiment. I was still puzzled as to why the police hadn't demanded to see her, if not flat out arrested her.

"You really think the Kellers are living there?"

"I doubt they'll be living there, but I wouldn't be surprised if they've staked a bit of a claim."

I held my hand out and made the international sign for gimme. Without a word, Doc pointed at the altar. The keys were in front of a pair of offering bowls, and I gave them a quick check before slipping them into my pocket. Other than a trio of ugly metal charms, and some ash, they didn't seem to have been anointed with anything nasty. My scrutiny wasn't lost on Doc, who had the audacity to look exasperated. Well tough. If you make a life study out of being weird, you're going to get funny looks.

"They might have changed the alarm code," Doc said.

"What I am I meant to do if the alarm does go off?"

"Sit and wait for the police." I waited for the rest. There was no rest and I asked if I was missing some subtle nuance of the plan. "Jan's had no official notification that she's not allowed on the property. If the police arrive, she just tells them she's there to see if she had any mail. If the Kellers rock up, same story." Click, click went his tongue. "If you get her talking, do you think you could use the recorder again?"

"No way to set it up."

I'd tried recording with the Dictaphone in my pocket – all I'd got was a recording of my pocket. And, I didn't want to. There was a limit to how much cloak and dagger I could stomach.

"Shame," Doc said. When I didn't reply he dropped back into his armchair and stared at me for a while. "Something on your mind?"

What was on my mind was the long, drawn-out confessional we'd had that night in the lay-by.

"You forgotten how lousy you felt after blackmailing Caroline?"

"No. Not at all." He regarded Ezulie Dantor stampeding across the wall behind me. "You think I'm about to do the same trick with Jan?"

"I'm not happy about you switching Jan's tarot cards. If I'd done that it'd just be a dirty trick. But you're messing with your beliefs, and hers. Doesn't that bother you?"

He pulled a face, the way you do when you want people to know you're about to say something you'd sooner not. I wasn't surprised when he got up again and walked behind me to Ezulie Dantor. Someone else might have lit a cigarette, or kissed a rosary. Or for that matter rubbed a mojo. I twisted round in my seat and watched him stare at the ugly artwork he'd put on the plaster. A few owners down the line, and some poor sod, cheerfully stripping wallpaper, was going to find these walls. Maybe he'd love it. It takes all sorts.

"There is no hell in the Voodoo tradition." He caressed the picture on the wall and I felt like a peeping tom for being there. I wished I hadn't brought the subject up. "I made a bad choice with Caroline, Yakky. We needed that police report and I thought it was more honest to lever it out of her than to charm it out of her. I was wrong. Jan's more complex, and yes, I'm playing it dirty again but if I get Chris out of this and they live happily ever after, I think she'll forgive me."

I didn't know if he was talking about Jan forgiving him or Ezulie Dantor granting absolution.

"And if getting Chris *out* involves putting Jan *in*?"

Doc turned and laughed. "I'll still sleep the sleep of the just, only I'll keep that shotgun under my pillow in case Chris doesn't forgive me."

He left the picture and moved instead to the crime wall. He leaned his back against it. He looked tired.

"Yak, I know you're not happy with a lot of the stuff that's been going on. If you want to bail out, I understand. Only thing I'd ask is let Jan stay with you, she – "

"I'm not quitting. I'm in this 'til the end."

So far, I'd lost my self-control, a week's worth of sleep and probably my girlfriend. If we didn't get Chris out of the clink, all that would have been for nothing. And I'd just be a lonely, knife toting thug with bags under his eyes.

And surrendering Jan to the grinning gears of the Doc machine wasn't an option.

Doc nodded and peeled himself from the wall so he could actually read it, or absorb it, or whatever he did to make it work.

"What if I can't get Jan talking?" I asked after I'd spent five minutes in silence looking at his back.

Without turning he said, "I'm pretty sure she'll talk. It's going to be emotional for her, going back there again. More so now the Big Guy's been nicked. And you'll be there."

"The knight in shining armour."

Of all the things I wasn't happy about, that was fairly high up the list.

"Exactly. A nice strong shoulder to bear the weight of all her fears." He considered this for a second. "I'm wasted as a tattooist you know, I should have been a poet."

"Okay, so once she's traumatised and sobbing her guts out, is there anything in particular you want me to find out?"

I was brutal on purpose. I wanted Doc to keep his eye on the cost to Jan, and to me for that matter. His flip comments might have been nothing more than gallows humour but they still rankled. He stopped scrutinising the wall and turned to me again, held his hands up in apology.

"The three things that really bother me. One, why did Jan pick Chris. If I'm any judge, she'll lay the mooey on a foot deep with that one, so take a shovel and dig. Alright?"

"Yeah, I get you. This ain't Mills and Boon so don't let her convince me it is."

"Exactly. Second ... "

He tapped the massive drawing of the knife. I got that too – what was with knife play? The third item on the list was the emails. I still didn't get why that was bugging him. He asked me if Jan used my laptop at all.

"Don't know. She's got the run of the place pretty much and I don't use a password."

Doc nodded, this was the answer he'd been expecting.

"Someone who spends every night for two months shagging somebody's brains out then starts sending them emails the moment they're out of sight would be wearing your keyboard away every waking moment. And you don't even know if she's used it. Anyone so besotted with emailing wouldn't move into your spare room without a computer, and the first thing they'd do is ask you about broadband and Wi-Fi access."

"Not necessarily, you can send emails from a phone."

"Not hers. It's a crappy little pay as go. I remember her telling us she didn't have any credit left on it. And she normally *talks* on the phone; she doesn't often *text*. It doesn't gel with all the emails."

I had yet another tea for the road and headed back to the house. Doc came down to the yard to let me out. I gave the mojo a rub and hit the starter. The Yam didn't spring into life but it grumbled its way to tick over without too much grief.

"Thanks, again, for the oil," I shouted through my full face. Doc gave me the thumbs-up. I was about to pull away when he put a hand on the bike's headlight.

"One more thing," he shouted at the side of my helmet, "See if you can find why they used the spare room instead of the master bedroom the night Peter died."

The drive to the Keller house took a lot longer than when Doc and I had made the journey by bike. That suited me; I had no real desire to arrive. If I'd been on a bike, I'd have taken one of my torturous routes to really delay things. Jan didn't talk a great deal and I left her to her thoughts. I didn't doubt they were all pretty grim. As we entered the private estate and the quality of the road began to worsen, Jan piped up.

"What do we do if Jeffry and Caroline aren't there? I don't have keys anymore."

"I've got a set. Doc had copies cut before he handed them over."

"Oh."

She didn't add *of course*, but I suspect she was thinking it. You didn't spend too long around Doc before realising that was the kind of thing he did.

"Yes," I said. "Resourceful chap isn't he?"

As we drew up at the gate Jan asked, "What if the alarm code's been changed?"

I repeated Doc's thoughts on that. I doubted the alarm code would have been changed. People avoided resetting passwords and codes, most people could barely set the controls on their central heating. I thought I'd been proved wrong when the gate didn't open, then I saw the structure was shuddering as the motor tried. I got out of the car and put my weight against the gate to help it along. Jan rolled through and we left the gate sitting open.

The grounds were looking neglected. Any gardener Peter Keller had employed must have been working cash in hand and moved on when the readies stopped. The blasting summer had scolded the lawn to yellowish brown and the flower beds were dying.

I pulled the keys out and was about to open the door when it occurred to me that Jan had more right than I did. She took the keys when I offered them and smiled when she saw the three metal charms. I think it was more about delaying her entry to the house than any delight with Doc's choice of key fobs.

She held them out for me to see.

"These are veve, they're – "

"Symbols of Voodoo spirits, I know."

I hoped that would end the conversation. I was no more eager to get inside than she was, but I got enough of Doc's nonsense from source.

"Papa Legba." Jan laughed as she fingered one of the

charms and I asked what the joke was.

Apparently, Papa Legba was in charge of the gate between this world and the spirit world. If you wanted to deal with any lwa, you had to go to him first so he'd open the gate. Jan said all this quite matter-of-factly as she inserted the key and added she'd have to start calling me Papa.

She was still speaking as she opened the door, looking over her shoulder and not where she was heading. So I saw what was waiting in the hallway before she did. When she did turn, she made a noise like someone jumping into cold water.

The big photo portrait of Jan and Peter had been pulled from the wall and leaned against the newel post at the bottom of the stairs. Peter still stood in the foreground gazing into middle distance, unaware that behind him his trophy wife had been slashed to ribbons.

I stepped around so I was leading and we padded softly into the hall, listening for any kind of sound. In hindsight, it wasn't very likely that the photo slasher would hang around waiting for someone to attack. At the time it felt entirely possible.

The other photo portraits of Jan were laid out on the floor around the main picture. A few of them had been destroyed, slashed into tatters of canvas, even the wooden formers broken. The rest had been given more consideration. In these the face had been cut through three or four times, but in only one direction so the picture could still be recognised. The only images of Jan that had escaped the edge of a blade were four informal prints in glass-fronted frames. These where on the floor – their glass shattered. It looked to me as if they'd been carefully set down and then stamped on.

We stood and listened, each of us barely breathing. Once it became apparent that we were the only ones there, we stepped nearer. I don't know why. I can't imagine Jan wanted a closer look; I know I didn't. Jan reached out to touch, or maybe pick up one of the pictures.

I put my hand on her shoulder.

"No, don't." She looked confused and I realised I spoken too softly to be heard. "Don't touch anything." The sound of my voice seemed overly loud and the slight echo, provided by the hallway, got me rattled. "Come with me."

I led us to the kitchen and the block of expensive knives. If I was going to be paranoid, I wanted to be armed and paranoid. I grabbed the first handle in the block, a serrated edge bread knife. I put it back and went for the next. A heavy-duty cook's knife, about nine inches long. Better.

We went from room to room. Opening doors like they were booby trapped, creeping up on furniture. After the first three rooms, the adrenaline levels dropped enough so that we could think straight, and we both got embarrassed and started to giggle. I went and put the knife back, used a sheet of kitchen roll to wipe my fingerprints from the handles I'd touched.

Jan announced she needed a drink and took us to the big reception room with the drinks cabinet. She must have noticed Doc's pilfering because she gave me a knowing look and told me there was no Tequila. When she found some bourbon, she took an impressive hit straight from the bottle, then did that shuddery thing people do. I had a flashback to Karla sitting next to me in bed knocking back vodka and coke. Maybe it was the adrenaline turning sour in my veins, but I suddenly felt sad and tired. I took a seat on one of the huge sofas and pulled out my mobile.

"You calling the police?" Jan asked.

She was still on her feet, looking around the room at the spaces where her pictures had been. I shook my head.

"Doc."

He picked up almost at once.

"Hello, Yakky."

"I think you ought to come over here." I told him about the house's new art installation. He didn't say anything for a while. "You still there, man?"

"Yeah, it just, this line's not great." His voice was coming to me loud and clear. He added, deliberately, "Maybe if you moved to another room?"

Jan was huddled on the end of the sofa with her feet drawn up, her arms clasped around her knees. I motioned her to stay there when I got up.

"Bad reception. I'll try outside. Won't be long."

I leaned against Peter's 4x4 with an eye on the front door.

"Okay, I'm on my own now."

"Good. How's Jan?"

"Shaken up, we both are. You coming over here, or what?"

"Yeah, but I'm going to hold fire for a bit. I still want you to talk with Jan," he added carefully. "You ain't going to like this Yakky, but now's a good time to do it. Take her upstairs, look around the spare room and the bathroom. Give her the big manly shoulder to cry on and listen to what she tells you. Remember: why did she pick Chris – "

"Yeah, yeah, I know. Why Chris, why the knife, why the emails?" I took a deep breath, I didn't like it, but I could see the truth of what he was saying. Distressed-Maiden-Jan was ripe for picking. "Just tell me something Doc, did you ride over here last night and set this up?"

"Yakky, I swear, I've got nothing to do with what's happening over there."

I finally decided I believed him. When I apologised for suggesting the idea, the mobile distorted his laugh into a cackle of static.

"Don't apologise. I would have done it if I'd thought of it. Careful where you put your fingerprints, okay?"

I noticed the keys were still hanging in the front door when I went back inside. Jan had left them there when she first let us in, too occupied with the tableau in the hallway to notice. I avoided looking at it as I walked past. It was more disturbing than anything Doc had ever put in his home.

Jan was still on the sofa but she'd uncurled herself at

some point and found a glass. She was sipping bourbon now rather than gulping. She looked rough. I felt bad for her but I found myself looking for faults in her performance, hated myself for it.

I knew Jan and the Big Guy had spent evenings on that sofa together but, even in the tight denim and the cleavage flashing tee shirt, I couldn't picture anything sexual about her now. I handed her the keys and she took them and fumbled through the charms until she found a particular one, sat rubbing it and sipping bourbon.

"Doc's tied up with something. He said to carry on without him. Careful about leaving prints."

She asked me what we should do, and what we did was go with Doc's plan. Not that I told her that.

I parked just across the road from the front door and saw dad's curtain twitch. It was surprisingly early. Still, if he put his mind to it, dad could probably fit a two-act drama in before dinner.

Jan had been crying when we left her old home. She'd stopped now but the floor of the Audi was littered with damp tissues. Because of the state she was in, and the dent she'd put in the bourbon, I'd driven back. It was the first time I'd been behind the wheel of a car since I failed my driving test. It hadn't seemed the time to point this out.

"You alright?" It must have been the tenth time I'd asked her. It was a stupid question the first time.

"I'll be fine," she said, more to herself than to me.

We sat in the car for a few minutes not saying anything. I was caught between not wanting to leave her alone and wanting to run away. Either way, I really didn't want to land her with dad. My options were limited: outside of professional contacts and clients my social world ceased to exist when Karla moved out. Doc's circle was likely bigger, but undoubtedly stranger with it.

"You know I'm going to have to tell Doc?" I said, Jan nodded and didn't say anything. She was staring at the roof lining of the car. "Would you rather tell him yourself? Do you want us to do it together?"

"God no. I don't ... I ... didn't want Chris to know."

I nodded, though she wasn't looking at me and wouldn't see.

I promised her Chris wouldn't hear about it from me. Which was no comfort. I was about to ask if she was alright again but stopped myself.

I left Jan alone in the house with dad but took her upstairs before he could commandeer her. In a fairly empty gesture I saved her the hassle of preparing a meal for him. Three sandwiches to ignore bound to a plate with cling-film.

I met her coming down the stairs as I was about to go up. She'd spent some time in the bathroom and looked better. I saw she'd also changed clothes, gone back into nurse mode. I asked her if she was alright yet again.

"I've been better. I've been worse too, I'll survive."

I put a hand awkwardly on her shoulder. Jan was less contact averse, and I found myself in a hug. In a strange way I wished Karla was there to be hacked off. Dad sensed someone was pulling focus from him and he let out a heart rending,

"Oh. Oh, oh!"

Bless him.

Jan unwrapped herself from me and mouthed, *I'll see to him.*

The Yam was leaking oil like a night sweat. Maybe it was an allergic reaction to Doc's high-grade lubricant. Before I rode to the shop, I gave the mojo an extra rub.

Gina's Jap hack was chained to the lamppost outside the shop. I chained my Yam alongside it and hoped they'd get on. Doc's front door was still open.

"Still no word from him?" I heard Gina ask as I hung my leather in the hall. When I looked into the front room, Doc was explaining the wall to her. It looked like he'd been working his way along the timeline. His finger was hovering over the Big Guy getting nicked. Gina hadn't taken off her bike jacket and was balanced on the arm of a chair, making a point of not getting comfortable.

"Still no word from him," Doc said.

"What do you think's happening?"

There was no answer for a moment, then Doc said, "I think he's playing hardball with the police. He'll demand his phone call once he gets fed up annoying them. Then he'll ring."

I was puzzled as to why he'd had to pause for thought. It was practically a word for word repeat of what he'd told me in the curry house the night before. If he was giving Gina an edited account of what we were doing, and watching what he said, I wonder if he might be doing the same with me. Gina got up to leave and something passed between them.

"Don't you want to hear what Yakky thinks?" Doc asked her.

"Just let me know. ASAP okay? See you."

Gina surpassed previous levels of cordiality by nodding at me as we passed.

The look on Doc's face as he watched her leave made me feel bad for intruding. We listened to the steel stairs ringing as she made her way down to the yard. I didn't say anything until I heard the gate to the alley shut behind her. Doc wasn't gazing starry-eyed at her wake, but she was on his mind.

"Sorry, man, were you two sharing a moment?"

Doc's grin had a touch of the rictus about it when he answered.

"Nah, brother, nothing like that." He sighed. "She's ready to quit the ink altogether. You ready to step up?"

The question caught me on the hop. "Step up?"

Doc pointed me to the kitchen and, more importantly, the kettle.

"Do the honours, eh?" He sat at the table and began unwrapping the tarot cards. I hadn't seen him collect them. He shuffled them straight, no fancy riffles or one-handed cuts, "You're good enough to work your own list. If you want, we start on it tomorrow, see how it goes for a couple of weeks and work out a schedule so Gina can move on."

It was the opportunity I wanted, of course. That was the point of being an apprentice.

Looking at Doc took the gloss off the offer.

"Yeah, we'll have to work the details, but I want it. It ain't looking like you do."

He looked over to where I was, at the sink filling the kettle.

"You're loaded with talent and you pick up the technical stuff quicker than anyone I've ever seen. Plus, you know how to keep things clean, and believe me that's almost a super-power. From now on, it's all about practice. Doing it hour after hour, day after day." He started laying the cards. "I want you to work with me, Yak. You'll do good work and get a good rep. And that'll be good for the business."

"But?"

He turned cards, laid out a cross, turned more cards.

"But, Gina's been looking for a chance to cut from the shop for a while. Having someone who can help bump up the profits allows her to do it."

The business gained a fulltime tattooist but Doc lost his last sliver of contact with Gina. Bittersweet.

I made the tea and thought about the offer while Doc frowned at the cards. He drank his tea still staring balefully at the spread. He hadn't moved any of them or turned over new ones. I assumed he'd finished doing whatever it was he did with them.

"Not what you'd hoped for?" I asked, when my nerves began to fray in the silence.

Doc shrugged. "Jan started talking?"

"She was being a bit cagey then we found this and the floodgates pretty much opened." I fished my phone out and opened the photo album, dropped it on the table next to the tarot cards. "Take a look. Took them in the master bedroom."

Doc scrolled through seven images. The first six pictures were the interior of the wardrobe. Jan's clothes, the stuff left behind on the night Jeffry laid his claim to the house, were still hanging in it. Like the photo portraits they'd been slashed to ribbons. The last image was of the mirror in the en suite. The word SLAG had been written on it in lipstick.

Doc handed the mobile back to me. "Story time, Yakky. I'm all ears."

I don't know the psycho-babble he'd have dressed it in, but Doc's plan amounted to scaring Jan until she was clinging onto me like a lifebelt. Then start asking questions while all she wanted to do was keep me close. I didn't like the idea, but I could see the reasoning behind it.

That said I didn't ask Jan to start with the bedrooms. It was about a fifty-fifty mix of compassion and caution. Doc, for all his expertise, wasn't there in the house with the mutilated pictures. If he had been, he might have shared my fears of pushing Jan into hysterics. I suggested we take a look around the garden. Fresh air seemed like a good idea.

We had to go out through the hallway again. The ground floor had plenty of doors, all of them locked. Doc's keys, copied from Jan's, only opened the front door. I kept an eye on Jan as we passed the heap of pictures. She didn't linger over the display, but didn't shy away from it either. For me the impact of that first viewing hadn't diminished. Now I was over the first gasp of shock, the details of what had been done began to worry at me. The desecration of Jan's image hadn't been a flash of violence; someone had executed it with heartfelt devotion.

I looked around the 'grounds' with Jan. The fence separating Keller's property from the golf course was hidden with a zigzag of shrubbery. Your garden party need never know your lawn stopped barely short of their gullibility.

None of the landscaping had ever been about pleasure. This had always been working soil, tilled to grow admiration. The boundary was clearer now the grass had died: Keller's money ended were the lush greens started.

A short trek around the corner from the pilfered view took us to a thin strip of turf and a plastic shed. This was the last bit of Keller territory before you were into the neighbour's garden. The properties were separated by a chain-link fence that had been allowed to over grow with some climbing plant. It shielded either party from seeing the other but I could hear children playing on the other side.

The plastic shed wasn't locked so I took a look inside. There was a petrol mower and some gardening forks. In one corner there was a plastic crate with a collection of mud-crusted hand tools in it and a pair of work gloves on top. I pulled one of the gloves on and picked through the tools, thinking again of Karla's remark about playing cops and robbers.

Kicking around the bottom of the crate was a Stanley knife missing its blade. I put the crate back in the corner where it'd been, then saw that I'd left a trial in the dirt on the shed floor. I wiped the prints away with my gloved hand. You could still see the floor had been disturbed but it wasn't advertising my shoe size anymore.

If my memory was correct from the night I'd been there with Doc, the bathroom where Peter Keller was found looked out over the front of the house. Before Jan and I made our way back inside, I looked for the en suite's window. It was the last one to the right, glazed with etched glass. To the left of it was yet another set of French windows. They should have led to a balcony, so you could sit with your morning coffee and gaze along the length of your driveway.

The driveway kinked almost as soon as it left the doorstep so its rapid termination at the gate needn't be witnessed. The suggested balcony wasn't there, only a cement ledge about six inches deep. Some wrought-iron work, reaching to waist height, stopped anyone from stepping out. Anyone who had would have taken a short but eventful trip down the sloping roof of the veranda that ran along the frontage.

"You okay if I take a picture?" I asked pulling my phone out. Jan looked bewildered and I realised she thought I was asking to take her photo. "Of the house."

She told me to go ahead and I snapped off a couple of shots of the windows and veranda.

"What do you want pictures for? Do you think someone got to Peter through the window?"

I directed us back towards the front door. "Well, suicide's not holding up."

Her reply was a reflex. "Chris didn't do it."

Back inside the hallway, I took some more pictures, at which point my mobile chirruped at me. I asked Jan if she had her charger on her.

"No. There might be one in Peter's study."

I almost strode off in that direction but decided to let Jan lead me to it. I wasn't sure if she knew I'd already been snooping around with Doc. I began mentally backtracking, trying to remember if I'd given the game away already.

It had been late evening when I'd been in the study before and it felt like the poor relation of the house then. Now in the mid-afternoon sunlight, it looked painfully shabby. We both looked around for a charger and Jan spotted a collection of cables nesting in a corner. I found one that matched my phone and spent some time tracing the lead to its plug.

Jan stood behind the office chair with her hands resting on its back. She wasn't comfortable in the room. She noticed I was looking at her and tried for a smile.

"Poor Peter."

I was already hyped up after finding the slashed photos, hearing her use Caroline's condescending name for her husband didn't help. Jan was staring at the framed poster of the yacht.

"Poor Peter?"

Jan nodded at the poster. "The first time I ever came to this house, he brought me in here and showed me that picture. It was his big dream: a fifty-metre super-yacht and a private mooring point in Saint-Tropez. He told me, 'that's where I'm going. When you get there, you've arrived'. He never talked about it again, but sometimes he'd sit here gazing at that picture. He never got there."

What she'd said should have sounded personal but didn't. When she talked about Chris there was a breadth of feeling that was almost desperate. She spoke about Peter Keller as if he was somebody she'd lost touch with years before. I double checked the screen on my phone to be sure the charging icon was flashing. On my way to the door, I glanced over the world map mounted next to the yacht. I'd wondered before why anybody would trouble to frame it; it was an ugly piece of work.

"Is that what the map's about, planning where to go in his yacht?"

"I don't know, maybe. He never talked about sailing. I think he just liked the idea of a yacht."

The room was thick with disappointment. Jan followed me out and I took us up the stairs. Mainly I was trying to get away from the hall.

"What did Chris make of this place?" I asked when we reached the landing.

It would have swallowed Chris's flat and his front yard. Jan laughed. "I don't think he liked it. He didn't say anything but then ... "

She looked embarrassed and I didn't press her to finish. Chris hadn't been there for conversation about the décor.

We drifted. I guessed Jan was playing it by ear, knowingly or otherwise following Doc's instruction. She gravitated to the spare room but drew short of going in.

"This is where it happened," she said, looking at the door, hand not quite on the handle.

I took my cue and gently moved her to one side so I

could go into the room first. The room was overly bright in the afternoon sun. The pale wash paint and cream fabrics looked more clinical then restful. The word morgue came to mind.

Jan was looking around the bedroom surprised at the state it was in. This would have been the first time she'd seen the room since she'd answered the door to the police. She clocked the prints on the mirrored wardrobe. I left her to her thoughts for a few moments.

It wasn't long before she said, "Can we go to another room?"

We drifted again and Jan gave me a mostly silent tour. The top floor had five bedrooms and a landing that boasted enough doors for twice that. The five spares hid an upstairs toilet and four cupboards. You didn't have to look too hard to see through the smoke and mirrors, but it gave an impression of grandeur that honesty would have lacked. The last room Jan took us to was the master bedroom.

She opened the door and went in ahead of me. The door was set close to the end of the hall; it hinged on its left and when it swung open, it shielded the view of the bedroom until you were through the doorway. I saw Jan step quickly backwards, away from something, and come up against the wall to my right. I was more on edge than I knew and when I pushed past, moving sideways, I missed my footing and fell over. Shaking, veins primed with aimless adrenaline, I was strangely disappointed that no one tried to kill me. Jan helped me to my feet and we both looked around the room. Without comment, she walked out.

The floor-to-ceiling wardrobe doors were all open. The trophy-wife outfits were slashed to tatters. Three or four long dresses had been ripped apart at the seams and thrown on the floor. I walked deeper into the room, taking a closer look at the carnage. I couldn't find an item of Jan's clothing that hadn't been wrecked but nothing else had been damaged.

I found the insult lipsticked across the bathroom mirror

when I went to gulp down some water. My breathing was too fast and my mouth had dried out. I sat on the edge of the bath, wondered if I should tell Jan about the mirror and decided against it. She'd have already worked out someone didn't like her. I didn't see any percentage in giving her more evidence.

I took another mouthful of water from the cold tap on the hand basin. I used my handkerchief to turn the tap on. It was hard to see a tap putting me in the bunk next to Chris's, but the house was full of paranoia.

The room hadn't been designed as the master bedroom. It had a view of the plastic shed and chain-link fence and it was smaller than the guest room where Jan and Chris spent their last night in the house. A generous spirit would have said Peter was making sure his guests had only the best.

Jan wasn't on the landing. When I called out her name, she answered from the guest room. She was standing in front of the mirror with the prints on it, staring at them.

"Do you think that's why the police arrested Chris?"

In daylight, the dusting of fingerprinting medium had a ghostly quality, as if the Big Guy was trying to reach us.

"I think there's a lot more to it than that," I said.

She moved closer to the mirror and pressed her hand to one of the marks Chris had left behind. It was a sentimental sort of gesture and I wanted to find it tacky and cheap.

"I shouldn't have brought him here," she said.

Part of me, the better part, wanted to leave her with her sadness. But the other part saw the chance to open the door. Or turn over the stone.

"Shouldn't have brought him to the spare room?"

Jan pulled away from the mirror and took herself over to the bed, sat on the edge of the bare mattress. She looked as desolate as anyone could and I braced myself for tears that didn't come. At that point I don't think she could have cried. Being numb was taking everything she had.

"I should never have brought him to this house."

It was horrible talking to her with Doc's agenda at the

back of my mind. With her seated and me towering above her, it began to feel like intimidation. I didn't want to sit beside her on the stripped bed, so I grabbed the straight-backed chair from the dressing table. It had been scaled down, presumably to make it feel feminine, and rather than fall off it, I straddled it backwards.

"You didn't know any of this was going to happen. It's not like you put a gun to his head."

"Didn't I?" She lifted her head and again looked at Chris's palm prints on the wardrobe. It might have been her helpless maiden look, but I felt embarrassed. I cursed Doc for not being there and myself for doing his dirty work. "Chris never wanted to come to this place. He only did because I asked him. He didn't know what was going on."

Her eyes hadn't left the palm prints.

"This isn't your fault. You've got to stop beating yourself up over it. Chris knew what was going on. He knew you were married." I paused, watching her throat work. Still, she didn't look away from the prints. "Look, I know about the website you were on, and Chris kept the emails you'd been sending him. He's good bloke but he's no saint. He knew the score."

Finally, Jan turned away from the mirrored door. The desolation had passed and now she was losing the fight not to cry.

She choked out something I could only just hear, "He didn't know the half of it."

Three things popped into my head that should have had no connection.

Chris bracing himself against the mirrored wardrobe.

The en suite bathroom.

Doc, in the lay-by, half-heartedly returning a salute to a group of Harley lovers.

It was like remembering a name that's been on the tip of your tongue for hours. No chain of reasoning leads you there, one moment nothing, the next, enlightenment.

I left my chair and went across to the wardrobe. Mindful of fingerprints, I pressed my knuckles to the point midway between Chris's ghostly palms. A touch of pressure and the reflection distorted as the door flexed. Seven foot of passionately grinding Chris would have gone straight through it. I looked at the bathroom door then back to Jan, who didn't look up.

"Peter was in the bathroom all along?" It wasn't really a question, but Jan nodded. "You knew he was there?"

"Yes."

Again, Doc and his gleaming Sportster came to mind, the way he soaked up people's admiration of her but didn't want to be part of the show himself.

"Peter liked to watch, and he knew about Chris all along?"

Jan nodded and her chest began to hitch up and down. I put a hand on her shoulder. She didn't grab onto me as I'd expected. She just rested her head against my arm, looked ready to fall asleep.

Barely a whisper, "It was his idea."

Neither of us cast a glance at the photos in the entrance hall. I think she'd maxed out on emotional turmoil for the day and, to my shame, I was on a bit of a high. I was getting something done, finding something out. I'd taken two bottles of lager from the fridge before we made our way back to the garden. Jan had grabbed the bourbon again, along with a glass that she ended up not using. We sat on the expensive patio furniture and looked over the burnt away lawn to the golf course.

The story started with intent eye contact and both of us hunched forward; Jan talking in rapid bursts. We didn't keep it up for long. Once the initial mortification had worn off, the things she said were almost predictable. Anyone on the golf course who happened to see us might have thought we were discussing some mundane domestic arrangement.

In a way, we were.

It had started at the beginning of the year, around the end of January. Peter began bringing up the subject of her affair with Jeffry. The immediate fallout from the affair was loud and angry then, by tacit agreement, it became taboo. Jeffry was taboo as well, a name never mentioned.

"I found the wedding album in the bin one day. Peter had started to go through it pulling out any picture with Jeff in it. What was left wasn't worth keeping."

The wedding album, not *our* wedding album.

The situation had changed only marginally after Jeff had bailed out his brother's failing business. His name still wasn't invoked in the home, but his presence was occasionally tolerated. The Keller brothers and their respective trophies were seen again at the appropriate gatherings. Jan, the Jan Chris would recognise, flashed into view as she took a swig of bourbon.

"Those functions, the events, were horrendous."

Jeffry was contrite, trying to make things right with Pete and struggling to understand that some things didn't have a price. Peter didn't have enough grace to spread any around. Instead he took the attention as his due and became obnoxious. Caroline loudly forgave her errant husband and was publicly magnanimous in the face of Jan's defeat. Jan was left to be the bad guy.

"You'd have to know the circuit pretty well to spot the difference," she said. Another swig of bourbon, another flash of ole' lady hardness around the eyes. "It was all, 'Darling, we must do lunch' and conversations about spa weekends."

Until there was no one there to impress. Then she didn't exist. Word got around, Jan was persona non grata and she was dropped like a stone. Caroline was head girl.

Then, Peter began to break the taboo. At first Jan thought he was getting over what had happened. He'd mention Jeffry from time to time, testing his pain threshold, poking the subject like a bruise. Jan was guarded with her responses, trying not to unbalance the remains of the marriage.

"He kept coming back to it. Started asking questions, little things to begin with. Where would we meet? Did Jeffry take me out for meals, which restaurants? Things like that."

The questions began to get more pointed. Instead of asking about meals, Peter worked around to asking whose bed they'd used. Then details about what they'd done.

Jan's voice flattened out, then petered out. She was staring in the direction of the golf course, but not seeing it. It would have taken a more perceptive soul than mine to have read her expression. Jan blinked, took another hit of the bourbon then noticed I was watching her.

"He showed me some revolting website he'd found."

"Seductive Secrets, the one Chris saw?"

"That came later, this was some chat room. Peter pulled it up on the computer one morning and said he wanted me to look at it while he was out."

She took another pull on the bottle and offered it to me again. I accepted it this time, kept it over my side of the table after pretending to take a swig. Jan had stopped talking again.

"Chat room?" I prompted.

She gave a laugh, low and sneering. "It was all these men swapping stories about their wives having affairs. I think most of them where made up, but they wanted them to be true."

Peter wanted the same truth. That evening he came home and asked Jan what she thought of the website. The correct answer was pretty obvious.

"You told him what he wanted to hear?"

"I took my lead from the stories on the site. Then I asked him if it turned him on." She gave another sneering bark of laughter. "I ended up wanking him off while I described getting fucked by his brother."

The bitterness made her voice harsh and for an instant it looked like her anger was going to carry her through. Then the floodgates burst.

We sat in silence for a while once the tears stopped. I'd handed Jan the bourbon again but she didn't want it. Telling me about pleasuring her husband had taken her beyond some landmark only she could see.

"He wanted me to try again with Jeffry but it didn't work out. Caroline was watching me like a hawk and anyway Jeffry didn't want to know. I don't know if he'd just got me out of his system or if he was scared of Caroline finding out. Either way he'd run a mile when he saw me coming."

"Did you want to get back with Jeffry?"

She pulled a face. "He's just another version of Peter really. Bit taller, bit older, bit more money. I didn't think sleeping with him mattered to be honest." She laughed at what she'd just said. "I don't suppose that sounds very nice does it?"

I didn't realise straight away that I was meant to respond. It didn't sound nice but than nothing I'd heard about her life with Peter did.

"The people around you don't sound especially likeable."

"It was hard to know what they were really. Everything was so much about keeping up and getting ahead. That's why I didn't think sleeping with Caroline's husband was important. I didn't imagine she'd care, not really."

The coffee mornings and fundraisers Caroline presided over were usually awash with chatter about the cliques' extra-marital dealings. Positions and rankings would move up or down accordingly. An affair with your personal trainer might get you a step up the ladder if he was a decade younger. A quickie with the masseur at an expensive spa retreat might be considered tacky and you could drop down a placing. Caroline never mentioned any such activities. In a rare moment of carelessness, Jan assumed this was because of her age.

A couple of nights after Pete had shown her the chat room, the brothers Keller and their spouses attended an evening performance of something involving ostentation, dinner jackets and a private box. Peter managed to engineer the absence of him and Caroline. Jan did her best to rekindle the flame. No dice.

"He looked at me like I'd crawled out from under a stone. Not very flattering."

Peter wouldn't let the subject drop and pressed her to try again. It wasn't on the cards. The rebuttal in the private box was the last time Jeffry allowed himself to be alone with her. The next stop was the internet cheating sites. I asked if they were another of Peter's finds.

"They came up in the chat room. He never said so, but I don't think Peter was just reading what other people posted. He was joining in, asking questions."

The chat room, like a lot of online endeavours, billed itself as a community. The exchange of information between members included a lot of advice and a few cautionary tales. Jan couldn't be sure if Peter was one of the online voices. People posted under usernames. Seductive Secrets was mentioned along with three or four other such sites.

"Did Peter suggest using it?"

"Yeah, the one I met Chris on, and two others." I asked if Chris was the only man she'd hooked up with. She nodded and allowed herself a small smile. "To be honest I didn't get many replies."

"What do you count as not many?"

Jan did a quick mental tally and told me seven in the first week.

Doc's little masquerade on the Seductive Secrets website had garnered nearly twenty replies in has many hours.

I finished the first bottle of lager and left the second one alone. I figured I'd be driving us home. Jan had forgotten about the bourbon but she'd already put a good chunk away.

"Was that why Chris was the lucky winner, lack of competition?"

Movement from Jan caught my eye. She was staring at me with a hurt look on her face.

"Why do you say that?"

"Chris and you were worlds apart."

I gestured around the garden. Even dried out and dying, it was a long way from the oil-stained hardstanding outside Chateau Rudjer.

"I suppose you're right." She cast her recently jaundiced eye over the gardens. "But a lot of people misjudge Chris. He's a gentleman in the real sense of the word."

Which might have been true but was unlikely to hold up in court. Twelve good men and true might struggle reconciling Jan's gentle giant with the accused standing before them. I was having trouble with it.

"And you got that from his online profile?" I asked without looking at her.

"Chris is a lovely guy."

I left a silence for her to fill but my silences lacked the potency of Doc's and I broke first.

"It's still a hell of a leap from designer dresses and black-tie to a pint down The Jericho."

"Peter helped," Jan finally admitted. "A couple of them were near retirement age, so they were out. One of them I vetoed because he wanted to explore the 'darker side of his sexuality'. Peter vetoed some of them because he thought they looked boring. We had it narrowed down to just two. I sent a reply to the first one but didn't go through with it."

The first choice had arranged to meet up at what he called an out-of-the-way place. Out-of-the-way translated to *dump*.

She waited at a table drinking bottled water for twenty minutes. When the date showed he suggested they go back to his place and order in a take-away. Alarm bells started ringing when he said they could take his car and he'd drive her back to the Audi later.

"I told him I didn't want to leave my car in an area I didn't know, so I'd follow him. At the top of the road he went right, so I went left."

"Why was it different with Chris?"

"It was the reply he sent to my email as much as anything. He suggested meeting for a drink at his local pub and said he'd wait outside so I could see him. If I didn't like the look of him, I could just drive past. That spoke volumes; he wasn't assuming I was just there for the taking. That's why I said he's a gentleman in the real sense of the word."

I remembered how nervous she'd looked on that first night in The Jericho. I wasn't sure that gelled with the image she was painting for me of gentleman Chris, but pointing it out wasn't going to do anything good.

"What was Peter doing when you were out on these dates, didn't he stay close to keep an eye on things?"

"He stayed at home, he was probably ... " She made a pumping motion with her cupped hand. "He told me he wanted me to come home as soon as we were ... done." Another flash of bitterness. "I'd thought he was worried about me but he just wanted the details."

So, Trophy-Wife-Jan would run home as soon as the smoke cleared and tell all. If what Chris had told Doc was true, she could show him the proof too.

"Was Pete here every time you had Chris around?"

We were both admiring the lush greenery of the golf course again.

"Not the first time. He was away in Manchester wining and dining a client. I didn't want to go with him so I suggested going to Chris's for the weekend. Pete said to bring him here."

"Wasn't he worried about the neighbours seeing?"

"I think it sort of added to it for him. Then he asked me to bring Chris over while he was here."

"Chris didn't twig?"

"That my husband was in the bathroom watching us? Who'd think that was going to happen?"

It wouldn't have occurred to me. And by Chris's accounts his attention was held elsewhere.

Pete spent most of the weekends camped out upstairs with a bottle of vodka, a load of junk food and his laptop. I asked if they'd moved the show to the spare room so Peter could have the run of his own bedroom. It turned out not to be the case.

Chris had spent three weekends there in total. The first, Peter had been away on business. The second, he stayed out of sight upstairs. Jan would go up ahead of Chris, on the pretext of getting ready, and tell hubby it was show time. Then Pete would hide himself in the en suite. Before the third and last visit, he told Jan to take Chris to the guest room, because of the silent flush.

"The what?" I asked. I turned back to look at her, expecting her to laugh or at least smile.

She was doing neither. The guest room was the biggest and the best and so was its en suite. To spare guests the horror of hearing running water in the night, it had been fitted with a flushing system that produced a low, dignified, hiss.

"Our en suite just had normal plumbing. Peter said if he needed to use the toilet in the night, the sound of the flush would give the game away. So it was best we used the guest room."

"What was the plan if Chris needed a pee in the night? If he opened the bathroom door and found a man in there he'd – " I almost said *kill him.* "He'd know something was going on."

"He used the toilet on the landing. I told him the en suite bathroom was my dressing room, said it was private." being the gentleman he was, he'd respected that. Jan looked away from me again then said something touching and ridiculous. "I hated lying to him like that."

"Was the knife your idea?"

Her voice caught when she said, "No, that was Peter's idea. He'd got a bit of a thing about seeing me ... dishevelled. He asked me to give it to Chris and ... "

She started crying again. I got up and walked around to her side of the table. I took the seat next to her, put my arms around her and let her cry it out.

She cried for what felt like a long time but probably wasn't, repeating again and again, "I didn't want Chris to know any of this."

Doc listened to what I said without interrupting, cycling his tarot ceaselessly through a variety of single-handed cuts. It began to annoy me and I asked him to stop. He looked surprised to find the cards in his hand and apologised, put them down on their square of linen.

"We're back to the Keller dynasty," he said when I'd finished.

I grunted in agreement. One of his hands crept down and stole the cards back while he wasn't looking. I let it ride. Doc fell silent again and stared into space, finally he announced he needed another cup of tea and stood up.

"Messed up family," I said as Doc set the kettle to boil yet again.

"The Kellers?" He shrugged then twisted left and right from his lower back. His spine let out an impressive barrage of cracks and snaps and he gave a contented grunt. "Most families don't fit together too smoothly. Spouses playing the away game with an in-law ain't exactly unheard of."

While the kettle heated, Doc wrapped the tarot cards in their linen and put them back into his leather. He went to his crime wall and made an addition to the timeline: *late January, PK wants Jan to sleep with JK.*

"You don't think that's messed up?" I asked. When he raised his eyebrows in question I pointed at his notation. "Asking your wife to have an affair."

He took a step back from the wall then drew a line from the centre piece, which was Peter Keller, down to the lower strata with all the questions. The connecting line answered why Jan had picked Chris. She hadn't, Peter had.

"Takes all sorts."

We heard the kettle come to the boil and we wandered back to the kitchen. I told Doc what was bothering me, the palm prints on the mirror.

"I looked at those wardrobe doors. If Chris was leaning his weight on them while he screwed Jan, they'd have gone straight through them. He must have been balanced on a knife's edge." It didn't look like Doc was making the leap I had. "It wasn't about good sex – it was about putting on a show."

"That's what Jan's just said."

"She also said Chris didn't know about it. That doesn't really fit with him choosing the wardrobe door for a landing pad."

"You think Chris was in on the game?"

I nodded and Doc changed gears on me. "Did you check for post at Keller's place?"

I didn't pursue the point. Even if Chris was aware of being observed, it didn't make him a killer. Though the switch, from being a pawn to taunting a man with his own wife, didn't put him in the best light.

"Yeah, I checked, no post."

The Keller's had an ornate mailbox next to the entrance gate. It didn't have a lock and it didn't have anything in it.

"Nothing, no junk mail, freebie papers?"

"Nothing."

Doc gave me a grin and made the spooling motion.

Someone had been clearing away the post.

I left Doc to his tarot and altar and headed home. My mobile started buzzing when I was about halfway there. I didn't bother pulling over to answer it. It was a nice evening and I wanted to ride. The extended route I took home was more industrial than picturesque but that's North London for you, and it suited how I was feeling. Once I got to the house and pulled out my phone I wasn't surprised to see a missed call from Doc. He'd been running on high octane when I left him. I dialled his number on the landline.

"You called?"

"Yakky, good. I thought you were ignoring me." There was an edge of excitement in his voice that I wasn't sure I was happy about. "Sorry if it's not a good time but can you make it over to Keller's house again, ASAP? If this works out, stuff's going to start happening in about thirty minutes."

The thirty-minute deadline wasn't a problem, I made it with ten minutes to spare. Sunday evening traffic was light enough to be ignored, at least on a bike. Jan hadn't asked any questions when I told her where I was going. Dad's questions I just ignored.

The steel gate was still open and unless someone paid to have it fixed, it was going to stay that way. When I got to the front of the house, the doors of the double garage were open too. The white Sportster was parked in there alongside Doc who motioned for me to ride in. As soon as I got off the Yam, Doc led me outside again. He pulled the door closed, hiding both motorcycles.

"I'm expecting Jeffry to turn up any time now. I'll give you all the details later but right now we need to get out of sight." He nodded at the big 4x4, meaning I was meant to hide behind it. "Wait for me to talk to him before you come out. Don't threaten him just put yourself between him and his motor. Okay?"

He headed towards the front door before I could offer any objections and vanished into an angle of the architecture. I sat on the drive, used the rear wheel of the car as a backrest.

We didn't have long to wait. The broken private road gave away the approach of Jeffry Keller's Range Rover before it reached the top of the driveway. I had a flash of paranoia as it drew up on the opposite side of the car I was behind. Sitting gave way to crouching, gave way to ready-to-spring.

In the event, Jeffry's footfalls moved straight to the front door without taking a security conscious prowl around the grounds. I risked looking around the wing of the 4x4 and saw Doc step into sight just before he spoke.

"Better you let me do that Mr Keller. The number you have for the alarm's no longer valid."

Jeffry jumped. He thought he'd been alone and Doc startled him. The older of the Keller brothers was a big guy – I agreed with Doc's description of a rugby player running to fat. While he was occupied with Doc, I walked around the back of Peter's 4x4 and leaned, arms crossed, against the driver's door of the flashier Range Rover. I saw Jeffery clock my presence and I stared into space as if bored. I was hoping to give the impression that this was just another day at work for me.

"What is this?" Jeffry demanded.

His voice was crisp, a man in control, or at least one who expected to be. It was one of those moments Doc worked like a conjuring trick. He left a tiny pause before telling Jeff that there was nothing to worry about. Most people would have tried for a menacing silence or an over-the-top bonhomie, Hollywood gangster style. Most people standing where Jeff was would be expecting a threat or – being the alpha male he wanted to think he was – outright contrition. Doc's subtle game of silly buggers put a spanner in the works. When Jeffry told Doc he wasn't worried, his timing was off, it made him sound like he was.

How we appear to others, Doc had more than once opined, largely dictates how we appear to ourselves. He'd normally follow such statements with a significant glance at my tee shirt and by inference, all the tattoos he'd never seen. He still hadn't seen them.

I didn't think I was any smarter than Jeffry Keller; I just had more exposure to Doc's bullshit. I could see when he was lacing up his Jiving shoes.

Jeffry, again his timing just off, said, "I suggest you get off my property before I call the police."

And nobody moved, at least not quickly enough. Keller hesitated over the keypad; he might have done the same even without the two of us watching him. There was no reason for him to be familiar with the alarm. But the slight hesitation left space for Doc to drive another wedge of uncertainty home.

"No need to call the police. They'll be on their way once you've set that alarm off." Keller found himself bathed in the dazzling glare of Cheshire. "Then you can explain to them all about lying to your brother's widow and throwing her out of her home."

Abracadabra.

Doc let us in.

Before he opened the door wide and let anyone through, he looked over to me and twitched his head. I knew it was part of the spiel; still, I planned on telling him if he wanted something that came when he whistled, he best buy himself a dog.

Jeffry Keller wasn't scared but he was on the defensive and a lot of the fight had left him. When I joined him and

Doc by the front door he gave me a slow up and down look. If the chairman of the board did it to a subordinate, it would have been devastating. But I wasn't his subordinate and it fell flat, and he knew it.

Jan's revelations earlier that day were still turning over in my mind, and my stomach. Jeffry's treatment of her didn't endear him to me. When he finished trying to look superior, I looked around, still bored.

"Nobody's holding you back. If you fancy your chances, give it a shot."

I saw Doc, who was slightly behind Keller, close his eyes and mouth: *oh fuck*. I don't pretend to know what was going through Keller's mind. And I don't know what would have happen if he had taken a swing. With his expensive suit and rolls of soft fat, he didn't look like a man you'd back in a fight, but he was still a lot heavier than me. And it would have been a fair fight. I win by cheating. It was academic in the end. He saved what face he could by snorting derisively and turning back to the front door. Then lost his composure all over again.

Doc had swung the door open and stood aside. The display of vandalised photos was still front and centre. I heard Keller catch his breath and mutter something, to me it sounded like he'd said *all mine*.

Doc nodded.

"Caroline, indeed." We entered the hall and Doc stopped for Jeffry to fully absorb what he was seeing. "Your wife's also been in Jan's bedroom. She's cut Jan's clothes up and written slag on the bathroom mirror. If anyone's going to call the police tonight, I think it's Jan."

Jeffry drew in a breath, let it out again through his teeth, his shoulders slumped a fraction.

"Where is Jan?" he asked.

Doc didn't answer straight away and I think he was considering what to say, rather than playing games.

"Jan's okay, she's staying with a friend."

He didn't give any indication that I was the friend.

"She sent me a text ... " Keller trailed off in the face of Doc's head shaking.

"I sent you a text. Jan doesn't know we're here. But I'm sure she'd appreciate the effort you've made. Love that suit."

I didn't know one suit from another but Doc had a point, Jeff was dressed to impress. I closed the front door, not hard, but in the silence, you couldn't miss the click.

The trap had been sprung.

We sat in the big reception room and Doc opened the drinks cabinet again. Jeffry had a glass of the bourbon. I didn't tell him Jan had been swigging from the bottle a couple of hours earlier. It wouldn't be the first time they'd exchanged body fluids. He didn't knock it back in one but he made short work of it. When it had gone he refused a refill, just sunk back in the sofa and yanked his tie open.

Doc sat across from him.

"What's with all the bullshit about the house, Jeffry?"

Jeffry made point of meeting Doc's eye. "I wanted the house."

I was stood in the doorway, staying just on the edge of his vision. Doc flicked me a look.

"You risk criminal charges for this place, Yak?"

"Not if I had his sort of money. No."

Keller cranked his neck so he could see me properly. I'd stayed standing on purpose – if he wanted to see me he'd have to look up, not down. He looked away again but didn't offer up a better answer. Doc leaned forward, closing the distance between them. He switched the grin off; this was business.

"Jeffry, let me tell you what I know. You do not have any legal claim on this house – moral claims or gentleman's agreements with your late brother I don't know about – but legally you've got *nada*. So, your little performance with Jan and me the other night amounts to fraud. And, I'd say we've both pretty sure that after meeting me for lunch and getting the keys, your wife came back here and trashed anything to do with Jan. I doubt very much if she bothered wearing gloves, at the time she thought she had a right to be here. If Jan wants to bring a case against the pair of you, it would cause you a damn sight more trouble than this place is worth. Lastly, I'd be willing to bet a fair amount that we can add straightforward theft to the charge sheet because you're the one who's been taking Jan's post."

I saw Jeff register surprise at mention of the post. Doc must have seen it too because he grinned, not unkindly. He didn't tell Keller he'd done too good a job of clearing the mailbox.

Doc gave Jeffry a few moments to think about what he'd done, then he leaned back in his seat, lowering the pressure.

"Now, that's what I know, *this* is what I suspect. I think you have some sort of *in* with the local plod or maybe a local journo, so you know Jan was here with Chris Rudjer the night your brother died. So, you're very much in the loop at the same time Jan's being kept out of it."

We both watched Jeffry as Doc spoke. He was being more guarded now, more poker faced. I think he was also beginning to see how smart Doc really was.

"The thing is," Doc said, "I think you're trying to protect Jan, which is all very admirable, but leaves my friend's head on the block."

Jeffry looked Doc over with a fair impression of equanimity. He might have been fooling himself but Doc wasn't buying it. He sat and watched Jeffry's composure fall into the pit of his silence.

"If you think all this, why haven't you gone to the police?" Jeffry asked.

"Speaking for myself, I don't trust policeman. As for Yakky, over there, I don't think he trusts anyone." Jeffry flicked another glance my way and when he turned back, Doc was leaning in towards him once more. Keller twitched back and his poise took another beating. "And dropping you in the shit ain't going to help my friend. I just want some questions answered. You're better off talking to me than the police at this point. Me and Yakky boast no official powers and don't keep records." He looked at me and said, "I mean it's not as if we're going to tape this conversation, is it?"

We didn't transcribe the tape of Jeffry Keller's conversation with Doc. Doc didn't want a record for study; he wanted the tape as a lever should the need arise. One of us, I can't remember who, dubbed it The Kellergate Tape. Doc's efforts at clandestine recording were more successful than mine, the results fully audible and the voices recognisable. In my defence, Doc had an easier time of it setting things up, and Jeffry Keller was nowhere near as upset as Jan was during the discourse.

Jeff was led to the end of the cream leather sofa and accepted a drink, blissfully unaware that the open magazine on the coffee table was hiding a Dictaphone.

Once he got started, he seemed to find talking cathartic. The world of psychology suffered a loss when Doc became a tattooist. Like a fair amount of his activities, I couldn't really see how it was done.

"I'm not trying to embarrass you Mr Keller but we're all men of the world, so let's not pussy foot around, eh? I know from Jan that the pair of you had an affair."

Jeffry laughed. "If you've had lunch with my wife you'll have heard it from her as well. No doubt Caroline went to great lengths to tell you she's forgiven me? I thought we weren't pussy footing around."

Doc looked slightly surprised, but he might have been acting.

"Yeah, she did. She told me how much you paid for her

forgiveness."

Jeffry laughed again and enunciated slowly, "You do not begin to know."

"You're still paying?"

"Does that look like Caroline's letting it lie?" He flicked his head towards the doorway and the display of ruined pictures beyond.

"You think that was meant for you, not Jan?"

"Of course it was meant for me."

Doc didn't say anything in response. Normally his Jive filled the room, throwing off ideas and misdirection in equal measure, making people's heads spin. This was different, slow and quiet. He was letting Jeffry cook his own brain.

Finally, he said, "Did your brother ever get over it?"

"Peter wasn't my brother, he was my half-brother. Fraternal."

"You weren't close?"

"Not in a good way. We were rivals."

It sounded as if he'd finished. Doc nudged him with another mention of his wife.

"Caroline said something about Peter being in your shadow."

Jeffry shook his head impatiently. Evidently it was a line he'd heard a lot and didn't swallow.

"Caroline's very loyal in her way. She always trots out the big brother little brother story. I think it makes her feel better about patronising him. What went on between us wasn't sibling rivalry, it was caustic. I think I'll take you up on that refill."

I saw Doc's face give a tiny twitch of annoyance. I was reminded of the night in The Jericho, when he'd given Jan the first tarot reading, and the way the pair of them seemed to occupy their own space. A corner of the universe where the normal rules didn't work. He cut a look across to me and, to save Doc bursting the bubble, I did the honours with the drinks. Keller surprised me by saying thank you, and I told him he was welcome. This drink lasted longer than the first but he was still drinking from necessity.

We listened closely as Jeffry started talking again. I didn't have Doc's specialist schooling, or his passion for people watching. Even so, it was clear enough that the surviving Keller had had mixed feeling towards his half-brother. Guilt was playing a part in his decision to talk.

Keller's birth mother had died when he was just shy of a year old. Cancer, massively aggressive. His father had remarried two months later, another four months and the union was blessed.

Jeffry managed a sour smile.

"Make of that what you will. Family lore had it that the old man married a woman already carrying another's child. When it was born, he selflessly raised it as his own."

Jeff didn't know whether anybody took the idea seriously, but by the time Peter was five, it was obvious whose child he was. He was the image of his father. Same hair, eyes, build, everything. They even sounded alike. Jeffry emptied his glass and put it firmly on the coffee table, telling himself no more booze.

"Peter never had the old man's flare for business. He didn't have his intelligence, to be blunt about it."

"Is that what you got?" Doc said.

Jeffry nodded but there wasn't any pleasure in the boast. "That's how it fell. I've been thinking a lot about me and Pete, since he died. If he'd picked up the business sense and not the looks I think we'd have had a better time of it. Everyone always said I took after my mother, at least in appearance."

Epiphany had come too late. He lapsed into thought and, though I didn't want to, I found myself feeling sorry for him.

Doc gave him another nudge. "Did it divide you, taking so strongly from each parent?"

Jeffry looked surprised when Doc asked that. It looked at the time as if he'd hit a nerve but when he answered he sounded calm, even grateful. I think he was startled by the depth of Doc's understanding; it wasn't a setting where many people would expect to find empathy.

"I think so. I was the favoured son, maybe because I looked like my birth mother. It was excepted wisdom, when I was growing up, that the old man's first wife was the love of his life."

"Was making you the blue-eyed boy his way of assuaging his guilt?"

Jeffry shook his hand and laughed again. I wondered if he ever laughed in a good way. "I don't think guilt was part of the old man's makeup. He played us off against each other but it was already so skewed in my favour that Pete spent his life just trying to catch up. I won't lie about it; I became a spoilt brat, and I never really stopped. Even when we grew up, I kept reminding him I was doing better."

Jeffry tugged at his already loose tie, taking it off completely. He wound the ends of it around each hand until his knuckles were almost touching. It looked like he had handcuffs on.

"I treated him like shit. That's why Caroline's so keen to tell everyone I'm the much-admired older brother. Sibling rivalry at our age sounds light-hearted, as if it was just banter. Sounds better than saying ... "

Jeffry trailed off, unable or unwilling to finish the thought.

Doc caught my eye and made like he was drinking, tilted his head very slightly to Keller. Once I'd given Jeff the refill he hadn't asked for, Doc, very delicately, motioned for me to take a seat.

Join the party, all men of the world here.

I nodded to let him know I'd got the message then disappeared to the kitchen. If Jeffry was going to become one of the boys, he probably wouldn't want to drink alone. I grabbed a pair of overpriced lagers from the glass fridge and opened them.

When I put Doc's bottle in front of him, Keller glanced my way. Before sitting down, I toasted him with tap water in a dark green bottle. He inclined his head a few degrees and sipped his bourbon. Doc took the barest taste of his lager.

"Was marrying Jan a bit of a coup for your brother?"

Jeffry looked at him and gave a nod. He also took another sip of his drink and copied my toast, impressed again with Doc's perception. Doc already had the inside knowledge from his date with Caroline, but that didn't occur to Jeff. We didn't enlighten him.

"A coup? I suppose it was. When she appeared with Pete the first time, a lot of people thought he'd hired her from one those agencies. When he announced they were engaged," he mimed a bombshell going off, "boom." Jeff forced out another of his horrible laughs. "We had more in common than we knew."

He let the statement hang, waited for me or Doc to beg an explanation. I obliged, asked him what he meant.

"Pete crowed. He'd managed what I hadn't – he married a younger woman, got the newer model. Jan was one of the youngest and best-looking women in our circle. When I say *our* circle, I mean *the* circle."

Doc took his turn, "The circle he was never let into?"

"He was only at the guest's table. There by the grace of my largesse."

Jeff took another sip of his drink and I thought again what a messed family this was.

Doc gently prodded him along, reminded him, "Pete crowed?"

"Yes. Not loudly, but he did it well. Back handed complements to Caroline." He pushed his voice up an octave to voice his brother, "'You're a classic beauty Caroline, a fine vintage'. Lots of boasting about his sex life, dressed up like self-deprecation, comments about not being able to keep up at his age." Another sip of bourbon. "Of course, Jan was his ticket into the circle, through Caroline."

Caroline, to judge from what Jeffry told us and from what I'd already heard from Doc, was razor sharp when it came to social politicking. With Jan came the possibility of a minor revolution. Caroline wanted her on side, or at the least wanted her where she could be watched. She was younger, prettier and she wasn't just eye candy.

"I know plenty of men my age who find a bimbo to be seen with. It can work if they've got the clout. People will admire you for buying a whore, provided you pay enough. Peter didn't have that sort of status, but Jan wasn't a bimbo, not by any means." Jeffry finished his third measure. Doc provided his fourth. "She ruffled Caroline's feathers. Jan has a natural style about her, poise I'd call it. Caroline's always had to work for those things. She felt threaten to begin with, in the end they became friends though."

He smiled to himself; it made him look stupid. He couldn't have been aware of half the manoeuvring that went on within his wife's ring of friends. I wondered if we'd over done the booze because he fell silent, lost in memories, happy or sad. It was hard to tell which.

Doc broke the spell. "Who started the affair?"

Jeffry's head snapped up, for a split second it looked like he was about to get angry, but he was too far gone.

"Jan did but I didn't need much persuading. Once Peter was part of a couple it was easier to extend invitations. We saw a lot of each other, talked a lot. She was, she is, an attractive woman but it wasn't just that. She ... " Jeff frowned and took a drink as words failed him. He shook his head, if he was trying to clear it I could only wish him luck. Neither Doc nor I poured short measures. "I can't believe I'm about to say this, it's such a cliché, but she ... well she ... "

"Understood you?" I suggested.

The pair of them turned to look at me. Jeffry Keller nodded and smiled. He smiled too long and it began to look like a dead thing.

Then said, "Exactly."

By Caroline's account the affair had amounted to Jeffry making himself a fool. She was nearer the truth than she knew. By Jan's account, she'd been scoring points, moving up the circle's hierarchy. Jeffry had thought they were in love. He didn't say this out loud, because men don't. Had Jan said the word, he'd have been ready to trade up to a newer model. They'd gone at it like knives for a couple of months. Then Caroline found out and it was over.

The details were different but the story sounded similar to Chris's. Discretion wasn't Jan's strong point. While Jeffry covered his tracks, and watched every word he said, Jan flaunted her indiscretion. Of course, Jeffry and Jan were coming at things from different angles. You don't scale the hierarchy by keeping your victories secret.

Word got to Caroline, Caroline got word to Peter and the great romance turned to ash. Give the man his due: he knew he'd acted badly and in his way, tried to make amends. Finding out he couldn't put everything right with a cash injection was a lesson he was still struggling with.

The next drink he poured for himself. I placed a bet with myself that he'd be a maudlin drunk.

While Keller started on his fifth, I watched Doc. He was focused on Jeff like a sniper but you had to look closely to see – until you got to his eyes you'd think he was about to doze off.

"If you were so taken with Jan, why the cold shoulder when she offered you a rematch?"

Doc swindled a laugh out of Jeffry with his phrasing.

"That was different."

Rather than elaborate, he sipped more bourbon. Doc was getting impatient, he bypassed gentle prodding and went for some needle. He dressed it up as sympathy.

"Different because Caroline was wise to you?"

He ground the ball of a thumb into his palm and shook his head. "Caroline was watching Jan, watching us both, but it wasn't that. Wasn't just that." He made the same under-the-thumb hand signal. "Caroline's a proud woman, and I hurt her badly, but she doesn't wear the trousers. And anyway, I love my wife."

"You're still here though," I said.

Doc's text to Jeffry had been pretty ambiguous.

Jeffry, please, I need to c u. Can we meet at Peter's this evening?

Don't tell C. Jan.

At the time, I imagined he'd been tempted with something a bit spicier. Even so, for a man with an innocent assignation in mind, he was very well dressed. Jeff turned to me and drew up that miserable smile again. "You know Jan."

He seemed to have me marked down as a fellow conquest.

"So why the cold shoulder?" Doc asked again.

Jeffry shrugged. It was a mannerism that sat well with the cut of his suit. "Call it pride."

The tattoo ink across Doc's face rippled with tension.

More needle.

"I think I'd call it pussy whipped."

This time Jeffry did bridle slightly, the tone of voice had probably been enough. I changed my grip on the bottle I was drinking from. If Jeffry was going to get difficult, I was going to cheat. After a few seconds of macho staring, he gave in and started talking.

"You're right, it wasn't pride." He made to take another drink but changed his mind with the tumbler half way to his lips. He put it back on the table with the same decisive thud he had earlier. "If Jan had made a pass at me because she wanted me, I would have taken it. But I knew why she was doing it and it wounded my fragile male ego."

He enunciated *fragile male ego* very carefully. I think he was repeating a phrase that had been thrown at him as an insult. Then he knocked back the tumbler of bourbon, did the shuddery thing.

"I was bloody stupid. I should have just jumped on and taken what I was offered." He swung his gaze back to me. It wasn't the sad smile this time; it was a man-to-man smirk. "You know Jan."

Doc made a small noise in the back of his throat. It sounded louder than it was because the room was quiet. When I turned to him he pointedly looked at my hand – he'd noticed how I was holding the bottle. Once he'd drawn my attention to it, I noticed how hard I was holding it.

I took myself back to the kitchen where I left the bottle on the draining board. The glass-fronted fridge had a few mixer cans of coke so I helped myself to a handful of them and adjusted my caffeine levels. I waited until I was sure I'd calmed down before going back.

I must have missed a good bit. When I returned, the atmosphere of confessional therapy had been reinstated. I decided not to sit down with the lads again but took a leaf out of Doc's book. There were various seats tastefully scattered about the room. I found a straight-backed chair, which was situated comfortably out of Keller's line of sight.

The needle had been put away and Doc had his concerned face on.

"When was this?" he asked.

Jeffry frowned and I saw his glass had been filled again. Thinking wasn't coming easy.

"It was just after New Year's. Another of Caroline's charity fundraisers. Don't ask me what for, the tickets cost an arm and a leg, then I had to pay out more to invite a guest, then again for the guest's partner."

Guest and partner being Pete and Jan.

"Free ticket and then he wanted to borrow more money?"

Doc whistled softly under his breath, sympathising.

"He wanted a lot more money."

"And this time, you didn't have it?"

Jeffry laughed his laugh again. "Oh, I had it, I was just sick of giving it away. The loan I'd given him in October was only the start. The bloody idiot lost the lot. I just wrote it off, told him to call it an olive branch."

Only Peter had got a taste for olives. The eagle's eye Caroline kept on her husband's finances wasn't as all-seeing as she thought. The loan-come-gift had gone; the hole in Peter's business hadn't. The next cash injection was definitely labelled loan – the one after that, a top-up loan. The one after that had been the limit. Peter played the guilt card but found he'd worn it thin.

"I told him he couldn't expect me to keep on bailing out his business ventures just because of what happened with me and Jan. Then I said, 'I think I've paid enough. Don't you?'" The tumbler went towards his lips and once more he thumped it down, without drinking. His iron resolve failed almost instantly. "Bad turn of phrase, wasn't what I was saying, but Peter, well, perhaps that's what gave him the idea."

Doc nodded and glanced my way. He spoke to Jeff but he was bringing me up to speed.

"The deal was he'd look the other way regarding you and Jan if you made him another loan?"

"In a nutshell. Peter was offering me his wife for money." From where I was sitting, I couldn't see his expression but the disgust sound genuine. The next thing he came out with threw some doubt. "I should have gone for it, cheap at the price." The crassness of what he'd said might have shamed him because he tried to back pedal. "I think turning him down hurt him as much as the affair did. The one thing in the world he had that I didn't, and he couldn't even sell that to me."

Doc caught my eye.

"How did you know about Chris getting nicked?"

Jeff tried to shrug nonchalantly, playing hard to get. "Contacts, business is about contacts."

Doc regarded Keller benignly, finally he nodded. Then he went to the drinks cabinet and pulled out a pair of shot glasses. He came over to where I was sitting. Slightly behind Keller's back he made to pour me a shot, clinked the neck of the bottle against the rim of the glass so it sounded.

"Thanks," I said, and I just went with the flow. Or lack of flow, since I was still holding an empty glass. He pulled the same trick on himself then topped up Keller's drink for real. Before he sat down again, he made a toast. Long fingers curled around the front of the shot glass, so his audience wouldn't see it was dry.

"To business," he said, tilting his head respectfully

towards Keller.

Then he threw back a measure of bugger all; he even faked the little shudder. Keller, caught up in the moment, emptied his glass. Doc poured the same again and looked to me to make the next toast. Keller twisted round on the sofa to see me, bourbon half raised in readiness, eyes bloodshot.

I thought for a moment before lifting my glass and quietly saying, "To Jan."

Keller froze and it looked as if I'd over played it.

Then he murmured, "Jan."

And threw the drink down his throat.

We had a few toasts. I don't remember them all, they weren't important, but we finished up on a toast to the Queen for some reason. After that, Doc dispensed with the niceties and just got down to the serious drinking. I didn't bother joining in anymore. Keller was too far gone to see, or care, that he was working his way down the bottle alone. Doc carried on with the charade, swept along with his own nonsense.

I'd been right about Keller being a maudlin drunk. More importantly from our point of view, he was a talkative one.

"You know I actually do feel slightly drunk?" I told Doc. He nodded and grunted, *rest.*

"It's auto-suggestion," he said, breathing hard. "All the trappings of getting pissed. Bottles, glasses, toasting, singing. Your mind filling in the blanks again." He put his hands on his hips and sucked in air through clenched teeth. "Look at this guy, bit of blokey chat, few drinks and his brain's telling him we're his best mates. Come on, lift."

I was glad Keller hadn't taken me up on my doorstep offer of a fight. Carrying his unconscious body up the stairs brought home how big he was. I'd have been flattened before I had time to surrender. We sat him on the top stair and rested again before manhandling him across the landing to one of the unused rooms. Doc had already made the bed up with the pillows and covers from the master bedroom.

Between us we managed to strip him to the waist and positioned him diagonally across the double mattress. Doc regarded the snoring man, with obvious dissatisfaction, and left the room.

He reappeared just as I was about to go and look for him. In one hand, he had a bottle of vodka, in the other a pair of skimpy knickers. He arranged them on the bed then pulled the sheets up just far enough to leave sleeping beauty's torso on display. After Doc had pulled out his phone and taken half a dozen pictures, I put Jeff into an approximation of the recovery position. I couldn't see a vomit-choked corpse doing anyone much good.

"You sure about this?" I asked.

Doc was reviewing the photos he'd taken. "Police ain't going to bust a gut to hassle this one, Yak. He knows that as well as we do. We drop the plod a line, it's just an inconvenience." He turned the phone so I could see the screen. "Send him a copy of this and tell him Caroline's next on the mailing list ... " He shut the phone down and put it in his pocket.

"I don't mean will it work, I mean are you okay with doing it. I'm thinking about the last time."

Doc took the props off the bed and ushered me out the room.

"That was different. I could have handled Caroline gently but I acted like a prick." We were heading back down the stairs and he jerked a thumb in the direction of the bedroom. "If we don't need matey boy, I'll just delete the photos and the only thing he'll have to remember us by is a hangover. I'll only wheel these out if he won't play nice."

When Doc put the bottle of vodka back in the cabinet, he realised he was still holding Jan's knickers. He threw them to me, but I stepped back and let them land on the floor. He laughed. "It's alright; they're clean."

He moved on to the kitchen, searched the cupboards until he found some tea bags, then spent a few minutes figuring out the science-fiction-style kettle. I didn't fancy black tea so

I opened another can of mixer. Doc looked up to the ceiling as he waited for the water to boil. "I can't believe he went ahead with the funeral."

Keller had talked a lot when the alcohol really took hold. It was possibly more than just the booze; he'd drawn short of getting tearful but there were things on his mind. Doc asked him when Pete's body was going to be released. Jeffry had shifted, trying to escape his own skin. He was slurring his words – it took him three attempts to say *cremated.*

It bothered Doc a lot more than me. Dead was dead. I'd watched my mother's coffin disappear through a curtain to get burned. It didn't bring her back. Doc didn't share my opinion.

"Jan should have gone to the funeral. It's part of the grieving process."

He said the same to Jeffry, who claimed he was thinking of Jan. Wanted to spare her the scene Caroline was bound to create if she turned up at the chapel. Better not to upset her by having her run the gauntlet of his wife's disapproval. Doc pointed out, coldly, that it would have been better to keep Caroline away. Whatever the balance of power had been pre-affair, post-affair, Caroline's goodwill held a lot of sway.

I think that's when Doc decided to set up the photo shoot in the bedroom. I didn't completely buy Doc's line about needing more leverage on the man. We already had a beautifully recorded account of his attempted fraud and his claims about contacts in official places.

I'd watched Doc as he questioned Keller. His contempt for the man was etched in his face like a hallmark. Twenty-four karat.

We stayed in the kitchen while Doc drank his tea. He let the subject of the funeral drop in the face of my indifference.

"One of us ought to stay here with Keller tonight," he said. I asked if he was volunteering. "I really want to talk to Jan tonight. I expect that asshole's going to ring her at some point and tell her what happened this evening. I'd sooner she heard it from me beforehand. I need to break it to her about the funeral too."

"You going to tell her about Peter trying to pimp her out?"

If the price of missing that little chat was staying the night, I'd call it a bargain. Doc asked if I was happy to stay. I told him happy wasn't the exact word but agreed to babysit.

"I don't see the point through. What do you think he's going to do, trash the place?"

"Un-trash it. I don't want him clearing up Caroline's little hissy fit. It shows there's more going on here than just Chris and Jan getting it on."

Before he left, Doc gave me the keys and told me the new alarm code. I listened to his Sportster rumble away along the drive, then locked up and went to the kitchen to see if there were the makings of a meal anywhere. I made do with tinned soup followed by half a tub of economy vanilla ice cream that left a coating of saccharin over my tongue.

I picked my way across the mess in the master bedroom. Its en suite was the most likely place to find some toothpaste. Predictably Peter's bathroom cabinet contained a tube of supermarket economy brand. I squeezed an inch of the stuff straight into my mouth and tried to swill it around with my tongue. After giving that up as a bad idea, it struck me that the cabinet in the guest room might have been window dressed with toilettes.

Going back into the guest room, now I knew what had been played out there, made my skin crawl. That didn't stop me pocketing the toothpaste and shaving kit I found there. I also found two toothbrushes still in their blister packs. One in pink the other in blue. How many high-flying couples had spontaneously extended their visit to an overnight stay, then been awed by the splendour of the guest room? My guess would be zero. Another sad detail about the house. Once I'd cleaned my teeth I pocketed the toothbrushes too.

I sat on the edge of the bath and looked round the en suite again. How did Peter work it? Jan had told me she came up the stairs ahead of Chris so she'd been able to tell her husband to get ready. Had he intended to wait in the bathroom all night or was the plan to tip-toe out once the Big Guy started snoring? Would Jan extract herself from the bed and go tell him it was safe to come through?

Getting into the mindset of someone who'd want to watch their wife with someone else was beyond me. Nurse training had shown me that empathising wasn't my strong point. I left the train of thought to derail itself and looked over the room again instead.

Doc, with his Miss Marple fixation, was hooked on the working of the people involved, the *why* question. For me the *how* of it was more vexing. The en suite had one door that led into the bedroom with the two lovebirds in it. The only window was a nine-inch transom. Someone Doc's build might have been able to get through it. Assuming they'd made it along the veranda's algae-coated roof without breaking their neck. Allowing that someone had got in without disturbing Jan and Chris, why hadn't Peter raised the alarm? They'd switched to the guest bedroom because the silent flush on the toilet meant Peter could use it if need be. If you could hear a normal toilet flushing between rooms, then someone shouting for help, or even just struggling, would be audible.

I sat on the edge of that bath for a long time. I had a list of questions the prosecution could ask and not a single answer from the defence.

I checked in on Keller before I looked for a bed to crash on. Once I was happy he wasn't about to aspirate in the night, I left him to it. I was no more enamoured of the man than Doc was and there was a certain satisfaction in knowing how hungover he'd be in the morning.

And knowing exactly how early he was going to be woken up.

For the Defence

Monday 25 July

I was back at my house before seven. Nobody else was up so I had a shower and sat in the kitchen with some decent coffee. It was nice to have the place to myself for a bit. Now I came to think about it, I'd spent most of the last two weeks in other people's pockets. The novelty of peace and quiet hadn't worn thin before Doc called.

"Morning, Yak. I meant to say last night, before you ship out this morning, get those keys back off Keller, will you?"

"I have."

"You back home already?" I told him I'd been back about half an hour. He let out a sniggering laugh, sounded like Dick Dastardly's dog. "When did he get his wake-up call?"

"It was still dark. He wasn't looking too clever when we left."

"Good. Any trouble?"

"No."

Jeffry and I were never going to be best buddies, and my five a.m. wake-up call hadn't improved relations, but we kept it civil. He climbed out of bed by force of will alone and took himself to the en suite shower. I treated him to a couple of aspirin and a glass of water for breakfast. Just to be sure he'd know he was at the limit of his welcome, I handed them to him at the bottom of the stairs when he came down. I was holding his coat in one hand. He thanked me for the painkillers. The pile of shattered images that his wife had left might have been taking some of the starch out of him. We were an arm's length away from Caroline's study in hate.

"Has Jan seen this?" He meant the pile of smashed pictures. I nodded and he drew a shaky breath that was almost a groan. It might have been the effects of the hangover. "Was she upset?"

"What do you think?" I took the empty glass from him, exchanged it for his coat.

"This is bad," he said to himself. "I'll have to call Jan, try and ... "

He couldn't think of what he'd try and do. I didn't offer any suggestions, couldn't see what he hoped to achieve with a phone call.

"I'll be seeing Jan later," I said. "If you give me her keys, I can hand them back for you."

We both knew I was telling him to give me the keys but making it sound like I was doing him a favour. He told me it was good of me and dropped the keys into my hand.

"Can I ask you another favour Mister ... ?"

"Just Yakky."

"Okay, Yakky. Can you apologise to Jan for me? I'll call her at some point but I ... "

Words failed him again. I found it strangely touching, so I agreed to apologise for him.

Doc snorted down the phone when I told him. "You should have told him to do his own dirty work."

I heard Jan moving about upstairs as I was getting ready to leave for the shop. I thought Doc would ask me to come in early so we could dissect what we heard from Jeffry, but that hadn't happened. I would have liked a reason to be out of the house before Jan got up. Pure cowardice – I was anticipating emotional trauma and wanted to be out of the way.

Jan appeared shortly before I left. She was red-eyed and puffy, the same look Jeff had been wearing when I woke him up. I offered her the last cup of coffee in the jug, but thankfully she declined. When I pulled her keys out of my pocket and held them out, she didn't react.

"Take them, they're yours."

She finally took them and let me get on with drinking the filter machine dry.

"I never liked that house."

There wasn't much to add to that so I hid behind a mouthful of coffee, and caught myself checking out how she was dressed. She'd gone for a hybrid – part old lady, part nurse. It crossed my mind that she might have been consolidating her various roles into one. Then again, she might have been low on clean clothes.

Before he rang off, Doc had told me he hadn't mentioned Peter's plans to branch out into pimping. I'd asked why not.

There was a long pause, during which Doc no doubt practised his one-handed cut.

"I'd sooner it's Jeffry that drops that particular bombshell. It puts him over the line with all the bastards, leaves us on the side of the angels."

I didn't like being part of *us* and after finishing on the phone, I felt like taking another shower.

"I take it Doc's spoken to you?" I asked her.

She nodded. She was in the same spot as when I handed her the keys, and she hadn't taken her eyes off them. I waited for an explosion. When she just stuffed the keys into her hip pocket and began making herself breakfast, I was almost disappointed.

Now she was downstairs with me, I didn't want to break for the door like I was running away. Rather than stand around like a spare one, I set the coffee machine up again and she accepted a cup this time. I watched her as she sipped it. She didn't like Ethiopian coffee. That upset me vaguely.

"Rough night?"

Jan took another sip and shrugged.

"Least you've got the house back," I said.

She looked up sharply, looked close to panic. "I hadn't thought about that, about living there again."

"I'm not throwing you out, stay as long as you want.

You've got something to your name, that's all I meant. That's a good thing."

I sat down at the table opposite her and waited while she calmed down again.

"I won't have it long," she said.

"You think you'll sell it?"

"I won't have any choice. That place costs a small fortune to run. Anyway, if Peter's business was in as much trouble as Jeffry claimed, it's probably mortgaged three times over."

Mention of Jeffry reminded me about his apology. When I told Jan he'd asked me to say sorry for him, she laughed and rolled her eyes.

"Worthless bastard."

"Yeah, you're well shot of him."

Jan nodded, jaw clenched tight, working hard at keeping a lid on things.

"I can't believe him. I really can't."

The ambiguity of her words might have gone over my head if she hadn't started crying. She cried with her eyes open again, watching. Watching me. I did my Sir Galahad bit, stood up, walked around the table and put my arms around her. Confirmed it was true, told her she could believe Doc. I judged it was safe to leave for work when she closed her eyes to finish crying.

"I think you're right about Jan," I told Doc as soon as I got to the shop. "She's got her doubts about you."

"And good morning to you."

He had some music on, old blues, scored for acoustic guitar and depression. I stowed my lid, hung up my leather. Doc's was on the rack too. He'd sat himself down by the laptop and adjusted the volume so the music became a background mutter.

"So, what happened with Jan?"

"She got emotional on the subject of Jeff, started saying she couldn't believe it. I thought she was talking about him. Then she started crying. She kept her eyes open."

"Watching for your take on things?"

"Waiting for me to back up what *you'd* said about Jeffry."

Doc pulled a face, like people do when they see something they approve of. "Good."

"Why good?"

"Mistrust goes hand in glove with disobedience. The way she'd been adopting roles, I think she's been getting into self-destructive behaviour. The cues she picks up on come from whoever she's close to. I don't think she's been able to see when those cues run counter to her own best interests. I think she's learning to be more judgemental."

He started clicking his fingers in time to the track that was playing. I pondered this theory and his reaction.

"Yeah, I agree: good. But why she's decided to question you?"

"Probably a lot of things. She's made a fairly drastic change of environment when you think about it. Keller and the big house, fundraisers and ladies-who-lunch ... " He didn't finish the sentence, just spread his arms to encompass Jan's new life: Chris, tattoo shops, bikers. "And life experience in general. She's had a lot of bad decisions to dwell on in the last year or so." He tapped the little leather bag nailed to the door frame of the back room. "I think the Voodoo's helped, too."

I wasn't planning on say anything, insulting his belief wasn't going to change it, but I could feel him waiting for me to react.

"All I've seen your Jive about spirits and tarot cards do is trick her."

Doc grinned and held up a finger, like I'd just proved his point.

"As I've told you, Voodoo is a practical religion, the religion of survival. It doesn't teach you to love your neighbour or turn the other cheek. It's more about taking control of things."

"If you say so. I'm going to make a start."

Doc stepped to one side to allow me into the back room.

I found his chair and work station had already been cleaned and set up. There was nothing for me to do. When I turned to ask Doc what was going on, I found he'd come up behind me. His expression was hard to read.

"You're not the apprentice anymore, so it's not your job. That one," he pointed at the other chair, the one I shared with Gina, "is still down to you."

The wall behind the chair now had a hand-drawn sign. Doc had lettered *Yakky* in an elaborate font and framed the result. Naturally, after he'd mounted the frame on the wall, he'd added a mojo just above it. Above that he'd drawn a strange symbol that I guessed was another veve. Doc's equivalent of the key to the executive toilet. Touching and annoying in equal measure.

"Thanks, man."

I held out my hand to shake. Doc took it, clasping it as if we were about to arm wrestle, and pulled me into a brief hug. I was surprised at his strength.

"Welcome aboard, brother. It's good to have you here."

When we broke free of each other, his face didn't quite match the sentiment. I thought I knew why.

"But not quite the same as having Gina here?"

He shrugged. "I spoke to her this morning. She's going to do one evening a week until Christmas."

He didn't add, *and that's it*, but I guessed it was. We still had the details to iron out, but by the time the first customer rolled in, we'd agreed most of it. Doc was generous with the appointment book that day. Any client who hadn't specifically asked for him, got me. It worked out a little over the half day's takings came my way. I tattooed for longer that day than any before. I could feel myself improving, and my muscles complaining.

Just after lunch, which I skipped, Chris's barrister showed up.

Doc was at the reception desk. I didn't know it at the time but he was up to his elbows in Chris's laptop and the obscene emails from Jan. He asked me to try and get Jan to talk about them the day before but in the midst of all that had gone on, it slipped my mind. For reasons I couldn't see, they continued to worrying him.

When I heard someone ask for Doctor Slidesmith I excused myself from the customer I was with and put my head around the door. I assumed anyone being so formal would be wearing a blue uniform and a stern expression.

"That's me," Doc said and gave a watered-down version of his grin. His first-time-customer face.

The young woman at the counter returned it with a professional smile and a business card.

"Good afternoon, I'm Priti Patel. I've been appointed as legal counsel for Christopher Rudjer. He asked me to contact you."

Priti Patel appeared frighteningly young. If I'd been in a cell for the last five days, I'd have wanted a legal rep old enough to have seen, done and known it all. This one looked like she'd just come from the job interview.

"Would it be convenient to talk, Dr Slidesmith?" When Doc told her *yes*, she glanced in my direction. "Is there somewhere more private?"

"Of course, but anything you say to me you can say to Yakky; he's a part of things."

At the mention of my name Priti looked at me fully, and sanctified me with the same professional smile. It was so quick I didn't have time to return it.

"Ah. Yes, Mr Rudjer told me Jan Keller is currently living at your home, but he didn't have your address," she said. "Also, he didn't know your real name." I agreed with her: *he* didn't. She blinked once at my answer. Back to Doc, "As I said, maybe somewhere more private?"

Doc shut down Chris's laptop then gave the appointments book a quick once over.

"You happy to take my three o'clock, Yak?"

I said I was and returned to my current client as Doc led Priti from the shop.

Thankfully my customer's piece wasn't too demanding because once I was on my own, the shop got busy. People drifted in asking what we charged, did we do cover-ups and, of course, does it hurt? An hour's worth of flash wound up taking over two. I was grateful when Doc's three o'clock phoned to say he was running late. Late or not, I'd barely got my chair prepped before he turned up.

I saw the tail end of the black Audi as it past the window. A second later, Jan ran by the shop going the other way. I assumed she'd parked up and doubled back on foot. She didn't cast a glance at the shop. I didn't waste time worrying about it; I didn't doubt I'd be back in the loop again soon. Instead I concentrated on laying down ink and tuning into the needle song.

I checked the clock when I heard the shop door open. It was one of Doc's teachings; check the time you start tattooing, check it again when you stop. If you charge by the hour you need to get into the habit of keeping track. Jan was at the counter, her eyes were red again, which was becoming a regular feature, but she didn't look upset.

"I'm fine, really. Doc asked me to look after the desk, so you can work in peace. Is that alright?"

I told her it was great and got back to work.

Doc's client left the shop, happy with his new tattoo and happy with the price. I had a feeling I'd just gained a regular. I tidied and cleaned the back room obsessively before talking properly to Jan. She found her way to the music store on the laptop and, based on her choices, her spirits were fairly high.

I asked her what was happening; she had her tarot set out on the counter and my question seemed to throw her. She may have thought I was asking for her interpretation of the cards. To short cut any of that crap, I pointed a finger straight up, to the flat above. She gave me my first genuine smile of the day.

"Doc rang me and said I should come over." She turned over a card and smiled again, this time not at me. "Priti thinks she's got a good case for getting Chris freed. She spoke to me and she thinks the police have made procedural mistakes that could make any conviction unsafe."

I didn't think she understood the full implication of what she'd been told. Priti was talking about overturning a conviction. Not avoiding one.

"Did she say how Chris was bearing up?"

"She said he's doing very well." She smiled again. It was beginning to get on my nerves. "It's going to be alright."

Jan was still buzzing when I closed the shop and locked up. It worried me; I'm not prone to great highs. I don't trust them. Higher you fly, farther you fall. As she made her way to the Audi, she asked if I'd be back for dinner.

"I reckon me and Doc will be burning a bit of the midnight oil, you know?"

I could feel the air turning cool as I walked around the shop to the flat, a hint that summer was coming to a close. Chris's bike skulked in a corner of Doc's yard, still waiting for the Big Guy to come home. Possibly that helped spoil my mood. Whatever the reason, the excitement of my first day as a real tattooist was quickly becoming a memory.

I found the door on the latch and announced myself as I went in. Doc told me he admired my timing, inevitably, he was making tea. I didn't feel light-hearted, but I forced a smile. Doc frowned with his head on one side, asked if I was okay.

"Yeah I'm good, just tired." I rolled my shoulders. "Bit stiff and achy."

Doc acted like he believed me and waved me to the front room. It didn't really surprise me to find Priti Patel still in Doc's flat. By the same token, it wouldn't have surprised me to have seen her running from the alleyway screaming. Doc was like that.

She was on the floor amidst the documents Doc had amassed. She'd taken a cushion from one of the armchairs and was sat on it, legs folded beneath her. The teenager-like posture was at odds with the uber-professional outfit. She didn't react when I dropped into the remaining armchair.

I said, "Hello, again."

And she lifted a hand in my direction without looking away from what she was reading. When Doc came in, he put a black tea next to her and got as little response. Doc handed me a mug and lowered himself to the floor, cross-legged with his back to the crime wall.

"You get on alright this afternoon?" he spoke as if it were just us in the room.

"Yeah, it was good. Good job you asked Jan to mind the desk."

He nodded thoughtfully. "Once you've got yourself settled, we need to see about a fresh apprentice."

We talked shop for a while. Agreed Gina was going to leave some big shoes to fill when she quit for good. We also agreed a female tattooist made sense from a purely business perspective. Not all women want to be worked on by a male artist. Neither of us wanted the shop to become a soulless safe-and-pretty parlour but scaring custom away was plain stupid.

Doc broke off mid-sentence and looked away from me to Priti, who was watching us. The conversation abruptly changed course.

"Miss Patel has been reading through our bits and pieces. She thinks some of it might be useful." He looked relieved. "Does anyone want more tea?"

While Doc was back in the kitchen, Priti stood up and took a couple of stiff-legged steps, pressing creases out of her skirt with her palms. I wondered again at how young she was; she looked tiny. She must have seen me scrutinising her because she squinted at me and asked if something was wrong, clearly meaning: *who do you think you're looking at?*

"Didn't mean to stare. I'm just knackered. I was up at about three o'clock this morning, sorry."

Miss Patel didn't say anything for a couple of beats. She was either thinking or wanted me to think she was. In the end she flashed that professional smile at me.

"I understand that. I've had a long day too, Mister Yakky. Or is it just Yakky?"

I felt cornered by the question, but she was on Chris's side and there was nothing to gain by being obnoxious.

"Just Yakky. My old man's about the only one who calls me anything else."

"Does Yakky mean something?"

"Short for Yakuza."

She must have got the reference because she asked, "Do you have the traditional tattoos?"

"I've got a lot of ink I don't show to people."

As Doc came back with her tea, she tilted her head to me, maybe as a kind of apology.

"Questions," she said, "force of habit."

She put the tea down on the floor and folded herself back onto the cushion. Doc slid gracelessly into his customary bag-of-bones slouch. He took a swig from his mug and waited for Priti to follow suit.

Once he was happy she had a mouthful of tea he asked her, "Do you know Neville Minton?"

She didn't choke, but being occupied with swallowing made it harder for her to hide that she'd been caught unawares.

Classic Doc Jive. In general, I didn't have any problem with ambushes, survival is all the honour I need, but the aesthetic of what was happening bothered me. The way Priti settled on the floor like a child, the size of her compared to the two of us.

I kept thinking about Jan as a little girl trying to hide from the face in the wardrobe doors.

"Neville's one the senior partners," Priti told Doc. "He's the one who assigned me to Mr Rudjer's case."

Doc produced the Dictaphone. "Then there's something you need to hear."

Scumbag

The night before, once Jeffry Keller was good and rat-arsed, Doc started talking about his contacts. He didn't mention the police report directly out of deference, he claimed, to his agreement with Caroline. I doubted it would have mattered. Come the morning after, Jeffry didn't look set to remember what was being said. Doc played to the man's arrogance, knowing he liked to flaunt his success as much as his brother had. The difference was Peter tried too hard and had less to work with.

The contact turned out not to be a cop but a partner in a law firm. A law firm that worked for the Criminal Defence Service. I had a hazy idea that people working for the CDS were professional do-gooders. Jeff shattered that illusion. According to him, his contact preached public service but lived the gospel according to cash flow.

"Think of the amount of people that get into hot water with the police. They all want a lawyer but none of them want to pay for one." Jeff winked at Doc. "If you want a nice, reliable income stream, you represent the low life, because tax money's going to pay their bills."

He laughed expansively, a man in the know. Doc listened to this, turning it over. Caroline hired Steve and Uncle Kenny to follow Jan before Chris's arrest. She had a copy of the police report to flash around before the Big Guy was shown a warrant card. If there wasn't a suspect in custody, why would a lawyer from the CDS have a report on the crime?

"When did your friend get involved?"

"I gave Neville a call as soon as I got word Peter was dead."

Doc leaned closer, all drunken goodwill and fellowship. "Neville?"

"Neville Minton," Keller said. "One of the big boys in Brookfield, Minton and Langdon."

Keller poured himself another measure. The brief abandon of the toasts was gone. Now it was the measured pace of miserable drinking.

"Why'd you call a lawyer though?" Doc asked him once he'd got his snout in the glass.

"Looking out for Jan. I thought if she'd gone and killed Peter, she'd need a bloody good lawyer. Neville knows who to talk to, so he gets to pick up the choice jobs."

As the bloody good lawyer that picked up that particular job was paid for with tax money, Jeffry's act of largesse wouldn't cost him. Keller laughed into his glass and had a coughing fit when he breathed in the spirit. Neither of us bothered to pat him on the back. When he could breathe again, Doc asked him why he thought Jan killed his brother.

"Everybody knew she was carrying on with someone. Caroline kept going on and on about it. It was all her witches' circle ever talked about. Of course, she wanted to tell him. Kept saying he had a right to know. She doesn't care about Peter."

He took a careful sip from the tumbler and fell into morose reflection.

Doc filled in the silence.

"She wanted to tell Peter so she could drop Jan in it?"

Keller nodded. "When I heard Peter had died in funny circumstances, I thought Jan might be in trouble. Called up Neville. He pulled a few strings, even got me a copy of the police reports."

Doc took the trouble to look impressed. I'm pretty sure Keller missed the act.

"You still think Jan was involved?"

"'Course she is. Obvious what she's done. She wants shot of Peter, and who'd blame her? Takes up with some thug and gets him to do the dirty work." He fell silent again, staring into space. I saw Doc move closer to prompt him, but Keller started talking again. "That's why I told her Peter signed the house over to me. I wanted her out of the way of the investigation. Pete's business is finished – no money, no house, no motive." He spread his hands and shrugged, the motion nearly unbalanced him. "I didn't think she'd move straight out the night I told her, though."

"And you've been taking the post so you can sideline any letters from your brother's solicitors?"

"I didn't take it myself, I arranged for it to be cleared once a day and brought to me."

"And so far it's working? No police sniffing around Jan?"

Jeffry poured another measure. "Neville's keeping an eye on things for me. The police are busy with Jan's thug and, according to Neville, he's not saying anything. He must be in love. It looks like he's going to take the blame."

Doc finally dropped the fellow drunk act. When he asked if Minton was pulling strings with the investigation, he sounded neutral. The look in his eyes said different.

"I don't know. I'm sure he's got friends dotted around the force but I don't think he calls the shots. He's still a defence lawyer. Different sides really, aren't they?"

He belched quietly and grimaced. Doc had reached across the table and taken the Dictaphone from its hiding place, held it between them to get the best results. Jeff was past the point of seeing, or caring, that he was on record.

"Will your friend's firm take the case when Chris asks for legal counsel?"

"Chris?"

"Chris Rudjer, Jan's thug. Will Neville's firm get his case?" Jeff nodded, belched again, grimaced. "And the plan is ... ?"

"The police get a successful conviction. Case closed. It all goes away."

Along with Jan's thug.

There was a long pause before Doc spoke again, "So Neville takes the case and throws it?"

"Not Neville. He'll just give it to one of the juniors and let them make a hash of it. He said he's got someone in mind." Jeff seemed to find this amusing.

We watched him empty the glass again. Doc refilled it but there was nothing friendly about the gesture. Jeff was sweating like a pig and looked miserable. People forget alcohol's a downer. Without the flow of prompts and questions from Doc, he lapsed into silence. For a while the only sound was Doc's occasional tongue click.

When Jeffry started mumbling, Doc and I both leaned forward trying to hear what he was saying. I realised he was singing and sat back, losing interest, but Doc got closer, trying to make out the words. After a few seconds, he looked up and pulled a face.

"What shall we do with the drunken sailor?"

It was probably just the come down after the tension but it struck him as funny.

"Maybe sailing's a family tradition," I said.

I was thinking of Peter's office and his photo of somebody else's yacht. It was meant as a sarcastic remark not directed to anyone, but Jeff heard it and laughed.

"That was just Pete's thing, boats. Thought if he had a yacht he'd be a real player, be one of the big boys. Bigger than me and Neville."

Jeff's breath caught and I thought he'd started to sob, then Doc pulled his face away abruptly. The smell of bile wafted over even to where I was sat. Jeff found the bottle again and cured the taste with more of the problem.

"That's why he bought this eyesore. It's on the golf course. I told him, 'it all happens on the golf course'. Golf course, that's where the big boys play. Waste of time." He barked out another laugh. "I black-balled his membership."

The tuneless singing started again and, soon after, he passed out. Doc regarded the snoring man for a moment before speaking directly into the Dictaphone.

"Conversation between Mr Jeffry Keller and, myself, Doctor James Slidesmith. Witnessed by Mr Andrew Miller, identified on tape as Yakky. Recorded at the former residence of the late Peter Keller, on July twenty-fourth." Then he clicked the machine off and added, "What a scumbag."

It was getting late when we finished up. The coolness I felt in the air earlier had gone, replaced by the sticky closeness of an approaching storm. Doc's front door was propped open again to circulate air. Noise from the street echoed in the alleyway.

Miss Patel had gathered up her notes along with selected copies of Doc's stuff. She also took the Kellergate tape. She said she'd get it back to him once she'd copied it. Doc wasn't thrilled about handing the tape over but we had no way of making a copy and Priti needed one. He may have given it as a display of trust; the same way he'd shown me the gun under the floorboards.

Priti stowed everything in an expensive-looking satchel. It was heavy and she strained to get the strap over her shoulder. It wasn't the only strain; there was a line of tension running along the edge of her jaw. It had been there since Doc had played the tape.

Doc asked her when she'd talk to Chris again.

"First thing tomorrow. All being well, you might be able to see him sometime in the afternoon. But, as I said, I'm not making any guarantees."

"Understood."

Doc held out his hand and there was a trace of hesitation before Priti took it. The movement dislodged the satchel strap so I offered to carry it down the stairs for her. Once we reached the yard, I realised I was hungry.

"I'm going to get a pizza," I told her, "I might just as well carry this to your car."

She consented without comment and we walked in

silence. She'd parked a little beyond the pizza place and, as we'd passed it, one of the lairy teenagers, who were becoming a regular fixture, looked us up and down. Decided against it. It was a wise move – Priti would have probably put him in the ground. The anger coming off her was palpable.

She opened the car's hatchback and thanked me when I handed her the satchel. I asked if she really thought the plod would let Doc in to see Chris.

"It's possible. Mr Rudjer's refusal to speak is driving the police to distraction. They may allow a visit to see if it breaks the status quo."

"But you wouldn't bet on it?"

She gave it some thought before saying, "A few hours ago I'd have said no. But since listening to your tape, I'm inclined to think it could work."

I told her she'd lost me. "Mister Miller, what Doctor Slidesmith has suggested is ludicrous. My involvement will undermine my position and damage my standing. However, as Mister Minton appears to have given me this case in the expectation of my losing, I think there's a good chance phone calls will be made and strings pulled."

The Big Guy was currently in a grey-walled limbo, in a cell but yet to be imprisoned. Visits while in police custody were more or less discretionary.

Doc wanted to talk with Chris.

Miss Patel hadn't thought that was likely.

The Cheshire Cat had made an appearance.

Chris Rudjer was surely allowed to practice his religion? It was agreed that he was.

"Well," Doc said, "I'll be willing to take responsibly for your client's spiritual needs. Assuming the police can't find another practicing Voodoo priest."

Priti was not amused.

"No one is going to believe Mr Rudjer is a ... " she waved a hand, irritated " ... a whatever-you'd-call-it."

"A Voodooist," Doc said. "If you ask for a list of the

items Chris was carrying at the time of his arrest, you'll find he was carrying a Voodoo mojo and his pack of tarot cards. Both of which I expect he's been denied access to."

I remembered Doc bestowing the trappings of faith just before Chris had turned himself in. Now legal counsel was going to plead for visitation on grounds of religious expression. And it might just work, because Neville Minton had set Miss Patel up to lose.

I told her I was sorry she'd been caught in the middle of everything and for the way her boss was treating her. She dismissed this the way you'd shoo a fly.

"I should have expected it."

"This Minton's a bit of a sleazebag, is he?"

She laughed, I thought at my description, then I realised she was laughing at me.

"No, Mr Miller. Neville Minton is a perfectly charming man. A charming white man."

She paused and held my eye making sure I'd taken that in.

"What's that supposed to mean?"

Priti sighed. Not despairing, venting. "When I was taken on at Brookfield, Minton and Langdon, my brother gave me the keys to a new car and told me I was a *double whammy*. An ethnic minority and a woman, all in one package. The firm could tick two boxes at once."

"Nice. I hope you told him where to stick his car."

"You don't understand. My brother is boorish and rude but he is also right. He is also male. If he gets what he expects, he pats himself on the back because he's done well. No one expects him to be grateful for being allowed to work twice as hard as everyone else. People expect men to be on top and white men ... " She ran out of words and made a guttural sound in the back of her throat. I was expecting her to spit, but she didn't, she just glared at me.

"Mister Miller, if you had my job, no one would think you were being given a free ride. Whereas I get charming white men patting me on the head and being amazed that I can do the job at all. Or I get alpha males, asking me who I slept with before the interview. If those – " she jerked her head at the teenagers buzzing round the pizza shop and said something that wasn't in English " – want to give you trouble, they give it some thought, think about what they're going to do. They see a woman and they just do it, because they don't need to wonder if they'll come out on top."

She hauled the satchel into the back of her car and forced herself to set it down gently. When she tried to slam the hatch closed, the pneumatic struts holding it up wouldn't let her. She had better luck with the driver's door.

I went back to the pizza place and ordered the biggest thing they did and two litres of cola. As I waited for them to cook it, one of the gobby teenagers peeled himself away from the pack and swaggered towards me. Priti had a point. I watched him weigh up his chances.

He was brighter than he looked. He got his sums right and swaggered right back again without saying a fucking word.

"Ah, nice one," Doc said when I dropped the pizza on the kitchen table.

He produced what looked like the world's oldest carving knife and began cutting it into eighths. I poured myself a mug of cola and put the rest of the bottle into Doc's fridge.

"Priti Patel's pretty pissed off."

"I don't blame her." Doc took an unusually small bite of pizza. "This is the first time she's been given a big case to handle. She thought the old boys' club at the top was finally showing a bit of faith in her. Wankers."

He took another bite; this one more his usual shark like affair.

"Yeah, well, I don't think we're much higher in her estimations." Doc made the spooling motion as he chewed. "She thinks all men are bastards."

He nodded and finally managed to swallow. "I don't blame her for that either."

Me and Doc were tattooing side by side, both deep in the needle song. Jan was looking after the front desk, and dad was looking after himself. It was one of those brief moments when the universe worked like it should.

Blink once and you'd miss it.

Jan called Doc to the phone. He wasn't gone long, and came back without comment, other than to apologise to his client.

Doc finished before I did and once the bill had been settled, he cleaned up his work station for the day. I took a break from tattooing and went to check the afternoon appointments. Jan was laying out her tarot cards; she happened to turn one over as I finished with the shop diary. It was the Six of Cups. I picked it up from its place in the spread and studied it at arm's length.

"I think the future holds Doc going out for the afternoon, you making phone calls to reschedule the customers, and me working late."

I meant it as a joke, but it rubbed her up the wrong way. She snatched the card back and told me I shouldn't mock things I didn't understand. Doc must have had heard this exchange, because he came out of the back room, bang on cue, and announced, "Listen guys, I'm heading out for the afternoon. Jan, would you ring round, see if you can reschedule some people? And Yakky, are you alright to work late?"

Jan's butterfly of a scowl fluttered against the chaos of Doc's grin. She herded the spread of cards back into a pack and wrapped them in Chris's old bandana.

"You're not funny."

"Yeah, we are," I said and headed back to my client.

Before I got back to the needles, I heard Doc telling her, "You need to get your head around something. Your faith is yours and only yours. It doesn't require anyone else to be a part of it. Let people laugh." Just before he left he called loudly from the door, "Put some blues on, he hates that."

Jan took him at his word and put on a selection of songs that Dignitas could have used for the company anthem.

I ached and stank by the end of the day. The air was still thick and close, but there was no sign of the storm promised the night before. What I wanted more than anything was to get home, make a gallon of coffee and drink it while I soaked in the bath. Doc didn't return, but his Sportster had rumbled passed the shop about an hour before we'd closed up.

After I double-checked the shop door I followed Jan, who'd disappeared into the alleyway. The door to Doc's yard wasn't lit and I could see she was playing the light from her phone over its surface. I asked what she was looking for.

"A bell."

By way of an explanation she pushed on the door. Doc had locked up for the night. I told her there was no bell and she tried his mobile. Not unexpectedly, it went straight to voicemail.

The surgery was closed.

I headed out of the alleyway and Jan came with me. I'd chained the Yam to the lamppost in front of the shop. With the extra light I could see she was worried, wanting news about Chris. I told her to stop fretting.

"If something drastic had happened, Doc would have been straight back to the shop to let us know."

She wasn't convinced, then neither was I. I took the lock and chain off my bike and put it over my shoulder like a bandolier, thumbed my mojo and hit the starter. The engine catching coincided with the start of the rain.

I used the landline to leave a message on Doc's mobile, told him to call me if he picked the message up at a decent hour. Me or Jan. We both wanted news of Chris.

I asked Jan if she needed to use the bathroom because I was going to have a soak. She told me she didn't so I went to set the taps running then came back down to get a coffee.

In the time I'd been gone, she'd settled herself at the kitchen table and laid out the cards. She met my eye with an expression I'd last seen on Priti Patel. Doc's counsel to ignore the doubters hadn't taken hold.

I got my coffee and as an afterthought poured a second for her. I put it on the table, careful not to disturb the cards. She nodded a thank you.

"I didn't mean to upset you earlier," I told her. "If this is what gets you through the night then, go for it."

Jan sighed, then took the coffee and sipped it. It was a gesture of a kind.

"Doc upset me more," she said flatly. "Sometimes I think he's really got some sort of spiritual wisdom to pass on, sometimes I think he's just laughing at everything."

"That's how the man is. He was giving people the needle long before he picked up a tattoo gun. Doesn't mean he isn't, I don't know, devout?"

Jan sighed again, continued laying the cards. She didn't say anything else and because I didn't want to leave it there; I asked her what she was reading for.

"Guidance," she said shortly.

The next card she turned was The Star. It showed a woman pouring water from an urn, which reminded me I'd left the bath running.

"Too late to call, Yak? I've only just picked up your message."

It was about quarter to one. I'd made small talk with Jan and sat with dad for an hour, eaten dinner without tasting it then gone to bed. I'd stripped naked and lay on top of the bed clothes. The rain had done nothing to draw the heat off and I didn't try to sleep, just lay and let the bitter feelings fade with the light. By the time Doc rang I was more or less numb.

"You there, Yakky?"

"Yeah. Hang on a sec."

I found my jeans and pulled them on. It would have felt

weird talking to Doc without clothes. Once I was dressed again, I asked him if he'd seen Chris.

"Yeah. All went to plan. The Big Guy's fine." I wondered what counted as fine sat in a cell with a murder charge hanging over you. "You up for getting in early tomorrow? Only I think I know who did it."

Revelations

Wednesday 27 July

I knocked on Jan's door at stupid o'clock in the morning and told her Doc called and Chris was fine. I didn't wait around for her to surface fully before I took off.

It was another sticky day. The puddles from the downpour were drying out and turning into humidity. Even wearing my leather, damp from the ride home the previous night, I was sweating by the time I got to the shop.

The backyard door was unlocked, so was the door to the flat. Doc was slumped in one of the armchairs, staring at the crime wall and cutting a pack of cards. He looked dejected, like he'd been there most of the night.

"Behold."

He made a grandiose sweep with his free hand. The crime wall was almost finished. Along the bottom strata the only items unanswered were: *??Emails??* and the picture of the lock knife with *WHY THEN?* written next to it. In the centre, the big *PK*, around which everything revolved, had been rubbed away, in its place was the word *HOW?*

"You should have left a space to put the answer in," I told him.

Doc shrugged. "This is just my working out. The police keep the sheet to write the answers on." He stood up and grabbed the printouts of Jan's emails to Chris, handed them to me. "Something about these isn't kosher. I've read the bastards so many times I'm getting a fetish. Just humour me, read them, see if something hits you."

I dropped into the other armchair and read the very personal emails. The pages I was reading had been printed from the folder in Chris's email account where he held them. It appeared to have been a one-sided correspondence. Chris either never made replies or deleted them from his account.

If you were given to tact, you might describe Jan's correspondence as love letters. I found myself glancing up periodically to look at Doc. I didn't like the idea of being watched while I read them. Doc, however, was tuned out, staring at, or past, the crime wall. He cut and recut the tarot deck endlessly.

I read the lot end-to-end. Other than the seediness of it, nothing struck me as odd. I started again and got no further. By the third reading I realised I was beginning to get favourite passages and stopped looking at the text. Instead I checked the dates and times they had been sent. What I thought that would tell me I couldn't say. After I'd checked half a dozen dates, my only conclusion was that Jan sent a lot of emails and didn't always fill in the subject box. Occasionally the emails to Chris would be titled *Morning Handsome* or *Hi Stud,* but most of them were marked *No Subject.*

I did another skim through, comparing the ones with titles against the ones without. Other than noticing that Jan was using two email addresses, nothing stood out for me. I put the pile of papers back in their place at the foot of the crime wall. Doc's focus changed to include me. I shrugged in defeat but felt I should say something.

"Jan's got a one-track mind and two email accounts. Sorry."

Then I jumped back. Doc had sprung forward in his chair, the one-handed cut became a shower of cards.

"Two accounts?"

I picked the printouts up again and gave him the top one, pointed to the header at the top of the paragraph where the sending and receiving account details were given.

"This one's Jan seven eight eight at such and such." I

scanned the next few sheets until the other address made an appearance. "This one's Jan seven eight eight underscore at such and such."

Doc laughed and pulled a charcoal pencil from behind his ear. He drew a line through the entry: *??EMAILS??* He stepped back from the wall and nodded.

I had the feeling I'd been a part in some kind of revelation but missed out on the epiphany. Doc turned to me and laughed, probably at my confusion. "Two email accounts, Yak. What does that mean?" He made the spooling motion, faster than usual. "Two different accounts?"

And I finally saw the light. "Two different writers. Jan didn't write half of these."

Doc pointed his finger and pretend to shoot me. The mannerism had lost its charm since I'd seen the shotgun. He drew in a huge breath and let it back out in a juddering sigh. I thought he was being theatrical but he sat down again and almost missed the chair when his knees buckled. I asked if he'd been keeping a bottle of Tequila company all night. He shook his head and took a few deep breaths.

"Nah, not a drop. I'm just knackered. And relieved. And I need something to eat." He got up, a little cautiously, and drifted off to the kitchen.

I trailed after him, holding the emails. The kitchen bin was overflowing with egg cartons and tea bags.

"Give me a clue, will you? I'm still catching up here."

Doc was in his fridge. He came out again holding a pint of milk and half a loaf of sliced bread.

"I was worried Chris was covering up for Jan. That's why I wanted to see him really, make good and sure we were singing off the same sheet." He sat at the table and drank most of the milk in one draft. "So, now I'm happy he wasn't shielding her; he genuinely believed she was on the level. Thing is, he's so gone on her I can't trust his judgement. He's sat in that cell willing to do fifteen to twenty so long as she's left out of it."

Jeffry Keller's comment from the other night: *he must be in love.*

"And you weren't convinced she was innocent?"

Doc was chewing on dry bread when I said this; it wasn't really a question, but he shook his head. While I waited for him to finish his breakfast, I filled the kettle. I wasn't surprised by his answer. I'd have been willing to believe she was involved when we'd first met. My lack of suspicion now had little to do with logic or deduction. I was just returning her trust.

"I'm convinced now, Yakky. For me those emails prove it."

I made the spooling motion at him; I was still in the dark. He grinned and took a huge bite of bread and began chewing slowly. I rounded up a couple of mugs and didn't react to his dramatics.

Eventually he said, "Check those emails, I'll bet you anything you like, I'll bet you my Sportster against your Yamaha, that all the real dirty stuff, and all the snide comments about Peter, come from just one of those addresses."

He stopped talking and started on the bread again, gesticulating to the printouts I was still holding. I didn't go all the way through the emails again. After ten or so it was clear Doc's assumption was right. All of them were fairly smutty but the ones received from Jan788_, the *No Subject* ones, were in a different league. They were also peppered with spiteful comments about Peter Keller. I told Doc he was right. He tilted his head in a miniature bow.

"That's two writers who weren't working together. If they were both in on it, there wouldn't be any point in opening a second account, they'd have just shared."

"Okay, who's the other writer?"

Doc frowned slightly when he answered, not impressed with how far behind I was.

"Peter Keller, of course."

"Jan's husband?" I sifted the emails and picked one out, "You reckon Peter wrote this?"

I turned it so he could see it:

Thank God for a real man. Peter's little cock barely touches the sides now you've been up there.

Doc nodded.

"That is fucking sick."

"I agree, he was, but the point is he wouldn't need to use a separate account if Jan was in on the deal. If the email porn was part of the game, they'd have sat and typed them out together. To me, this says Jan was out of the loop. She didn't know what Pete was really doing – she thought they were just playing out his sexual fantasy." Then the spell of excitement fizzled out and be looked flat again. "Clever as all this is, it won't get the Big Guy out of that cell."

By Doc's telling, the phone call from Priti Patel the day before had been not unlike the woman herself: short and angry. It amounted to, get over here quick before they stop laughing and change their minds. They being the police, with a side order of Neville Minton. Who, at least in Miss Patel's opinion, had probably been instrumental in getting the request for a visit to go through.

She was spitting blood and pissing vinegar by the time Doc met her outside the cop shop where Chris was being held. Doc had supplemented his uniform of festering white leather and jeans with an ageing Gladstone bag.

Before being allowed into the non-denominational chapel, Doc was required to open the bag. It contained a Dictaphone, three pewter bowls, a candle, a nine-inch nail wrapped in a stained cloth, a framed pen-and-ink drawing of woman with a scarred face, half a bottle of spiced rum, six eggs and the heads of seven Barbie dolls. After much wrangling between the officer in charge and Chris's legal counsel, the bag was allowed into the chapel minus the nine-inch nail and the bottle of rum.

The audience of admin staff and cops were greatly

entertained.

In the chapel, as they waited for Chris, Doc set up his altar while Priti Patel sat at the back and quietly fumed.

The solitary police officer who escorted Chris from his cell waited outside the door while Doc attended to his congregation. Chris was possibly more surprised than anyone to find that he was required to sit through a Voodoo service. I asked if Doc had been winding him up but he denied it.

"I made offerings to Ezulie Dantor," he said with dignity.

If Chris found the scene at all comical, Doc's next move wiped the smile off his face. Doc put the Dictaphone on the altar and pressed record.

"If you give me anything in here today that I even think is bullshit, I'm walking out and leaving you to it. Understand?" Chris blinked a couple of times in the face of Doc's cold appraisal. Once Doc was satisfied that Chris was just confused and not thinking of how to proceed he asked again, "Understand?"

"Yeah, I understand. And when have I lied to you?"

"I need to be sure. I need to know what the score is. Okay?"

Chris looked Doc in the eye, "I ain't going to lie to you. I got nothing to hide."

Doc rewound the tape and played it back to gauge the quality.

"Okay brother, I just had to know."

He pressed record again and put the machine back in front of the Big Guy.

Doc – When did you find out Jan's husband was dead?

Chris – The tenth, Sunday.

Doc – Time?

Chris – Don't know exactly, sometime in the afternoon.

Doc – Where were you?

Chris – I was back home by then, crashed out on the sofa. Some cop called me. Asked if I knew Jan and wanted to know if I'd go over to her house, said to get there quick.

Doc – Was this the one that brought you in when they arrested you the second time? Joan Rix?

Chris – I guess it was Rix. Rix was there when I got to the house. She told me Jan had found her husband dead in the bathroom then she took me through to the front room. Jan was on the sofa, white as a sheet.

Doc – And this was the first time you heard about the death? You heard it off the police?"

Chris – Yeah.

Doc – Did you go upstairs, go into the bathroom, or the bedroom again?

Chris – No. No, I didn't.

Doc – You sure about that?

(There's a pause while Chris thinks.)

Chris – I didn't go upstairs at all. I sat with Jan in the front room, told her she could stay at my place if she wanted to.

Doc – Didn't she go upstairs to pack a bag or something?

(Silence while Chris considers the question.)

Chris – Yeah, she did.

Doc – Didn't you go with her?

Chris – No. I was going to but that cop stopped me, Rix. She was flitting about quite a bit, in and out. When me and Jan went to go upstairs she told me to wait in the front room, and she took Jan upstairs.

(For a few seconds the only sound the recorder picks up is Doc's tongue clicking, then Chris continues.)

She wasn't strong arming it. She just said it'd be better if I waited downstairs, said she'd take care of Jan.

Doc – Okay. There's a set of palm prints on the wardrobe doors that look like yours. What's was all that about?

Chris – Well I was leaned against it while ... well you know.

Doc – No. I don't.

Chris – Christ man, we were getting it on. What do you think we were doing?

Doc – You're what, twenty-three, twenty-four stone? And you brace yourself against a mirror on a plywood door?

(Chris doesn't answer for a time. His breathing is heavy; it's hard to tell whether he's angry or embarrassed)

Chris – It wasn't ideal but it was how Jan wanted it. What the fuck has this got to do with anything?

(Long silence, then Chris sucks air through his teeth.)

Jan wanted to watch us together in the mirror. She was really getting off on it.

Doc – Jan wanted to watch? Just Jan?

Chris – (Sounding confused) Well, I wasn't objecting. It was a dirty weekend, Doc, that's why we were there.

Doc – So where was Peter Keller when all this was going down?

Chris – Not a clue. I thought he was off on some poxy business trip.

Doc – Did you go into the en suite bathroom that night?

Chris – No. I never used the en suite. Jan asked me not to.

Doc – Why?

Chris – She just said it was private. It wasn't a problem, that house is full of bloody toilets and showers.

Doc – Jan's all over you but doesn't want you in her bathroom? Didn't that strike you as odd?

Chris – A bit, but the whole set-up was odd, wasn't it?

Doc – Were you in the bedroom the whole night? All night, you didn't leave it at all?

Chris – No. We went upstairs around eleven. Then we went at it 'til we collapsed.

Doc – And you didn't leave the room at all until the next morning?

Chris – No, once we flaked out, I was dead to the world 'til about ten o'clock.

Doc – So Jan could have done anything? All you can really say for sure is you *didn't leave the room all night?*

(There's a long pause.)

Chris – I suppose so. I was out cold.

Doc stopped the playback and gave me a twitch of a smile.

"You get that?"

"Yeah, Chris wants to give Jan an alibi but he's already told you he was asleep."

"But he doesn't back track or give me any bullshit. He thinks about it, but he doesn't. I'm happy he's giving me the truth."

He stared at me, waiting for a reply.

"Okay. Good."

"Yakky, do you believe him?"

"Yeah, he sounds genuine. But you know him better than I do."

He nodded. "I just want everyone on the same sheet."

Assured that Chris hadn't known he had been co-starring in a private sex show, Doc was tasked with telling him.

Doc – Chris, you ain't going to like this, but I think it's better you hear it now off me. You need to get your head around this in case it comes up in a courtroom.

Chris – Go on.

Doc – Jan wasn't cheating on Peter, not with you at any rate. The whole thing was set up by her husband. He wrote out the posting on that website, even took the photo. I'm pretty sure he sifted through the replies and more or less set the pair of you up. The business with the mirror, that was so he'd have good view. He was watching from behind the bathroom door.

(No sound on the tape for a long time)

Chris – How do you know all this?

Doc – Long story short, Jan told Yakky. She didn't want you to know.

Chris – It explains a few things.

Doc – Like?

Chris – When we were at my place she was quiet. Not quiet in a bad way, just not noisy, sort of intense.

Doc – Different at her place, yeah?

Chris – Christ, yeah, like something out of a porn flick, some of the stuff she'd come out with. Putting on a good show, I guess. It's probably why she wouldn't clean up before she left my place. Showing hubby what she'd been up to.

Doc – Jan knows I'm here. She asked me to tell you she loves you.

(Long pause.)

Chris – It's funny. I'm sort of glad. I mean glad her husband was in on it. It never felt quite right knocking around with a married woman.

Doc – No one had a gun at your head, brother.

Chris – Thinking with my dick. Look where it's got me. Does Jan know we're having this conversation, I mean you telling me about her husband?

Doc – I'm not planning on keeping it from her.

Chris – Look Doc, do something for me, okay? Let Jan know that you've told me, tell her it doesn't change anything between us, alright?

Doc – Yeah, I'll do that.

(Sound of Chris clearing his throat then the tape ends.)

As Chris had cleared his throat he'd drawn his finger tip across his neck then pointed at the Dictaphone. Doc shut the machine off.

The Big Guy said softly, "And tell Jan, if I see her with

another man, she's dead to me. I'm no Peter Keller and I don't play these fucked up games."

The Miss Maple Appreciation Society of North London

Doc rang Jan and asked her to come to the flat before the shop opened. We'd agreed that we'd both be there when she heard about Doc's conversation with Chris. Telling her that Chris now knew about the role he played in Peter's fantasy, would fall to me. I'd been the one she confided in and the one who passed it on to Doc. I wasn't looking forward to it.

Doc's wall had nearly run its course. There were only two outstanding points left. Front and centre, the big one, *HOW?* The other, down the bottom, was next to the picture of the knife Jan had given to Chris. The notation said: *WHY THEN?* As in why had the knife been produced then, during the second weekend spent in the Keller house?

The crime wall looked strange to me now, or maybe less strange. With so many crossings out and items attended to, it had lost some of its disturbing beauty. The more of it that was solved, the less of a mystery it was, with the loss of its abstraction it became just an ugly tool. Maybe because of this train of thought I came up with another question to ask it. Why *that* knife?

Doc's head snapped up when I spoke; he'd been dozing off. I don't think he slept the night before. He shook his head blinking and asked, *what knife*? I pointed to the foot-long rendering of the lock knife Jan gave Chris.

"If Keller wants to see Jan get her dress cut off, he could have given her a pair of nail scissors or a Swiss army knife. Why a ceramic knife?"

Doc gave it a moment's thought. "Perhaps it was just what he had to hand."

"Skeletal handle, ceramic-bladed, lock knife? How many of them do you see in a day?"

The more I thought about it, the less sense it made. We'd seen Keller's house, public face and private office. No blades outside the kitchen, certainly nothing exotic. Nothing that indicated any interest in knives, no collection, no Samurai swords on the wall. So why something so unusual, just to cut off buttons?

I fired up Doc's laptop and did an image search of *ceramic knives*, found the one I was looking for on the third page. It was available through an American tool supplier that serviced the explosives industry. The ceramic blade was non-conductive, so you didn't accidentally short anything out if you were working with a detonator. The skeletal handle was to keep it light; presumably you wouldn't want extra weight on your hip if something started ticking and you had to run.

We both spent a long time looking for a UK supplier and couldn't find one. Doc folded the laptop away and exchanged it for his tarot. He shuffled them without any fancy one-handed stuff.

"You're right," he said as he started to deal. "You don't go to that much trouble just to cut off a few buttons." Then, to the cards, "What was that all about, Peter?"

Despite Doc's asking her to come to the flat to see us both, I intercepted Jan at the shop and ended up talking to her on my own. Time had crept up on me and Doc, and he wanted to concentrate on his reading. When I left he was making adjustments to the altar.

The shop was thick with damp heat when I let myself in. I opened every window that had a hinge and turned on the desk fan we kept in the back room. It made no difference. When I spotted the Audi cruise by, I went and stood by the door to catch Jan before she dipped into the alleyway.

"Doc's going to be a while but I need to talk to you."

I led her to the back room so we wouldn't be seen from the street. I didn't lock the door behind us because I could imagine she might want to leave once I'd told her about Chris and Doc.

Jan perched on Doc's stool and gave me a knowing smile. I didn't dress it up. I just apologised for having told Doc and she guessed the rest.

"He knows then?"

I could see the muscles set in her face, fixing the smile on. It was horrible to witness.

"He knows, but he said to tell you, it doesn't change anything between you."

The dead smile grew wider as Jan squeezed her eyes shut, failing to keep the tears back.

"I feel so ashamed. It was a horrible thing to do, he'd been so good to me and all the time I was doing that to him." I thought she was talking about her husband but then she said, "Oh Chris, what have I done to you?"

There was nothing to do but let her cry it out. I put a hand on her shoulder and gave her a couple of paper towels to blow her nose on. Doc came into the shop before she'd finished. The sound of the door opening triggered some deep reflex and her eyes snapped open. I left her in the back room and stopped him before he came through.

"I've told her Chris knows. She doesn't seem angry."

Under his breath he said, "That's something."

If Jan was keeping a list, subconscious or otherwise, of people she trusted, then Doc evidently hadn't made the cut. When she looked up, she was still crying, eyes open. She carried on crying without closing them. I stood myself beside her with one hand lightly touching her back. Doc perched on the edge of my work chair. No one spoke for a while. It felt like a long time before Jan got herself together.

"How did Chris take it?" Jan said. "I mean when you told him about ... about being watched?"

Doc caught my eye and signalled me towards the door. I shook my head and stayed where I was. He didn't react to this and Jan didn't give any sign of having seen the exchange, though I doubt she missed it.

"Well it came at him out of the blue, but he wanted you to know it doesn't change anything. The other thing he said," Doc was speaking slowly and I was aware that his attention was on me. "Chris wants you to know he's not like Peter – he's never going to ask you to do things like that. He doesn't want you to do things like that. I think for Chris, infidelity's a deal breaker, if you know what I mean."

Jan nodded and it looked as if the tears were about to start again. Doc flicked a glance to the door, again asking me to leave. I was still reluctant to go but my hand was forced when the shop door opened and a hesitant voice called out.

"Hello?"

My first client of the day had turned up early and found the door unlocked. They offered to come back in ten minutes, official opening time, but I waved them to a sofa and put the kettle on. As Doc would say: show time.

Doc and Jan vanished to the flat soon after I had my customer in the chair. I was surprised but not overly bothered. The customer was happy to listen to the music I'd put on rather than chat, and I was getting the knack of splitting my concentration between the tattoo gun and the waiting room.

An hour or so later, I heard the heartbeat of a Harley engine. I wasn't surprised when Jan appeared a minute later and told me she was going to start ringing around; see if she could persuade Doc's morning customers to come in later that afternoon.

He'd taken off and hadn't told her where. When he still hadn't appeared by two, I asked Jan to ring around the afternoon punters and see how many I could cover. I had a light afternoon list that looked like it might expand.

Doc showed up at the end of the day and just had time to fit in an hour's session, finishing off a sleeve someone had been growing for the last year or so. He looked near dead with tiredness but had a slightly manic air. He worked slower than usual, forcing himself to be methodical and careful. I kept stealing sideways glances at him as the needles buzzed, expecting him to make a mistake. He didn't, but that hour shredded my nerves. When the last client on the list showed up, Doc started prepping his chair, in readiness.

"Doc, go and get your head down; you're putting me on edge."

He looked comically startled at the comment then seemed to sag as the truth of it became real.

"Yeah, yeah alright, I will. I'll wait for you, got stuff to talk about. Big news breaking, brother, big news."

He did a piss poor clean-up of his work station then finally left me to work in peace.

By the time I came out to collect the last customer, Doc was sprawled across one the sofas, dead to the world. Jan was watching him.

"Should we take him up to the flat?" she asked.

"Nah, let him sleep."

I took my leather off the rack and draped it over him.

Once my last customer was set up, Jan brought me a mug of tea and said she was heading back home. I locked up behind her and turned off the lights in the front, so no one would think we were open for business. Doc had curled into a ball, snoring loudly.

The customer was an old hand, with leather for skin. He didn't register pain and told me to carry on 'til I was fed up or finished. Finishing became a point of honour and it was gone half ten when he left. Like mine, his tattoos were for selective viewing only. The ink I put into his chest joined a plethora of other work that you'd never guess was there. When we were done, all the unfathomable script and designs were hidden under a shirt and jacket. As he left the tattoo shop he seemed to vanish, I was sad to see him go. It felt like a kindred spirit had gone, leaving me in a foreign country.

Doc hadn't moved. I cleaned up my chair and did a quick

inventory of stocks. Before I left I emptied the cash box and put a note in it telling Doc the day's taking was safe with me. Then I retrieved my leather and locked up for the night. I left Doc asleep on the sofa.

The household was still awake when I got home. The feeling of being somewhere I didn't belong hadn't left me, I pulled the bike into the front garden and sat on it wondering why.

It took me a while to admit to myself that I was missing Karla. It shouldn't have been a surprise. I had my own chair at the shop and the money was coming in. The future I wanted with her was beginning to roll out in front of me, but she wasn't going to be in it. Caffeine addiction eventually coaxed me into the house.

Jan had put the filter machine on when she heard me pull up. Now she was reading tarot.

"You eaten?" I asked. She told me she had, without looking away from the cards. "What happened with you and Doc? You didn't look happy when you two went back to his flat this morning."

"I was a bit shaken up. Wondering what Chris must be going through."

She made it sound like that was all there was to say on the subject. I didn't pry. At the end of the day it was between her and Doc.

The draining board was full of freshly washed dishes and the fridge was full of sod all. Dad and Jan had been busy. She carried on turning over cards while I sat with a bowl of cornflakes.

"He was very sweet," she said, seemingly at random.

"Who?"

"Doc."

She turned a fresh card as she said this and laughed, turning it so I could see. It was the Magus. It was also a coincidence. I wanted to tell her that but didn't have the heart or the energy.

"Doc was sweet?"

Jan laughed again. "Really." She hadn't added the Magus to the spread of cards in front of her. She was playing with it, rotating it with her fingertips. It was the sort of thing Doc did. "He told me he wanted to apologise."

She left the statement hanging, waiting to have the story teased out of her. Another of Doc's traits.

"For telling Chris about what you and Peter were doing?"

She shook her head and finally put the card in its place in the spread. "For suspecting me, I suppose. He said he didn't have any doubts about me anymore."

For the first time, she looked at me as she spoke. Possibly because I was looking for it, she appeared more confident. The smile was too old for her face and I could see Doc's Voodoo acolyte more than dad's nurse or my shrinking violet.

"Then he said I shouldn't have any doubts either. He said it wasn't my fault, nothing I did put Peter where he was." She got back to the cards and said, "Sweet."

I finished the coffee and rounded off the cornflakes with a couple of cream crackers.

"Any idea where he went today?" I asked.

"Not really. He just said he had something to do."

Thursday 28 July

I was woken by my mobile. I ignored it and let the call go to voicemail. When the tone started up again a few seconds later I gave in and picked up. Doc was calling and it was two o'clock in the morning.

"Doc? You alright?"

"Yeah, but you locked me in the shop, you dozy fucker. I can't get out."

He'd left his shop keys in his leather, in his flat, which he'd gone back to before returning to work that afternoon. I scribbled out a note to Jan, telling her what happened, and rode over to the shop.

The lights were on when I got there but of course Doc

was staying out of sight. I let myself in and found him tucked behind the counter with a sketch pad. He was filling the page with flash designs, each about four inches square. They ranged from traditional stuff, with a slight twist, to stuff that was plain twisted.

He was in a better mood than I would have been and appeared to find the episode funny.

"Sorry, man, I assumed you had keys. I didn't want to wake you up you looked like you needed some kip."

Doc waved off my apology.

"You were right, I did. I was getting strung out." After he watched me lock up again, he asked, "You want to hear my big news, or you want to head straight back to bed?"

Sleeping well wasn't my forte. We headed back to the flat and Doc led me to the front room before I had a chance to take my leather off. He bowed and gestured to the crime wall. There was another change to the centre piece. The desperate *HOW?* had been rubbed into a grey smudge, in its place, fixed with a thumb tack, was a clear plastic sandwich bag. In the bag was a ceramic-bladed lock knife with a skeletal handle. It was identical to the one the police had removed from Chris's cutlery draw.

"I take it that ain't the one Chris had?"

Doc's grin was probably visible from space. "Nah," he said. "That one is the murder weapon."

We disagreed on what we should do next. Doc wanted to put the knife back where he'd found it. I doubted the wisdom of this. But at the end of the day Doc had a plan and I didn't.

We'd hit the point where most people, normal people, went to the police. I did put the idea forward but only because I couldn't see any other options. I was glad when Doc took the suggestion apart.

"If we go to the police with that" – he jerked a thumb to the knife, which was still hanging from the wall – "all we've got is a story and a knife that we could have bought off the internet. They'll ignore us."

"What about prints?" I said. "Chris ain't touched that one. Whoever's prints are on it, they won't be his."

Doc rolled his eyes and did a slow turn of the head until he was staring at the knife. Half an inch of water had puddled in the corner of the sandwich bag, the clear plastic clung moistly to the contours of the handle.

"You want to risk there being any prints on that at all?"

I held my hands up, surrendering that point at least. "How about we put it back but tell Priti you've got this mad theory. She takes the theory to the police and that way they can find the knife."

Doc gave me a smile and said nothing. The holes in that idea were too big to need explaining. Assuming the police followed up on the information, as evidence went, the knife would still leave a lot to be desired.

The crime scene had been out of the police's control for weeks. There was nothing to say the knife hadn't been planted. If the police got it into their heads that the course of justice was being perverted, then going to them was as likely to put me and Doc *into* a cell as to get Chris *out* of one. Since Keller's death we'd been in and out of the house half a dozen times. I'd spent a night there and Doc had raided the drinks cabinet. I held my hands up again. Total surrender.

"Okay," I said, "we'll go with your plan. But tell me, honestly, are you going for this because you think it's the best way?" He gave me a puzzled look that I needed to believe was genuine. "I mean this isn't just some bizarre tribute to Miss Marple is it? Gathering all the suspects together in the library for the grand finale?"

Doc got to his feet. He carefully unpinned the sandwich bag from the wall. I took it from him when he handed it across to me. The knife inside was amazingly light. I nodded at him, equally impressed by its lack of weight. After folding the bag tightly around its contents, then wrapping it in a faded bandana, Doc answered my question.

"I yield to no man in my admiration of Miss Jane Marple."

He paused and seemed to be searching my face. At first, I wondered if he was waiting for me to laugh then realised he was checking I wasn't. "And if *she* was trying to get Chris sprung, I think this is what she'd do." He saw I was about to object and he held up a hand to stop me. "Because this is the only way to do it. If we take what we've got to the police, they'll look at it, weigh up the odds and go for a conviction. If it gets to court we've got next to nothing and Chris will go down. Even if Priti's right and she can go for an unsafe conviction on technicalities, it'll take years, and on a murder charge he'll be waiting on the inside. Chris ain't got the temperament for nick, he'll have a bad time. God knows what it'll do to Jan.

"I want to put the players together, the people up close and personal with it, the ones who knew Peter. And I want Priti Patel and this prick Minton there. Lay it out for them, in all its toxic glory, and produce the evidence while they all watch. Then we hope Minton and Keller put enough store in their reputations to try and keep the whole business under the radar."

"And you reckon you can sell this to Priti?"

"Her back's up, and I think Minton's seriously underestimated her. She's smart and she's angry and at the moment, she doesn't think she's got much to lose."

Doc rode back to the Keller house to replace the knife. I tried to doze in the armchair for a few hours before going to open up but it wouldn't work. In the end I opened the shop early and spent the extra time cleaning until the place shone. I tried to keep myself busy enough to avoid thinking about Doc's plan. It didn't really work. I could see all the faults in my suggestion of going to the police, but that wasn't the same as seeing anything positive about Doc's scheme. My main worry was his love of The Jive.

Doc had been back to the flat before joining me in the shop. He must have had a shower because he smelled of soap. He offered to give me the keys so I could go and freshen up before starting work. I didn't bother but I helped myself to one of the shop tee shirts to replace the stale one I was wearing.

Around nine Gina rolled up in a taxi. She nodded at me but didn't say anything. While he'd been in the flat Doc must have pulled that floorboard up because he handed her a massive roll of notes.

"Sorry you'll have to change it up at the airport," he told her. Gina peeled off about a hundred pounds that went into a man's style wallet, the rest disappeared somewhere into her jacket. "If you need more when you get there, message me and I'll send some over."

"Okay." She was turning to leave but she hesitated. "You sure you know what you're doing?"

Doc laughed. "Not really." Gina remained blank faced. "You've got the details?"

"Of course. I'll call you when I'm back."

And she walked out.

The cab drove away again with her in the back.

Doc gave me one of his half smiles and said, "Insurance."

RSVP Not Required

29 Friday July

Priti Patel, myself, Jan and, of course, Doc were sitting around the dining table in my back room. We met at my place because there was more space and it didn't appear to have been decorated by a serial killer. Doc was in his interview-with-the-bank-manager clothes.

For the first meeting with Priti there'd been an advantage to not having things too cosy. For the hard sell, more comfortable surroundings were called for.

I'd pointed out dad was likely to make his presence felt. Doc told me it would add to the ambience. I couldn't see it myself.

Priti was in a difficult position. On one hand, she could stay on side with Minton and his boys' club, cementing her place as the firm's nod to employee diversity. On the other hand, there was team Slidesmith. But I think the die was cast the moment she heard the Kellergate tape. The few objections she put forward were mostly for form's sake. The big one was, why should she bother?

"What's to stop me defending my client in the usual manner? If I do the job well and he's still convicted, it's hardly likely to damage my standing in the firm. Mr Minton hasn't given me this brief with any expectation that it can be won. I can use this as an opportunity to demonstrate what I can do. It's only in films that legal careers hinge on a single case."

Doc didn't respond straight away. He looked away from Priti, as if he was intent on listening to the light classical playing on the radio.

Eventually he said, "There's nothing to stop you at all. Go back to your desk tomorrow, and slog your guts out fighting a fight you've been set up to lose while Minton laughs at you. Then, when they've watched you lose, all the old white men can pat each other on the back and tell each other how right they were. Meanwhile Chris sits in a cell and hopes you can prove everyone wrong on appeal."

No one spoke after that and the stare Priti was giving Doc could have stripped paint. Doc wasn't bothering to return it. He was fiddling with his phone. When Jan's mobile bleeped at her, she glanced at Doc who nodded, confirming it was from him. Jan opened the message and took a moment to work out what she was seeing. It was one of the photos Doc had taken after we'd poured Jeffry Keller into bed and set a post coital stage.

"Store that in your phone and get it ready to send it to Jeff," Doc said.

Jan's mouth opened, probably to ask why, but she changed her mind and fiddled with the mobile, then she nodded at Doc. Doc told her *thank you* and returned his attention to Priti.

"Miss Patel, going back to your firm and letting things play out the way they're expected to is the smart move, at least from your point of view. You don't make ripples, you learn from the experience, you keep your position and hope it gets better." He twitched his cheek into a smile. "Smart thing to do, the safe option."

Priti scowled at him. "But?"

Doc shifted in his chair and leaned forward on his elbows, grinning like he was about to give up a big secret.

"But, if you wanted to go down that route I don't think you'd have made a copy of this."

The Kellergate tape materialised in his hand like a magic

trick. Priti had returned it earlier, when we'd all sat down at the table. He folded his long fingers around it again and it vanished from sight. Priti's expression wasn't showing much either.

"What's on that tape, at the very least, is likely to cause the firm huge embarrassment. There's a good chance it could end the Criminal Defence Service contract. It's not impossible that Neville could be struck off. Having a copy of that tape gives you something to hold in reserve." Doc grinned. "And without witnesses to the conversation it's all but worthless."

Priti nodded, part agreement, part defeat. She didn't contest the statement. She'd known that was where the speech was going. Doc spelled it out anyway.

"If me and Yakky don't want to play along, all you've got is a drunk slurring his words. And your tape goes from major problem to minor annoyance."

"But?"

"If we play this my way, we can put the fear of God into Minton. Then you can make it look like you're saving his bacon. Your client gets out of nick. You get to keep your copy of the tape and, if at some point, you want to nail Minton to a tree then I swear me and Yakky will stand in the dock and talk all day long. And, by-the-by, the police get to find out what really happened to Peter Keller. And as a cheeky bonus, you come out of it a hero. Wrongly arrested man facing a life behind bars, in walks Miss Patel and solves the crime the police didn't even see. Minton's not a fool; he'll see you're more use working for the firm than against it."

I knew Doc well enough to guess he was on tenterhooks. Priti clenched her jaw and finally nodded.

Jan said, "Thank you."

And gasped. She must have been holding her breath.

Doc borrowed my mobile to make the first call. He'd used his phone to send Jeffry Keller the bogus text from Jan, enticing him to his late brother's house. Doc didn't want to chance the number being recognised. We all heard the conversation because Doc put the mobile on loudspeaker.

"Hello, Mr Keller. James Slidesmith here. How's the hangover?"

"What do you want?"

Jeffry didn't sound delighted to be in touch again.

"We're having a little party, thought you might like to come."

If you listened carefully you could hear the gears turning in Keller's head. He wasn't sure how to react to the invite. He was taking a while to conclude that the amiable tone was fake.

Doc helped him along, telling him, "We thought we'd have it at your brother's old place. You remember the address?"

"I have nothing further to say to you."

The line went dead.

Doc turned to Jan. "Send him that picture and a text: Ring me now, or I ring Caroline. Sign it Doctor Slidesmith."

I stepped out of the room to make some drinks. I knew the plan, and it was going to stand or fall without any input from me. Besides, the sheer pressure of Jive in the back room was making my ears pop. If Jeffry Keller thought we were bluffing, he'd got it badly wrong. He had five minutes to ring back or the photo of him in bed with an empty bottle and a pair of Jan's knickers was going to his wife. Once he knew Doc didn't bluff he'd get another phone call talking about recordings and contacts and cheating Jan out of her home.

Priti Patel came into the kitchen as I was loading the filter machine. She looked like she wanted to be somewhere else. She wasn't wearing the business suit now, but the dress she had on might have been borrowed from somebody twenty years older than her. In the back room, I heard Jan's ring tone. One point to our side. Priti looked back towards the sound and almost smiled.

"I owe you an apology, Mister Miller. The other night I was upset and you took the brunt of it. Sorry."

I waved it off. Priti was chewing at a thumb nail, the anger she'd been running on was fading, now she was worrying instead. It wasn't an improvement.

"Take it easy," I said. "Doc's a lot smarter than you'd think."

Priti flashed me that professional smile I didn't like. "I know a lot of clever men. It doesn't stop me worrying."

I let her have that one. I knew what she meant.

We carried the mugs through to the back room. Jan was smiling to herself as she watched Doc talking on her phone. Doc's voice was jovial but he wasn't grinning; it was like seeing him naked. He was wrapping up the call with Jeffry.

"Okay. Yeah. I'll be in touch with the exact time ... She won't hear it from me. You have my word." Doc gave Jan her phone back. Finally, he grinned. "He wants to keep Caroline out of the loop."

Jan laughed. I suspected Jeffry's life was going to get complicated.

"He's agreed to the meeting?" Priti asked.

I expected some clever reply but Doc said, "Yeah he agreed. I've told him I just want to talk to him about the case against Chris."

I sat down at the table then got straight up again; I hadn't offered dad a drink. I could have saved myself the trouble. He was sulking. After I'd asked him if he wanted a cup of tea three times, and still not got an answer, I gave up and sent Jan in. She was sucked into his orbit without preamble and I left her to it. I met Doc in the hallway when I came out. He'd left Priti to make her phone call to Neville Minton in private. It was a spur of the moment decision, one of his displays of trust.

Priti Patel left about twenty minutes later. She'd arranged for Neville Minton to join the party at the Keller house. She told us the time they'd agreed. Doc told Jeffry the time of the meeting and left soon after. He also retrieved the

Dictaphone from its hiding place under the table top.

He wanted to be sure his display of trust in Priti had been justified.

Gina's flight had been due in just before eleven p.m. Jan had offered to drive to Heathrow and collect her. Doc had said he'd go with her and I ended up joining them.

The approaching endgame was causing a ripple of excitement that carried me along. Everyone seemed to be having a similar buzz. We left way too early and got to the terminal with an hour to kill. The flight arrival time was then pushed back another hour and excitement faded to boredom. I bought myself something to read and we found a coffee shop. Jan sat on the padded bench seat next to me and fell asleep leaning on my shoulder. Doc had a paper beaker of tea that didn't impress him much then said he was going to stretch his legs. He wandered away and drew a flurry of interest from a pair of airport cops who were probably as bored as we were.

An hour before the new arrival time, Doc drifted back and put another beaker of coffee in front of me, where it joined four empties. He'd bought one for Jan as well but we decided it wasn't worth waking her for.

When the arrival of her flight from New York was announced, Doc went to meet Gina. Jan and I waited in the coffee shop. I got another couple of coffees, one for me the other for Gina. I'd figured she'd need one and I wasn't wrong. When she came over to us she was wearing the same clothes I'd last seen her in and she was grey with fatigue. She acknowledged the coffee I handed her with a nod and took a mouthful gratefully.

Jan announced she needed the toilet before we headed out and Doc did the same, leaving me and Gina sitting with our paper beakers. Gina was chatty, at least by her standards. She pulled a sheet of A4 from her jacket and passed it across to me.

"You think this is going to work?" she asked.

It was a webpage printout showing one of the ceramic-bladed lock knives. The supply house that sold them was based in New York.

"God knows. We just got to trust Doc, I guess." I folded the paper into four again and gave it back. Gina buried it deep in a pocket. There's no a law against looking at a picture of a knife in an airport coffee shop, but the circumstances gave everything a clandestine feel. "You got one I take it?"

"I didn't fly across the Atlantic for the hell of it."

The knives – she'd bought two to be on the safe side – were in her hold-all wrapped in a pair of jeans. She handed them over once we were in Jan's Audi and driving away from the airport.

The Party Line

Saturday 30 July

The three of us were in our Sunday best. Once again Doc was dressed for chatting with a bank manager, although he hadn't bothered to cover his facial tattoo. I was wearing my clean combats and a tee shirt sans oil stains. Jan wasn't quite in trophy-wife rig but she outshone the pair of us.

Doc had said we should *make an effort*, and Jan had pointed out that Caroline destroyed all her posh frocks. He'd pulled one of his remaining rolls of floor-lagging from the side of his boot.

"Some change would be nice," he said and handed it over. "I'll leave it to your judgement but we're going for conventional and demure with a touch of style."

Jan took off in her Audi. I asked Doc if I was due a clothing allowance and he told me to fuck off.

That was in the morning just before we opened up. We debated closing the shop for another day but decided against it. Everything was set in motion; we had nothing to do but wait. Keeping busy and making money made more sense than sitting on our hands.

Now it was early evening and we were all in Peter Keller's kitchen. Doc was singing, or chanting, or praying. Whatever he was doing he wasn't doing it in English. Or in key. Jan watched him with an air of approval for a bit then took her cards from her bag and began dealing. It's funny how the mind works; after all the weeks that had passed, I recognised the bag as the one she'd brought to The Jericho the first time I'd seen her.

The meeting was for six but we turned up early for no particular reason. When we arrived, we settled in the living room with the big screen TV and drinks cabinet. It made me uncomfortable, like I was sitting centre stage. After fidgeting and changing seats a dozen times, I moved to the kitchen. Doc and Jan may have felt the same, because they followed me. Doc, acting on reflex, filled the kettle.

We drummed our fingers and made jokes about waiting being the worst part. Then Doc found a corner to commandeer and started his keening. I asked Jan what he was doing.

"It's a song to Ezulie Dantor, it's a bit like a hymn."

"What language is that?"

"Creole," she said and turned back to her cards. Believers only beyond that point.

We all heard the crunch of gravel as Jeffry's self-important car pulls up. I hadn't gone to let him in immediately. I turned to Doc to see if he had stopped singing to himself. He felt me looking at him and turned on the Cheshire Cat, mouthed, *show time.* Then he motioned at Jan's tarot spread and she shepherded them away out of sight.

"Yakky, would you do the honours?"

Doc turned the grin down a bit, so he looked like he only needed mild sedation. I nodded and made to leave the kitchen but turned back to ask where I should put Keller.

"Sit him in the front room," he said, adding maliciously, "offer him a drink."

As I turned away, I saw Jan press a key on her mobile then slip it back into the tiny clutch bag. She wasn't hiding what she was doing, but she wasn't advertising it either.

I'd assumed she was just checking the time. She hadn't handled the phone long enough to do much else. Unless of course she'd prepared a message beforehand and only needed to press *send.*

Jeffry pressed the bell just as I opened the door. He gave a start when he saw me, then recovered himself.

"Good service."

It wasn't the usual breaking-the-ice noise people make. Keller turned it into an insult you could pretend was a joke. Once in the entrance hall, he was faced again with what Caroline had left there and it took some of the cockiness from of him. The pile of shattered images perhaps reminded him how much grief his wife could dispense.

I took him to the living room and let him find a seat. He sat where he'd passed out a few nights earlier. I didn't offer him a drink, instead I reclaimed my spot from that night, a little way outside his line of vision.

Jeffry spread himself out on the sofa and drummed his fingers. It was a passable impression of indignation, rather than nerves.

After a short time, he said, "Where's the other one?" I told him Doc was about and he forced a dramatic sigh. "I really don't have time for this nonsense." When I didn't answer he craned around awkwardly to look at me. "I said: I don't have time for this."

"Well you can go if you want, spend some quality time with your wife."

He tried to glare at me. It didn't work because he had to twist to meet my eye. He gave it up and turned back to the wall opposite. Drummed his fingers a bit louder. After he'd tapped out about thirty bars he addressed the empty room again.

"I don't appreciate being blackmailed."

Enter Doc, stage left, bang on cue. "And I'm sure Chris Rudjer doesn't appreciate sitting in a cell while the likes of you and Neville Minton do your best to keep him there."

Keller sprang out of his seat ready to fight but his nerve failed him and he went for morally-outraged instead. I think it had as much to do with Jan walking in as it did with being outnumbered. I wasn't sorry he backed down. He was a hell of a size compared to Doc.

Doc sidestepped him and dropped into an armchair, watched the mini drama in comfort.

"Hello Jan," Keller's voice was neutral.

For her part Jan looked at him like he'd stuck to the sole of her shoe and sat in the place he'd just vacated. He tried to think of something to say and failed, when he made to sit next to her, another look forestalled him. He sat on the sofa opposite and drummed his fingers again.

"Why did you ask me to come here?" he asked Doc.

He was doing his best to be alpha male but it wasn't working. His instinct was probably to get up and either storm out or throw some weight around but he didn't have the option of doing either. Doc grinned, showed no sympathy for the man's discomfort.

"As I said on the phone, bit of a party. Exclusive, not many guests. You're the first to arrive."

"Who else is coming?"

Doc cupped his chin and frowned. "Let me see, there's your golfing buddy Neville Minton. Oh, and Miss Patel, do you know her? Delightful woman, delightful, wouldn't you say, Yakky?"

"Delightful."

I felt Keller looking at me. I wondered how he liked his own medicine. Nothing was being said that couldn't be passed off as innocent banter.

"Oh yes, and we're hoping Joan Rix can make it."

Doc paused, either for effect or to gauge Keller's reaction. The mention of Rix triggered nothing but when Doc told him she'd been the arresting officer, alarm registered. It was momentary and I only saw it because I was expecting Doc to find a nerve. Doc saw it too and once he'd got his reaction he relaxed into the armchair.

"That does leave us with an awkward number I'm afraid – four gentlemen and only three ladies. If everyone stays for supper the seating plan's going to be a nightmare."

Doc meant this to be one last jab of the needle but Jan stole the final line. She gave a contrived laugh. "No need to worry, I've invited Caroline. She'll even out the numbers."

I realised what she'd been doing in the kitchen with her mobile. Doc's grin froze and I knew he'd been sideswiped. It didn't take him long to recover; he gave a soft chuckle and turned back to Jeffry, who'd gone the colour of bad milk.

"Now isn't that nice?"

Jeffry didn't have Doc's bounce. It looked like someone had thrown a switch and turned him off. I'd have been willing to swear he stopped breathing for a while.

Jan must have been hoping for a more animated response. She gave Jeff one of those slow up and down looks that *he* did so well, then reached into the clutch bag and pulled her mobile out. She brought up something on the screen and placed the phone on the coffee table so he could see it. He picked it up, looked at the screen for longer than he needed to, then dropped it back on the table.

"You vindictive little bitch," he muttered and flopped back, face to the heavens, eyes shut.

He stayed that way. Jan didn't make any move to retrieve her phone and Doc picked it up. He looked at the screen, didn't react other than clicking his tongue. Before giving the mobile back to Jan he passed it to me.

It was the last message sent: the picture we'd taken of Jeffry in bed and an accompanying text.

Where did Jeffry tell you he slept on Sunday night? He's at my front door again now. Why don't you pop over and see how to keep a man coming back for more? Jan X

It was shaping up to be one hell of a party.

I went to the kitchen and dug through the cupboards until I found a jar of instant coffee. No one had spoken in the living room since Doc had given Jan her phone back and the silence hadn't taken long to start grating. Jeffry came into the kitchen just as the kettle boiled. Sitting in silence with Jan and Doc couldn't have been any easier on his nerves. He should have turned up fashionably late.

"Is that coffee?" he asked, probably just to avoid more silence.

"Only just." I showed him the jar, own brand powder. "Want one?"

"Please."

We both grimaced when we tasted the stuff and dumped sugar into our cups to kill the bitterness. I sat at the breakfast bar where Jan had laid out her tarot earlier. Jeffry stayed on his feet but came over to where I was sitting. He put his cup down and stood too close. Maybe he was trying to assert himself. I pushed his cup along the surface, away from me.

"You mind giving me some space?"

He retreated a step and contrived to look offended, asked if it was *far enough?* It came out wrong and he sounded like a child. I sipped my excuse for a coffee and ignored him. It wasn't long before he spoke again, the silent treatment in the other room must have really been getting to him.

"I can't believe Jan did that."

My instinct was to ignore him again, but in truth the sour atmosphere of the house was getting under my skin as well. That didn't mean I had to pander to him.

"You treat her like some old whore then you try and take her home off her. You don't even have the decency to let her know when you cremate her husband. What did you expect?"

Jeff wanted to come on strong. I could see it in his face, the arrogance coming back to the surface. But arrogance and stupidity are different things and he didn't bother getting on his high horse. He knew nobody was going to be impressed.

He deigned to explain himself to me. I still wasn't impressed.

"It was Peter who tried to make her a whore. And I didn't try to take this house from her. I was trying to distance her from my brother's murder. I've been protecting her."

I gave him the same look Jan had. I saw his lips tighten.

"That's what was on your mind the other night was it?

When you thought she'd texted you. You came over here on the QT all booted and suited to offer your protection."

It rattled Keller sufficiently that he went for the alpha male spot again.

"Who do you think you're talking to?" He jabbed an index finger at me, voice raised, dander up. I noticed the flesh under his chin wobble. The thought of him and Jan in bed together was revolting. "Just who the hell do you think you're talking to?"

When it was clear he didn't have anything else to say, I told him evenly, "I'm talking to the playground bully who's shitting himself because his wife's coming over."

I didn't imagine my answer made much impact on his ego but bringing the spectre of his wife back to the table took him down again. He dropped his gaze and shook his head. If he was looking for understanding, he was out of luck.

"Once everything was settled, I was going to call Jan, tell her she could come back here."

"I bet you were. Here you go Jan, have a big fancy house, I'll drop in now and then, so you can be properly grateful. Believe your own bullshit if you want but don't hand it to me."

He surprised me by having enough shame to avoid my eye.

He started to say something then just mumbled, "Shit."

He must have heard the car before I did, or at least recognised it for what it was.

Caroline's silver-blue Porsche came into the driveway at speed. I stepped back into the living room just as it flashed past the window. Caroline began hammering on the front door barely a second later.

Doc flashed me a grin.

"I think another guest's arrived."

He didn't make a move to answer the pounding and Jeffry had frozen. I was about to get the door but Jan beat me to it. As she went, she gave Keller the smile cats give mice.

Neither Doc nor Keller budged as she left the room and I was a couple of steps behind her as she got to the hall.

Jan stopped first in front of an oversized mirror and checked her hair. My first thought was she was waiting for me, so she wouldn't have to face Caroline alone. But before I got to her she gave me a grin – not dissimilar to one of Doc's – and threw the door open.

In every film I've ever seen, a fight between two women kicks off with an open-handed slap. Apparently, Caroline wasn't much of a film buff. As soon as the door opened she punched Jan in the face. Jan, clutching her mouth, reeled back and the following hook punch came short of making contact. Caroline almost over balanced as the momentum of her swing pulled her round. Whatever her boxing technique lacked in skill, it made up for in enthusiasm. She found her feet and punched Jan in the face a second time before I got to them.

I was only just able to keep her off Jan, who was now on the floor scrabbling away backwards. Caroline was shouting a stream of abuse and threats while I held her round the waist and did my best not to get my face clawed open. The commotion finally pulled Jeffry from his stupor and he came running out. I hoped he was going to take over from me but he froze again as Caroline switched targets and began hauling abuse at him instead.

I was craning my head trying to see if Jan was alright, so I didn't have a great view of events. I was only aware that Doc had come to the hall when he crossed my line of sight on his way to Jan. Maybe Caroline noticed him too, or maybe she was just catching her breath, either way she stopped struggling. I relaxed my hold and tried to judge if it was safe to let go completely. She looked past me, from her husband to Jan and Doc, then back again. After calling Jeff a bastard one more time, she pushed me away. It caught me by surprise and I nearly fell on my arse. Caroline wouldn't meet anyone's eye. She was close to tears.

"Yakky, I think you've got some work over here."

Doc was down on his haunches in front of Jan, who was still on the floor.

There was blood down the front of the pale-green blouse she was wearing. Her head was bobbing slightly, as if she was about to fall asleep. I dismissed the bleeding. She had a split lip, painful and messy, but nothing a tea towel and ice cubes wouldn't take care of. Looking like she was about to lose consciousness worried me more.

I tilted her head back to get her eyes into the light, watched the pupils contract, checked they were both the same size. I put a hand on her shoulder and quickly dug my thumb nail into the thin skin across the collar bone. She gave a jolt and her focus snapped into line with my eyes, then despite the blood and the beginnings of some good swelling, she pulled a quick smile. Then zoned out again.

"Let's get her up," I said to Doc, and we gently got her to her feet.

I'd had my back to the door and didn't see the new arrivals until Doc and I began steering Jan from the hall. Priti Patel was standing just inside the entrance and a man, I assumed it was Neville Minton, was blocking the doorway. Priti looked comically surprised at the scene but Neville was thinking fast. You could see the wheels revolving. As I led Jan to the reception room, Joan Rix pushed her way through the door, shunting Minton aside without ceremony.

"What's going on here?" She was in her civvies but her voice was pure cop. She saw me and a flash of recognition crossed her face. "What's going on here?"

"Let me deal with this," I said, meaning deal with Jan, my patient. Some of the nurse training must have rubbed off after all.

Of course, before I finished tending to Jan, Doc started to Jive. I didn't hear it at the time, or at least didn't listen. I took Jan back to the sofa and sat her down.

"Don't lay it on too thick," I said under my breath as I took a closer look at her lip.

The split was fairly small and I was happy it didn't need a

stitch. I went to the kitchen and pulled open drawers until I found some tea towels, took a glass and filled it from the ice maker in the fridge door.

There was another cut on Jan's cheek bone – Caroline's follow-up swipe. It looked to me like the mark had been made by the stone of a ring. An inch higher and we might have been on our way to A&E; the dig was just below her left eye.

I kept my eye on the door to the hall, checking we weren't being observed.

"You plan all this?"

She shook her head but then said, "Sort of. I thought she'd create a scene. I was hoping Joan would be here to see it." She grinned with one half of her mouth. "This is a bonus."

The original idea had been for Doc to open the door to Priti Patel. Priti was primed to expect the display of vandalised photos at the foot of the stairs and knew to step smartly through the doorway so as not to interrupt her boss's view. Before he'd even got through the front door, Minton would get to see the level of embarrassment the Kellers could expose him to.

Jan's unscripted interlude with her sister-in-law dovetailed nicely with Doc's plan. The mutilated pictures, that were to have been centre stage, had been relegated to back drop, but Doc wasn't unduly upset: the tail end of Caroline's assault became the main feature. Rix pushing past Minton, and putting on her policewoman's voice, had been a standing ovation.

From where Jan and I were sitting, Doc's showcasing of events was clearly audible. Happy that Jan wasn't at risk of anything worse than a few bruises, I sat back on my heels and listened. I could hear Caroline oscillating between hysterical despair and straight hysterical. Priti told me later that Jeffry's attempts to explain, or comfort, had earned him at least one smack round the face.

Doc was ignoring the galleries and playing direct to Joan Rix. The blood splashes Jan trailed along the hallway floor upstaged him. Minton came into the living room while Doc was still holding force.

Minton came straight over to where we were sat. He didn't give any indication that they knew each other but he asked Jan if she was alright by name. Jan nodded and winced. I wondered if they'd met at some function or other and Minton had committed her to memory, along with everyone else he'd ever met. I'd come across people over the years who collected names and faces the way some people collected stamps. They get called charming a lot.

He was bent at the waist resting one hand on the sofa, not touching her but just close enough to show his concern. I could see what Priti Patel meant when she said Minton was a perfect gentleman. His clothes were high-quality and expensive but he didn't expect a round of applause for wearing them. The man had style.

He kept his attention on Jan for a moment then turned to me, silently asking for me to agree her diagnosis, acknowledging an authority I didn't have. If I hadn't already decided I didn't like him, his flattery would have probably worked.

"There's no sign of concussion and the bleeding's stopped."

I had the impression that he was trying to get a handle on me. He shifted his weight and I saw his hand move towards me, debating whether to pat me on the shoulder. He made the right decision and didn't.

"Should we call an ambulance, have someone examine her?"

Jan said, "I'll trust Yakky, he trained as a nurse."

Minton bowed to my expertise with a small smile, just a hint of whitened teeth. He sat on the opposite sofa and set his face to concerned. Those wheels were turning again.

Next in the room was Rix. She went straight to Jan too but didn't bother asking what I thought. I expect she'd spent plenty of weekends looking at fat lips and black eyes and didn't need a second opinion.

"Are you okay?" she asked.

Jan told her she was then pressed the ice to the side of her face. I figured I was just cluttering up the floor, so I took up my customary spot slightly behind things.

The police were there, Jan had been firmly established as the victim, Minton was calculating the cost of doing favours for friends. Apart from the lack of decent coffee, it was all going swimmingly.

When Doc came in just behind Priti, he left the hall door open and we could all hears the Kellers arguing. Caroline wanted to shout; Jeffry kept trying to whisper. It got embarrassing. Minton excused himself and went into the hall. He pulled the door shut behind him.

"What the hell is going on?" Rix asked Priti.

"Doctor Slidesmith here claims the case against my client has been wilfully comprised. He also claims to be in a position to shed some light on the real events that led to the death of Peter Keller."

Rix was in her civvies so I figured she was there on her own time; she had stepped outside the normal chain of events. Whatever line she'd been fed by Priti must have found a willing set of ears. Still, a cop was a cop and I could see her reverting to type.

She turned her attention to Doc.

"If you had information about Peter Keller's death, you should have contacted the police."

"As Miss Patel just said, I believe the investigation has been wilfully compromised. So, let's just say I have trust issues when it comes to the handling of information and evidence," Doc said before adding, "I'm also inclined to think you're less than happy with way things are going. That's why you're here, on your day off."

Rix sat down on one of the straight-backed chairs. She'd taken a position similar to mine, outside of things. Only with her it was about keeping everyone in sight. She gave Doc the once over. She didn't do it like Keller did; she was looking for information not trying to juggle status. She pulled off something few people did: she got Doc to break silence first.

"I'm going to guess here," he said. "Dead body in a big house, in an upper-middle-class area. An upper-middle-class widow who seeks comfort in the arms of a scruffy-arsed biker. Who has a history of violence, no less. And you know about his history of violence ... "

Doc made the annoying spooling motion. Rix didn't look as if she was going to oblige at first but then she decided to go with it.

"Because I arrested him last time." She stopped but when he started with the spooling again added, "I don't think the man's a thug."

"No, he's not," Jan said with a certain edge in her voice. "That toe rag he punched deserved what he got."

The short version of Chris's previous brush with the law was that he'd got into a fight and put a man through a window. This was more or less the whole story as it appeared on the charge sheet.

Doc's account was that Chris had seen a couple arguing. He hadn't taken much interest until the boyfriend started getting his point across with a series of backhanders. When Chris crossed the street and suggested the guy calm down, he gave Chris a backhander too. The right hook he got back put him through a shopfront.

Rix had been one of the attending officers. By that point the couple had reconciled, agreed it was all Chris's fault and charges were duly brought. Rix knew the boyfriend and had a fair idea of the true situation. She also reasoned that if Chris really wanted to hurt the guy, he'd have put him through a wall, not a window.

The law, however, blindly ground along its paper rails.

"I'll make another guess," Doc said, but this time there was no grin, no Jive. He spoke quietly and directly to Rix without any showboating. "If Jan called someone in a nice suit and tie to provide a shoulder to cry on, no one would have thought to get suspicious and go through the bathroom, looking for a crime."

I don't know how Rix reacted to that because I was too busy watching Doc. He was probing, hoping for something from Rix.

"That may be true," she said, "but, whatever the reasons for looking, we did find evidence of a crime."

"Then they found Chris and they stopped looking."

Before Rix could answer, the door was pulled open and Minton led the Kellers back into the room. I noticed that where Jan had chosen to sit – and bleed – was the spot you were faced with as you came through the door. The effect was lost on Caroline who glared balefully at her, unmoved by the bloodstained upholstery. Jeffry was a different matter. He couldn't look at her at all.

Minton came in, the wheels still moving. He selected a seat that put some space between him and Jeffery Keller. His closest neighbour was WPC Rix.

"Sorry to keep everybody waiting," Minton said. Before he sat down, he offered Doc his hand. "I'm assuming you're Doctor Slidesmith?" Doc confirmed he was and they shook. Minton gave him a warm smile. "Neville Minton, pleased to meet you. Miss Patel tells me you may have some unusual information relating to her client's case. You believe you can help Mr Rudjer?"

"I hope so."

Minton turned away to take his seat but on the way down caught sight of me and straightened again. He held his hand out to me.

"Sorry, didn't introduce myself properly before. You're Yakky, Mister ... ?" He put a very slight frown on, struggling to recall my real name. I didn't doubt he got my name off Priti, I didn't doubt he also remembered it. Being the perfect gentleman, he wasn't using it until I gave him the okay.

"Just Yakky."

"Yakky, then. Neville."

We shook on it; he flashed the warm smile again. Priti

could have learned a lot from his technique. Although, I didn't like his smile any more than I liked hers.

Minton finally settled himself into an attentive posture: *shall we get on.*

"If Peter Keller had been beaten to a pulp or left lying at the bottom of a staircase, I would have paused for thought. Chris is a big fella and if he lashes out, people can get hurt." Doc glanced at Jeffry Keller and his wife, who were looking at Doc rather than each other. "You'd know that from his police record."

Caught by surprise Jeffry nodded then compounded the slip by looking guilty. Doc shot a glance at Rix and Minton. They both kept blank expressions but the lack of reaction said enough. I chalked up a point to the good guys.

Doc had positioned himself behind the sofa where Jan was showcasing her wounds. He put his hands on the high back leather, one either side of her shoulders. He looked like a lecturer behind a podium. Or maybe a priest.

"Chris was on hand when a crime was committed. Then he was there when Jan needed a shoulder to lean on, and he stood out. He looks like he was born guilty and, lest we forgot, his DNA's all over this house along with his fingerprints."

He paused, probably for dramatic effect, but it gave Rix time to slide a comment in.

"You accept there's evidence then?"

"There's evidence that Chris was in this house and that he was carrying on with Jan. I don't accept it's evidence that he killed Peter Keller."

"There's a good many things about Peter Keller's death that don't point to suicide."

"The bottle of Scotch with all the prints wiped off it, the unconvincing note and the blade that doesn't fit the wounds?" Doc allowed himself a smug moment.

Rix didn't reply. Neither of them gave anything away.

It was Priti who broke the stalemate. "Doctor Slidesmith is familiar with the details of the case against my client. He is acting, on a voluntary basis, in an investigatory capacity on my behalf. My client has given his express permission for Doctor Slidesmith to be included under the umbrella of client confidentiality."

She sounded like she was reading from a textbook. Or a script. Rix nodded, if not satisfied, then at least resigned.

To Doc, she said, "Then you know why he was arrested."

Doc stumbled on what he was about to say. I think he was going to let loose some comment about lazy policing but changed his mind at the last moment. When he regained his stride, he divided his attention between Rix and Minton. The Kellers didn't look upset to be left out.

"Bear with me for a second," he said, "Is the scenario you're going with something along these lines? To make Peter Keller's death look like suicide, Chris gets a bottle of Scotch and plants it in the bathroom after wiping off any fingerprints, so he doesn't incriminate himself. He also plants a suicide note with the signature obscured by blood; he even plants the pen, again completely devoid of prints. But now, rather than wiping his prints off the murder weapon and leaving it at the scene, he turns the house upside down to find a Stanley blade that he presses the dead man's thumb against to provide a single fingerprint. Is that the case for the prosecution?"

Minton said, "I would assume that's a reasonable sketch of the case against your friend, yes."

Doc turned to Priti, who answered for the defence, "The official investigation centres on the absurd idea that my client took the time to clean up a crime scene, while leaving an extraordinary amount of evidence in an adjacent room." She wasn't as good as Doc at addressing a group of people. She spoke to Rix, "I've spent a lot of time with Mr Rudjer. I really don't know if he's a thug or not. I'll concede he looks the part, but he has, at no time, given me any indication that he's an idiot. I would imagine if my client were trying to hide a crime, he'd have made an effort to clean the bedroom."

"Maybe he didn't have time," Minton said.

I think he was playing devil's advocate, not lodging a real objection, but Jeffry took his remark as an in. "He'd have been panicking, rushing to leave, before the police arrived."

This observation was swallowed whole by the silence that followed. Jeffry looked from face to face, wanting one of us to respond. Minton finally ended, or compounded, the awkward moment by clearing his throat and countering the point that he'd raised to start with. He didn't look at Jeffry as he spoke.

"There wouldn't have been any urgency. The police only came because Jan called them, and the forensic evidence gathered from the adjacent bedroom indicates that Mister Rudjer had already been in the building for some time." He made a small movement of his head in Jan's direction. "With Jan's knowledge."

A lot of people, I'm one of them, would have embarrassed everyone in the room saying that. Minton left you thinking you'd just witnessed the apex of discretion.

Caroline suddenly stood. Jeffry must have tried to stop her because she made an irritated slap at his shoulder, told him to get off her. She crossed the room to the drinks cabinet, took one of the bottles – I'm pretty sure at random – and poured herself a measure that she knocked straight back. With the exception of her husband, everybody watched her. Her movements were slow, overly controlled. I recognised them from my own movements when dad was playing me up.

"I'm going to tidy myself up a little, I won't be long. Please, carry on without me."

I was impressed with the degree of dignity she salvaged. I don't know why but nobody spoke until we'd all listened to her heels click through the hallway and up the stairs. Jeffry stared at the door long after she'd gone through it. He gave a start when Priti broke the spell and began talking.

"If we rule out rushed panic measures, or stupidity, neither of which is likely, there seems to be no reason for making such a hash of concealing a crime."

With that, she handed the baton back to Doc.

"So, look at it from another angle," he said. "If there was no reason for the stage to be so badly set, then perhaps it wasn't."

Doc stopped and left the idea hanging. He didn't do the spooling thing but Rix finished the thought for him anyway.

"You're saying it's a set-up."

Doc anointed her with a Cheshire Cat grin. "Bingo."

Minton's wheels were turning again, if they'd ever stopped. I think Rix saw that as well; she was focused on Doc, but keeping an eye on the lawyer. Priti, who had her back to me because of where I'd chosen to sit, turned slightly and gave me a wry smile, which surprised me. Jeffry had tuned out, too uncertain to leave and, suddenly, too far down the pecking order to join in. I finally felt a thread of sympathy for him.

"This is farfetched," Minton said. "Mr Rudjer and Peter Keller inhabited completely different worlds. Other than Jan, I doubt they shared any acquaintances. Nobody with a motive to murder Peter Keller was likely to have known Chris Rudjer even existed."

"I agree," Doc said. "By the same token nobody in Chris's circle would know Peter Keller's movements well enough to set a trap. Chris wasn't really the target. He was collateral damage." He paused with his head cocked to one side. Caroline's heels were clicking across the hall again. Doc, and by extension the rest of us, waited for her to come back in. As the door swung open, he said, "The real targets were Jan and Jeffry."

Caroline froze in the doorway as heads turned. She looked startled then affronted in quick order. Jan, not surprisingly, was still the focal point of her ire and she fixed her with a nasty look.

"It's easy to throw suspicion around, isn't it?" Doc said and Caroline looked daggers at him instead.

She'd scrubbed her face, losing her makeup in the process. She'd also undone a lot of expensive grooming by raking her hair back with wet hands. As styles went, I preferred it but I doubted I was her target audience.

Caroline looked away from Doc and made to sit down without comment. Jeffry moved along the sofa to give her more room but she blanked him and took one of the armchairs. When she produced a near empty pack of twenty and lit up, the trembling cigarette tip betrayed her nerves. It was the only thing that did. After she'd taken a powerful draw, and tapped ash onto the floor, she made an impatient gesture at Doc to get on with it. He nodded to her gravely, it was almost a bow.

"Jan and Jeffry, together, were meant to come under suspicion, be plagued by guilt, lose their social standing. They were meant to suffer."

Rix looked from Jan to the Kellers. Her gaze lingered on Caroline's cigarette, she obviously wanted one.

"Jeffry Keller's never been a suspect," Rix said, as if that put an end to Doc's Jive.

"And Jan?"

"It was decided not to pursue that line of enquiry."

She sounded like she was quoting directly from an official memo and wasn't happy about it.

Doc directed a grin at Minton and said, mildly, "Fancy that." The comment washed over Minton without a ripple. Doc didn't bother chasing the point. "Regardless, I think both Jan and Jeffry have suffered, don't you? And the fact Chris happens to be bearing the brunt of the grief isn't surprising. He was chosen as a proxy."

Minton and Rix both made to speak at the same time.

Minton, ever the gentleman, allowed the lady to go first.

"Who are you talking about? If Chris Rudjer didn't kill Peter Keller, then who did?"

"Peter Keller wasn't murdered," Doc said carefully, his attention fully on Rix. She was the hard sell, the one he needed to convince. "He *did* kill himself. He hid in the bathroom and watched his wife having sex with another man, as per his request. Then he carved open an artery and bled out. Knowing Jan would find his body and hoping the police would ask questions."

Minton didn't say anything but he looked pointedly at Jeffry, prompting him to reply. That was as far as the landscape of their new relationship allowed him to go. Jeffry didn't say anything. He may not have even seen the look he was getting, but his wife did and picked up the torch.

"Really, Doctor Slidesmith, or whatever you call yourself, is that why you called us here? You honestly think Poor Peter arranged to watch that little tart with one of her men, then killed himself? To make Jeffry feel bad?" She sucked down about a third of her cigarette, blew smoke in Jan's direction. "You're more idiotic than you look."

The end of the cigarette still trembled.

Doc waited for a better objection, but none came. He grinned hugely, no humour, no Jive, something baser.

"Not one of Jan's men, Caroline, the man," He turned back to Minton and Rix. Caroline, like her husband, had been deemed too small to keep. "One man. And Jan didn't even choose him. Peter set up an account on a cheater's website, put Jan's picture on it, wrote her profile and offered her up. The account's in Jan's name and all correspondence from it goes to an email address, again in her name, set up solely for that purpose. Or so we thought, but really everything went to Peter first. He created two email address that were almost identical, just one character's difference between them. That's all it takes, and unless you're looking for it, you'd never spot it. What Jan saw in her inbox was what Peter wanted her to see. The replies and offers she was getting were the ones he wanted to steer her towards, plus a few creeps and weirdos to muddy the waters. Jan met up with Chris after Peter made sure he was the best offer she'd get.

"He picked Chris for a couple of reasons. He stands out, he's hard to forget and easy to describe. And he's big, just like big brother Jeffry, big and intimidating. I think that was the most important thing."

Rix glanced at Jan, maybe waiting for a reaction. Jan was looking at her hands, still clutching the tea towel I'd given her to mop up the blood. Meanwhile her sex life was held up as exhibit A.

In her cop voice, Rix said to Doc, "You think Peter Keller was a submissive or whatever they call it?"

Doc shook his head.

"Peter wasn't a submissive. Everything I've heard about him points to the opposite, even the way he got Jan and Chris together: he ordered it all from start to finish. Took the picture, dictated what appeared on the posting and filtered the replies. He was even giving out instructions on the sex, the where, the when. How Jan should dress, should act." Doc compounded the preacher's image by raising his hand heavenwards. "Look around this house. Every inch of it is about making Peter Keller look impressive. Expensive booze, off-the-shelf good taste. All those photos of Jan in the hallway out there. Not one of them was about Jan; they were all about showing what a success Peter was."

Rix jerked her thumb in the direction of the hallway.

"You know anything about what happened to those pictures?"

Caroline tipped another inch of ash on the floor. She was left holding just the filter tip and avoiding everyone's eye.

"It's not directly connected to Keller's death." He paused to cut a quick look towards Minton and Jeffry. Both men would have thought he was singling them out, but from where I sat, I could see he'd glanced at a point about midway between them. "I don't think we need to get into it, just yet."

Rix blinked, taking a picture of her own, and her face tightened. It might have been a grimace but I suspect she was swallowing a smile.

Caroline looked straight at Doc now. "If Peter was such a powerful character, why would he be setting that little whore up with men, and not just kicking her out?"

The dead filter tip she was holding joined the ash on the carpet and she pulled out a replacement.

"He wasn't a powerful character, not in any way. I don't want to talk ill of the dead but, look at his legacy." He gestured around the room once again. "The man was a loser who couldn't be happy with what he had if someone else had more. Even his marriage was only good enough if it made less of his brother's."

"Is it really necessary to pull Mister Keller's lifestyle apart?" Minton chipped in. "You said you didn't want to talk ill of the dead."

"I don't, but nothing I say or do is going to hurt Peter now. I'm concerned with the living, specifically with Jan and Chris. Peter brought them together and used them. The *how* is easy but I want you to see the *why*."

Minton regarded Doc for what felt like a long time. He was weighing things up and, I think, making the tiniest of power grabs.

Doc didn't need his permission to talk, but Minton granted it anyway.

"If you can shed light on what happened here then, please, continue."

"Pete had been on the edge for a long time, maybe for years. Business was failing and his brother's handouts had stopped. The one thing he'd ever had that Jeffry wanted was Jan. So he offers a deal – Jeff can have the use of his wife, again. Provided he pays. When Jeff said no, that was the tipping point. The only asset he had, and it – she – wasn't enough. Peter loses and, knowing that, he can't bear to live.

"Suicides tend to be a furious gesture. That's why most of

them fail; careful planning takes a cool head. Peter had a cool head. The planning he could do but he needed to build up the fury. That's where Chris Rudjer got dragged in.

"Jan didn't know Pete had tried to pimp her to his brother for money. He'd spun a story about being turned on by the affair. So when Jeff gave her the brush off, she was already primed to try with someone else. Peter was orchestrating the situation and himself. I don't know if he picked Chris from a cast of thousands or if Chris was the only one who came close, either way he was pure gold. He's big and intimidating like older brother Jeffry, only more so.

"Seeing Jan with a man like Chris wasn't Pete's fantasy – it was his nightmare. Knowing another man took his wife, in his house, in his bed. He wasn't exciting himself by pushing them together; he was fuelling that rage. The affair and Jan's lack of discretion were all directed by Pete to cause him as much pain as possible. Chris's neighbours had seen the expensive redhead leave his flat in the mornings and seen the state she was in. Caroline's coffee circle knew about Jan's bit of rough. Everybody was seeing what they were meant to. And it dovetailed with presenting his death as a murder.

"On that final night, he had Jan invite Chris over for the weekend. If Chris looked in the bathroom, he'd have found Peter waiting for the big show. I suspect it was one hell of a show.

"God knows what Pete did in there. Maybe a few minutes were enough and Jan played porn star to a corpse for most of the night, maybe he tortured himself for hours. All I know is he set the stage before he left it. I hope he got some sort of peace as he bled out, even it was only the satisfaction of knowing the trouble he'd cause."

Doc had spared some of Jan's blushes. She'd told Doc that Peter's last words to her had been, "Don't hold back, let me know how much you're enjoying it. Let him know how good he is."

She'd done just that. As Doc said: hell of a show.

When Minton spoke up I jumped slightly. "Doctor Slidesmith, your assessment of Peter's character matched what I knew of the man. He was a hard worker, very determined, I'd even say driven, but he lacked resilience." Minton tried to meet Jan's eye but she couldn't look away from her hands, still twisting around the tea towel. "I can imagine him ending his own life, but that doesn't explain how he could have opened the wound in his arm without some sort of weapon. The police have ruled out the blade found at the scene."

Caroline, who was striking up her third cigarette, paused with the lighter just short of its target. When Doc grinned, she rolled her eyes and carried on lighting up. I was beginning to warm to her.

"A knife, matching the wound, was found in Mister Rudjer's flat," Rix chimed in.

Doc turned the Cat on her. "Has anyone asked Chris how he came by that knife?"

It was Rix's turn to roll her eyes. "He's playing it dumb, as I'm sure you know. The only thing he's said to date is that he wanted legal representation."

"Then let me fill in the blanks. Chris got that knife the weekend before Peter died. Jan gave it to him to cut her clothes off, but knife games weren't his thing. Jan turned up at my shop wanting to talk to me. I didn't know it at the time, but she was worried about Peter's new interest in blades. I had things to do, so I put her off."

That wasn't quite the full story of that Thursday. Jan had rolled up wanting him to do another tarot reading. His Jive when he'd first met her in The Jericho producing The Fool and synchronising it with her husband had hit a nerve. He made a comment, off the cuff, warning her The Fool was a wild card.

The Fool already had her taking other men to the marriage bed – now he was upping the ante and throwing weapons into the mix. Jan had run to a Voodoo priest for guidance. I didn't rush to amend Doc's editing of the details.

"I arranged to see Jan on Monday the eleventh. She didn't show, by then Peter was dead. As long as I had the notion in my head that it had been murder, that knife didn't make sense. As a suicide dressed as a murder, it fell into place. Chris was meant to handle the knife and put his prints on it so it could be found in the bathroom. That part of the plan went belly up. Chris put the knife in his pocket and took it home. So, instead of planting incriminating evidence, Peter planted obviously fake evidence to raise suspicion."

Doc paused, giving everyone time to catch up. Or maybe just for the drama. Rix used the lull to ask Caroline for a cigarette. She lit up from Caroline's expensive lighter and sucked down smoke with relief. Then she told us she'd been trying to give up and looked daggers at Minton as if her lapse was down to him.

She told Doc, "There was nothing at the crime scene that could have produced the wounds. The only matching blade we've found, that has any connection with this case, was in Mister Rudjer's kitchen."

She coordinated her next lungful of nicotine with Doc's next grin. "It's a very specific type of knife that's hard to get hold of. Why? Any knife would have done to collect fingerprints. Why something so special? That particular knife folds away very small and weighs next to nothing."

Doc came out from behind the sofa and strode over to one of the room's straight-backed chairs. He pulled it around so when he sat in it, we could all see him.

"Peter had two knives. One was a plant to be found at the scene of the crime. The only prints on it were going to be Chris's, maybe with a couple of Jan's thrown in for a bonus point. The second knife was going to do the cutting."

Doc, sitting on the straight-backed chair, mimed driving a knife into his left arm then twisting it. The type of action we thought most likely to have produced the killing wound. Then he held up the mime weapon as if at a loss to know what to do with it.

"Now what? This knife, knife number two, has to go

missing. It doesn't matter if the knife with Chris's prints was found in the bathroom or found in his pocket, this knife mustn't be seen again."

Doc did a sudden gear change, "And why use the guest room? The other nights, Jan had taken Chris to the master bedroom and the bed she shared with Pete. That had been another feed to Pete's anger and bitterness. He was even sending emails to Chris, pretending to be Jan, making comments about sex on the marriage bed, torturing himself. Yet, for the final showing, Peter wanted them to use the guest room. Why?"

He grinned again, looked down at his lap and let his knees fall open. He mimed dropping the knife between his legs.

"Flush. All gone. That's why he needed *that* knife. Big enough to provide a proper handle, so he could cut deeply enough to ensure a fast bleed out. Then it folded away into a neat little package, small and light enough to flush away. That's why they weren't in the master bedroom; it didn't come with a silent flush toilet. If Chris heard the toilet flushing, the game would be up."

There was silence for a while, then Caroline snorted, "Good luck proving that in court."

Priti answered, "We don't have to. The burden of proof is on the prosecution. All we have to do is show a reasonable doubt. Doctor Slidesmith has offered a plausible explanation of the events surrounding Peter Keller's death."

"Plausible, but far from compelling," Minton's was the voice of caution. "This is a theory with a great deal of supposition and nothing in the way of supporting evidence."

He turned to Priti and when she didn't offer anything, he smiled sadly. I could feel that pulse of anger coming from her again.

"I think the knife may still be in the bathroom," Doc announced and waited for the room to focus on him again. "When the toilet was flushed the flow of water would have been enough to push the knife out of the pan and into the U bend. But I don't think there'd have been enough force to get it past the U bend and into the sewer." He stood up and pulled a pair of the black latex gloves from his pocket. "Shall we?"

Everyone made their way back to the hall except Jeffry and Caroline. When we left, Jeffry was sitting with his head in his hands while Caroline pretended to be alone. She didn't have her back to him but she might as well have.

We lost Jan at the door of the guest room when she excused herself and went to clean up. The rest of us followed Doc into the room's en suite. Doc pulled on one of the latex gloves and rolled up his sleeve, put his hand into the toilet bowl with a pinched expression. We all watched him in silence, five of us in a space designed for privacy, watching a man shove his arm down a toilet.

Doc braced his left arm against the wall while he twisted his right into the pan. The flush on the toilet didn't use a handle, it worked by waving your hand across an electronic sensor. Wriggling to work his wrist into the U bend, Doc touched it and the toilet flushed. He jumped back as the water began to cascade. It wasn't totally silent but it hissed gently rather than roared. Everybody stared at the toilet and Doc closed his eyes as though in pain.

He turned, everyone was now staring at him.

"Well I guess if there is a knife still down there after that, then I'm right."

When no one said anything, he knelt in front the toilet and inserted his arm again, now carefully avoiding the sensor. After a minute or so of twisting and turning, he slowly pushed himself back onto his heels.

In his hand was a folded lock knife.

I heard the car pull out as we left the bathroom. Downstairs we found Jeffry on his own.

"Well?" he said shortly either to Rix or Minton, I wasn't sure which.

Rix answered by holding up the knife; she'd put it in a plastic evidence bag. Jeffry must have had a set-to with

Caroline while we were gone. He was riding a wave of adrenaline and the shell shock from earlier had been replaced with indignation.

"That proves nothing. He was in the house before any of us. He could have planted it before we got here."

Minton spoke politely, but knowing the back story, I could guess the subtext. "Doctor Slidesmith accidentally flushed the lavatory before retrieving that item. That the knife stayed where it was and wasn't lost in the sewer gives his theory a lot of heft and if any trace of forensic evidence has survived it will assist greatly the case Miss Patel is putting together."

His tone softened when he said, "Jeffry, I think you should accept your brother's death was a suicide, tragic but nothing more. Caroline should be your main concern now."

I thought Jeffry was going to throw a punch but he just clenched his jaw and nodded at Minton. Before he left he glared at and Doc and Jan.

"Have you any idea how much trouble you've caused me?"

Jan didn't deign to speak to him but Doc gave him that tight little smile.

"Go home, Jeffry."

"I still don't get why he wanted to frame Chris," I said once Rix, Priti and Minton had left. "He was only there because Pete set it up."

Doc shook his head, he had a mouthful of lager. Jan was holding a cold bottle against her face where Caroline had punched her. She'd ditched the blood-stained blouse for a sweatshirt. It was too big on her; I assumed it had been one of Peter's.

"He didn't really care about Chris. He wanted to hurt his brother but Jeffry had put himself out of reach. Chris was his brother in spirit if you like, the big man who took his woman. A focus for his bitterness."

He took another mouthful of lager and examined the

label, obviously not impressed. I asked Jan if she was alright. Even allowing for the beating she'd taken, she looked drained.

She smiled and nodded, then winced and pressed the bottle to her cheek again. "I'm just tired. You think that'll be enough? You think they'll let Chris out?"

Doc was still examining his bottle; now the show was over, he looked deflated.

"I think we've done what we can. It's not in our hands anymore."

I finished my drink and made my excuses. Jan had her tarot out by then and I didn't want to hang around. I did my best not to rub the mojo in my pocket before starting my bike, but I didn't quite manage it.

Priti Eyes

Sunday 28 August

It wasn't instant. We didn't all ride down to the police station the next morning and lead Chris to freedom. But once things were in motion, it was fairly quick.

Before they'd left the Keller house that day, Doc spoke in vague but loaded terms to Rix about the damage done to property. He hinted at Jeffry's attempt to claim the house. Jan said she wasn't sure if she'd be making a formal complaint. I don't know how much of the undercurrent Rix was aware of, but Doc was careful to say it all in front of Minton, who would know trouble when he saw it.

Priti got to land the knockout punch. She waited until Rix was out of the room before telling Minton that Jeffry boasted to Doc about his connections and his efforts to hamper the investigation. Minton did little more than raise an eyebrow when she said Doc had the conversation on tape. Eyebrows must be high currency in the offices of Brookfield, Minton and Langdon; the case against Chris fell apart in the renewed onslaught of Chris's legal counsel.

Once the police investigation got underway again, other evidence supporting Doc's theory was uncovered. The Met's IT division went through Peter's computer and found the correspondence with Seductive Secrets. They confirmed everything was sent into one email account before being filtered and arriving in a second account with an almost identical address. Peter's banking records also revealed the purchase of three ceramic-bladed lock knives from

Mertone's Blasting Supply House, NY. When that detail filtered back, via Priti, we surmised that the third knife had been for a test run and was probably still sitting in a u-bend somewhere.

Peter had wiped his browsing history regularly, but the IT boys still found he'd frequented a chat room used by men who fantasised about seeing their partners with someone else. They'd also found he made repeated visits to a site providing information and tips on committing suicide.

The official line was that the case against Chris Rudjer was not being pursued due to lack of evidence.

Jan moved back in with Chris the day he got out. Dad was practically in mourning. The Big Guy rocked up at the shop a couple of days after his release to pick his bike up. I was in the back room working and Doc was out front, talking to a very intense woman who had ambitions to be the new apprentice. Chris surprised Doc with a bear hug that pinned his arms to his sides. I heard him say thanks just before he put him down again. When he put his head around the door of the back room, we exchanged nods, biker style.

"My next piece, Yakky." Chris patted his left flank and pointed at me.

We didn't hear from him or Jan for over a week. According to Doc, who kept his finger on the pulse, they were holed up in Chris's flat. I figured they were either having a lot of deep and frank conversation or a lot of deep and frantic sex. Neither of which were any business of mine.

Now, Doc and I were sat waiting for them. Jan called the shop number and told Doc they wanted to take us out for a meal to say thank you. Doc read a lot into this, but then he would.

"Did I tell you Priti rang me?" Doc asked as we ate poppadums and assured the waiters everything was fine.

"What did she have to say?"

"This and that, I think she might put some work our way. She was rather impressed with our ... resourcefulness." I was a beat behind so I made the spooling motion. "I think, now and then, the great and noble firm of Brookfield, Minton and Langdon employs people to gather information in ways that may not be strictly legal."

"People they can deny all knowledge of should they screw up?"

Doc toasted me with his lager. "I like her you know, she's a smart cookie." I didn't doubt that but his next line still startled me. "And she's got the eyes of a crow – she spotted me palming the knife."

I was grudgingly impressed. I knew about the insurance knife and I still missed Doc's set up. He pulled it off so smoothly that I asked him afterward if he'd gone through with it.

After Doc reasoned that Peter could have disposed of the real murder weapon by flushing it, he went back to the Keller house and checked. The knife he showed me, pinned to his crime wall in a wet plastic bag, was the knife Peter had cut himself with.

Doc's first thought had been to call the police and tell them, then paranoia dictated otherwise. The house hadn't been under police control for weeks and any new evidence found there was open to dismissal. Likewise, pulling it out of the toilet in front of witness proved nothing. But as Priti was fond of saying, we didn't need proof, just reasonable doubt.

Doc wanted the witnesses to see the process in action. Toilet flushes, just not hard enough to wash away the evidence. He wanted it fixed in their minds as a spontaneous event, something unplanned and, to their eyes, new. Accidentally flushing the toilet then producing the knife might be enough.

Problem was the flush couldn't be relied on not to flush the knife away. So Gina had taken her trip to New York and brought back an identical knife. The latex glove Doc had put on had the new knife inside it. Doc knelt by the toilet, set off the flush accidently on purpose, looked horrified, and said: if the knife's there, I'm right. With that idea implanted in everyone's head, he reaches in again and produces the evidence.

If the original knife wasn't there, he'd produce the new one. The lack of any prints could be chalked up to the weeks it spent under water, we hoped.

The decoy wasn't needed. The knife Doc pulled out and presented to Rix was the one Keller had used. While everyone was intent on that knife, Doc slipped out of shot to wash his hands, peeling off the glove with the decoy still inside it.

"Did you tell her the knife she saw you palm wasn't the knife you gave to Rix?"

Doc shrugged. "I did but she just laughed. I don't think she cared. Proof or plant, her client's out on the street again, so she's won."

"And that's all that matters to her?"

Doc looked surprised at my tone.

"What's your problem?"

"Doesn't that strike you as a bit sordid? She just wants to win, doesn't matter to her if Chris is innocent or not. At least me and you did shitty things because we believed him."

"She represents her client, that's her job." He broke off a piece of poppadum. "This time the good guys won. Don't knock it."

His gaze shifted to a point somewhere behind me, Chris and Jan had just walked through the door, both laughing and holding crash helmets. They made a striking couple.

"You think those two are going the distance?" I asked.

Doc gave me his Cheshire Cat grin. "Don't ask me, brother. I'm not a fortune teller."

THE END

Doc Slidesmith will return in

INK TO ASHES

Also published by Fahrenheit Press.

About the author

Russell Day was born in 1966 and grew up in Harlesden, NW10 – a geographic region searching for an alibi. From an early age it was clear the only things he cared about were motorcycles, tattoos and writing. At a later stage he added family life to his list of interests and now lives with his wife and two children. He's still in London, but has moved south of the river for the milder climate.

Although he only writes crime fiction Russ doesn't consider his work restricted. 'As long as there have been people there has been crime, as long as there *are* people there *will* be crime.' That attitude leaves a lot of scope for settings and characters.

One of the first short stories he had published, *The Second Rat and the Automatic Nun*, was a double-cross story set in a world where the church had taken over policing. In his first novel, *Needle Song*, an amateur detective employs logic, psychology and a loaded pack of tarot cards to investigate a death.

Russ often tells people he seldom smiles due to nerve damage, sustained when his jaw was broken. In fact, this is a total fabrication and his family will tell you he's has always been a miserable bastard.

More books from Fahrenheit Press

If you enjoyed The Paris Ripper by Seth Lynch you might also like these other Fahrenheit titles

Boondoggle By Mark Rapacz

Jukebox By Saira Viola

Hidden Depths By Ally Rose

In The Still By Jacqueline Chadwick

Printed in Great Britain
by Amazon